SEP 19 2018

ECHOES
of EVIL

HEATHER GRAHAM

ECHOES of EVIL

mira

ISBN-13: 978-0-7783-6874-8

Echoes of Evil

For questions and comments about the quality of this book, please contact us at CustomerService@Harlequin.com.

BookClubbish.com

Printed in U.S.A.

For Aaron Priest, Lucy Childs
and the Aaron Priest Agency—
making my life better for years and years

CAST OF CHARACTERS

Dakota (Kody) McCoy—she's a native Key Westerner, or "conch,"
and curator of a new local museum and festival

Brodie McFadden—the youngest of the McFadden brothers
is in Key West to clear his head and plan his future

Cliff Bullard—this middle-aged musician is an old friend of Dakota's family,
and is beloved on the island by locals and tourists alike

Ewan Keegan—a retired navy SEAL who works for Sea Life,
a nonprofit organization committed to the presevation of sea mammals
and the history of the sea

Sonny Atherton—Miami artist helping Kody with her festival

Emory Clayton—runs a research facility

Bill Worth—"conch" who writes historical nonfiction

Rosy Bullard—Cliff's wife is a retired schoolteacher and a visual artist

Liam Beckett—a detective on the Key West police force

Kelsey Beckett—Liam's wife and Kody's good friend

Colleen Bellamy—Kody's assistant at the museum; very shy

ECHOES
of EVIL

PROLOGUE

The rhythmic sound of his own breathing through his regulator was, to Brodie McFadden, the sweetest music; there simply was nothing like diving. The light he carried, attached to his buoyancy control device, illuminated the world of darkness around him.

His dive partner for the day, Ewan Keegan, motioned to him that he was moving up to the next deck; Brodie motioned back that he would continue where they were, here, deep in the hold, where the tragic "cargo" of the ship had been "contained."

He was getting an early peek at a historic discovery and was now in the bowels of the wreck of the *Victoria Elizabeth*. Even here, though, fish darted about. The *Victoria Elizabeth* was yet to become a fine reef home; eventually, she might well be so. Barnacles covered much of her wood, even within the ship. In the cargo hold, very little light filtered down. He was careful. He'd already discovered a moray eel had made itself a home in what had been a cupboard.

Brodie had come down to Florida for a vacation—and to mull his future. But he had wound up on this dive because his old

friend Ewan Keegan, who had been a Navy SEAL, asked him
to come along. Ewan was fifty, with steel-gray hair and still in
rock-solid shape. Brodie was a good diver himself, but Ewan
knew the waters here like few other men did. He was also one
of the finest divers Brodie had ever known, but then, not many
were as skilled and experienced as navy divers. Ewan had retired and gone to work for an amazing salvage company and
had been part of the crew that had finally discovered the *Victoria Elizabeth*, a ship that had gone down in the Florida Straits,
just southwest of Key West, in 1827.

The *Victoria Elizabeth*, out of England, had not been high on
the list for most treasure-seeking divers; she had not carried gold
and riches, but rather an entirely horrible and cruel cargo: she
had been a slave ship. Her value was historic rather than mon-
etary; in Brodie's mind, she was an important monument to the
concept spoken once by the great philosopher, George Santa-
yana—*Those who cannot remember the past are doomed to repeat it.*

The ship wasn't on any of the tourist dive books yet. Ewan's
company, Sea Life, was still charting and exploring the find. Bit
by bit—and with the help of the proprietor—they intended to
sponsor a room in a new museum that had just opened in the
island tourist town that focused on both local history and the
legends and stories that arose from that history. Ewan had told
him about it before they'd gone down that day.

There would be artifacts found that would be fascinating,
though not a treasure by standards set by such ships as the Mel
Fisher discovery, the *Atocha*. Gold and jewels would likely not
be discovered. They had, however, found trinkets that allowed
them to trace the human cargo held so cruelly in the hold—and
some owned by the crew who had manned the ship.

And the ship was not in bad shape—not considering the hundred and fifty years plus since she had gone down. The water,
and therefore the seabed deep beneath her, constantly shifted.

Ewan had only discovered her because a storm had shifted a huge bank that some previous storm had shifted before—the first all but covering, the second clearing a bit of the broken main mast that had led them to the hull.

The *Victoria Elizabeth* had once been a cargo ship with four decks; she had carried four-hundred slaves—the British Slave Trade Act of 1788 had decreed that numbers be limited. There had been a time when her decks had carried as many as six hundred. It was believed that there had been a handful of survivors from the wreck—but where those survivors had ended up, no one knew.

Iron ballast blocks and encrusted shackles had been discovered, along with the remnants of shell necklaces. The ballast blocks had been an emotional find, Ewan had told Brodie—they were the ballast to counter the moving weight of the human cargo. They hadn't found many remains, but they had found a few partial remains along with the shackles. Ewan had told him, "Not to worry—you won't come across any skeletons just floating at you through the water." Ewan had given himself a shake—the discovery of the ship was disturbing. Ewan had been career military; Brodie had served four years. They'd both seen their share of very bad things. Still, it was hard to imagine the terror and misery of the men and women who had perished in the ship, shackled together, one atop of the other, trying to survive in wretched conditions—until a watery death had claimed them.

And now Brodie was working with Ewan's company, and so he had free rein to find whatever he might—to be turned over as salvage, of course, and then taken through the maritime courts.

Something appeared before him, a dark shadow. It was quite possible that a shark had wandered in or even a massive grouper—there were plenty of gaping holes in the wrecked hull. But there was something more familiar about it. The shape looked like the shadow of a man.

The Sea Life ship *Memory* was high above them—where it would remain until salvage and discovery on the company's part were complete—so he and Ewan were the only divers working now, and Ewan was working on the deck above.

Brodie followed the shadow; it seemed to float to an area of the hold blocked off by a narrow fire door.

Brodie reached the door and then checked his air; the shadow had disappeared.

He paused. The shadow, he thought, had not been part of the sea, or anything that belonged in the water. Something akin to resignation and a bit of dread filled him.

He went on.

The door was partially open, as it probably had been when the ship had gone down. Brodie doubted he'd be able to move it. Yet, he pulled on it, wondering what lay beyond.

It was something of a struggle against water and pressure, but then the door gave.

Brodie had seen a lot in his day, and was an experienced diver. Still, he committed a cardinal sin of diving. For a moment he stopped breathing. He was so stunned.

There was no skeleton coming at him, but what was there seemed quite impossible.

There was a man.

A dead man.

Eerily facing him, as if he were just suspended in time.

Barely decomposed; nibbled a bit, perhaps...

His eyes were open. The cotton of his tourist shirt drifted up a bit, displaying his abdomen. He'd been fit, but his hair, close-cropped to his head, had been graying, and his face was somewhat weathered, suggesting that his age had been mid-forties to mid-fifties.

Hard to tell precisely with such a corpse.

He might have been a space-camp participant, just floating.

Except he was not.

How the man had been killed, Brodie had no idea.

And how the hell he had gotten down into the bowels of the *Victoria Elizabeth* seemed impossible, and yet...there he was.

Brodie remembered to breathe.

Then he went in search of Ewan. They'd have to figure out the proper means by which to bring the very recently dead man on the very old ship up to the surface.

CHAPTER ONE

A song ended, and Kody McCoy smiled. She was satisfied with the past few days, and just glad to be listening to the music.

"That was John Denver, for my fine young friends who might not remember the man—great songwriter and balladeer, gone too soon. A little thing called 'Annie's Song.' And before that, a number by the late great Harry Chapin, and before that, one of my own numbers—I call it 'Living on the Isle.' Oh, I see you out there, Marty Madrigal. Fooling around, eh? Oh, wait— sorry! Matilda Madrigal, you're just looking so good tonight… I thought Marty was with some hot, young chick!"

Laughter followed the musician's words. Marty and Matilda were regulars; now in their fifties; they'd been together since high school.

Cliff Bullard had broken his string of songs to joke for a minute with the audience, as he often did. He teased his old-timers and new clientele with a gift for saying the right thing to the right people, and he was loved for it. He was a staple on the island of Key West, and many of those who lived there came out especially on the nights he was playing.

"Say goodbye to my wife, guys! She's off to paint—I guess she's heard me sing one time too often."

"Never!" Rosy Bullard, his middle-aged blushing bride of one year, called out, waving. The little bar was a friendly place—everyone there waved back to her. Rosy was slim and attractive, with short blond hair and a quick smile. She was also fierce about caring for her husband; she made him eat well and watch his drinking.

As she left, Cliff began to strum again. He called out, "Hey, Kody, this one is for you."

He went into a rendition of a song Dakota McCoy loved and seldom heard. It was called "Seminole Wind." She'd heard it the first time at a powwow in the Everglades, and had it on a CD she'd bought while staying up at the Seminole Hardrock Hotel in Hollywood. It had been written by country artist John Anderson, and it seemed to convey a lot that was beautiful about South Florida with some of the errors of history, all with both a nostalgic and rhythmic sound.

Cliff was doing a great job with the song, and Kody sat back for a minute, just enjoying the tune—and smiling because he had thought to dedicate it to her. Of course, Cliff was a friend, and his wife, Rosy, was a wonderful artist. When the new museum got really underway, Kody intended to feature some of Rosy's work in the gift shop. Tomorrow would be busy; tail end of closing down the festival, and working out kinks with her staff—consisting of her one assistant. The museum had only been open three weeks now.

Tonight, she was glad of the breeze, the swaying palms and the music.

Live music was one of the best things about Key West. There was always somewhere you could go to watch one or two performers, some doing rock, some country and mostly a mix.

It felt wonderful just to be here tonight—kicking back, as the

expression went. The Drunken Pirate was a small bar attached
to the Tortuga Shell, a boutique hotel on the water, accessed off
Front Street and not far from Sunset Pier. The bar was in the
center of the little hut with tables surrounding it, all shaded beneath a roof comprised largely of wood beams and palm fronds,
but open to the breeze. Even in summer—when Florida hot became hottest—the little establishment was comfortable. Breezes
came in off the water, and when they didn't, the management
had strategically set fans that kept the air moving.

Trees swayed around the hut, from great banyans to kapoks
and gumbo limbo—or "tourist" trees—so nicknamed because
they had a reddish bark and peeled, as tourists' skin was known
to do. Boats were clearly visible out on the water, and when
sunset came, it did so with colorful brilliance that rivaled any
other place on the island—or the world, for that matter.

The bar was fairly full that night with locals and lingering
Sunday-night tourists. Lots of locals: Kody had greeted Captain James Vick—a dive boat operator—and a few of his dive
masters; Bev Atkins and her husband, Dan, owners of the Sea
Horse bed-and-breakfast; and Liv Jensen and Truman Aberna-
thy, sales personnel at the Wandering Tourist over on Duval.

"How nice! This place is always just perfect."

The words were spoken by Sonny Atherton, a friend of
Kody's, down from Miami. Sonny had been one of the team
members who had just put together the first History, Mystery,
Art and Music Fest to have taken place in Key West. Sonny was
an artist, and while she officially lived in Miami, she might as
well have lived in the Keys, she was down so often. She did
beautiful watercolors of the boats on the water, the sunset, the
trees, the old Victorian homes and the many things that made
the place so exotic, unique and wonderful. In her late thirties,
Sonny was one of the most striking women Kody had ever seen;
her parents had come to the states from Brazil, and her heritage

included Portuguese, Kenyan, Chinese and Native American. Her coloring was exquisite; her skin was a café au lait color, her eyes were a crystal green and her hair a deep, dark brown.

She was also a bundle of well-focused energy, currently directed into the festival that brought so many artists of so many disciplines together.

Key West was a great place for a fest such as they had created. Kody—who now owned and operated the newly opened Haunts and History Museum right off Front Street—had been one of the locals to come up with the idea, and had been grateful for Sonny's help. Sonny had recruited songwriters, actors, artists and musicians from the Miami-Dade and Broward County areas, and done much to make the event a success. In the world of the internet, names from the far south had helped draw names from more northern reaches—they even had attendees from England and from as far away as Australia.

Not that it was that hard to coax people to what many considered to be an island paradise—one with a booming nightlife, she thought dryly. And, of course, delightful water that one could enjoy most times of the year. All right, she wasn't that fond of the water even in Key West in the dead of winter, but Canadians and other northerners always seemed to enjoy it.

But right now it was late summer, almost fall, and the dead heat was slacking off a bit. It was a great time of year in Kody's mind—a bit before the influx of the winter snowbirds who sensibly left bitterly cold climates for the balmy months that could be found here. Of course, retirement helped with that, but many savvy younger businesspeople had figured out how to love their northern homes *and* escape snowplows.

"It's always perfect, especially for a wind-down," Kody said, looking around the table. Besides Sonny, she had brought Bill Worth, who wrote historical nonfiction, and Emory Clayton, chief administrator of a research facility on the island—and a dabbler in watercolors. Although he wasn't a scientist, Emory looked like one. He was in his late forties, tall and thin—with a headful of wild pale blond hair that went whichever way the breeze was going.

"And they serve the best margarita in the world," Emory said, sighing happily. He quickly turned red and apologized to Bill, who didn't drink at all. "Sorry!"

"No problem—best mock-tail in the world, too," Bill said. He looked at Kody with a self-deprecating grin. Twenty-odd years her senior, he'd gone to high school with her mom, and been there for her when she'd lost her dad to a sudden heart attack in his sleep when Kody had been eighteen. Bill had spoken honestly to her, and instead of saying that her dad had looked great or at peace in his coffin, he had said, "He was tired, Kody. He went quickly. No pain."

Michael McCoy had been a 1980s rocker—famous around much of the world for a time. He'd almost destroyed himself, imbibing heavily of all manner of substances. But then he'd met Kody's mother—who was around twenty years younger than him—and a true love had begun that had saved his life. Sally McCoy had loved him with all her heart—but he was going to have to be clean if he stayed with her, and he became just what she wanted. Their time together had been just two decades, but they had been beautiful decades. Despite her father's fame, he'd cleaned up and lived quietly in Key West, where he'd been born and raised, and until her father's death, she'd been blessed to have an amazing down-to-earth childhood.

Bill had once told her that the hardest part about being sober was that people were afraid to ask him places—afraid they couldn't have a cocktail if he was around. "And there's the thing—you need friends. And it's up to me to keep the path and not care what other people do. I order something that looks like a drink wherever I go—then people aren't awkward."

She knew and she understood; Bill's friendship had helped save her dad once, as well. Her father had called him in the midst of a jam—other musicians had been imbibing, and Bill had talked him through his temptation. Her dad had remained clean and sober.

At just over fifty, Bill was fit as the proverbial fiddle, with snow-white close-cropped hair, bright blue eyes, and a clean-shaven and well-tanned complexion. He loved the water.

"We've got the best bartender for any kind of mixed drink, one with or without alcohol," she said, indicating Jojo Paige, the young man behind the bar. Jojo had come down from Canada for spring break when he'd been in college; two years later, with a marketing degree, he'd come back and helped turned the tiki bar into one of the most successful venues on the island.

"Darned good," Bill agreed.

Sonny smiled suddenly. "To the bartender," she said, and then added, "I know how you feel—or how any of us feels—when they're not sure if you may face prejudice or awkwardness. We're friends here. Emory—enjoy your drink."

They all laughed. And it was all easy again.

"Kody, how's your mom doing?" Emory asked. "She wasn't here for this."

"I know, and she felt very bad," Kody said. "But she's in Tampa with Frank—there was a statewide meeting on the care of sea mammals. They had to attend."

"And how is Frank as a stepdad?" Emory asked.

"Emory, I'm twenty-seven. A bit too old for a stepdad. But how is he as a person? Remarkable. I love him, and here's what's funny—my dad would have loved him, too," Kody said.

"Not so funny, really—makes sense. We all like a certain kind of person," Sonny said.

Emory smiled. "Rock star, animal activist," he said. "Just alike."

"No," Bill said. "They were both down-to-earth guys. Hey, Michael McCoy was born a Conch and he took some of that with him, even in his wild years. He was a good man."

"Do anything for anyone," Sonny agreed.

"Had integrity," Bill said. "Like Frank."

"I'm lucky to have had both good men in my life," Kody agreed. "I adore Frank—he was very supportive of my dream to open the museum. Obviously, I didn't do it alone. I was good with the history of the island, but I had a lot of help when combining it with the history of the chain of the Keys. We're trying to show a picture without politics involved, the truth and all the truth, and where we go from there."

"What about the discovery of that ship—the *Victoria Elizabeth*?" Sonny asked.

"I'm already working with the salvage company. It will be in there, too," Kody assured them. "I can't think of an uglier period of history than what Europeans and then Americans did as far as slavery and the slave trade went. Well, wait—let's see. There is the treatment of American Indians. But remembering is how we don't do horrible things again."

"We're always doing something horrible," Bill muttered.

"Yes, but in remembering, we can point out what we did, and strive to do better in the future," Kody reminded him.

"From your lips to God's ear and the world," another voice muttered.

Cliff had taken a break and was coming over to join them, drink in hand. "Sad, huh?" he asked, lifting his drink. "I guess I'm not a very manly man. I love the fruity things, and these creamy drinks and all that kind of stuff I shouldn't!"

"You're a beachy kind of song-fellow almost-manly man," Sonny assured him.

"And, Sonny, you know I love you, too—hell, can't think of

anything to tease you about, my friend. You are the ultimate lady."

"Hear, hear!" Emory said, and they all chimed in.

"Love my gang," he said. "Two-minute break. How y'all doing?"

"Great. Hey, great set tonight, Cliff," Sonny said.

"Yeah, ya think? I didn't make Kody go up yet." He looked at her and grinned. Years ago, her dad would come and sit in with Cliff. He'd worked with him on his first album.

"You loved the old man, right, sweetie?" Cliff asked.

Kody laughed, shaking her head. "You use that all the time. We just finished with—"

"Yeah, yeah, your big arts festival. Do his number-one hit, huh?" Cliff asked. "Come on, make me look good."

"You don't need me to look good."

"I don't, do I?" Cliff had a great smile. Weathered face, soft blue eyes, and an always genuine grin. He'd known her family forever, too.

"But I'd go for her rendition of 'Ghosts are Walking Bone Island, Girl,'" Sonny said. "We're all so proud that your dad was from here." She beamed. "He's a claim to fame. Major rock star."

Kody laughed. "He was in a band. They came out about the same time as Queen, Bon Jovi and Duran Duran. They were good and they made a name for themselves, but they were never that big."

"The world had heard of them—that's big enough," Cliff said. "And your dad, well, he made it past his troubles, and that's a damned good thing. He had you."

"Cheers!" Sonny said, and it was echoed.

"He had my mom," Kody said.

"And he's in the museum," Sonny said.

"Of course."

"Even I knew about Mike McCoy," Emory said. "As to anything else about the Keys… I'm still just learning. I'll always be a bit of an outsider, you know."

Emory was what they called a "freshwater" Conch; he had lived in Key West for ten years now, and a mere seven years gave you freshwater status. Bill was like Kody; he had been born on the island, and that made him a Conch. Cliff was "freshwater," even after twenty years.

Key West had the rare distinction of having once been a sovereign republic—for a matter of a few hours. On April 23, 1982—protesting a US Border Patrol blockade up on US 1, where it met with the mainland—the mayor had declared that Key West was seceding from the Union. Things had been rectified in a matter of hours—Key West officially surrendered and asked the federal government for a great deal of money to "rebuild."

Kody knew she was prejudiced about Key West—her many great grandfathers had come down here soon after businessman John Simonton had more or less officially bought the property from Juan Salas (who more or less had officially been granted the island by the king of Spain). Following lines of ownership was dicey at best, but the United States did eventually control the Florida Territory. Though all the details were lost to time—the facts and speculations were available in the first room of the museum—her roots in the island city went back to the early 1800s.

"You change it to 'Ghosts are Walking Bone Island, Boy,' right?" Sonny asked.

Kody grinned. "Sometimes, and sometimes not. Did you know the oldest version of the lyrics to 'House of the Rising Sun,' by Robert Winslow Gordon, 1925, has the singer as a 'poor girl'? The song matters. It was one of my dad's first, and yes, one of his biggest hits. With the Bone Island Boys. Anyway…"

"Isn't your dad's song about that ship they just found the wreck of?" Sonny asked. "Everyone knew that it was lost off the coast. Or possibly wrecked on purpose, that kind of a thing?"

"Basically, it's about man's ability for cruelty to man. My dad was as far left as they came—when it pertained to social issues and justice for all. Even in his worst days—when he was heavily into alcohol and drugs—he was a huge believer in equality. He was on tour once in Portugal where they had a display of the way slaves were crammed in ships—no room whatsoever. He was naturally horrified. Talked about it for weeks. He visited Auschwitz when he was in Poland on tour, and he was really affected by it. He found it very upsetting, but also was glad the Polish people kept the camp so that we could all learn to never allow such inhumanity again. But he also hated the way we—I say we, generally, meaning European colonists—treated the American indigenous population. Justice and music—they were both passions with him."

"An incredible man," Bill said. "And he is always with us." He raised his glass in salute.

Kody wished that he was.

"I wonder what he would think of the *Victoria Elizabeth* having been discovered," Emory said.

"He wouldn't have whitewashed it," Kody told him. "Hey, speaking of the ship—there's Ewan Keegan—finder of said treasure!"

Ewan Keegan was the man Kody had met with earlier about his salvage company and the amazing find of the lost ship.

He wasn't alone. He was accompanied by Liam Beckett, another old-time friend, and one of Key West's six police detectives, as well as a tall man with dark hair who Kody didn't know.

"Hmm. And he's with Liam. Our good and serious island defender. And who is that he's with? Most intriguing fellow," Sonny said.

Cliff leaned in toward Kody with a sparkle in his eyes. "I think she means *hot*," he said.

Sonny waved a hand in the air. "Too young for me. Such

a thing, however, does not prevent me from enjoying such a striking sight."

Bill laughed. "I think she means *studly*."

Kody thought the man was definitely—as Sonny had said— intriguing. He was probably in his early thirties; the kind of fit that came from being either a gym enthusiast or an outdoorsman. He was tightly muscled without being bulky, bronze from the sun, and with good features that were nicely sculpted with a touch of ruggedness about him.

Intriguing, yes—great word for a description. She didn't know him; she'd never seen him before. But he was with Liam.

Ewan Keegan had been in the Keys for several years, working with Sea Life. Kody thought he was a nice man, and one clearly dedicated to his work. Liam was a friend Kody had known as long as she could remember, just several years older than she was.

As a member of the small police force on the island, he had his work cut out for him. While Key West offered history, incredible water sports and more, it was also a party destination. Officers had to learn to cope with absolute craziness on many levels—to let go what was youthful folly and deal with what was real crime or situations that could become dangerous. For a while, in the '80s, with the drug smuggling and everything else going on, Key West had been a strange version of the wild, wild West. Assaults, rape and robbery were higher, she knew, than the national average.

But murder was rare.

Liam visited the bar often enough; seeing him wasn't at all unusual. But there was something grim in his expression this night.

The stranger also appeared somber—as did Ewan.

Liam saw Kody, and she waved. He looked as if he'd rather find his own table, but then she thought he winced slightly and decided to join them.

"Evening, all," Liam said, drawing up with the other two men. "You guys have met Ewan. This is Brodie McFadden."

They rose as a group to greet everyone. "Bill, Emory, Sonny, Kody—and our entertainer, Mr. Cliff Bullard," Liam told the man.

They shook hands all the way round. The newcomer, Brodie McFadden, had a strong, warm grip.

"I gotta head back up," Cliff said. "Hope you like the music."

He left them. Liam brought up another few chairs, and he and Brodie and Ewan sat down.

Seeing he was still frowning, Kody asked Liam, "What's wrong?"

He hesitated, looking around. "Brodie is a diver. Here on vacation."

"Nice!" Bill said.

"But as a friend, he's been working with me," Ewan said.

"And not so nice, I'm afraid," Liam said.

"I found a body," Brodie said quietly, looking around the table.

His eyes were very blue; Kody had the feeling that he was reading them all in some way.

"How horrible," Sonny murmured. "They say that time and decay work their way on human remains and that…well, the ship was all split up. But I guess remnants of humanity remain."

"He didn't find an old body," Liam said wearily. "He found…"

"A victim. Someone killed in the last day or so," Brodie said.

"A murder victim? In an old slave ship?" Kody asked incredulously. "But—Sea Life hasn't opened the ship to divers. How…"

"In the dead of night, I imagine," Ewan said. "A good diver off a nearby boat… We don't work the site at night. We use what pale sunlight they get down there."

Kody felt sick. She stared at Liam, horrified that anyone had been murdered—praying it wasn't anyone they knew.

Key West could be a small community.

"Who?" she asked.

Liam shook his head. "I have no idea, as of now. The body is up at the coroner's office in Marathon. It's not someone I knew… nor did anyone working with Sea Life know him."

"So," Emory said, "you went diving down to the *Victoria Elizabeth*—and found a dead man in the hold?"

"That's the gist of it," Liam said.

Brodie McFadden wasn't talking. He was just watching them all—as if they were suspects and he was waiting for them to make a slip and spit out the words that they were guilty of murder.

"Dear Lord," Sonny whispered. "But how…how…"

"How did he die?" Bill asked.

"We don't know yet," Liam said. "He wasn't shot or stabbed. The medical examiner will have to answer that question."

"Well, he didn't swim down a hundred feet to die in the hold of natural causes," Brodie said. "Someone did kill the poor bastard and dragged him down to the hold of that wreck."

"Maybe…maybe he did die of natural causes and whoever was with him panicked and brought him down—afraid that they would be accused of murder," Kody said.

Brodie McFadden looked at her as if she had said the most ridiculous thing in the world.

Maybe she had.

He leaned forward. "I believe it might have been some kind of a statement, actually. He was left in an old slave ship. There are dozens of good ways to get rid of a body in South Florida. Take it up to the Everglades, sink it in the swamp. Toss it out of a boat and let it float to the surface, or, weigh it down out in the Straits and let it sink until nothing else can be found."

"Interesting," Kody murmured, looking at him, "that you… know how to get rid of a body here so…well."

No one had a chance to reply—or, if they did reply, Kody didn't get a chance to hear what the reply might be.

Cliff Bullard was calling her name from the stage.

She grimaced but decided not to make a big thing out of it. She wasn't her father. As a child, she'd been studious—and probably way too quiet. She'd known enough about her father's younger years and sex, drugs and rock and roll to not want to live them. He'd never cared that she hadn't wanted to follow in his footsteps—but he had been proud she'd been in the church chorus.

"Sorry! Gotta do this, can't help it," Cliff was saying. "You know how I loved your dad—and love you." He took a sip of a drink and then tossed the contents, and the cup, just behind the stage.

Kody gave him a weak smile. "'Ghosts are Walking Bone Island, Girl,'" Cliff said.

"Wouldn't you rather do something you were in on—or maybe your song that dad played with you—'Love in the Sun'?" she called out as she walked toward Cliff.

"Naw, your dad's song tonight, Kody!" he said.

"Friends, I've a special treat for you all—you regulars know my girl, but for all of you Sunday-night newfound friends, this is Kody McCoy, daughter of the late great Michael McCoy. Welcome her, please, for a rendition of her dad's first big hit, 'Ghosts are Walking Bone Island, Girl.'"

There was a burst of applause. The original published version of the song had been enhanced with drums, a violin, a bass and a rhythm guitar. But she knew her dad had written the song on his Fender, and he'd played it that way at home. Cliff had played with her dad often enough; she had to admit that doing the song was as easy to her as reciting the Pledge of Allegiance.

She started the song, with Cliff playing:

Ghosts come down Duval, my friend, listen to their words,
They haunt us for the things we've done, and whisper softly
Bone Island, nevermore, and I whisper back, Bone Island,
I have heard, and nevermore...
Nevermore...
Nevermore...

It was on the tail end of that last "nevermore" that Cliff Bullard suddenly stopped playing.

Kody turned to look at him.

He stared at her, eyes alive with confusion, his face constricted, his body taut.

Then he keeled over, falling in a contorted ball on the little platform stage where he'd been playing.

Kody screamed; a man in the audience hopped up.

"Let me through—I'm a doctor!" he cried.

Kody leaped off the platform, giving the man room. She reached in her pocket for her phone, but she didn't have it. It didn't matter; she saw Jojo, the bartender, was already calling 911. Then she watched, unaware of anything around her but Cliff and the doctor working so strenuously over him.

Cliff had allergies! He was always so careful, and he usually kept an EpiPen in his jacket pocket. His jacket was lying over a chair near the bandstand. She hurried to it and searched through his pockets.

No EpiPen.

"He has allergies...he may have eaten something, gotten something that...he needs an EpiPen!" she cried.

The doctor nodded to her.

"Allergies? What are his allergies? Anyone carry an EpiPen?"

No one did.

But they heard sirens almost immediately. It was a small island.

The next minutes were a nightmare and a blur. Liam took

charge and cleared the area. They left her alone. Moments passed that were endless, so long, and so short.

The EMTs had epinephrine, but it was too late. Then she saw the paramedics and the doctor step back, defeat in their postures.

"No," she whispered.

Tears instantly sprang to her eyes. It was impossible. But the doctor was checking his watch and conferring with the paramedics. And she knew that they were establishing time of death.

She sank down on her knees, sobbing softly.

Someone was behind her. Liam, she realized. He drew her to her feet. "Come on, Kody, I have to stay here, but I'll get Brodie to bring you home, or to my house—you shouldn't be alone."

"I can go to the hospital with Cliff, until they can reach his wife. I can stay with him—"

"Kody, he's dead," Liam said gently.

"No...he was playing, we were singing..."

"Kody, we're all so sorry. We all loved him. I have to stay. The coroner is coming."

"I... This can't be, Liam. It just can't be. He was fine, Liam. He was just fine. And then—he was dead."

"His heart must have given out."

"He didn't smoke. He seldom drank. This is—"

"Kody, I'll be here. I'll be with him."

She looked around. They had cleared out the tiki hut. She didn't see Sonny or Bill or Emory—or anyone. Her handbag and phone were no longer on the table; someone had taken them for her.

"He was allergic to nuts, but he knew it. He carried an EpiPen. Liam, it isn't possible!"

Liam looked at her sadly.

Because it was possible. Cliff was on the floor; dead.

She suddenly felt the touch of strong hands on her shoulders.

"Miss McCoy, I'll get you home."

She still just stood there. Her knees were weak. She remained in disbelief.

"Miss McCoy," Brodie McFadden said softly.

Liam was still watching her. The doctor who had been in the audience moved over to her, looking at her sympathetically. "I can give you a prescription for something."

She shook her head. "No, no, thank you."

"Come away, please," Brodie said quietly. And she didn't have much choice. His touch was still gentle, but he firmly turned her away, and they left, walking down the little hotel path that led to the public parking lot.

It was extremely courteous and gentle, but he was a stranger. She wasn't sure where he was taking her, and she didn't care at that moment.

"It's not right. There's something wrong. I know Cliff…knew him. He didn't just die like that."

She was surprised when Brodie looked at her. "What do you think happened? You were next to him on the little stage."

She glanced over at him, wondering if he was speaking just to let her talk, to help and let her say whatever was on her mind.

But his question was serious.

"I—I don't know," she said. "We'd been there an hour or so. I remember he did bring a drink to the table… He usually has a beer when the set is over, but before that, it's usually water. He wasn't inebriated by any means."

"Hard life in his earlier years?" Brodie McFadden asked her.

"Like my father?" She couldn't prevent the bitterness in her voice. "No. Cliff's always been a moderate man. No hard drugs, ever. Probably smoked some pot in his day. Moderate drinker. He never needed to drink—he always had a soda water with lime when he was out with my dad."

"Did he—have any enemies?"

The question startled her.

And the way that the man was looking at her...

He wasn't behaving as if she was crazy or torn by grief, grabbing at straws. "He had a drink—up there?"

"He tossed the drink—and the cup, in the little area behind the stage. The drink in some foliage...he tosses them all the time."

"I'll find the cup," he said. "Can you think of anyone who would want him dead?"

"God, no! Everyone loved him. Everyone loved his music. He was easygoing—the kind of man everyone got along with." She stared at him. He was a stranger, and that was hammered home by the fact that he didn't know Cliff Bullard. "Have you ever been to Key West before?"

He gave her a little smile. "Of course. I dive. Who could resist Key West?"

She was surprised that she almost smiled in return.

"I just meant that...you didn't know him. *Everyone* loved him. How long have you been friends with Liam?"

"Stay right here. I'm going to tell Liam to look for the cup. It might help the coroner."

He stepped away, heading back toward the stage to talk to Liam.

Liam looked perplexed. But then he nodded, and Brodie came back to where Kody was waiting.

"Are you—friends with Liam?" she asked.

"I'm friends with Ewan Keegan. And, yes, through him, I'd met Liam before."

"And you wound up with him here tonight because...?"

"Because of the body on the boat," he said.

For a moment, she felt an irrational anger. They did have trouble in Key West; for far too many of the criminal ilk, it was a great place to prey on the unwary—and the inebriated.

But it was still a small community. People died, yes. Usu-

ally, it was through natural causes. Their average murder rate
was one per year.

This man, this tourist, had found a victim on a ship that was
over a hundred feet down in the Straits.

And now…

"Cliff was murdered?" she whispered.

"No, no, I'm not saying that," he said. He opened the passenger door to his car and gestured for her to get in. She seemed to
be having trouble moving herself, so he guided her to the seat. "I
was here. I saw him. It looked as if he just keeled over. His heart
giving out, or, perhaps, somehow, he did die from anaphylactic
shock. He ate something he didn't know was tainted with nuts
and therefore didn't think to use his EpiPen. Miss McCoy, we
won't know until there has been an autopsy." Brodie shut her
door and went around to the driver's side. He got in and started
the car. They drove in uncomfortable silence for a few minutes.

"He didn't just die!" she said suddenly, passionately. She
couldn't help it; she spoke the words as if death were a choice.
"He was smart about life and his allergies. He carried an EpiPen
and I couldn't find it. And he loved his wife!"

"Miss McCoy, Liam will look for the cup. Other than that,
there's nothing I can say right now. We'll wait."

"Someone killed him," she said. "I know it, I know it, I
know it!"

"Careful," he warned her.

"But—"

He pulled off the road; she saw he had brought her home, to
her old house on Caroline Street.

"If anyone did try to kill him or make him sick, that some-
one is out there. So, please, be very careful of what you say.
We'll probably find there was a natural reason for his death.
And if not…"

"And if not?"

"Well, then…apparently, he did have an enemy. I guess it would mean that someone out there did want the music to end."

CHAPTER TWO

"Should you be alone?" Brodie asked Kody, frowning as he studied her.

It was a really stupid question. No one should be alone after a friend had just dropped dead in front of them. He wanted to kick himself.

"I'm fine," she said. "Well, I'm not fine. I'm incredibly sad. Cliff was an amazing guy—and a very good friend. And he was so in love with Rosy—the two of them are still kind of newly-weds, in a way. He was so much a part of my life for so many years…" She paused and looked at him apologetically. "Thank you for getting me home. You must have had a rough day all around."

"It's a sad thing to find someone who was evidently murdered, yes. But while I can feel bad about what happened…it's not the same thing that you must be feeling. It's not like losing a friend."

"It's all right. I'm really all right."

"You live alone?"

"Yes. But I'll be fine. Truly. And, actually, I'm not alone—I do have Zilla, or Godzilla, my cat. He's huge—over twenty pounds—and he's almost as good as a dog—he's an attack cat. I got him from the shelter up in Key Largo... He's what we call a 'Hemingway' cat—he has the six toes. I swear I'm fine. You need to leave me and get on with...with what you need to be on with."

She started to jump out of the car. He quickly exited the driver's side and walked around.

"At least let me walk you to the door."

"It's not necessary."

"Please. My parents taught me that you always walk a young woman to her door."

"They're not here right now, are they, though?" she queried.

"They're deceased, but believe me, they had three sons and we were taught certain behaviors and—trust me—they might still be all-seeing."

She managed something that was almost a smile. "Lovely. I mean—not that they're gone. But those we lose live in our memories, right? By all means then, please, walk me to the door."

He couldn't help but be curious that she lived alone. Kody McFadden was stunning. Her eyes were a distinct color—not hazel, not green, not brown, but something of a golden color that matched her hair—although she wasn't really a "golden" blonde; there was a deeper color, a warmth to it. Her features were fascinating, too. Her eyes were very large and her mouth was generous, and yet she seemed to have a delicate face. He was about six-four, and she was, perhaps, just five inches shorter, with her height all in the legs, it seemed. And she was definitely a Keys girl: tanned, fit and obviously a fan of the outdoors and the water.

She stood awkwardly when they reached the door. "I think I'm supposed to invite you in."

"No, that's okay," he said softly. "Unless you need company. I'm a stranger down here—and to you. If you need me..."

She shook her head. "I guess I do want to be alone."

She swallowed—as if her words made her feel a little guilty. But she glanced at the house as well, as if there just might be someone in it.

So, she lived alone.

Didn't mean she always slept alone.

"Take my number," he told her. "If you need me…if you need anything, please, let me know."

She took the card he handed her and smiled grimly. "I'm sure we'll meet again. My museum is all wound up with Sea Life right now, and you're here with Ewan, so…"

"Ewan is an old friend, and it was great to get out with him. Not so great to have to call Liam about a dead man, but…yes, I'll be down here for a while."

"You know Liam, too, right? That's what you said, I think."

"I've met him a few times. This is one of my favorite places to get away. Whenever I can, especially when…"

"When?"

He shrugged. "I'm a PI."

"Oh!"

"In Virginia. I like to come down when something…difficult has been solved. Get in the water."

"You just solved something difficult, then," she said softly. "Then found a dead man, and…watched another die."

"I'm so sorry about your friend," he said.

She lifted the business card he had given her and said, "Well, then, I look forward to seeing you again—whenever, and under happier circumstances." Tears suddenly welled in her eyes. "I imagine I'll be helping Rosy with the funeral and… Anyway. I hope to see you again on a better day."

"I hope so, too." He hesitated. "Can I do anything for you? I know that you just opened your museum about a month ago. I know it's small."

"I have an assistant. She's smart as a whip, great with everything," Kody assured him. "Colleen Bellamy. She was up in Fort Lauderdale, working for a museum there. But she wanted to be closer to her aging grandparents...anyway, she knew Cliff, of course, but she'll handle things tomorrow. And as long as I need her to. Thank you again," she said. "I'm really all right. I'm brokenhearted, but truly, of sound mind."

"I can see that," he said with a smile.

She opened her door and went in. He waited, and he had the sense that she knew he was waiting. He heard her lock the door, and then he walked down the path back to his rental car.

He stared back at the house. It was an old place—not one of the mansions built when Key West had held the highest per capita income in the country because of wrecking and salvage rights, but a bit older. He reckoned that it might have been built right around 1820 or so. It was a shotgun house, he saw, meaning that the front door would lead to a hall that would head straight to the back door, allowing for any sea breezes to cool the house during the wickedly hot days of summer. Somewhere along the line, a second floor and little wing had been added on. She had a small patch of land around the house—the whole of it, house and yard, probably taking up about a third of an acre.

He watched the house for a minute and then gave himself a shake.

Hell of a day.

Two dead men.

One, obviously murdered. You didn't wind up in more than one hundred feet of water without dive gear by accident.

And the other...

Kody thought that Cliff Bullard had been murdered. But why in God's name would anyone want to murder a singing guitarist?

And how on earth could that connect with their finding of a body on a slave shipwreck?

Or did it?

Even with thoughts of the dead filling his mind, he couldn't help but wonder about Kody.

It wasn't easy being the child of famous parents; he knew that too well. Both his parents had been well known actors. Kody's dad had been major in a few decades of music that still lived on and on. Brodie loved the man's work himself.

He headed back to the bed-and-breakfast where he was staying, not far from the house on Caroline where he had just left Kody McCoy.

Kody walked into the long hallway that stretched from entry to end of the house and turned left, into her parlor. She couldn't help but note her eclectic decorations; she had framed posters of a few of her father's rock concerts, old street markers and signs, and pictures—her family, her friends...

Including one great picture of her dad with Cliff Bullard. They'd been playing at a small Irish bar up in Marathon; both men were wearing kilts, holding their guitars as if they were bagpipes, arms around one another's backs as they grinned at the camera.

She sank down on the sofa, not adding more light to the room, and not turning on the TV or the sound system or anything else.

She just sat. She wondered if she should have stayed with people.

She still couldn't believe Cliff was gone. He had died in the middle of playing his favorite Michael McCoy song—while she'd been singing along.

She wondered if she was in shock. She wasn't crying anymore. She was staring into the shadows in the house.

She felt something beside her. Her cat, Godzilla, coming to instinctively give her what comfort he could.

She stroked the cat. And then she realized that the captain was there, too. As much as a ghost could be there.

Captain Blake Hunter had been killed off the coast of the Keys in 1864.

From the time Kody had been in high school, she'd saved to buy a house, and when she'd managed the down payment three years ago, she'd discovered that the captain came with the house.

That was all right; the dead had never frightened her. She'd been just a child when her grandfather had first appeared before her, shushing her with his finger to his lips in a mischievous way. She had learned quickly that mentioning his presence only upset her mother. He'd told her that only certain people—lucky people—got to see the dead. He would stay around awhile, and make sure they were all okay. Then, he would move on.

And he did move on—the minute her grandmother passed away.

Kody had never doubted her own grip on reality—she knew what she saw and heard, and she had a few friends on the island who also had the ability—her friend, Liam, for one, along with his wife, Kelsey.

It was just something unspoken around others. She'd always been very careful not to talk about the people she had seen before—the dead people, that is. Even to her closest friends—other than those who were like her.

That the captain enjoyed the house was fine with her. He was fascinating; he was a large part of the reason she had wanted so badly to open her museum.

Captain Blake Hunter had been born in the house back in the 1820s. Why he stayed in spirit, he didn't really know—but the decades upon decades that had passed since his demise had been incredible, in his mind. He spent his time watching people and studying human nature. His death had been lamentable—

certainly, to himself, he had assured her—but fair. It had been a time of war. Maybe he'd needed to learn; maybe he'd stayed to help others. He was kind and wise, but not particularly humble. He'd told her at times that he'd helped many a person through the years, those who had died suddenly, or been cruelly and unfairly taken from life—murdered.

The cat sat at her one side. The captain took a seat on the other. She couldn't really feel him, and yet she could, since she sensed him. And she sensed the warmth and comfort he tried to give her, setting a ghostly arm around her shoulders.

"Kody?"

"A friend died tonight," she told him softly. "Cliff. Cliff Bullard. Captain, he…died right in front of me. I was with him onstage."

"Oh, Kody, I'm so sorry." He was quiet a minute. "Cliff—there was a good man. I know how it must hurt to lose him, but that is the way of our existence. We're given so many years on this planet." He was silent for a minute. "Trust me, I know this well."

"Of course," she said softly. "It's just that…"

"Hmm?"

She looked at him. "There was something wrong with him dying. I mean, the police came, there will be an autopsy because…because he did just drop dead. But…"

"Perhaps a heart attack?" he asked.

She shook her head. "I don't know." She frowned. "Cliff was deathly allergic to nuts, but he knew it. He was very careful."

"Kody, maybe it was just his time. You lost a dear friend. You want to deny it—that's natural."

She let out a sigh. "There was a murdered man found today. Out on the slave ship."

"Out on the slave ship?"

She nodded.

"A diver who…who shouldn't have been diving? Anyone you knew?"

"I don't know. They haven't identified him as yet. But I doubt it. Liam was on the call, and if he was from here, or frequently down here, Liam probably would have known him."

"Ah, I should have been out and about today. So much happening. I didn't even turn on the television."

Kody smiled, glancing at him. Blake was a practiced ghost. She hadn't known him, of course, in his early days. But he'd been around quite some time. He materialized easily; he could make all kinds of ghostly sounds which she knew he enjoyed. He wasn't beyond playing tricks. She often wished that he was alive—flesh and blood. The history he'd gone through since his death had taught him so much. He was careful in his thoughts and judgment; she thought that he could have been a great statesman now. He'd learned so much about people, their differences and all that made them alike, as well. He was tolerant, and while he did enjoy his practical jokes, he was careful not to frighten the elderly or anyone who wouldn't be delighted by the possibility of a ghost.

Flickering lights, going bump in the night—and turning on a television—were nothing for him.

"I'm so worried about Rosy," Kody murmured.

"She will endure—people do," he said softly. Then he asked, "Who drove you home? Such a strapping man! I'd have loved to have had him in my command. Except I've seen that we were wrong—though, you must remember, back then, men were loyal to their states. It's good that the Union was preserved. And slavery was an abomination, truly. That's so clear to me now. And that ship being discovered…maybe it upsets some people."

"Captain, I really don't believe that there is a person out there who doesn't realize slavery was a horrible thing—wherever and whenever it took place, from Ancient Egypt down to the European trade and certainly here, when it existed. It's an important discovery—it's important that we remember the bad so that it's never repeated."

He nodded. "You didn't answer me. Who drove you home?"

"Oh. A stranger."

"You took a ride with a stranger?"

"No, no, sorry. He's a friend of Ewan's—you know, the guy from Sea Life. He's been here."

"Of course, of course. Does he have a name?"

"Brodie McFadden." She hesitated. "He behaved as if…"

"As if?"

"As if he might have believed me. About Cliff being murdered."

The captain made a sound as if he sighed—which of course, he couldn't possibly do. Inhaling and exhaling were things that not even such a ghost as he could manage.

And yet the soft sound came to her.

"You need to try to sleep. You're somewhat in shock, and in terrible pain. Please, go to bed."

"Yes, I know."

"I will be watching over you," he told her.

She smiled again. He was a valiant captain. Stalwart, kind, courteous…

Everything she wanted in a man. Maybe she was searching for someone who didn't exist; she didn't fully understand why she couldn't seem to find the right relationship. She was always looking for something special. She'd even dated really nice people. Just never the right ones. Maybe she was looking for someone out of the past, someone who admitted mistakes, who looked to learn as time went on…who was careful of others…

Yep. She was looking for someone just like him.

Except that she was looking for someone who was alive.

Captain Blake was dashing, charming—perhaps too excellent a companion. Even as a ghost, he cut quite the figure with his long curling hair, jaunty, feathered hat, bright blue eyes and aquiline features. And he had never been anything but courteous and completely respectful. Maybe she had been a little bit in love with him at first; now, of course, she just loved him. But he was dead—

She couldn't help but wonder if people did fall for ghosts.

"I will watch over you," he repeated. It was almost as if she could feel a gentle finger on her cheek, brushing away a tear.

She did have to try to get some sleep.

Tomorrow would be a very long day.

She started to get ready for bed; then she remembered someone who was living.

Her mother.

She hesitated, not wanting to make the call. But she didn't want her mother hearing about Cliff's death from anyone else.

So she dialed.

Sally McCoy—Frampton now, Kody needed to remember—answered the phone quickly. "Hey, darling. I would have called you, but I thought you might be celebrating. A friend of Frank's came up last night—left Sunday morning early, trying to get everything in—and he said that you did a fantastic job. I wish I could have been there, Kody. But what we're working on is so important. People are so divided on sea creatures these days. Frank's starting that documentary about the amazing care sea mammals receive at a lot of the facilities under attack for keeping them. Take Jax up at the Dolphin Research Facility. He was chewed to pieces by a shark. He wouldn't be alive if they hadn't saved him and he couldn't live as he is now. There's a baby up here—a dolphin—her mother was killed by idiots out on the water. They're trying so hard to save the calf, and Frank—"

"Mom. Mom! We talked about it. I was fine with you being up there, honestly—I love what Frank is doing and agree it's important. The festival went very well. That's not why I called."

"Oh?"

"Cliff… Mom, I'm so sorry. Cliff died tonight."

"What? How?"

Kody tried to explain.

She could hear Frank, comforting her mother. He was a good man; she really liked and respected him.

He took the phone. "Kody, we'll get right home."

"No! No, there's nothing you can do here. There's going to be an autopsy."

"Of course," Frank said. "A sudden death like that. Did his heart just give out?"

"Maybe. They don't know. Frank, don't let Mom come yet. When there are funeral arrangements, I will make sure you all know. Okay? Please, there's nothing either of you can do. I'm just going to do my best to help Rosy. Okay?"

"I'll do my best to keep her here, Kody. Cliff was a friend to your family. A dear friend to all of you."

"And he loved dolphins and sea creatures, too."

"Your mom is going to be worried about you, Kody."

"I'm fine. I have Rosy and Colleen and a host of friends down here. I promise I'll let you know when you need to be here."

She spoke to her mother again, and she managed to convince her at last that there was nothing she could do for the moment.

While Kody loved her mom, she just didn't really want her around right now…

Not when she was wondering if Cliff Bullard had been murdered.

Inconceivable! The man had been loved.

And still…

Maybe someone hadn't loved him all that much.

★ ★ ★

Brodie woke just as the sun was brightening his room and lay awake for a while, contemplating his day. He wouldn't be heading out with Ewan—the Sea Life crew was off for the day; police divers were still investigating the site. But there was no way to be the kind of man who has a PI license, to have discovered a dead body, and not want to know who the man had been and how he wound up dead in a newly discovered wreck.

Brodie wondered if he'd be able to tack himself on to the local police investigation. He had met Liam Beckett a few times before on his trips to the Keys, but he didn't know the detective well. He was someone Brodie had liked immediately. One time, he had actually been able to help him on a case. They had a tacit understanding: they were both "gifted" with a sixth sense, that of sometimes being able to see the dead.

Like the dark shadow on the ship, a remnant of the dead man who had led Brodie straight to his body.

He supposed the dead man would have been discovered eventually, but the shadow had been something.

He hoped that the man—whoever he might be—would find substance in something more than shadow. And point the way straight to his murderer.

It seldom proved to be that easy.

One dead man…and then another.

Naturally, the night haunted him—the musician he'd barely met dropping dead mid-song. And then, Dakota McCoy. Was she right? Had her friend been murdered? If so, his murder had been planned out and carefully executed. It was a stretch. Cliff Bullard had probably quite simply dropped dead from natural causes.

If Kody hadn't suggested that something wasn't right, would he even be questioning it?

He was incredibly curious about Kody. Attracted, yes.

Why had she been wary of her house when he'd walked her to the door?

She'd said that she lived alone. Maybe she hadn't planned on being alone that night? He didn't think that was the case. It didn't seem as if she would watch a friend die and then head home to meet someone.

He rose, wishing that he did have authority in Key West. He felt incredibly restless, as if he needed to be involved in the cases. Last night, when the body from the water had been sent to the medical examiner up in Marathon, and Liam and his officers had gone as far as they could for the night, Liam had suggested that they grab a beer and something to eat at the tiki bar.

It was supposed to be a way to chill out after the long afternoon of corpse removal and what investigation could be done so far beneath the water's surface.

Water. It was a great way to dispose of evidence. Especially salt water; it had a way of removing what little trace evidence that might have been discovered.

He was surprised when his phone rang; he glanced at it. He didn't know the number, but it was local to South Florida.

Kody?

No, she wouldn't be calling him. Not today, he was certain. She would be seeing Cliff Bullard's wife and doing what she could to help.

It was Liam.

"You have plans today?" the detective asked him.

He should have plans. He'd taken himself on a vacation to decide what to do. He and his older brothers—Bryan and Bruce, both equally gifted—had talked about becoming a three-man investigation company. It would be easiest to work with each other. No explanations needed.

But first Bryan and then Bruce had decided that they wanted

to join a unique unit of the FBI—a place where there would be no explanations needed, either. The Krewe of Hunters, as it was known, had been put together by a man named Adam Harrison—a very rich man and philanthropist who had learned after the death of his son that there were forces beyond what was scientifically known and accepted. He'd called upon a seasoned agent, Jackson Crow, to pull it together.

Bryan and Bruce had to apply to the academy and go through all the regimen that went with being a federal agent. But upon graduation, they'd go right into the Krewe—which even had its own offices.

Brodie had come down here, where—usually—time diving and out on the water helped him reason through his next steps in life.

He'd been given an invitation to join the Krewe, as well—assuming he graduated from the academy.

"I don't have a thing in the world planned," he said.

"Good. I'm heading up to Marathon—it's about an hour's drive."

"Sure. I'm doing nothing but spinning my wheels," Brodie said.

"I'll pick you up in thirty minutes. Enough time?"

"More than ample. And, hey, thanks for letting me in on all this."

"My partner is up in Alaska, fishing, for the next three weeks. I like a back and forth conversation, a pro and con. We've kind of worked together before, and it went well. As far as solving the situation went."

"Yeah. Thanks. Hey, did you find the cup that Cliff Bullard had been drinking out of?"

"No. In fact, three different people went through every bit of foliage anywhere near Cliff. There was no cup."

"I think I even saw Cliff throw it down."

"In all the melee, friends, the EMTs and the cops, it's possible that someone just picked it up absently and threw it in the trash."

"Possible," Brodie said.

"You don't think that's likely?"

"I'm just saying that it's possible that there was something in it—something that caused him to have a reaction. And it's possible that person made a point of seeing that the cup disappeared."

Liam was silent.

"You think that Cliff was murdered?" he asked. "Brodie, you're not a local. I can't think of a soul down here who didn't like the man."

"But there might have been."

"Well, we'll see."

Brodie hesitated. "We won't see," he said softly, "if we don't look."

Again, Liam didn't reply. "We'll look," he said after a minute.

They finished the call. Brodie headed into the shower. He was grateful to be involved.

It would be impossible for him not to want to know answers.

And it was more than that.

It was Dakota McCoy.

Waking up was painful.

Sleep had eased the loss of Cliff Bullard; morning brought back to her the fact that it was all far too real.

She had just showered when the phone rang.

It was Rosy. She spoke in a teary whisper, breaking Kody's heart into even smaller bits.

"Can you—can you come over? Oh, I forgot…the museum. You need to be working."

"No, I need to be with you," Kody assured her.

"But…so much is happening with that wreck they discovered. Oh, Kody, that poor man. And my poor Cliff…"

"I'll be right there, Rosy," Kody promised.

Hanging up, she quickly dressed and went on downstairs.

Coffee was brewed; the captain was excellent at pushing the on button. He couldn't manage the pouring of a cup of coffee, but he could manifest strongly enough to push buttons.

"How are you?" he asked her.

"I'm okay. But I do have to go see Rosy. Cliff was really the longtime resident here. Well, you know that. You know almost everything."

"Not at all. I know what I've observed over time. And, you know that even dead, I actually have to be somewhere to have observed what went on there. I do know that Cliff was an amazing man, dearly loved down here. And his poor wife must be devastated." He gave her a sad smile. "The man was a fine musician. Through the years, I spent many a night wandering down Duval to Front Street and then heading in to hear him. He will be missed."

Kody nodded, pouring coffee and drinking it quickly, looking at him.

She hesitated. "Captain, can you…feel him, or sense him?"

"No—if his spirit has remained, he hasn't dropped by this house. But I do think I'll do some wandering myself."

She nodded. "I know it sounds extreme, but…it wasn't right."

"I'll see what I can see. And hear—and sense," he assured her. As if to prove his point, he tipped his sweeping hat, and left.

"Thank you," she called after him.

She finished her coffee quickly and headed out. Rosy's house was on Simonton; it was an easy walk. Kody owned a car, and she liked to drive, but there was no sense driving when it was just a matter of blocks. It was the same with the museum. Parking was always at a premium in Key West, and she was just accustomed to walking when places were close.

As she started out, she realized that she hadn't called Colleen, her assistant and helper in all things at the museum. She pulled out her phone.

Colleen was amazing. But she was shy. She was an incredibly hard worker, but she had little faith in herself as a woman. She never dated; though, in truth, she was attractive enough. She had a way of drawing in on herself and wearing clothing that did little to flatter her form.

"Kody!" Colleen said, answering the phone. "I've seen the news, and right off—you must not worry. I will take care of everything. I don't know how busy we'll be anyway on a Monday morning. I'll be working on displays and archiving all the artifacts. And greeting guests we might have! I'm already here— seriously, you must not worry. And I'm so, so sorry."

"Thank you, Colleen. What are you doing in there so early?"

"I—I couldn't sleep last night."

"Oh, did you hear…last night?"

"No, this morning. When I turned on the news. A dead man on the ship! Police investigating—and then…well, poor Cliff. There's little I can say…"

Colleen sound strangely disconcerted. Organization and a calm look at any situation were usually her forte.

"Are you all right?" Kody asked her.

"Of course, of course. I'm fine."

She was lying, but Kody would have to find out why later.

"I'll be in to see you by the late afternoon, okay?"

"You don't need to—"

"I'm restless. At some point, I'll be there."

"Oh…okay. Whatever you like. But I want you to know that I am here for you."

"Thank you," Kody said softly. She hung up, then picked up her pace, steeling herself to go see Cliff's widow.

"Where are we going?" Brodie asked. "The morgue?" He tried to keep his voice flat. Sometimes, if a dead man's spirit remained, you could actually feel it by touching the body.

Few spirits, however, hung out at a morgue. Too painful. Except once he'd had a case in which the deceased in question had been a detective. The detective had actually remained to watch his own autopsy—he hoped to solve his own murder and then lay it all out to those in authority—as soon as he could find someone with whom he could communicate.

Easiest case Brodie had ever worked. Sadly, it didn't usually work that way.

"Yes," Liam said. "They haven't gotten to start on Cliff yet. Everyone is assuming that it was a natural death, one way or another."

"One way or another?" Brodie said.

"Heart attack, massive stroke...we don't really know anything yet."

"Anaphylactic shock?" Brodie suggested.

"Maybe," Liam said. "But it seems obvious that it was natural. You don't think that it was?"

"He showed no signs of an imminent heart attack."

"Well, we need a complete autopsy on Cliff, which won't be now. At least we'll find out about our victim on the boat."

The drive up took almost an hour. By that time, Brodie learned that Liam and his wife, Kelsey, were doing well, still living at the Merlin estate Kelsey had inherited from her grandfather, who'd left a houseful of incredible artifacts, many of which would now find their way to Kody's museum. Without explaining the entire dilemma, Brodie talked about his current reason for being down in the Keys where the warm water and time in the sun and sand might help him determine himself if he wanted to stay on his own, or join the FBI, as his brothers had done. Liam, he discovered, also had two brothers.

He felt that, although they chatted almost as two old friends who had been close for years, they were both sticking to small talk and skirting around getting too deep into anything. It felt odd to Brodie, but it made the drive pass quickly.

The medical examiner on duty for the case of the body in the water was Dr. Clyde Bethany, a short man with neatly cropped snow-white hair and an easy manner. They quickly learned that the man in the water had been somewhere between his late thirties and early forties. He'd been in good shape with no obvious health issues. There were defensive bruises on his arms—he had most probably fought his attacker. A wallop on the head had certainly stunned him, but not killed him. Cause of death had been strangulation, performed most likely with an electrical cord or something similar. "We've taken fingerprints and done all the things we can do to find out his identity," Dr. Bethany said. "This isn't going to help much—his last meal was grouper, probably consumed less than an hour before his death. I'm going to suggest therefore that he was killed in Key West."

"Impossible for our murderer to have gotten him right after dinner, then down to the Keys, and then down into the water, if he'd been farther away," Liam said.

Brodie kept silent; he'd been asked to join as a courtesy. But he noted Liam touching the body, setting his hands on one of the bruises.

He'd made a point of doing that himself. Certainly, the spirit of the man was not there—not haunting the bright lights of the morgue, witnessing the last chance for his remains to speak.

But Brodie couldn't forget the dark shadow he had followed on the shipwreck.

Brodie had a theory. "By what you're saying, Dr. Bethany, he was probably struck, then he went down, and maybe managed to roll. The attacker came at him when he was on the ground. This man tried to fight him off, but the attacker had weight and leverage on him, slipped the cord around his neck. There's bruising and scrapes here on his fingers, so it seems he tried hard to fight against the cord but wasn't able to dislodge his attacker."

"I'd say that's a good example of what might well have happened," Bethany agreed. "He fought, so the attacker didn't just get him down with the blow to the head. Some kind of hard object—I have an impression, but I haven't determined yet what might have been used to deliver the blow. Florida Department of Law Enforcement people, sheriff's office, and of course, Liam, your office, will receive my findings. The lab might have better luck in determining the object used." He moved the victim's hair around. "Whatever it was, the object was broad. I keep thinking something like a restaurant napkin holder, a large paperweight— does anyone still have paperweights? Yes, actually, I have one. I'm not a spring chicken these days, so...yep, I have one. But not as big as this would have been." He looked at Liam and indicated Brodie. "This is the man who discovered our victim?"

Liam nodded.

"I was diving with the Sea Life crew," Brodie explained.

"I see. Must have been quite a shock. And yet here you are."

"Brodie's a PI," Liam explained.

"And you were there when Cliff keeled over?" Dr. Bethany asked. He shook his head. "Sad thing. I enjoyed the fellow's music quite a bit. Loved his way with people. A good man. A sad loss for us all down here in the Keys."

He was eyeing Brodie speculatively. Well, hell, yes, it was odd that Brodie had been around for two deaths. People weren't murdered in the Keys every day, nor did they just drop dead every day.

"Yes," Brodie said simply.

Liam asked if they could see Cliff.

"You saw him last night, didn't you? I hear you were there when he died," Bethany said. "You and Mr. McFadden here."

Was the old man suspicious of him, Brodie wondered?

"I was. I'd like to see the body today, though," Liam said.

"As you wish. I guess there was a lot of hoopla going on at the time, and you detectives and investigators... Well, I'm going to suggest natural causes, Liam, but you go ahead and see what you can see," Dr. Bethany told him.

They left the ship's victim, and Dr. Bethany led them to a room where three other corpses awaited autopsy.

"Mrs. Delany of Marathon," Dr. Bethany said, pointing to one. "Ninety-three, but she died alone. And Harvey Martin, retiree from Grassy Key. He was in his eighties, a snowbird. He, too, was alone in his trailer." He sighed. "And here... Cliff Bullard."

He pulled down the sheet.

There was little to see. Cliff, in death. Cold, eyes closed, as if he slept. But there was actually nothing of life to the man, though there were no gashes or bruises or anything that would indicate that the man did anything more than sleep. Didn't matter. There was life, or there was not.

Once again, like Liam, Brodie reached out to touch the corpse. And while there was no sense of him in the morgue, there was something that hinted to Brodie that he might not be quite as *gone* as his stone-cold corpse indicated.

Do you know? Could you even know just what happened? Brodie wondered.

"Thank you," Liam said softly. "Goodbye, old friend," he said softly to the corpse. "You'll always be with us—the stuff of local legend."

They thanked Dr. Bethany; once again, the doctor assured Liam that he would receive reports on all his findings.

When they were back out by the car, Liam asked, "What do you think?"

"Maybe the killer—of our ship's victim—hoped that he'd douse the life out of his victim with one swipe."

"But he was prepared—with a cord."

"Okay, so he meant to knock the victim out—and then finish him off."

Liam nodded and sighed softly. "I think you're right. Hopefully, as soon as we learn his identity, we can find a motive—and then a killer."

"Hopefully."

"And what about Cliff?" Liam asked.

Brodie shrugged. "I think… I think you're right. I think he's still with us—as a musical legend in the Keys."

CHAPTER THREE

Kody was happy to see that Rosy Bullard had gotten out of bed, gotten dressed and brushed her hair, even applied makeup.

Of course, the second she saw Kody, tears formed in her eyes and she hugged Kody fiercely.

Then she drew back, and began speaking quickly.

"I don't believe this…we were…we were still newlyweds, really. Okay, well, it was over a year. Oh, he took me on the most romantic sail for our anniversary. He was such an amazing man. His voice, Kody…at least I still have his recordings. I'll always be able to hear him. Oh, I can't believe this! If they'd only give him to me. I have to go to the funeral home. I mean, I don't know when I get his body, but I feel that I must be doing something. I must take care of all the arrangements. We'll have a funeral at the church—he would have wanted that. He was a good man, a religious man. But I'm not sure whether he'd have rather been in the cemetery, or if I should have him cremated and scatter his ashes out on the water—he loved Key West and the cemetery, but he also loved the water so very much. I just don't know what to do… Oh, Kody! It was the oddest thing. I felt that he was with me when I slept, that he was smoothing my hair back, telling me that it was going to be all right. Of course, that would be Cliff, too. So giving. Him dead, but assuring me that he was all right!"

Kody was at a loss. "I'm so sorry, Rosy. So sorry."

"I know you loved him, too."

"Very much."

"And he was playing when he died. Playing your song—your dad's song. You were singing. At least…he was doing what he loved, with someone he loved. That's a bit of comfort to me. I just thought…well, I thought we had years to go."

"Rosy, you were his happiness."

"I hope so. I truly hope that, at the very least, I made his last year a very happy one."

"I know so," Kody said. "Is there…is there anything I can do for you?"

"It's so soon…it just happened. I don't know… I don't know how I'll ever go through his things. His clothes… There are charity foundations that can make good use of them. I just don't… I'm lost, I'm afraid. I feel that I should be cleaning, or working, or doing something. Moving, being busy."

"Being busy isn't a bad thing, but I don't know if you have to go through all Cliff's belongings yet. That would probably be painful. Painting makes you happy. Maybe you want to draw, or perhaps even find a picture of the two of you and create a painting from that," Kody suggested.

Rosy nodded thoughtfully.

"Coffee," she said.

"Coffee?"

"Yes, let's have coffee. And then maybe… Kody, this may sound strange, but would you mind going through the bedroom, folding up his clothing… I had a friend who lost her husband, and a year later, she hadn't touched any of his things. I don't want to go that route. I'm going to have to live without him—I have to become accustomed to that without, without…"

"Not to worry, Rosy. I will do anything you need."

"Coffee first. Then…"

Rosy brewed coffee, talking all the while. About the way she and Cliff had met. The way that Cliff had serenaded her. How it had been, getting to know his friends, the community of the Keys, the way that Cliff had made everything so easy for her.

Finally, she seemed to be talked out.

"I think I will do a painting," she said.

Rosy set up; Kody went on into the bedroom to start collecting and folding Cliff's clothing.

And as she did so, she thought of the man who had been her father's friend, and her friend, and she thought about the music, and how different her personal world would be without him.

"My friend, my dear, dear friend. I thought there would be so many more years. No, in truth, I never thought about losing you at all," she said softly.

There were pictures on the dresser. She picked up one that was of her as a child with Cliff and her dad. She was between the two of them, holding a hand of each man. There were more pictures: Cliff playing at the bar hut. Cliff with a giant fish he'd caught in the Florida Straits. Cliff, just holding his guitar.

Cliff with Rosy. Smiling, holding her tightly. Loving her so much.

Kody went back to work.

"I'm going to help Rosy, however I can," she vowed out loud. She waited.

But if Cliff had somehow stayed on, he didn't answer her. And he didn't appear.

She prayed he was at peace.

A police artist had done a sketch of what the dead man from the ship might have looked like in life; it had gone out in local media.

By the time Brodie and Liam arrived back in Key West, they'd identified him.

His name was Arnold Ferrer. He had come down from Georgia after the discovery of the shipwreck.

His great-great-great-great grandfather had been on the ship; he had survived the sinking. He hadn't been a slave, chained in the bowels of the ship. Ferrer's antecedent had been a slave trader from Portugal. Arnold Ferrer had documents that he'd wanted to turn over to Sea Life and/or the new museum.

A woman named Beverly Atkins was waiting for them at the Key West police station when they arrived; she had information.

Beverly owned the Sea Horse bed-and-breakfast on Simonton Street.

Brodie recognized her.

She had been at the bar the other night.

She was sitting in Liam's office with Detective Al Garcia, a man Brodie had met the day before, when the police had arrived in force after he'd discovered the body.

Al was listening as Beverly, a silver-haired little slip of a woman, talked a mile a minute. The man—late twenties with a pleasant manner and sympathetic dark eyes—was looking a bit frazzled.

He seemed glad when he saw that Liam had returned.

"Detective Beckett is head of this investigation," Al said, rising as Liam and Brodie walked into the office. "Perhaps, you can tell him…"

"Oh, Liam!" Apparently, Beverly Atkins knew Liam well. She stood and threw her arms around him; Liam was a big man. The tiny woman looked like a little elf creature clinging to him.

"Bev, Bev, it's okay," Liam said gently.

"No, no, it's not okay. What a wonderful man he was. I was welcoming people in the parlor when he arrived, and we chatted quite a bit. He told me exactly what he was doing down here.

He told me that he felt it was so important in this country that we remember the good and the bad. He's always been ashamed that he had an ancestor who was involved not just in owning slaves—but in procuring slaves. I told him that was just silly—his ancestor lived well over a hundred years ago. But, Liam, it meant so much to him. He was with me for two nights. All he talked about was that he had an appointment with a man from Sea Life, and that he was incredibly anxious to get by our new museum and speak with Kody McCoy. Liam, how could this have happened to him?"

"Bev, I don't know," Liam said, soothing her. "But I will find out."

Al Garcia cleared his throat, nodded to Brodie in acknowledgment, and then said, "Excuse me!" and made an escape.

Bev suddenly noted that Brodie was in the room. "Oh. Hello," she said, swallowing, standing on her own and flushing.

"How do you do," Brodie said.

"This is Brodie McFadden," Liam said in introduction. "Brodie, Miss Beverly Atkins."

"Oh, Mr. McFadden, you've come at a bad time for us, a very bad time."

"Brodie found Mr. Ferrer, Bev."

"Oh! Well, thank you. Is thank you the right thing to say? Can I be grateful that you did find the poor man's body rather than leaving it to the nasty ravages of the sea?"

"I'm sure he would have been found by someone from Sea Life," Brodie said. "But I happened to be exploring that deck and... I'm glad he's been found, as well. As quickly as possible. And, of course, we'll hope to solve this quickly, as well. Ease whatever pain can be eased for the family."

Bev Atkins sniffed. "He was the last of his family. Except for his little daughter, five years old, who is being raised by a very good friend. Well, actually, the child's mother. All I know is her first name—Adelaide. Mr. Ferrer was a different persuasion, sexually, and he told me that he'd had a fling trying to prove that he wasn't… Oh, he was such a lovely man! I can't believe the way we came to chat when he was with me such a brief period of time. People do terrible things to other people."

"We will do our best for him, Bev. And you've helped so much. We didn't know who he was," Liam said.

"We had nothing on him at all, and now, thanks to you, we have someplace to start," Brodie added, and then flushed slightly. He was still just a guest here. No, he decided. Liam was letting him in.

He had found the body.

This was his case, too.

"You might talk to the people at Sea Life," Bev said. "Oh, and Kody! He must have had an appointment with Kody. He wanted her to have the documents and everything for the mu seum. I mean, it's her museum, but she's done all the right legal maneuvering to make sure that what she has there that's precious and historical is not lost, but turned over to other institutions in case she has trouble. Arnold had talked to her—had to have been her, I'm pretty sure. Her little assistant doesn't do the talking to folks about what does and doesn't go in the museum. Oh, dear. Kody worked so hard for that museum. She's such a great girl…and Cliff Bullard last night, too. Poor thing. It's all just horrible!"

Kody McCoy again. But of course, Key West could be a very small place.

"Do you know of anyone we can contact?" Liam asked Bev.

"No," Bev said sadly. She brightened. "But I do have his home address."

"Thank you, Bev. Thank you so much," Liam said.

"I guess… I guess that's it," Bev said. She turned toward the door that led from Liam's office. She paused and looked back at

Brodie. "Welcome to the Keys!" she said dryly. Then she shook her head. "I'm so sorry that you came here for all this!"

"I've been here before," he assured her. "I love Key West."

"But all this…"

"All this will be solved," he told her.

She glanced at Liam.

"Brodie is a private investigator," Liam explained.

Bev was still just staring at Brodie. She took his hands in hers. "Yes, well, I guess that's it. But there's something more. Something special about you, young man."

"Well, thank you."

"I'm psychic," Bev assured him seriously. "I know," she added in a whisper.

"Again, thank you," Brodie said.

When she left, Liam shook his head. "Well, we know who the victim was—I wish to hell I knew why someone would want to kill him. The ship? Something to do with the ship?"

"He wanted things in the open—he wanted his documents given to the museum. He wanted to feel better about himself—and his family."

"Maybe someone didn't want those documents out in the open? But it's so far in the past."

"Then again, maybe it doesn't have anything to do with the ship."

"What else then?" Liam asked, shaking his head.

"Damned if I know—just playing the devil's advocate," Brodie told him.

"Well, nowhere else to start. Want to come with me?"

"Where to?"

"Time to check out Sea Life."

And Brodie hoped, maybe, in a bit, time to talk to Kody McCoy again.

Because they needed to find out if she knew anything.

And because he wanted to see her again.

Kody had gone through Cliff's clothing, folding it all in little piles for Rosy. While it seemed that Rosy was trying to move forward—at a frantic pace that might just get her through the loss—Kody wanted everything as neat and easy to see as possible, just in case there was something Rosy wanted to keep. Kody couldn't know if there was something that had more significance than the rest.

She left at last, realizing that the hours had gone by very quickly. The afternoon was waning. She'd been there since early morning, and she'd barely seen Rosy.

She left the bedroom and hurried out to the porch sunroom in back.

Rosy had been industriously painting, just as Kody had suggested.

"What do you think?" she asked happily.

"I think it's great," Kody said, studying the painting. Rosy had found a great snapshot of Cliff to work from. He was standing in front of the brick walls of Fort Zachary Taylor in dashing pirate attire, a sign reading "Pirate Days!" behind him.

Cliff had loved playing pirate.

There was even a stuffed parrot on his shoulder.

Rosy had turned the snapshot into a colorful and fun painting. Cliff's enthusiasm for life seemed to be fully visible in his eyes. His stance was cocky—Cliff could be cocky. Shy, too. He had been fond of fun and teasing others, but never in a way that was hurtful.

"Seriously—it's really great," Kody repeated.

She almost jumped at the sound of a knock at the door. Rosy frowned and looked at Kody, a hint of panic in her eyes.

"I know I should have people in. We should all sit around. We should talk about Cliff. But I'm not ready. I don't want neighbors bringing casseroles. I… I need to be alone right now. Oh, not you, Kody—being with you is fine. Or if one of our close friends came by…"

"I'll get it," Kody assured her.

She went to the door. Peeking out the peephole, she saw that Emory Clayton had come; he was, as usual, dressed in cargo shorts and a T-shirt, a sailor's cap pulled low over his forehead. Emory was a shoo-in for the Hemingway contest each year. He refused to enter, saying that he might be a "freshwater Conch," but, in his mind, he was all Conch, and the contest was to bring down more and more tourists.

He was rubbing his bearded chin thoughtfully, which meant he was uneasy. Sometimes, it was difficult and uncomfortable to be a friend—and to worry about saying the right things.

She quickly opened the door and gave him an encouraging smile. "Come on in. I know that Rosy will be anxious to see you."

"Kody, I'm so glad you're here. Is it all right if I come in?"

"Absolutely."

"You're sure?"

"I am."

He walked in just as Rosy came out to the entry. "Emory," she said softly. "Thank you so much for coming over."

"Oh, Rosy, I'm so sorry!"

"I am, too."

They stood apart for an awkward moment, then Emory took a step, and Rosy moved over to him, and they hugged. For a moment he was stiff, and then he was natural. "Rosy, we all loved him. But of course, none of us was…you."

"And he loved you. He was blessed with such good friends," Rosy said.

"I just thought that I'd come by…sit with you for a while," Emory said.

"That's lovely. Kody just went through Cliff's clothing… I'm painting."

"Will it make you nervous if I sit and watch?" Emory asked.

"It would be lovely," Rosy said.

It was a cue to be able to leave if Kody had ever heard one, knowing Rosy wouldn't be on her own.

"Okay, then… I'll go on and get some things done," Kody said. "Rosy, you call me if you need anything," she added.

"I'll be here," Emory said, as if assuring her that she had done her time; it was his part now as a friend to be there.

Kody gave Emory a quick kiss on the cheek and then hugged Rosy back. "He loved you so—like the daughter he never had," Rosy told her.

Kody slipped outside. The sudden feeling of relief made her ashamed, but sad to say, it was true—it was hard to handle someone else's grief.

"Where was I?" Ewan Keegan asked, appearing perplexed.

They were at the Sea Life offices on Whitehead. Ewan was at his desk; he'd greeted Brodie and Liam with a bit of anxiety and expectation, but now he was realizing that he was actually being queried as a possible suspect.

"The night before last was when our victim was killed, according to the best time schedule our ME can give us," Liam said.

Ewan stared at Brodie—as if he, as a friend, should have been able to explain that, beyond a doubt, he hadn't murdered anyone.

"Ewan, forgive us," Brodie said. "It's standard procedure. The man's name, we know now, was Arnold Ferrer. He was here with documents pertaining to the ship. You're one of the main contacts for Sea Life. These questions have to be asked. They'll eliminate you as a suspect and help lead to the right direction."

Brodie hoped that he had managed to be truthful—and placating.

"Night before last… I called you at nine," he told Brodie. "You had just driven down from Miami, and we were talking about the dive."

"What about before and after nine?" Liam asked.

"Before?" Ewan blinked, thinking about the question. "I ate in the hotel restaurant off Sunset Pier—and the waitress was Lizzy Smith. I know she'll remember that I was there. Oh, I was there when I called Brodie and found out that he had arrived, and then…" He was thoughtful, and then he perked up again. "I was out late. There was a great band at the Irish place on Duval. I was there until about midnight. And then—then I went home. And I live alone. In a house. I don't know how to prove anything beyond that."

"That's all," Liam said. "What about your coworkers?"

"We have six full-time divers—that includes me, head of the dive team. We also have four men on board working with the equipment, and I know that they can attest for one another, but I'll give you a list of the names of everyone involved. After we finish for the day—around seven most of the time—the divers usually chill out and head to the island. Only the four techs stay on board overnight. Thing is, the guys on the ship—unless they all conspired to murder this man, and God could only know why they would—are pretty much dumbfounded. Well, you know, Liam, you were there when we assisted the police divers bringing up the body. It was sad and interesting, what with following the PADI rules for rate of ascension. But, on top of one dead body, we didn't want anyone having decompression sickness. If you recall, we talked about it with the staff on ship after we brought the body up."

"I know," Liam said.

"Thing is," Brodie added quietly, "the body got there somehow. When you're diving with your guys, most of the time, the techs can see you, right?"

"One of us travels with a camera—and I always have a communication mask. We don't all have them. One day we will. Sea Life is nonprofit. We work on low budgets."

"I'm sure we'll discover that Sea Life wasn't responsible," Liam said. "We have to talk to everyone. You understand that."

"Yeah," Ewan said. He didn't sound sure. "What kind of documents did he have? Why would anyone kill him over that? He was trying to make sure that people saw how horrible that history was—just how cruelly people were treated. He wanted to expose his ancestor... It's not as though he was trying to hide anything."

"We'll study the documents soon. We just found out his identity and where he was staying," Brodie said.

"We have people in there now, acquiring his things. Maybe the documents will give us a clue," Liam said.

"And maybe we'll find out that he was killed for a reason that had nothing to do with the ship," Brodie said.

Ewan just shook his head. "Tragic. Whatever, however, just tragic. And then..."

"And then?" Liam asked.

"Well, Cliff dropping dead the same damned night."

"Cliff is a major loss to all of us. But this man, Arnold Ferrer...he was murdered. In cold blood. We have to find the truth."

Liam was a good cop, Brodie knew. A really good, dedicated cop.

But he couldn't help wondering himself if it wasn't too much of a coincidence.

Both men dead on the same day.

Then again, how could they be related?

Ewan passed a paper across the table. "Four techs, six divers. These are their names—along with the places they're staying. Only Josh Gable and I are at our own residences. The others opted for the Sand Castle—it's just off Front Street. Easy for them to get to the ship and back, and close enough to restaurants, groceries, all that. You should be able to reach them all easily. No one was at the site today except for the police divers."

"Yes, I know. And I'll be going down myself tomorrow," Liam said.

"Not to be a jerk when a man died, but...when are we able to get back down?" Ewan asked.

"Should be the day after," Liam said. "Don't worry—we will figure it all out."

"Wish to hell I believed it would ever make sense," Ewan said.

"It may never make sense," Brodie told him. "Murder—it seldom makes sense. But I believe that Liam and his team will get to the truth—however senseless it might be."

It was hard for Kody to imagine that just a day ago she and her friends had been congratulating themselves on a first-time festival that had gone so incredibly well. Everyone from musicians to visual artists, writers to performers, had been so willing and ready to collaborate with one another.

She'd been busy keeping a hundred plus people happy—but she'd been so happy and amazed herself.

She was proud of her museum.

It has once been an old Victorian house, complete with a porch and columns, whitewashed and inviting—even if it was almost flush with the building next to it.

The door was open—as it should have been, it wasn't six o'clock yet—and she went in. Colleen was seated at the desk, working on an inventory sheet. She looked up, ready to greet the public—as in a paying customer—and then her smile turned a little sad as she saw Kody.

"Hey. I did tell you not to worry," she said.

"I wasn't worried. Emory is staying with Rosy now. I was there all day and… I guess I just wanted to come by. The place is still new to me and sometimes, I can't believe it myself that I actually got it open."

"Well, if it helps you, I'm glad you're here."

"You look especially pretty today," Kody told her. Colleen was a pretty girl—she just usually seemed to have that knack for downplaying herself.

Colleen flushed, glancing toward the door that led into the exhibit rooms. The main rooms included one dedicated to pre-European times, one dedicated to the colonists who arrived from Europe and various nearby islands, one to the changing flags of Key West, one dedicated to the pirate days that became the rich time of the wreckers, one room to the 1800s and the Civil War, and one dedicated to the sinking of the *Maine* and modern days. Two fun rooms were dedicated to the strange events that had occurred in Key West, and the hauntings and ghost stories, and there was a big gallery for local artists and musicians, the many creators in all their forms who had come from the island or spent time there, working and contributing to the culture of Key West.

Her father's history and work were included in that room.

"We have guests still?" Kody asked.

Colleen smiled proudly. "Ten still in there. I told them not to worry—we don't let anyone in after six, but they were welcome to stay. I'm not going anywhere tonight, so it doesn't really matter. I mean, that's all right—right?"

"That's incredibly nice of you," Kody assured her.

"No, it's just… I love this place, too," Colleen assured her.

"Thanks. I'll just see how they're doing."

A single man in his late thirties or early forties was in the first room—one that described Key West from the time Ponce de Leon sailed by the southernmost islands and called them "Los Martires" or island of martyrs, to the time, about a hundred years later, when the island appeared on most maps—called Cayo Hueso, or Bone Key. Early indigenous tribes had been pressed south as European settlers arrived on the Eastern seaboard of North America. The Calusa were forced south until they fought a last battle with other tribes—and their bleached bones were left upon the sand and those who survived found refuge in Caribbean islands and were swallowed into history. The British wound up with possession for about twenty years; the islands were then inhabited frequently by Cuban fishermen, new Americans and the British, with none of the above really exerting any kind of control. At the end of the American Revolution, Florida, along with the Keys, was ceded to Spain. In early 1819, all of Florida was then ceded to the United States.

And it was time to go on to another room.

Kody caught up with a family of four in the "Arr! The Pirate's Place!" room. The kids were playing at a table where she left bandanas and sweeping hats and plastic swords specifically for children. The parents were studying a poster on Commodore David Porter, who had rid the Keys of pirates but who had also been almost as disliked by the residents as he was by the pirates.

She greeted them, and they told her what a great time they were having—the museum had been designed with work tables for children in every room—and the kids were having fun while they were learning about the island.

She thanked the family for coming and, as Colleen had, told them they were welcome to stay as long as they liked.

Her next stop was in the room that focused on the Civil War—a tough time for Key West, though no battles were fought there. Florida had seceded from the Union; the Union held staunchly to the forts. And, of course, Union ships out of Key West played havoc with Confederate blockade runners. The end of the war once again started a new era for the area.

The young couple there was admiring the display that held uniforms from the day. Kody smiled and left them to look.

In the Artist's Corner, she found another family, a teenaged son and mother and father. They were fascinated with the intimate information on her father, even more so than with the display on Hemingway.

She quickly left them, lest she get into a conversation about being her father's daughter.

Back at the entrance, she praised Colleen. "I'm so pleased. They all seem happy."

"Well, of course. Kody, few people love this island the way that you do, and it comes through in the museum. You've done a beautiful job here."

"Thank you." She couldn't help studying Colleen. The girl looked so different. Blushing, bright—pretty.

"I can't get over how nice you look," she said. Then, of course, her words sounded terrible to her own ears. "I mean, you always look nice. Just especially today. Did you do something... go somewhere...see someone?"

She was startled by the flush that crept over Colleen's cheeks.

"In my dreams, I guess," she whispered.

"What?"

"Silly, huh?"

"Um, what's silly?"

"Last night... I had an amazing dream. There was...a man. He was by my side. Oh, I mean, it wasn't an X-rated dream. Nothing like that. He was just there, touching my hair, telling me that I was beautiful and that I was sweet and that I needed to let my beauty shine. Kody, please, don't laugh at me. It was so...real. I could have sworn that...whatever. It was nice. He said that he would write a song about me. I felt like this incredible person was there flirting with me and... Please, don't laugh."

"I would never laugh. Dreaming was apparently great for you."

"I may even go out tonight."

"That's great."

"Oh! Is that wrong? I mean...with what's happened here..."

"No, it's not wrong. Go out and have a good time," Kody told her. "In fact, go now. I'm restless and at loose ends. You go!"

"Really? I mean, it was just a dream."

"Use it!" Kody told her.

Colleen smiled as she picked up her things and walked to the door. She hesitated. "I didn't know Cliff the way you did, but he seemed like a great guy."

A great guy—Cliff had been a great guy. But suddenly Kody wondered...was he now running around flirting?

She'd seen it before; ghosts often appeared as if they had regained health—in appearance younger than the age they had been when they'd died.

Or maybe Colleen had simply had a dream in which she'd met a flirtatious musician.

"Hey, it's okay," Kody assured her.

Colleen left and Kody took a seat behind the desk.

She thought about the room on the era of the Civil War and the slave ship. Soon after the *Victoria Elizabeth* had gone down, the importing of slaves had become illegal. Kody drew out the work pad where she had been planning the movement of some pieces so that she could dedicate one wall to the ship and the horrors of the slave trade.

The front door opened and closed. She'd forgotten to lock it behind Colleen.

She looked up, about to apologize and say that the museum had closed.

But the words froze on her lips.

It was the man she had just met last night; Brodie McFadden. Maybe it was the way the light created a silhouette of him in the doorway, but she felt something shoot through her body.

She felt an instant attraction—and was then ashamed that she did so. She had just lost a friend; Brodie had been there. That was it.

Still, the man was compelling in every way. She didn't feel this way any time she met an attractive man.

"Hello," he said.

She gave herself a strong mental shake.

"Hi. I'm sorry. We're not really open anymore. I'm just waiting for some visitors to leave. Okay, that was rude. How are you?"

He smiled. "I'm doing fine. I just came by to see how you were doing. I was walking down the street, and I saw the museum and I thought I'd just pop in and see if you were here."

"I'm here."

"I see. I'll get out of your way."

"No, no, no! I need to ask you—what about the cup? Did they find Cliff's cup? Are they going to test it for what might have been in it?"

"They couldn't find it."

"What? I saw him—he had a drink."

"Liam believes that in the hoopla going on when Cliff died, someone just picked it up and trashed it."

"That's—that's..."

"Not impossible," he said gently.

"No. Not impossible. Just improbable," she said. "Well, thanks. Sure. Thanks. I... Wow. I am being rude. I'm sorry. Thank you. And thank you for coming by."

"Do you have dinner plans?"

"Pardon?"

"Dinner. It's that meal that we all usually eat sometime around now. Do you have plans?"

"Are you asking me to dinner?"

"I guess I am." He was quiet a minute. "We've made some discoveries. Liam is going to be talking to you soon…but it's been on the news, so it won't matter if we talk. Say yes—it's just a meal."

No. She shouldn't go out with him. It just somehow seemed…

Dangerous.

But there was something that had happened; she hadn't seen the news. Liam was going to talk to her, but since it had been on the news…

"I still have people in the museum."

"I can wait. There's no particular exact time established for this dinner meal."

She flushed and was annoyed with herself for flushing. Just say no. She wasn't up to it.

"Sure," she told him. "I do have to wait for…"

"I understand. Mind if I wander a bit myself?"

"Um…not at all."

"Thanks!"

He moved through the hallway to the exhibits and she just sat, staring after him, wondering what it was about the man that she felt something so strongly…

Even though they had met just minutes before a very dear and old friend had suddenly dropped dead.

CHAPTER FOUR

Dakota McCoy's museum had been planned out extremely well. She had managed to set out history era by era, and add some fun.

Real pirates, of course, were not fun—and the exhibits showed that they lived under harsh and hazardous conditions—and frequently came to a very bad end.

Wrecking had once been king—and for a span of time, had provided the city with one of the highest per capita incomes in the nation. Some made their money very legitimately—some were suspected of having caused wrecks, luring ships to the ripping danger of the reefs.

Brodie moved quickly, seeing that most of the other guests were leaving.

He had been to the Keys many times—Key West, specifically. It was often thought of as a party town—and the bars and establishments on Duval and elsewhere did welcome many a bachelor and bachelorette party, reunion and celebration. But the history of the island was rich; it had always been a melting pot.

He loved the room on the "Conch Republic," the declaration that had created a little island nation—if only for a matter of hours.

The room that drew him now because of his curiosity regarding Kody featured the arts and artists. She had an exceptionally fine tribute to Hemingway, but in Key West, that was almost mandatory. There was a wonderful dedication to Jimmy Buffett, and to the many other natives and visitors who had given their expertise in some ways to the island.

Of course, he found himself most fascinated with the wall that featured her father, the late Michael McCoy.

He was studying the wall that explored his early days playing in local establishments, and the rise of his band to worldwide recognition.

He felt her walk in as he was reading dates and times and places.

"Your dad," he said, without turning.

"I was very proud of him. Proud of his music, and then prouder that he turned his life around. He adored my mom, of course, but friends like Bill…and Cliff…really helped him."

He nodded and turned to her and smiled. "I'm glad you have this here," he said. "Honest, and in the open. Your father was human, and therefore, like all of us, he had his frailties. You've managed to honor the man without putting him on a ridiculous pedestal."

"Thanks."

"He was an amazing songwriter and musician. He set the bar high."

"And for his only child. I loved him, love music and I can carry a tune—but I have different passions. I'm not my father. There have been times in my life when I've felt the need to explain that, but that's not his fault. And even if I weren't his daughter, I'd have to do a display for him—he was a major contributor to the music scene here."

He nodded. "I know what you mean."

"You do?"

"About the influence of famous parents," he said. "McFadden. Maeve and Hamish McFadden."

"Oh!" she said, startled. "Wow. I should have made the association. Your folks were so talented—together and apart. You're one of their sons. They had three—I mean, you have two brothers, right?" She waved a hand in the air. "When I was in my teens, I saw a movie called *Strive*. They were both in it. Well, I guess you know that. Anyway, I thought they were amazing. A 'Hollywood' couple who really made it. I read up on them, and I probably should have known your name, but..."

"That was a few years back. Hey, it's okay. I always felt a little badly. Three of us—and not an actor among us."

"What do your brothers do?"

"We are all licensed private investigators. My brothers are in the academy now."

"The academy?"

"FBI."

"Oh. Well, good for them. Excellent." She shrugged awkwardly.

He smiled. "We really don't act. Trust me—we'd be horrible. But I heard you doing your dad's song. You, at least, have a talent."

"I was younger when he died. I did sit in with him now and then. But I love people, places and history. He always understood that. My dad told me that each person had to move in the direction that most beckoned to them. He was... Well, I'm sure he was a total ass for many years of his life. But by the time I came around, he was great."

"It's wonderful to hear that."

"I miss him very much."

"I—um—miss my parents, too," he said, looking away and trying to awkwardly smile.

It wasn't as if he was actually able to miss them. Maeve and Hamish had never left. In actual spirit, they were absolutely determined to remain and watch over their sons.

He remembered after they'd died—it had been a freak accident in a theater—and how neither he nor Bryan nor Bruce had wanted to admit that they could see and hear them, that they were...there!

His mother, still breezing in and out, opinionated, determined; his father, ever patient, kind, smiling over her antics, even in death.

"Well..." Kody murmured. "I think the last of my guests just left. Shall we go?"

"Whenever you're ready."

"Just going to check that I locked up the back."

"Sure."

He followed her. There were two restrooms in the rear, he discovered, and a hallway door that led to a staging room. There were desks, boxes and artifacts—some of them old Key West signs, some in boxes marked "art," and a few old gravestones among other things.

Interesting, but not what drew his attention at the moment.

The back door had two bolts—no one would easily break in that way, certainly.

"You usually keep this locked, right?" he asked her, indicating the back door.

"Yes, always, really. Unless we're having a delivery of some kind," she told him.

"Sorry. The PI in me, I guess."

"Not a problem."

She headed out then, pausing to lock the front door as they reached the street.

"Where to?" she asked.

"You know that better than me."

"What are you in the mood for?" she asked him.

He laughed. "We're in the Keys. Seafood."

She smiled at that. As they walked down the street, she pointed out things that had changed since she'd been a child—and things that hadn't.

"The water is always there," she said, smiling. "I do love the water."

"You dive?"

She laughed. "I was born here. Yep, I dive."

They moved on, and she led him to a place not far away and right at the dock. It was a large restaurant; she greeted the hostess and the waiter who came to their table.

"You know everyone," he said.

"Nope, I'm just friendly. A lot of immigrants come here to work in the restaurants and shops. Cubans, South Americans, Central Americans—and a lot of young people from places like the Czech Republic, Albania, the Ukraine...you name it. Actually, I do get a lot of new friends that way."

"Nice," he told her.

They ordered, then she looked at him, growing very serious. "So what is it? What does the rest of the world know that I missed? Should have checked the news on my phone, at least."

"It might not be world news. We discovered the identity of the dead man. He was Arnold Ferrer. His forefather was Mauricio Ferrer, a Portuguese man who had an interest in—"

"Oh, my God!" she broke in.

"So—you did have an appointment with him?"

"I'd forgotten... Yes. I think I was supposed to see him tomorrow at the museum. Oh, he would have been to see Ewan or someone with Sea Life, too. I only met him over the phone, of course. Oh! I think Ewan—or someone with the company—

referred him to me. He had a fantastic notebook filled with his ancestor's observations and... Oh, no. He sounded like such a wonderful man. He said that he had friends who told him that he should never mention anyone in his past who was so horrible, but he thought the world needed to see how bad, how cruel it had been. This is so, so sad!"

"I'm sorry to add to what you're already going through."

She was quiet for a minute.

"He was murdered," she said.

"Yes. The autopsy showed that he was hit in the back of the head. He tried to fight back, but he was probably dazed—nearly knocked out by the blow. He was then strangled with something like electrical cord."

"How horrible. How truly horrible."

Her voice faded. Her face was knit with taut concern.

"Yes. Horrible," Brodie agreed.

"Why?" she wondered.

"Maybe someone didn't want the truth out."

"But...who would go against him on something like that? Especially in the Keys. Here's a great thing—we tend to accept people for who they are. We don't care a lot about ethnicity here, or religion, or sexual orientation, or...anyone's past! It's a tragic waste..."

"I'm sorry. Wish I could have held off until after we'd eaten," he said.

"No, no...you had to tell me. Liam wants to talk to me, right?" she asked.

He nodded. "He's hoping to find a clue somewhere."

"I have emails we exchanged. I can get them to you." She hesitated, studying him. "Were you...working with Liam today?" she asked.

He nodded. "Not officially."

"But...can you investigate things here?"

"Yes, Florida and Virginia offer reciprocal privileges."

"I see."

"I'm afraid there's no way I wouldn't have an interest."

"You found the body."

"Right."

She exhaled a long sigh. She'd ordered iced tea to drink and she took a long swallow of it.

"No wonder Liam is..."

"Determined?"

"Distracted," she said. She was silent a minute. "I'm concerned, of course. Horrified. And I totally want the truth to be discovered. But I don't think that Liam is giving enough attention to..."

"Cliff."

"You think I'm being ridiculous?" she asked.

"No. But when we left the morgue this morning, Cliff was still awaiting autopsy." He hesitated. "Why would anyone want to kill Cliff? Our Mr. Ferrer... Maybe his documents would incriminate someone who didn't want to be known as the descendant of a slave trader—at least, there's somewhere to follow with that. Cliff—from everything that I've seen and heard, from everyone that I've met—the guy was great. And loved."

"I know," she said softly. "He was loved."

"Well, we'll find out more tomorrow."

"Right."

"So..."

He paused, and they both thanked the waiter as their dinners arrived.

After the waitress left, Brodie smiled at her and asked, "What made you come up with your 'haunted' part of the museum?"

She looked down, pretending great interest in the shrimp dish she had ordered.

Then she looked up. "Well, we have some of the best ghost

stories in the world here. Any place this old is bound to be haunted—well, you're from Virginia. You must know that."

"We have 'Washington Slept Here!' signs all over," he agreed. "And there's a charming place—privately owned and opened now and then—that Jefferson had purchased for a relative. People claim that he can be seen sitting by the fire, contemplating, now and then."

"Nice," she murmured. "We have poor Elena de Hoyos—a man named Carl Tanzler fell madly in love with her. He was working as an X-ray technician and tried to convince her family he could save her. She had tuberculosis and died, and he bought her a beautiful mausoleum...then stole her corpse and lived with it for seven years, saying it was just fine—he had married her. And we have an old theater where a fire took the lives of many—pirate ghosts, soldier ghosts...you name it."

"A bevy of activity."

"Of course."

"And Robert the doll, of course."

"Yes, I've seen Robert. At the East Martello Museum. Creepy doll."

"Yes, well, Robert Otto—who grew up in and inherited the Artist House, a beautiful Victorian B and B now—blamed everything on that doll. It is a creepy as hell doll. We have that story in our 'haunted' area, as well. But of course, time...time lends to ghost stories."

"It does."

"Your house is historic, right?"

"It is. It belonged to a Captain Blake Hunter. He was a Confederate—and on a blockade runner when he was killed. Sad, of course. The thing is, he was a Floridian. Back then, you owed your first loyalty to your state—remember, the US was formed as a union of states. United States. But we didn't have the internet and constant news and travel and when Florida became part of the Confederacy, he went with the Confederacy."

She seemed determined that he understand that her house had been owned by a good man.

He smiled. "It's a nice house."

"It is. I love it." She quickly turned the conversation away. "So, how do you like where you're staying?"

"Love it."

"And you came to relax. Boy, do you know how to have a vacation," she murmured, her tone dry and sad.

"So it seems."

She hesitated, looking at him.

"Will you…will you look into Cliff's death, too? Please?" she added softly.

He reached across the table, placing his hand on hers.

It had just been a kind gesture. But he found he loved touching her.

He withdrew his hand.

"Of course," he promised.

She tried to get him to talk; he tried to get her to talk. He listened, realizing that he was often lost in her eyes.

He didn't touch her again.

He told her about the mountains in Virginia, about living near DC.

She talked about fishing and diving with her parents, and how her mother had recently remarried a remarkable man. And she talked about the festival where they had paired performers with musicians and writers with artists and every mix within.

But in doing so, she came back to Cliff.

At last, they had coffee.

And then it was time to leave.

"You don't have to walk me home," she told him.

"I do."

"No, really, you don't. I live here. I walk these streets all the time."

"I had dinner with you. In my family, that makes my walking you home a commandment. Hey, you wouldn't want me in trouble, would you?"

"With the dead?" she asked. "Lord, no!"

He smiled. No, she really didn't understand.

They walked on to her house. She paused on the sidewalk before the little stone path that led to her porch.

There were lights on.

He could see a strange silhouette within the house.

She wasn't going home to a lover, he felt certain. But she wasn't going to say anything, either.

Neither did he.

"Good night. And thank you."

"I'm sure I'll see you."

"Of course. You promised to investigate…everything."

"I did, indeed. Hey, I'm not leaving until you're inside," he told her.

She stepped back. "Okay, okay."

She walked up the steps and unlocked her door.

Before she stepped in, Brodie saw him. Tall, wearing a sweeping plumed hat—and dressed in an 1850s frockcoat.

He had been waiting for Kody to come home.

Watching over her?

Captain Blake Hunter?

Had to be.

Brodie watched the door close, and then he headed down the street, making his way to his own bed-and-breakfast.

Kody was right.

He didn't know how he knew, or how—under the circumstances—he could be so convinced.

There had been two murders in Key West.

And he knew that no matter what, he wouldn't leave until he knew the truth.

"You're all right?" the captain asked Kody as she entered. He sounded anxious.

"Of course, I'm fine. I spent the day with Rosy, but then Emory came and I went to the museum. Brodie McFadden came by and we went to dinner," Kody assured him. "Why?"

"I don't like what's going on," the captain said.

"Blake, no one likes what happened. But please don't be worried about me."

"I have to worry about you," he said indignantly. "That's what I do!"

"Well, thank you, but I'm fine. Honestly."

"Hmm."

"Were you here all day worrying?"

"Oh, no. I went strolling around town, and I stopped into a bar or two." He shrugged. "Ah, even for a seaman in the day, I wasn't much for rum. But it's good now and then to sit and listen to the music—not that I could imbibe the rum now anyway. Not the point. I listened. And everyone is talking about the murdered man. They know who he is now."

"Yes, I know."

"He was involved with the ship."

"I was supposed to meet with him," Kody said.

"And there's the rub!" he announced. "Why I should worry—you're involved with that cursed ship!"

"I'm not involved with the ship itself—I haven't—"

"You are planning a display. For the museum."

"I already have a segment on the Civil War. And slavery," Kody reminded him.

"Maybe you should take it down."

"I will not! What—you'd actually want me to take out an era of history?" she asked incredulously.

"No," he admitted. "It's just that times are tense. People attack one another over small and imagined slights these days. Over the past. Over any perceived insult." He hesitated. "Kody, someone murdered that man."

"They'll find out who, Captain. They'll catch him," she tried to assure him.

For a man who was already dead, Captain Blake Hunter seemed incredibly anxious.

"Hey," Kody said. "Captain… Blake. You're worried—so you keep doing what you're doing. Travel the streets. See what you can, listen to tourists, locals, anyone. There has to be someone out there who knows something."

He swept off his hat and bowed to her. "I'm off then. I haven't quite got the qualifications of your newfound friend, but I shall do my gallant best."

He left her, disappearing through the closed front door.

It was so strange. She could sense him when he was there.

And she could feel it when he was not there, as well.

She glanced at the hands on the grandfather clock in the parlor to the left of the hallway. It was past ten. Not late at all for nightlife in Key West.

She walked down to the stairway and made her way up to her room. Ready for bed, with the lights out and room quiet, she lay down to sleep.

She couldn't.

The questions kept running through her mind. Why was Arnold Ferrer killed?

Why did Cliff die?

She lay awake a long time. Somewhere in there, she knew that the captain had returned.

He never entered her room, but she knew that he was near.

He had taken up a stance in the hall, just beyond her door. Regardless of whatever he could or couldn't do, he would be standing guard throughout the night.

The sun was out, but the water was deep. With flashlights attached to their masks, Brodie and Liam could see an extended view before them and around them. It was a strange feeling being down there.

Brodie's last dive had been when he'd worked with the police divers to bring up the corpse of Arnold Ferrer. He had waited on the boat with Ewan and Liam while the divers had then searched and searched for anything else that they could find.

There had been nothing.

Just the man. No wallet having fallen elsewhere, no murder weapon. Just a floating dead man.

Today, he was back with Liam. Tomorrow, they would reopen the dive to the Sea Life crew and return it to those searching for history—not clues. Then again, what they would find were clues to history—artifacts that either gave credibility to or disputed the truth that had been assumed.

Under the sweeping glare of both their flashlights, they searched the ship, deck by deck.

Brodie saw tiny pieces of metal in the hold, and he was certain that he was seeing the time and sea-encrusted remnants of chains. He didn't touch them. He would report to Ewan on anything that he had seen, so the Sea Life crew could follow up.

Brodie moved through the darkly shadowed decks, listening to the sound of his even breathing through his regulator. Parts of the ship were eerily intact—as if a ghost army might move about daily, striding over the deck to take part in daily chores.

Parts were gone completely; time, the sea and the whimsy of the winds and tide had stripped away full pieces of the hull and the inner workings.

A crab, having found a home in a layer of sand on the deck, scurried by. A flash of silver moved before him: a lone barracuda, seeking a meal.

He saw Liam's light behind him; he turned. Liam beckoned that he was heading one deck up. Brodie gave him the "okay" sign.

When Liam was gone, he stared at the spot where the body had been.

He held still in the water, allowing his buoyancy vest and a slight movement of his flippers now and then to hold him in place.

If you're here in any way, Mr. Ferrer, help me…

Brodie might have seen the dead many times, but he didn't really believe that he could communicate telepathically with a ghost that may or may not exist.

The words were to himself.

Dr. Edmond Locard, 1877-1966, had coined the Locard's Exchange Principle.

Every contact made left a trace…of something. Every criminal brought something to the scene of his crime; he took something away, and he left something behind.

What could a killer have left behind?

Of course, in modern forensics, that often included minute skin cells, tiny drops of blood, little bits of fabric or fluff…

None of which had been found down here. None of which could have remained on a body, drifting deep in the sea for more than twelve hours.

He thought he saw a shadow. Maybe a large fish moving across a shaft of light coming in through a tear in the hull.

But Brodie knew it wasn't.

He still didn't think that his thoughts had summoned the remnants of a human soul. But he did believe that Ferrer did somehow remain…a spirit lost in the depth of the sea, not manifesting completely, though not really managing to move on. Perhaps, at some point, he might.

The shadow seemed to shift.

Brodie moved. He thought about the logistics of someone bringing a body down here. If the men on Sea Life's ship *Memory* were as innocent as they appeared to be, whoever had brought the body had done so from another boat. There might have been dozens of boats in the surrounding area. The men who'd been onboard the *Memory* that day couldn't remember anything specific. But the killer had to be a diver. This was Key West: many people were divers. Many visitors came specifically to dive.

But dragging a buoyant corpse down wouldn't have been easy. It must have been weighted down.

The shadow flickered.

Brodie saw a glint in the sand. He reached down for the object.

CHAPTER FIVE

Kody wasn't sure if she'd tossed and turned all night and so over-slept because she was tired, or if circumstances had just dragged her down. She tended to be an early riser; not because she didn't wish she could make greater use of the night, but simply be-cause she seemed to awaken—no alarm needed—soon after the sun began to rise.

That morning, it was almost ten o'clock before she cracked open an eye and noted the time.

She swore, leaped out of bed, and dashed right for the shower. She'd barely gotten out before her phone started to ring.

She made a dive for it on the nightstand.

It was Rosy.

"Kody, they're going to release Cliff's body to me. I have to go to the funeral parlor today and make arrangements. Will you come with me?"

"Of course, Rosy. When do you want me?"

"Eleven? Meet there?"

"Perfect," Kody said.

She ended the call. But before dressing for the day, she dialed Colleen.

Colleen was already at the museum.

"I'm so sorry. I just woke up," Kody said.

"Good—you needed sleep. And I told you not to worry. I have it all planned out for the week. I'll be here, okay?"

"Thank you, Colleen."

"I wish I could help more."

"You're the best. Hey, how are you doing yourself? How was going out last night? Did you do something touristy or hang with friends?"

"Well, I'm not that…brave. You know O'Hara's? I went up there. They have a great karaoke host. I knew some friends would be going, too."

"And you had a good time?"

"Yes, but…"

"But?"

"Oh, I don't know," Colleen said, and laughed softly. "Yes, I had a nice time there. But when I came home, I wondered why I hadn't had the nerve to try a single song. And when I was falling asleep…"

"Yes?"

"You're going to think I'm crazy."

"Never."

"Oh, trust me!"

"Colleen, come on. You can't leave it at this kind of a tease."

"I've invented a dream lover, I guess. With the softest blue eyes and sweetest grin. Oh, it's not…not *tawdry* in any way… just…nice. Sweet. Gentle. A guy who touches me, and tells me how lovely I am, how sweet and how wonderful, and that I deserve so much. He strokes my cheek. It's… I don't know, Kody, this sounds ridiculous, but this man I'm creating in my imagination… It seems so real sometimes. He's such a flirt. But oh, so sweet! And sexy, too. Maybe one of these days... Oh, I didn't say that. I mean... Oh, I just really can't wait to go to sleep at night these days."

"You don't sound at all crazy," Kody assured her. "You're finally gaining the self-confidence that you should rightly have."

"You think?"

"Absolutely. Okay, I'll see you later."

Kody broke the call and smiled; Colleen definitely deserved to get out there and have a life. She was all the right things, sweet, smart, loyal, dedicated—and pretty, as she finally seemed to be recognizing herself.

Kody quickly dressed and hurried toward Simonton Street and the funeral home.

"It's a piece of gold chain," Brodie said. He held it before Liam, not worried that he was touching the inch-and-a-half piece of links.

He'd seen it time and again, mostly with new divers. It wasn't that earrings, chains and rings couldn't be worn, and, of course, most people did wear wedding rings when they went diving, but dangling earrings and chains could easily be tangled up in a regulator or buoyancy vest.

Liam studied the piece of jewelry.

"We'll have to find out if any of the Sea Life crew lost a chain," Liam said. "Someone could have been down there working and lost this."

Ewan was just a few feet away on the deck of the *Memory*, staring at them.

"If they admit to it," Brodie said.

"So we don't start out asking if anyone has lost a chain. We ask if they know of anyone working with them who might have one."

"A subtle difference, but, yeah, it matters," Brodie agreed.

Ewan, who had been watching them since they'd divested themselves of their dive gear, walked toward them.

"Okay, what now?"

"We need to talk to the guys," Brodie said.

"Liam sent his officers out to the *Memory* and all around town yesterday afternoon. Every man has already been questioned," Ewan said.

Brodie noted that his old friend was wearing around his neck the same medallion he'd worn for years and years. The chain was gold, and good, but old—and didn't shine like something newer. The medallion on the chain was a St. Christopher—the same one he'd worn as long as Brodie could remember.

"Come on in to the galley. Most of the guys are there," Ewan said. "Biding their time," he added dryly. "Nothing else to do until we can get back down."

In the galley, two men were engaged in a game of chess; three were sprawled about reading. One was working on something at the stove, and the other three were grouped around the galley table, engaged in a game of poker.

"Hey, guys, you all know Liam, our local cop—Detective Liam Beckett—and my friend, Brodie McFadden. Seems like we all have to talk again. You all down with it?"

Cards fell on the table.

The crew wasn't *down with it.*

They knew there was no choice.

"Sure," one man said. He was thirty, wiry strong, a good diver, and a local who'd been in the water since he'd been able to stand. Brodie already knew Josh Gable; they'd met on his initial dive—same as he'd met all the men.

"Want me to go first?" Josh asked.

"Sure. Go with Brodie," Liam said. "Mr. Greenwood," he added, pointing to the head tech, one of the two chess players, "mind coming with me? I swear, I'll be brief."

Josh Gable accompanied Brodie topside. He pulled a pack of cigarettes from his pocket. "Shouldn't smoke, huh? Did you want to start with that?"

Brodie shrugged. "You're an adult."

"So, what's up now? The cops checked me out. I wasn't on the ship. I do have roommates at my place. Two of them. And we sat around catching up on that dragon TV show, and then we all went to bed. My roommate woke up at about two in the morning and closed my door—that's not what I remember, that's what she said. She was going to play some music and didn't want to wake me. Liam knows all this."

"I don't think you're guilty of anything."

"Then why the hell are you questioning me?"

Brodie shrugged again. "I've been known to be wrong. But seriously—I don't think that this was any of you guys. I'm not even sure it has to do with the ship. Stuff a body in the ship—and who do we have to look at? You—divers, techs, people involved with the salvage."

"Right." Josh nodded vehemently. "I want whoever did this to be found and found fast. This is my island. This discovery is important. Anyway, it pisses me off big-time. Some jerk doing this…making what should have been an important discovery into an ugly thing like murder."

"Hey, any of you guys break or lose a chain down there?" Brodie asked casually.

"Not that I know about. And none of these guys wears chains—except for Ewan, of course. He says he's being buried in that St. Christopher medal of his. But…of the divers, well, you know. You've met all of us now. Ewan, me—and then Gary Wall, Sly Cormack, Jimmy Martinez and Trevor McDonald. We're the kind who don't mess with jewelry down there. Hell, Sly wears a big gold earring when we're not working, but when we're down deep, he doesn't want it on. I mean, of course, it's a matter of choice. Some people take their jewelry off to dive, especially big, flashy jewelry. Some people don't."

"Thanks. You really have no reason to suspect any of these guys, right?"

"Hell, no. Go back—not one of us has a record of any kind and we're all about as unpolitical as men can be."

"How come there are no women on this team?" Brodie asked.

"Chelsea Yarborough was supposed to be diving with us— she got a major offer to go off with one of the science channels out in the Pacific. She took the offer. Genna Maberry was to lead on tech—she wound up in the hospital. There was nothing sexist intended, I assure you. It's just the way it fell out when we lost a few of our original people. In fact, Lucy Lee, one of the women working with the artifacts, is going to take Gary Wall's place next week. Gary's wife is having a baby back up in Georgia. He's going home to be there for it."

"Thanks," Brodie told him.

"You're not a cop," Josh noted.

"Nope. Private investigator."

"Who are you working for down here?" Josh asked him.

"Myself," Brodie said.

Josh studied him and nodded. "You're all right. And I get that. I get it. I mean, you found a dead man. Guess that means something."

"To me, yes."

"Are we through?" Josh asked.

"Yeah. Thank you. Of course…"

"Yeah, yeah, there's an investigation going on, all that stuff. Don't leave town. Hey, this is my town. I'm not leaving it."

Brodie smiled. "No, I was just going to say that I hope you won't mind if we need to speak again. You are a Conch, and a diver, and, when we have a suspect, we may need more help."

"You know where to find me," Josh said. "I'll send the next guy."

The next guy came. Trevor McDonald, a big man, muscled, bald, African American—and the kind of man so striking that, Brodie imagined, both sexes noted when he walked into a room. He had a sense of command about him.

"All right, hell, I'm pretty damned sure I'm descended from somebody owned up in the Carolinas. But come on, give me a break here. I didn't kill a man trying to get the truth out there— no way in hell."

Brodie found himself smiling; he liked Trevor. He was ready to say anything the way he felt it.

"You were at the B and B the night Ferrer was killed?"

"Hell, yeah. We weren't partying too hard. I've got my wife and little boy down here. We all sat at the pool with some of the other guys for a while, then we went to our little bungalow thing and I put my kid to bed. I could hear other fellows out there—well, you know that the tech guys stay on the ship, and Josh and Ewan live down here. Jimmy, Gary and Sly—none of them are married. And there were some pretty girls hanging at that pool. I'm sure I heard them all out there until at least midnight. You're barking up the wrong tree. And too damned bad—I liked you."

"Hey. It is what it is. You know of anyone who lost a piece of jewelry on a dive?"

"If you found something, it isn't ours. We don't wear stuff down there. Oh, except for Ewan."

"Yeah. His St. Christopher."

"That's right. You through with me?"

Brodie nodded.

Trevor turned to head back down to the galley, but he paused and turned back. "Okay, so, you're still all right. Come by the B and B sometime. We'll barbecue. You'd like my kid."

"I bet I would."

Trevor nodded, and headed out.

One by one, he spoke with the rest of the divers—Jimmy, Sly and Gary. None of them had lost jewelry or broken a chain—none of them noted anything missing from anyone else. They all appeared to be honest in their answers.

Liam had spoken to the technicians; they hadn't seen anyone who had lost jewelry. Everyone knew that they'd been in their bunks on the *Memory* the night the body had been taken down to the wreck. They swore they hadn't conspired to kill anyone.

Half an hour later, a police cutter swung by to bring Brodie and Liam back to the dock.

"Thanks for being on this with me," Liam told Brodie.

"You do have your other detectives and a host of officers working on this," Brodie said. "I want to thank you—for letting me in."

"You found the body. You had been on the *Memory* already. I think those guys may have a certain sense of camaraderie with you."

"I was with that crew one day."

"And you know Ewan," Liam said.

Brodie lifted his hands in the air. "*Ewan*—he was one hell of a career soldier. Passionate about causes. I sure as hell don't see him as the perpetrator."

"No, I don't either."

Liam shrugged and looked away. "I don't know. Gut feeling, I guess. You're going to help crack this thing."

"Okay, thanks, so…what was found in Arnold Ferrer's room?"

"That's kind of curious," Liam said.

"What?"

"I don't think that the killers were ever in his room. They must have taken him by surprise out in a public place. It doesn't seem they tried to rifle through his belongings. Everything was tidy in his room. Want to study the documents? Come on by the station tomorrow."

"Will do," Brodie assured him.

He started to walk away. Then he paused and turned back. "Liam?"

"Yeah?"

"Did you talk to Kody McCoy yet?"

"I never needed to call her. She'd spoken to you. She forwarded all the emails she'd gotten from Ferrer. We're going through all those, too, now, along with what we found."

Liam's phone rang. He excused himself and answered it, and listened, and then thanked the caller.

He looked over at Brodie.

"Official from the ME. Cliff Bullard died of anaphylaxis. Somehow, the man imbibed something that he shouldn't have. He'd definitely gotten hold of something with nuts—stomach contents are still being analyzed."

"Nuts," Brodie said. "You know, I don't know why, don't know how, but…"

"You're saying Cliff's death was suspicious, too."

Brodie nodded.

Liam just shook his head, and then he sighed. "Yeah, well… he knew it. Knew he was allergic to nuts."

"Somebody could have gotten them to him on purpose."

"Somehow, yeah, maybe. Oh, hell," Liam said. He waved a hand in the air and started walking; then he turned back.

"You know, I'm trying damned hard. Sure—if you wanted to kill Cliff, it would be easy enough. Everyone knew he was deathly allergic. But he carried an EpiPen. He was careful of what he ate—and drank."

"And the only way he could have gotten ahold of anything," Brodie said flatly, "was through someone he knew and trusted."

★ ★ ★

"This is called Majesty," Shorty said, indicating one of the coffins on display. "Really top of the line—mahogany with an ivory velvet lining, and you'll notice the fine carving of the crosses."

Majesty cost many thousands of dollars.

Shorty was professional even in his speaking; Shorty wasn't short at all—he had earned the nickname for being six-feet-five inches. He was a big man, and looked the part of a horror movie mortician; in his handsome suit he might have been the evil servant of a vampire king or some other such creature.

He was actually a nice man, a "snowbird" who had eventually stayed for good. His real name was Conway Finch, he said, but everyone called him Shorty.

Kody found herself smiling; Rosy was looking at her.

Rosy was smiling, too.

They both knew that Cliff would have an absolute fit—no one should spend that kind of money on a coffin.

"I think he would love that simple little pine coffin we saw first," Kody said.

"It is eternal rest," Shorty said sadly.

"He would be eternally restless if Rosy spent that on a coffin— trust me. I knew Cliff well," Kody said.

"Very well, now, as far as interment—" Shorty began. "Mrs. Bullard, let me explain the options to you."

"My family has a vault in the cemetery. Cliff will go there."

If he was disappointed that he wasn't going to make a good sale, Shorty managed not to show it.

"All right, for the viewing…"

He went into their options. They even had to choose which hearse would be used. But while Rosy had decided on the inexpensive pine coffin, she also determined that she would help

Shorty somewhat, and ordered a number of flower arrangements through the funeral home.

When it was time to leave, Rosy turned to Kody and thanked her—smiling. "I can't believe it, Kody, but that did make me laugh. Cliff would have had a coronary and probably passed on—if—if—he wasn't already gone…hearing the price of that coffin."

Finances were always an uneasy thing. "He left you okay, right? I mean, Rosy…if you need help with anything, you'll let me know?"

"Of course, and thank you, Kody. We both had a little insurance. He was so good about that, always so concerned about me. But for now, I'm fine. And it's really, really kind of you to offer space in your family mausoleum. Which…thankfully… I mean…heaven forbid, if something happened to you or your mom… I wouldn't want to take your space."

"Frankly, my family was lucky in that, if one can say lucky about anything to do with the loss of a loved one," Kody said. "There used to be graveyards in different places—there are still a few at the church and around—but the Havana hurricane that struck Cuba and the lower Keys in 1846 sent coffins flowing down Duval from the beach, and the cemetery was set aside. My family was here then, and there wasn't anywhere near the population, so they bought a big plot—and built a large mausoleum. Through the years, some family members have asked to be cremated and have their ashes distributed places that they loved. There's lots of space in our mausoleum."

"Still, it's deeply appreciated."

"Cliff was a great friend to my dad."

"Your mom said okay?" Rosy asked anxiously.

"Of course!"

Kody realized she had barely had a chance to discuss anything with her mother yet.

But she knew her mother well.

The family tomb had come to them through Kody's father's family, but the slot right next to her dad was naturally held for her mom. She and Kody's new stepfather had made arrangements for just about everything, including final resting places.

She wasn't at all worried; she was feeling guilty. She should have called her mom again today.

"As soon as we know when the funeral will actually be, Rosy, I'll get it all set with the cemetery."

"That's lovely, Kody," Rosy began.

"I'll walk you back to your place right now," Kody said.

"My place? No, no, Sonny Atherton has come back down, and Emory and Bill are going to meet us for a late lunch. We're supposed to meet them down the street at the Hard Rock Cafe. It seems fitting—Cliff loved music so much. And he said he loved our Hard Rock best—incredibly haunted building, and great music playing all the time. You can come, right?" Rosy asked anxiously.

"Um, sure," Kody said. She wasn't sure she was feeling that social, but she didn't want to tell Rosy no.

It was the middle of the week; there were tourists on the street, but it wasn't nearly as crazy as a weekend. The walk wasn't long at all from the funeral home on Simonton Street to the restaurant on Duval, and Rosy explained to the hostess that she'd made a reservation for a private room.

They were quickly led to the second floor. There was a very large round table in the room; if they wished, they could probably seat ten people.

Kody wondered how many others were coming to lunch. Then, she thought, whatever it was that made Rosy happy, that got her through all this, was the right thing to do.

"We are the first to arrive, so choose your seat," Rosy said.

"Okay. Who did you invite?" Kody asked.

"Let's see. Emory and Bill, Liam and Kelsey—and that friend of Liam's, Brodie—you've met him, right?"

"Yes, I've met him. I think he was actually friends with Ewan Keegan, and met Liam that way."

Rosy waved a hand in the air. "I invited him, because of course, I was inviting Liam, and I thought it would be rude if I didn't invite his friend. Sonny—that sweet woman came back down here just to see if she could help me."

"That was nice. Sonny is amazing."

"An incredible dynamo of a woman. But then, this whole group is so…well, interesting. I was so delighted to get to know Cliff's friends. Kelsey Beckett is so incredibly talented with her children's books…" Her voice trailed and she asked softly, "Kelsey wasn't with you the other night, though, right?"

"She's on deadline. She went home to work. I hope she will be able to come today."

Rosy nodded, looking around the room. "Well, hopefully, yes, she can come," she murmured. "So strange, Key West. Strange and wonderful. This building is supposed to be haunted."

"Most of our old buildings are supposedly haunted," Kody said.

"You have information on the Curry family in the museum, Kody," Rosy said, nodding her approval.

"Of course. William Curry came here from the Bahamas and, if legend is true, the man was Florida's first millionaire back in the 1800s. And the mansion where we are now was the house he built for his son, Robert, as a wedding present."

"And Robert committed suicide here—in what is now the ladies' restroom, so they say. Have you ever felt creepy in there?" Rosy asked Kody.

"No, I haven't. Poor Robert, he's probably long gone on. He was ill. He inherited the fortune, and he was too ill to manage it all. I feel so sorry for him. I hope that he went on and found peace."

"Oh, Kody. Come on. All the ghost tour people love this place."

"I love it, too. I'm just saying I've never felt anything creepy here."

Rosy shrugged. "Neither have I." She looked uncomfortable. "Kody, do you believe in ghosts?"

Kody froze for a moment. "I…guess that they could exist. We're composed of energy, and supposedly energy doesn't die. And something does make each of us unique, be that a spirit or a soul. But I'm not anyone who could say… But I'm open. Why?"

"Cliff should know… I am such a coward. He shouldn't come to me as a ghost. I've said it. I've said it out loud in the house… Kody, I am such a…really pathetic chicken. I thought he might have come back. That he might have touched me at night…"

She fell silent. They sat for an awkward moment, and just then Sonny arrived. Kody stood to greet her; Rosy did the same.

"Oh, baby, we're all so, so sorry," Sonny said, hugging Rosy tightly. "And don't you worry, I'll go back to the house with you from here. Oh, Kody, were you already going to Rosy's? I just thought that maybe you needed some time.

"You must have so much work with the museum. And the news is all over Miami about the man murdered. Oh, and how can I forget, Kody—you've been in the news, too."

"Me?" Kody said.

"Yes, yes, they mentioned the museum and how you were supposed to be receiving the documents that Mr. Ferrer would be giving to Sea Life first for their quest—and then to you," Sonny told her.

Great. "Oh," she murmured. Others were now arriving, Liam and Kelsey Beckett—and Brodie.

"Liam," Rosy said, hurrying over to give him a hug. "And

Kelsey… I'm so glad you could take the time. I know that you're on a deadline, but thank you so much for coming to this little lunch. I think that things will get a little crazy once we have the wake and the funeral. Cliff was loved by many people on the island, and it seemed important that we…his people, I mean those really close to him, were able to have a little time together before…before the funeral."

"Oh, Rosy, of course," Kelsey said. She looked over Rosy's shoulder at Kody as she returned the woman's hug. "We all loved Cliff, and of course, we all love you, and want to give you all the support that we can."

Liam's wife was a friend of Kody's, as well. Kelsey had inherited a great house on a little spit of the island that was barely attached; it was a wonderful and historic place. Her grandfather had been quite the collector of rare objects—so rare that he had lost his life to a killer intent on possessing one special piece. His death had brought Kelsey back to Key West after she had been gone many years. And it had been in finding the truth that she had reunited with Liam—and they had married soon after.

Bill Worth arrived and then Emory Clayton. The last to join them were Bev and Dan Atkins—who had also been present at the bar, Kody remembered, when Cliff had dropped dead.

There was a lot of commotion as everyone greeted each other and then took seats at the round table. Bev wound up by Kody. "So sad," she said, "but so nice to do this…just a few of us who were close to Cliff and Rosy getting together. I think she's holding up well, don't you?" she asked.

"Yes, she's doing okay," Kody agreed.

Bev shook her head. Tears dampened her eyes. "Cliff… Oh, we'll miss Cliff so much. But it seems that God called him. It was his time. And it's such a loss to all of us. And, yet, Kody, I tell you, it's just terrible about that nice Mr. Ferrer."

"Arnold Ferrer? The murdered man found on the wreck? You knew him?" Kody asked.

Bev nodded solemnly. "Kody, he was staying at our place. Oh, he was absolutely lovely. Such a bright and charming man. It's just heartbreaking."

"Yes, it is. Bev, I'm sorry. I didn't realize he'd been staying at your B and B."

Bev nodded. "I feel like I'm still reeling. Oh, not like poor Rosy! But we were there, at the bar, and saw Cliff...and then we found out that our lodger had been *murdered*."

"Bev, I can just imagine how you must feel. I never met Mr. Ferrer in person."

"But you knew about him? You'd corresponded?"

Brodie McFadden was across the round table from Kody. She saw that he was watching her and Bev. She hadn't really greeted him.

He hadn't really greeted her. But then, he was being very quiet. Polite and courteous, she noted, when he spoke to Bill Worth, who was next to him.

But most of all, he was watching. And listening.

"I knew about Mr. Ferrer. I had corresponded with him. And his emails were certainly forthright and very courteous. I never met him," Kody told Bev.

Two servers came in to take their orders. Kody knew the young woman on her side of the table—Adia Martinez. They'd gone to school together.

"Hey, Kody," Adia said, pausing by her. "Great to see you, though I'm sorry about the circumstances."

"Of course, but it is good to see you," Kody told her. "How are you doing?" she asked, her question a little awkward. Adia's husband had been killed while he was on active duty with the military. She'd become a very young widow at the age of twenty-five. And she was raising a toddler alone.

But Adia smiled, ducking down for a minute to talk to Kody. "I'm okay. I'm really okay."

"I'm glad to hear that," Kody said. When Mario had died, Kody had made a point of offering to watch the baby if Adia ever needed, and to help out any way she could. But Adia hadn't called on her—she really hadn't needed to. Her mom had come down from Tennessee to be with her. "Is your mom still here?"

"She went back about a month ago. I love my mom dearly and so appreciate what she did. But she has a life, and I had a great opportunity through another friend to acquire a nanny—sweet girl just here from the country of Georgia. She's very happy to have room and board and what I'm able to pay her. She's great and working toward her citizenship."

"Wonderful to hear that," Kody told her.

"Anyway, what will you have?"

"Um…the grouper, please," Kody said.

"How's the museum going? I haven't had a chance to come by yet."

"We're doing well—but we're a work in progress," Kody said.

"I've got to get moving. Hopefully, we can chat a minute before you need to leave."

"I can wait until you have time," Kody said.

"Great!"

Adia moved on. Kody made eye contact with Brodie across the table. She glanced away, but she'd noticed that Brodie was watching her—and everyone else.

When drinks had been served and orders placed, Rosy stood up. "I want to thank you all for being here. I know that you were all friends with Cliff, good friends to Cliff, and you've been incredibly welcoming and warm to me. I didn't ask you here to cry. I want us all to celebrate his life. He was an incredible man. An awesome musician, but an even better man. So, thank you! And, today, I would love to hear any stories you all have that were special to you and Cliff."

Bill Worth stood up and lifted his glass of iced tea. "Cliff was a hell of a musician, but one bad fisherman. He and I went out one day and Cliff kept thinking he had a big one—all he was doing was tangling his line with mine!"

Emory rose as Bill sat.

"He came to visit the facility—I asked him over. He was fascinated with research we were doing on lemon sharks. He bent over to listen to one of my lab techs—and knocked over half the vessels on the table. Poor Cliff, he was so upset...but it turned out they were all empty, my guys were starting out fresh. He made the day for everyone working."

Quips and remembrances were spoken around the room. When it was Kody's turn, she couldn't think of anything funny. "He was there for me when I needed him," she said. "He was... he was a true friend to my father. I loved him so much."

There was silence for a minute. She wished badly that she'd been able to think of an anecdote; she felt tears in her eyes and feared that she would start Rosy crying, too. But Bev stood up quickly. "Cliff managed a surprise for Dan and me on our anniversary. We were having dinner—champagne, surf and turf—and we were startled when he suddenly walked up with his guitar and played and sang 'Chances Are,' the first song we danced to at our wedding."

"Ahs" and laughter went around the room. And as they did so, Kody suddenly became aware that something was different. A shift in the air.

She looked toward the door.

Something...someone...

And then nothing.

Cliff. She was sure, and she had the strong feeling that Cliff had been there.

He had remained in spirit. And he was here…loving this. Wishing he was alive to love it, of course, but probably loving the tributes that were coming away.

There was nothing now; he *had* been there, though.

In spirit.

Why hadn't he tried to haunt her, and would she be able to see him again?

She was so sad about what had happened; she didn't know whether to be thankful that he had perhaps stayed, or just regretful that he was, no matter what, no longer a part of the flesh-and-blood world.

She looked across the table; Brodie McFadden was watching her again. There was something curious in his eyes. She had no idea what he could be thinking as he studied her.

The lunch went on. Kelsey spoke about the way Cliff had been so good to her grandfather.

Liam said that he'd been like an uncle to so many of them— and a singing uncle, at that.

Brodie McFadden stood then. "I was lucky to meet the man for a brief moment. And to hear him sing, and play. And I have to say, it is truly heartbreaking—such a wonderful, intelligent man…to die from a reaction to nuts when he knew that he was allergic to them. Rosy, we've barely met—but I want you to know that even to a stranger, he was incredible."

"Nuts?" Dan, on the other side of his wife, said. "Allergic reaction? We… I guess we all thought it was a heart attack."

"No," Liam said. "Cliff actually died of anaphylactic shock."

The room was dead silent.

"Cliff…" Rosy whispered. "Such a dear man, but too confident in his own good luck…"

The room remained quiet. Kody realized that only Rosy— and Liam and Brodie—had known that Cliff had died of anaphylactic shock. Most of the people in the room hadn't known that the cause of death had been definitely determined.

Kody had suspected it—and that, somehow, someone had caused it on purpose. She wasn't sure that she was happy to have in confirmed.

Brodie McFadden's words had been spoken kindly—with the right empathy.

And yet...

He'd put it out there.

Nuts.

Tragic for such a man to die—over nuts.

That silence...a strange quiet...lingered after he spoke, maybe some of the group not realizing what he said—while for some, the implication that he'd been too smart to have imbibed nuts on his own subtly slipping into their consciousness.

Brodie McFadden definitely believed her, she thought—that something was wrong, that maybe...just maybe...

Cliff Bullard had been murdered, as well.

CHAPTER SIX

When the lunch broke, Brodie saw that Sonny Atherton was going with Rosy Bullard.

He excused himself to Liam and Kelsey, and he followed Kody—who had shot out of the room as if she'd been propelled.

She was downstairs, speaking with their waitress. Kody listened, smiling. Brodie moved a little closer—close enough to hear what the waitress was saying.

"Sometimes I prefer dreaming to waking—so much fun. This guy tells me I'm the best, and that he should be writing a song about me."

"Well, dreams can be good, and...you are the best," Kody said. "But I think perhaps your dream is telling you to get out there and enjoy your life," Kody added. She hugged the girl—and then hurried out.

He followed.

She was headed south on Duval. He kept pace behind her. She turned on Simonton. He followed.

She went into the funeral home.

He gave her just a minute, and then went in.

A very tall man came toward the door to greet him. "Sir, may I help you? We don't have any viewings or services at this time. But if you're interested in our services..."

"I'm a private investigator, working with the police. A young woman just came in here. Can you tell me where she is?"

"The police? But..."

"Sir, there's no problem here. If you'd just be good enough to tell me where the young lady has gone?"

The tall man sputtered. "That was Miss McCoy, and she's involved with a funeral that will take place here shortly—"

"Where?" Brodie asked. "Has the body of Cliff Bullard arrived yet?"

"I...yes...but—"

"Thank you. Where?"

"Sir, Miss McCoy was a close friend. She chose his coffin. It's highly irregular for her to be with the body of the deceased now...before we're ready, but she is part of the proceedings here and—"

"Where is she?"

Brodie wasn't sure how he intimidated a man who was a couple inches taller than he was, but somehow, apparently, he managed to do so.

"In back, sir. We haven't had a chance yet to embalm—"

"Thank you."

Brodie strode down the hall to the door marked Employees Only. He opened it quietly.

Kody didn't hear him come in.

A sheet covered Cliff Bullard's yet-to-be-embalmed body. Kody had evidently pulled it down just enough to see his face.

She was speaking to him—speaking as if he were alive and well and lying there, as if his closed eyes suggested he was just resting.

"What are you doing?" she whispered. "I know you're here

somewhere, Cliff. You came to the restaurant—you would love any tribute, right? Cliff, this is serious—someone murdered you. I don't know what you're doing, but please, let me see you, talk to me. Instead of helping to let us know what happened, you're… you're cheating on Rosy! Two women thus far, Cliff, have told me about seeing you—in their dreams. They don't know it's you, but blue eyes, great grin, and that you want to write a song about them… I'm sure it's you. Oh, yes, of course, you visited Rosy. She said that she felt you…and then that she was such a coward that she'd be terrified if she really saw you. But! Even before that…you were fooling around with Colleen. And then I just talked with Adia—and you went to her at night, too. Cliff, please, let me see you, talk to me, I'll hear you!"

The corpse lay still on the table.

The body was an empty shell.

The spirit of Cliff Bullard was somewhere…

Just not here.

"Cliff, please!" Kody said. "I know that you were murdered. Doesn't that infuriate you? Oh, Cliff, you should still be here, with us. Alive. Please…"

Cliff wasn't going to answer. Brodie could feel that he wasn't there. And, he knew, Kody would soon realize it, too. She just wanted him to be there so badly.

He stepped back out and walked to the front of the funeral home.

"I'll just wait for Miss McCoy," he said.

"All quite irregular!" the tall man said. "Miss McCoy, insisting that she see Mr. Bullard before we are prepared for a viewing. And, sir, I assure you, we are a very established, reputable place of preparation and mourning."

"You are in no trouble, sir," Brodie told him.

A moment later, Kody came out. She was surprised to see Brodie—and a little worried, maybe.

"Um, hello. Prep for the funeral," she murmured. "Did you need me?"

"I do," Brodie said.

She wanted to ask him why—but not in front of the funeral director.

She simply nodded and headed out, and he followed.

"What is it?" she asked, walking briskly. She was heading toward her house, moving quickly down the street. She cast him a glance. "Definitely anaphylactic shock. And so you *definitely* believe me now that he had to have been murdered. You didn't know Cliff— He knew since he was a child that he was allergic. I can't believe that Rosy isn't freaking out and demanding that Liam and the police do something. Someone gave him something with nuts in it. Someone killed him. Okay, yes, I understand that it's truly terrible about Mr. Arnold Ferrer, and I know that the police need to find out what happened with him, but... Cliff was murdered, too!"

"Yes, I do definitely believe you," he said.

Kody was nervous; she was almost running.

He kept pace. He had long strides and could move damned quickly himself.

"So...find out who did it!" she snapped.

"I am intending to find out who did it," he assured her.

"Then why are you following me?"

"Because I don't know the people here. If I'm going to find out who did this to him, I have to understand more of what is happening on this island, the dynamics among the people who knew him. A murder like that was carefully planned. Most likely by someone in that room today."

She stopped and turned around to stare at him.

"No."

"I'm sorry, but probably, yes."

"The people there today...they're some of Cliff's closest

friends. No one there would have hurt him. There has to be someone else."

"Who? And why?"

He caught her arm when she started moving again.

"I was going home," she said.

"Yes, I'm going with you. We need to talk."

"You didn't tell me that you knew where Arnold Ferrer had been staying."

"Let's get to your place," Brodie told her.

She quickened her pace again. When they reached the house, she twisted her key in the lock with a vengeance.

The door swung open.

Her ghost was waiting for her; he backed away from the door, looking curiously at Brodie. Brodie smiled his way.

"You're all right?" the ghost asked anxiously.

Brodie figured Kody wasn't going to answer—not with him there.

The ghost stared at Brodie.

Brodie studied the ghost.

He must have been Captain Blake Hunter, the Confederate blockade runner killed during the Civil War. He wasn't, however, decked out in his military uniform—he was wearing a gray velvet frockcoat, red silk vest, black trousers, white shirt, and a sweeping plumed hat. His hair was long; the man had golden curls, much like the Union cavalry man, George C. Custer.

The ghost didn't acknowledge Brodie.

Brodie didn't acknowledge the ghost.

Kody took the first door off the hallway; it was the parlor. A grouping of handsome Victorian furniture—sofa, love seat and armchair—faced a large screen TV. An old ship's trunk in front of the sofa served as a coffee table.

Kody swept out a hand. "Please, have a seat. Can I get you anything?"

"I'm fine. Thank you. Have a seat with me."

He waited for her. She perched on the chair. He took a seat near her at the end of the sofa.

Her body language was, at best, taut. Absolutely rigid.

"Kody, you've been convinced that Cliff was murdered. People are seldom killed accidentally by ingesting nuts when they know they're highly allergic. That would mean that Cliff was murdered by someone who knew exactly how allergic he was. Someone with a motive. I don't know these people. Who could have a motive?"

"That's just it—you're going in the wrong direction. Rosy—his wife. Adored him. They were still basically newlyweds—they were married just a year ago. Sonny? She doesn't even live down here. Her home is up in Miami. Cliff admired her, and she respected him, too.

"Bill Worth is an exceptional man, in my opinion. He and Cliff were close. They'd have the longest conversations about history —argue sometimes. Bill says he finds the most fascinating stories—truth *is* always stranger than fiction, so if you twist it around, you've got great fiction. They loved to uncover some new bit of trivia to share with each other.

"Emory... Emory is an administrator at Granger Research—they do marine studies. He supported Cliff, was always at his shows, especially his Sunday-night-close-out-the-weekend shows. Bev and her husband, Dan, own a B and B. They're lovely people—they were regulars, too. Liam—he's a cop. I've known him ever since I can remember— Oh, well, he's not on your suspect list, right? He's your friend. And Kelsey is Liam's wife. Had you met her yet? She does great stories for children. Oh, yes, she did inherit a historic or "haunted" house, but then again, everything here is haunted, you know. Age does that to places!

"Who did I miss? Me. I really loved the man. He was my

father's dear friend, always there, always supportive—ignoring any kind of fame and fortune *and* misfortune, keeping his feet on the ground at all times. I don't imagine that you also meant the waitstaff at the restaurant today—some of them were there the night that Cliff keeled over."

"Kody," the ghost of Blake Hunter said softly. "You're being very defensive."

"You *are* being defensive," Brodie said.

Kody appeared to be perplexed. "What?"

"I agreed. You are being defensive."

"I..."

"He sees me," Blake Hunter said. "Kody, he sees me."

Kody blinked. "Really, I'm honestly not being defensive."

"I do see him," Brodie said.

"Who?"

"Captain Hunter."

She stared at him as if he was a snake. She stood. "Are you making fun of me? Because a Captain Hunter owned the house? And you know that. Did you look him up?"

"Kody, it would really help if you quit fighting me," Brodie said patiently. "I can see Captain Hunter. He is standing right there, behind the love seat. Great hat he's wearing—love the feather. And the velvet coat is pretty amazing, too."

"I—I don't believe you. You're..."

"Kody, come on, you have to know that there are other people like you."

"Of course... I have friends on the island, but..." She sank back down in the chair.

Brodie rose and looked over at the captain. "How do you do, sir? It's a pleasure to meet you."

Captain Blake Hunter swept off his hat and bowed low in return. "Mr. McFadden. The pleasure is all mine," he said.

Kody had found her seat on the chair again—Brodie wasn't sure if she sat, or rather fell back into it.

"This can't be real," she whispered.

"Really? You know that ghosts are real."

She was quiet for a minute, absorbing his words. "So," she said finally, "you really are a seer."

"I'm whatever you call it." He glanced at the captain.

"Dear Kody, most obviously, the man is," the captain said. "And quite nicely, too! I personally find it to be delightful—there just aren't enough people on this island who can see."

"There are others?" Brodie asked.

"Your detective friend for one—not as strongly as Kelsey, his wife. But...yes, there are others. Perhaps it is Key West. Perhaps there are many others, all afraid—some too afraid to accept it. But now that we understand each other...sir, what is going on here? Kody is indeed overemotional over all this—"

"I am not overemotional!" Kody protested.

The captain went on as if she hadn't interrupted. "But the thing is...while he didn't see me, I saw Cliff Bullard quite often. He was no fool—he was very aware of how serious his allergy was, and would ask every time if something contained nuts. Even here in Kody's home, when she hosted and she'd tell everyone that she didn't want any nuts of any kind in the house. Someone out there must have wanted that man dead—for whatever reason, I do not know."

Kody was nodding in agreement. Captain Hunter continued, "Now that we're all out in the open... Sir, you must do something. Aye, and indeed. I am distressed over the man killed and left down on that wretched ship. God forgive me. I did not own slaves, but I did nothing against those who did. What I am saying here, sir, is that both events were murder—and in each situation, a killer must be brought to justice."

Brodie lowered his head, trying not to smile. He liked the

man very much. The captain was wonderfully passionate; he must have been a man of tremendous integrity in life.

"Bravo, sir," he said softly. "Captain, a true pleasure to make your acquaintance."

"Likewise, sir," the captain said.

Kody turned to Brodie with new respect in her eyes, as if she hadn't denied his capabilities—almost as if she had just been given proof that he was indeed a private investigator. "I know that I felt from the start that something wasn't right. But I can't begin to figure out why anyone would want to kill Cliff. It just makes no sense. None of the people who were at lunch today would have wanted to harm him."

"Here's the thing, Kody. Whoever killed Cliff had to know that he was so violently allergic to nuts—that would suggest someone close."

"Yes, but it wasn't a secret."

"All right," Brodie said, and rose.

She seemed startled that he had listened to her so quickly. She rose, as well.

"Where are you going?" she asked him.

"Back to the bar."

"Okay...and?"

"I'm a private investigator by trade. I'll start doing that now."

Kody frowned, shaking her head. "I can't begin to fathom how the two deaths—murders—could be related."

"I can't, either. But I don't believe in coincidence. I'll call you later. All right? You going to be here?"

"I'll probably go by the museum," she said.

"I'll find you there." He started back into the shotgun hallway, then popped his head back through the doorway.

"Lock your door."

"Yes, I will."

He paused, looking at the captain. "Sir, I'm so glad to have met you."

The captain lowered his head courteously. "No, sir, the pleasure was mine."

She followed him, and, when he was out, she locked the door.

The day outside was Florida warm, but a breeze was coming in off the water. The sun had already begun to slide toward the west; the afternoon would wane soon.

Brodie made his way through groups of tourists and locals, pausing to help an elderly woman move her garbage can.

Soon enough, he came to the Drunken Pirate bar hut at the Tortuga Shell Hotel and found a perch at the bar. He ordered a beer.

"Thanks, Jojo," Brodie said as the young bartender set a sweating bottle in front of him.

"Yeah, no worries. Uh—have we met?"

"I saw you the other night. I heard someone calling you Jojo."

"Oh, right, you were here with Liam," Jojo said. "Bad night, huh?"

"Very sad."

"Hey, buddy," someone called.

"Excuse me," Jojo said, starting to turn away. But he hesitated just a moment and then said, "I'm so sorry about Cliff—ah, man, it's so rough—and sorry you were here for that. I'll check back with you later."

Brodie nodded.

He noted that the tables surrounding the bar were filled with couples and a few families, and a group of four men—possibly captains of dive or fishing boats, all bearded with ruddy skin—were seated around on the other side of the bar.

After a minute, Jojo returned. He appeared to be maybe just under thirty. He had curling brown hair and a neatly kept beard.

"Are you doing all right there?" he asked Brodie. "So, are you friends with Liam and Ewan?"

"Yup," Brodie said simply. Then, wanting to create a friendly feel, he added, "I've known Ewan a long time, and Liam a few years, too."

"Ah, man, cool. Heard Ewan was a hell of a military man."

"That he was."

"You're a diver then? With Sea Life?"

"Not officially. Ewan was still in the service when I was. He retired, and I wasn't career military, but I served under him and he was a good guy then—good guy now. He's head of the dive, so he had me in to work with him."

"Cool," Jojo said. "Ewan's a good guy. And Liam—salt of the earth, eh?"

"And you're Canadian?" Brodie asked him.

"I give it away every time, somehow," Jojo said. "Yeah, Canada is home. But when I came here… I fell in love."

Brodie nodded. "Easy to do."

"You're not from here."

"Virginia," Brodie said.

"It's good here. Paradise. Usually. It's been a weird few days. A good friend dying in my bar, and hearing about the man on the ship… Weird."

"Strange anywhere, I'd like to believe," Brodie said. "Really sad about your musician here, though. Hey, did Cliff eat here often? You know, he died of anaphylactic shock."

"No! I thought it was a heart attack."

The man's surprise seemed real.

"No. Allergic reaction."

"Oh, no, no, no, no. Cliff was careful. Always asked the waitstaff what was in food if he ordered it—and the waitstaff knew about his allergies, and I knew."

"So, he would eat here?"

"Yeah, it was a perk. He was always offered a meal. Every night before he played."

"What did he eat the other night?"

"Mako taco—it's a specialty. Not really shark meat—fish tacos. Mako taco just sounds fun—people order them frequently."

"What do the tacos come with?"

"White rice, black beans and plantains."

"No nuts in them?"

Jojo shook his head. "Please—the cops put everyone through a third degree already—though we didn't know yet that he had died of an allergic reaction. The only place we even have nuts around here is at the salad bar—inside, at the restaurant. We don't serve anything out here that has nuts. Trust me, we did not accidentally or otherwise let the man get them."

"But inside—on the salad bar—there are nuts."

"Sure. But Cliff knew it. He never went inside anyway. He came in early, put in his order, and set up his equipment."

"Where did he eat?"

"Right there at the end of the bar, where those guys are now," Jojo said.

"The server brings him his food?"

"Server brings it out, sets it at his seat, and when Cliff is— was—ready he'd come on over and eat. We'd talk. He was a good guy."

"So I understand. I only met him briefly."

"Sad."

"Did you see anyone near his food the other night?"

Jojo solemnly shook his head. "No."

"What about drinks? Heard he wasn't much of a drinker."

"No—but people always wanted to buy him drinks. Of course, he accepted. Said it was rude not to take a drink. Most of the time, he'd take a few sips and dump them."

"Lots of people bought him drinks that night?"

"More than ever—the festival thing had just ended. Friends. Other folks. Some of the fishing captains who have known him forever. I know Cliff. He never got wasted—never even got close to drunk."

"People use credit cards?"

"Sure. But a lot of people use cash, too."

"So…someone might have been around his food—and tons of people were buying him drinks."

"Sure, I guess." Jojo looked puzzled for a minute, then his eyes widened. "Oh, no. You think that someone spiked his food or a drink? I mean, hell, you'd notice a nut in a drink."

"Might have been a different form," Brodie suggested. The ME had determined that Cliff had died of anaphylactic shock, but as yet, Brodie knew nothing about stomach contents. Surely, they'd been tested.

And the tests would come back.

"You have almond milk back there?"

"Hell, no. Too trendy for us." Jojo shook his head. "However he got hold of nuts, it had to be accidental. No one would want to hurt Cliff. I swear, the man had no enemies."

"He apparently dumped a cup that night, behind the stage. The cops couldn't find it. You didn't happen to toss it, picking up?"

"We all help clean up, but no. And I asked all the serving staff who were on that night—and the cops asked them, too. No cup. We have no idea what happened to it. Probably some do-gooder. In the Keys, people kind of look out for things like that. Litter. Most locals, anyway. I'm telling you, Cliff had no enemies—no one would have hurt him on purpose."

Brodie was thinking of calling Liam; they'd need to go through the credit card receipts, even though they might not be definitive at all.

Liam came striding out to the bar, as if right on cue. He took a seat next to Brodie.

"Hey, Liam," Jojo said. "You off duty? Can I get you anything?"

"Thanks, Jojo. A beer. Local draft."

Jojo went to pour the beer.

"Anything new?" Brodie asked him.

"One thing that I thought was interesting—but could be nothing at all."

"What?"

"Ferrer. He was a guitarist, too. Loved his guitars. He played with a local group out of one of the service clubs in his area. He wrote a few songs, as well."

Brodie accepted that information.

"You know anything else about Ferrer?"

Jojo set the draft before Liam. "Thanks," Liam said, and then swiveled on his bar stool to look right at Brodie.

"Adelaide Firestone, the ex-girlfriend, mother of his daughter, is coming down tomorrow. As soon as she can, she wants to bring Arnold Ferrer home—bury him with his family in their Savannah plot. We can talk to her."

Liam was quiet for a minute. "You might be right, my friend," Liam finally said.

"That the deaths are linked?"

"Maybe. I repeat, just maybe. I mean, half the guys I know fool around on the guitar."

"Yeah, but are half of them dead?"

"I still say it might have something to do with the shipwreck."

"It might," Brodie agreed. "If only…"

"If only one of them had a ghost walking around who could simply tell us?" Liam asked him flatly.

Brodie stared at him, frowning.

"I just saw Kody," Liam said. "Oh, I guess she forgot to tell you. I'm one of you guys—you know, a seer, the way she calls it. My wife is better at it, her sister is best. Thing is… I'll be damned if I can get a read on either of our dead men. If their ghosts are running around Key West, they have yet to make it known."

Kody walked quickly toward the museum.

She didn't know why she was still so surprised that Brodie McFadden was able to see the dead. *A seer.*

She knew that others existed. It was Key West, and her hometown was open-minded about all things spiritual. But they were all very careful. In fact, she hadn't known about Liam and Kelsey until it had come to the captain, when they had been at her home and *seen* him, and then she had learned about a pirate ghost by the name of Bartholomew who had been around for years, helping out first with Liam's sister-in-law, Katie, and then with other relations until he was ready to move on, having apparently done all that he could.

Sure. Those who could see the dead existed. She'd never figured it was just her.

Why was she so surprised Brodie was one?

Because he wasn't from here? Had she assumed it might just be a thing in Key West? The locals did have a reputation.

Liam hadn't been surprised at all.

"I thought so," he'd said.

"You thought so?"

"There's something about him. He's bright, he's even-keeled. And he always seems to be paying attention."

It had been easy for Liam to accept Brodie McFadden's *gift.*

Why not? She had her own.

Except that she hadn't been able to find Cliff again after her one brief sighting.

"Cliff, where are you?" she muttered aloud.

A passerby looked at her curiously.

Great. One of the ghosts of Key West wasn't even taunting her—and she was still managing to appear completely eccentric.

She sped up, arriving at the museum just as Colleen was about to lock the door.

"Hey," Colleen said. "Are you all right? You're looking a bit like a thunder cloud."

"Oh, sorry. I... I don't know what I was thinking," Kody lied. "How was today?"

"Wonderfully busy. And so many compliments. One lady was a little bit bitchy. She said it was false advertising that you called the place 'The Haunts and History Museum.' She wanted more haunts, I guess. I explained to her that our haunts came from our history—and that we did have an entire room dedicated to hauntings, ghosts and the weird. I think she wanted something like a haunted house."

"You can't win them all," Kody told her.

"Right. I was pleasant, though. But I didn't give her her money back!"

Kody laughed. "She'll skewer us on the travel review sites. One star—or no stars."

"Oh, no. I didn't think about that."

"That's okay—we're very lucky. Most people give us five stars and call us 'a Key West must!' We will occasionally have people who won't enjoy the museum."

"Another man wanted more info on the *Victoria Elizabeth*."

"Did you tell him that the ship is still being explored and archived?"

"Yep. He asked if you had any hidden information."

"And you told him that I didn't?"

Colleen nodded proudly. "I said that we were working with Sea Life, but that we didn't have any information as yet. When we did, it would be displayed for all the world to see."

"Thank you. Do we have people still in there?"

"Nope. I was just locking up."

"Thanks. Go home…or out. Are you going out again?"

Colleen flushed. "I think… I'm not sure yet. I may go home and go to sleep early."

"And dream again?" Kody asked her.

The bright red color that flooded to Colleen's cheeks assured Kody that she was right.

"Colleen, you need a life—a real life, not a dream life. You're young, you're pretty—and you're very sweet and bright! Meet someone—go on a date."

"Oh, yeah, look at who is telling someone to have a life."

"Colleen—"

"Never mind. I'm not listening to your excuses. Maybe I will go out," Colleen said. She laughed suddenly and went to collect her purse. "There's the kettle calling the pot black, as my mom would say. We should go bar hopping together one night."

Kody gave her a smile—she'd never been a bar hopper.

"Maybe we'll find a concert to go to or something," she said.

"Okay…a concert!" Colleen said. She smiled and gave Kody an air kiss.

When the door shut behind Colleen, Kody spoke to the air. "Cliff Bullard, where are you? You have to stop making a young girl's dreams better than having a life!"

There was no answer.

Angry, Kody sat down behind the counter and logged on to the computer. She pulled up the name "Arnold Ferrer" from her email list.

She went back to the first message, written to her and Ewan Keegan just after the wreck of the *Victoria Elizabeth* had been discovered.

Dear Miss McCoy and Mr. Keegan, having read about the discovery of the slave ship Victoria Elizabeth, I find it incredibly important that I write to you—and offer up documentation and a few artifacts that have come to me through my family. I am sorry to say that one of my ancestors was aboard the ship, as an investor in the human cargo. With so many so tragically lost when the ship went down, I believe I must share my family's history with the world upon the historic discovery of the wreck. I am interested in meeting with you, if you would be so kind as to reply to this message.

She started to move on to her reply—and Arnold Ferrer's next message. But a sudden thump from the far back of the museum startled her.

She sat still, wondering at first if Colleen was certain that everyone had left.

She rose and walked into the hall. "Hello? Is anyone still here?"

She heard nothing at all.

For a moment she stood still.

"Cliff?"

There was no answer.

She returned to her chair behind the counter and the computer.

She read her reply. Thank you so much! Ewan Keegan and I would love to meet with you, sir, and certainly to see your documents. And we thank you for contacting us.

Ewan had sent a similar message.

Ferrer had answered, I have long been haunted by the terrible cruelty of the slave trade—and shamed that a family member had been involved. Even though it was long in the past. I am not seeking any kind of financial reimbursement; I wish only to share what I have—lest we ever come close to such a cruelty again. As Americans, we must face and admit our massacre of native peoples, our cruelty and ignorance in the slave trade, and even our interment of our Japanese citizens during World War II. I truly wish to help in any way that I can, and plan on making a trip to the Keys in the very near future.

She started to look at her next email.

But she heard a sound again. She wasn't sure what it was.

She walked back into the hallway, but an intuition of danger began to creep up her spine. She turned, ready to grab her bag and run out into the street.

She had her phone; she might be paranoid, but she was going to call Liam and wait until he could get to her.

Or she could call Brodie McFadden. She knew he would come.

She heard a sudden whisper in her ear. It was strangled, and barely a sound.

"*Get out…*"

She sprinted to the door, and out to the street.

And right into the arms of Brodie McFadden.

CHAPTER SEVEN

Kody McCoy flew into Brodie as if she had been propelled by the fierce winds of a storm.

He braced himself and caught her, holding her tightly for an instant, then setting his hands on her shoulders and steadying her as she straightened. There was a turmoil of emotions in her eyes, and her words came tumbling out. "I'm so sorry. Something... there was something in the museum...a noise. I thought someone was still in there...but it scared me. I didn't mean to knock you over! I heard a whisper. I don't know who was speaking..." Her voice dropped to a whisper. "Dead—I think. But...there's something back in the museum. Something...someone... I thought guests, at first, someone hadn't realized we were closed. But that whisper... I mean, I wasn't being stupid or anything—really. I was headed out to call Liam. Or you. But then that whisper..."

"Okay. So, you were alone in the museum—or you thought that you were alone in the museum. But you heard noises. And cautiously and reasonably you were just going to walk out and call one of us—but a spirit seemed to whisper a warning to you?" Brodie summarized.

She nodded her head firmly. Her eyes were stunning pools of trust at that moment, luminous amber. The silky softness of her hair teased over his fingers.

He gave himself a mental shake.

"Stay here. The street is pretty busy. You should be just fine. I'll check it out. Wait for me?"

She nodded.

"Yes, of course. Oh, I just sounded like a babbling idiot, but honestly, I'm not. I'm fine."

He walked into the museum, glancing at the reception and ticket area. He went into the hallway and through the exhibit rooms one by one. No one was there, and nothing seemed disturbed. He went to the back, in the storage and setup area, and then he checked out the two restrooms.

In the second, a window was open. Curious, he walked over.

The museum was in an old building—the historic marker at the front recognized that it had been built in 1864. The bathroom obviously a later addition/change in the original structure. The window frame was still original to the building. The glass panes in it, however, were not—it was good glass, storm glass.

But the window could be locked—or slid open or closed. It was wide open.

A fair-sized person could have opened the window and scooted over the ledge.

There were no screens on the windows; Brodie assumed they were usually kept shut—the museum was air-conditioned, and the restroom was extremely clean.

He looked out. In back was an alley and then a wire fence— behind the fence was the backyard of another house, one that was probably circa 1930.

There was no one in the alley—which would not have fit vehicles, just pedestrians—nor was there anyone in the yard of the house behind.

Brodie closed and locked the window. He walked back out to the front.

Kody was waiting.

"There's no one in there now," he told her.

"I heard something, I swear," she told him.

"I'm not saying you didn't. I'm just saying that there is no one there now. One of the bathroom windows was open."

"It shouldn't have been," she said, alarmed. "We keep them locked."

"All right, so someone may have been back there, and they opened the window and crawled out to escape. Or, someone was in there who—who decided the restroom needed fresh air when they were finished."

She almost smiled, but her humor quickly faded. "I heard something. I don't imagine sounds."

"I believe you," he said. "But then, someone whispered to you, right?"

She nodded.

"But you didn't see anyone—living or dead?"

"No."

He shrugged. "I don't think there's much we can do now." She was looking at him as if she wanted more—expected more.

"Kody, we could try to get fingerprints. But you're going to have fingerprints from the dozens of people who might have been in there. And while I believe you completely, it would be hard for any officer to justify such a search when you just heard a noise and there's nothing out of place and nothing missing."

She nodded. "Okay. You did lock the window?"

"I did."

"And you're certain that there is no one in there now?"

"Absolutely certain."

"You checked around boxes and everything? No one was—hiding? I mean, you do carry a gun."

"I do have a permit."

"Of course, I wasn't implying that."

"You don't like guns?"

"Oh, no. If someone is running around the Keys strangling people and causing them to die from anaphylactic shock, I'm incredibly glad that you carry a gun."

"Well, I guess that's…good. Anyway…"

"Were you coming to see me?" she asked him.

"I was. I wanted to tell you that I talked to the bartender at the Drunken Pirate."

"Jojo was working?"

"Yes. He said that almost all of your friends bought Cliff Bullard drinks the night that he died."

She waved a hand in the air dismissively. "People buy him drinks all the time. He doesn't say no—it helps the staff and the bar and therefore, the little hotel. He drinks one or two sometimes, but he usually managed to very discreetly dump them. I'm sure my friends weren't the only people buying him drinks."

"No, they weren't."

"Maybe he got something on his way to the bar, Brodie. He had to have inadvertently picked up something that had nuts in it—God knows, we have coffee shop chains and other little places where he might have seen something that he decided to munch on."

"He would have asked if it had nuts."

"Most probably. But sometimes, Brodie, we have language barriers here. People come from all over to work here. Maybe someone didn't understand what he was saying."

"I thought you were the one convinced that he was murdered."

"I… Oh, I don't know! Maybe I don't want to believe that he was murdered, and if so, someone else—not a friend who knew him—did it. If it was at the bar, how did someone buy him a drink—and slip nuts into it? You'd know a nut if you hit it in liquid."

"In its original form. Almond milk or nut oil or something like that could be added to a drink."

She was silent, studying him. He found himself fascinated again with the color of her eyes, not quite green, not brown, not hazel…amber or tawny or gold, depending on the moment, the way she was looking, the environment around her.

He turned. "Uh, did you want to lock up for the night?"

"Yes, yes, of course, thank you."

He opened the door for her; they both walked back in.

"Oh, before all the drama, I was checking the email correspondence I was having with Arnold Ferrer. I don't think that it ever got that deep, but…"

"I've already gotten it all."

"And have you spoken with Liam?"

He nodded. She let out a long breath. "Well, so we all…know. And we all know that we know, and we all see ghosts—and neither of these damned ghosts is talking to us!"

"So far," he said. "You think that Cliff is here, right? I mean, somewhere."

"Oh, yes—a promiscuous ghost!" she said. "The big brat is visiting women by night."

"Oh?"

"Nothing…nothing too…weird. Both Colleen and my friend Adia—our waitress from lunch—believe that a man is coming to them by night. They've both been thrilled to meet him. They don't seem to know that it's Cliff."

"Maybe it isn't Cliff," Brodie suggested.

"Arnold Ferrer? No, because Rosy thinks that he comes to her, too. Which, of course, would be more of a natural thing… she is his wife. Except that Rosy doesn't want Cliff to be a ghost—maybe she's just in so much pain."

"Maybe Cliff doesn't feel that he needs to go by the rules—now that he's dead."

"But where is he? Why isn't he helping us?"

"I don't know. Anyway, let's lock up. I'm starving."

"All right. We could just go to my house—"

"There's a shrimp special in that little place by my hotel. Let me take you out."

"Really, I can cook something—"

"Next time." He smiled at her, enjoying the idea that there would be more than one dinner together.

He wasn't sure that he wanted to go to her house; he wanted to talk with her alone. Brodie saw Captain Hunter as a good presence—but a third wheel nonetheless.

"Sure."

As they walked, Brodie told her what he knew about Arnold Ferrer. "He has a child, five years old."

"Oh? Bev told me that he was gay."

"Gay men do have children, you know that."

"Of course." She frowned. "I think I remember hearing that he had a great friend—an old friend. Must be the child's mother."

"Maybe she can give us a clue about him. Oh, here's something else—not sure if Liam told you or not. He was a guitar player and singer, as well."

"Do you think they were both killed for being entertainers? That seems…a stretch. And if someone has a vendetta…well, the Keys are filled with entertainers."

They reached the restaurant. For once, it seemed, Kody didn't know the server.

"Not a friend?" he asked her.

"I don't know everyone," she said. "We're just an island. And tourists are everywhere all the time, but residents do get to know one another. I've known Liam forever. And his family. And I have a really good friend—she's moved away, up in

Northern Virginia now—who owned a bed-and-breakfast and had her own ghosts. Her husband now is an FBI agent—a man was killed in her backyard and he was the agent investigating and…anyway, she comes back down when she can, but the thing is…we're close. Especially those of us who…well, who can see the dead."

Brodie realized that he was staring at her, frowning. She went silent and stared back.

"The Krewe of Hunters," he said.

Now she frowned. "Yes. How do you know? Are you really a PI? How do you know about the Krewe? That isn't their official title. It's considered a rather elite group—they have their own offices."

"Yes, I know."

"How?"

He leaned closer. It seemed that Key West was rife with those who saw the dead—still, those who didn't tended to think that there was something seriously wrong with those who "thought" that they did. There was no need to share with the other patrons of the little seafood restaurant.

"Both of my brothers are joining the Krewe of Hunters."

"Oh!" she said, and then, "Small world," she added dryly.

"The Krewe is run by a man named Jackson Crow, but it was created by Adam Harrison—a philanthropist who had a son who was gifted differently and…well, anyway, I've known Adam since I was a kid. He loved the theater—in fact, he owns one now—so my parents worked with him, back in the day. But Jackson Crow is the special field agent in charge, and his wife, Special Agent Angela Hawkins works with him and… I was thinking about calling one of my brothers and mentioning this case… I think it might be right up their alley. And they have unlimited resources."

"You were thinking about it?" she said. "You have a connection like that? Yes, call them!"

"Right after dinner," he promised.

"Will this be important enough?"

"I believe so."

She puckered her forehead again. "It's complicated, right? The FBI has to be asked in, and I think that might be through the sheriff—who is wonderful—but based up in Marathon. Or, of course, the chief of police—who is also great, but..."

"But doesn't see the dead," Brodie finished.

Their shrimp arrived. She didn't speak again until the waitress had left them.

"Have you—seen the dead all your life?" she asked.

He shook his head. "Not until I was just about eighteen, and my parents were killed."

"Oh, my God, right. I was even a bit younger, but I remember—it was an accident at a theater."

"They were both killed—by a falling chandelier."

"But they weren't...murdered."

He shook his head. "Freak accident. Anyway, after the funeral, they kept walking around the house and talking to me and my brothers, and we all kept pretending we weren't seeing them. Until I couldn't take it anymore. I confronted Bryan and Bruce about it, and then we all admitted we could see their ghosts. My parents were ridiculously happy when we finally acknowledged that we saw them. They're both a bit dramatic, to say the least. And my mother was always incredibly giving, but very much a diva in her way. My dad adored her in life and adores her in death. They're happy, they're together...they just haven't moved on." He took a long swallow of tea and told her, "You never know. You just might meet them. I meant it when I said it was like they were still watching over me."

She smiled and it seemed to light her entire face.

Her smile faded slightly and she said softly. "I see the dead—but not my dad."

He set a hand on hers. He felt a ridiculous stream of heat arise within him at that small touch. He didn't draw his hand away; it was just a sympathetic gesture. But maybe he shouldn't have done it. He was far more than attracted to Kody McCoy. He was fascinated, as if under a strange spell.

"Your dad went on—to where we're all supposed to be. Maybe he didn't linger because he'd raised you right. You loved him, he loved you. And you were strong, and you were going to be okay."

She smiled ruefully. "Maybe. But when I bought my house... Blake Hunter was there. He—he scared the hell out of me at first. He was the first ghost I ever saw, but he was so reassuring and gallant. Anyone the captain loved is long, long gone. And, oh, he is so attuned to history, and so sorry for the war—but also reconciled to what the world was then. He's learned so much, and he seems to really consider all that he learns. And he participates in our world as much as he can, and I share with him as much as I can...but I think he must be lonely."

"He has you," Brodie said, watching her. In fact, he couldn't look away. It was bad—very bad. He even thought that her every move in consuming shrimp was hypnotic.

"Me. I suppose. We do get along great—except that he's dead and I'm alive."

"And what about your life with the living?"

"I'm fine with the living." She sounded a bit defensive.

"No...companion out there?"

"Not at the moment."

"And is the captain the reason for that?"

"Not really. Okay, so, yes, dating with him judging anyone I bring home is not an easy thing. But more than that..."

"More than that?"

"What about you?"

"I've been busy."

"Afraid to bring a girl home to meet the parents?" she teased.

He smiled. "They are equal opportunity haunters—my brothers and I agree on that. They had three sons. Each of us still receives their love and attention."

Kody laughed. "Interesting lives we lead," she said.

Dinner was ending. But they were right by his hotel, he couldn't help but think.

Still, he was on a case—or cases.

And she was involved.

"I was thinking coffee, and we're right next to a specialty café. We can grab a couple of cups and head up to my room, and I'll give Bryan a call and see what he thinks."

"Perfect," she said. "Anything—anything at all that will help with this."

He insisted on paying the check. She said it wasn't a date. He reminded her that he was haunted by his mother, and that his mother was very traditional and would have a fit if her son didn't treat a lady to dinner.

She tried again with the coffee. He didn't have to speak that time; he just gave her a stern look.

Yes, he was haunted by his mother—who would insist that he buy coffee, too.

When they headed through the outer courtyard of his lodging, Kody whispered softly to him, "I think you may be making this up about your mom."

"I would never."

"I did see her in so many films. She was something. And your father, too, of course. He was in a Shakespeare play that I remember particularly. He was phenomenal."

"He was," Brodie agreed. "Anyway..."

He opened the door to his little suite. He was right on the

ground floor—poolside. It was pretty; darkness had fallen and there were lights on the palms and in the pools.

His room had a little kitchenette, a bath and a large living/dining/bedroom combo. He had a good-size desk and great lighting. He'd stayed many times in the past, and it was perfect for him.

The sofa bed was out and freshly made. Kody perched in a chair by the desk.

He opened his computer and pulled out his phone.

He was afraid that his brother might not answer, but Bryan picked up on the fourth ring. He was enthused to hear from him.

"Anything come to mind, like a light bulb in the head?" he asked Brodie.

"Have you see the news?"

"Are you involved with the murdered man on the shipwreck?" Bryan asked.

"I found the murdered man on the shipwreck," Brodie told him.

"Aha." Bryan was quiet for a minute. "And thus this call?"

Brodie went on to explain about Arnold Ferrer and then about Cliff Bullard.

"Nuts?" Bryan asked.

"Well, the nuts brought on the anaphylactic shock," Brodie explained.

"Hey, hang on," Bryan said. Brodie could hear him speaking with someone else.

A feminine voice came to him next. "Hey, Brodie, it's Angela."

Apparently, Bryan was with Jackson Crow and Angela and maybe others on the team—and with his other brother, Bruce, as well.

"Angela, hey."

"Bryan was just filling us in—we've seen the news about

Ferrer—thankfully, they don't have your name in any of the reports."

"I told Ewan just to say that a diver with Sea Life discovered the body," Brodie said. "He kept to his word. And the cop working the case is good—I've actually met him before. Thing is, another man died that night. I'd just left the dive site and gone to get something to eat—and he keeled over onstage."

"Heart attack?" Angela asked.

"No—anaphylactic shock. Severe allergy to nuts." Brodie paused, looking over at Kody. "Thing is, he had a very good friend who is insisting that he didn't just die—that someone spiked something he had with a nut mixture—could be in a cream form in a drink, ground up in a taco... I don't know."

"Was there an autopsy? Stomach contents?" Angela asked.

"Not back from the lab yet. It doesn't seem that the murders connect. In fact, the ME has Cliff Bullard's death down as accidental."

"But you don't believe it—or the friend doesn't believe it?"

"His friend doesn't believe it—and I believe her." Brodie looked up at Kody, and she smiled at him.

"Send me any information you have. Any possible enemies."

"Well, as we know... Cliff Bullard had to have had one enemy. But doesn't matter who you talk to, they all swear the man was loved. Oh, and the only connection I can find to the man on the ship so far is that they both loved guitars. Everything else is different. Cliff Bullard a local, Arnold Ferrer a Virginian. Bullard married, Ferrer is unattached, though he has a daughter from a previous relationship. Ferrer was involved with the discovery of the slave ship, as you probably know from the news. Bullard really wasn't associated with the *Victoria Elizabeth*, other than hearing about it from friends. And one more thing—Cliff's good friend, Dakota McCoy—was in correspondence with Arnold Ferrer. She owns a newly opened museum down here—*Haunts and History*."

"Got it," Angela said. "I'll take anything else you have. Email me. I'll see what I can find out." She was quiet a second. "Dakota McCoy—any relationship with the Key West musician, Michael McCoy?"

"She's his daughter."

"Ah, that's right. I remember reading about his death…and that he had a daughter. She must be interesting."

"Ah, yes, interesting," Brodie said.

"Send it all. I'll give you back to your brother."

He spoke quickly with Bryan, and then with Bruce for a moment.

Then Jackson Crow was on the line. "You need help, let us know."

Nice. Jackson was generous with his team's time and resources.

It was easy to see how his brothers had determined on the Krewe.

"Thanks."

"We'll see what Angela can come up with."

Brodie thanked him again and cut the call, turning back to Kody. To his surprise, she sprang off the chair and rushed over to him, throwing her arms around him. "Thank you," she began.

The momentum made him step backward and brought him falling back on the bed.

Her with him.

And it was…perfect. She looked down at him with those incredible and enigmatic gold eyes of hers. He wasn't sure if she kissed him or if he kissed her.

Maybe it was just supposed to be a thank-you kiss.

Maybe it was just what she had intended, because it quickly became hot, open-mouthed, very wet and overwhelmingly arousing.

They rolled; he was over her, the kiss continuing. He struggled to remove his jacket without letting his lips leave hers. She tried to help. The jacket made it to the floor. His hands slipped beneath the spaghetti straps of the little cotton dress she was wearing. Her shoulders were bared, and he kissed them while her fingers were tangling in his hair. She pushed against him, halfway rising, and together, they managed to get the dress over her head…fleeting seconds when they were apart.

They didn't stop to talk.

There were no discussions, just the moment, no matter what it might mean.

There was no talk of later, or the next morning, or if it was what either of them really meant.

There was just an urgency to make love, to strip one another of the annoyance of their clothing as quickly as possible. Kissing, touching…

Clothing was strewn where it lay.

She was finally naked, on fire in his arms. This was no slow seduction, just a desperate need to be together.

His lips slid over her body. She was tanned and sleek. She tasted sweetly of some subtle soap; the taunt of her hair brushing against him with her movements was equally evocative. They rolled and caressed, side by side, on the bottom, on the top, each anxious to touch and kiss and savor the other's flesh. And then, incredibly, he was with her, within her, and he knew he was holding her exactly as he had dreamed of holding her since he had first seen her, seen the gold in her eyes, the way she watched him…

The way she moved…

Poetry. He thrust and she arched. Liquid enchantment beneath him, a hunger growing in him until he was ravenous. Their gazes met all the while, and he felt power in her eyes, the honesty of her longing, all of it coming together to lift them ever higher until it broke in a kaleidoscope of physical climax that was powerful and volatile, leaving them to quake in one another's arms in continued sweet spasms that were a bit of heaven all in themselves.

He held her close; her body was sleek and still warm and so incredible next to his.

Neither of them spoke for very long moments.

At last, he brushed back her hair. He wasn't sure if he should be serious, if he should joke or tease—if he should thank her, or apologize.

"I would have made that phone call earlier if I'd only known what a response it would elicit," he told her.

He was glad that she smiled, that her eyes still met his with honesty.

"Hmm. I'm not sure that the Drunken Pirate or the Haunts and History Museum would have been the right venue for this," she said lightly.

"Ah, so all is well that ends well," he said. Face-to-face, they lay there, neither really surprised by what had happened.

Neither one dismayed.

For a moment they lay there, smiling.

Then she suddenly gasped and jerked up to a sitting position.

"What?" he asked, alarmed, getting up, as well.

"Do you travel alone? Please tell me that you travel alone."

It took him a minute to comprehend what she was talking about.

He laughed softly, easing back down. "I travel alone. No ghosts with me."

"You're laughing, but this would not be the way to meet your parents!"

He reached for her; she was still angry with his laughter.

"Kody..."

She drew the pillow out from behind her and smashed him

with it. Laughing, he wrested it away from her. He struggled to bring her back down beneath him. One look from her reignited him, and he kissed her, and the whole thing began again…

With equally erotic results.

As they lay together later, Kody said, "You're really on your own? I mean, I would know of course, but…they could be traveling the streets, they might have stopped in at Two Friends for karaoke, or gone up to O'Hara's or…"

"They are in Virginia. I believe they're…happy haunts at the moment. Happy with my brothers, because my brothers are happy."

"And you?" she asked softly.

"They knew I needed time. That every man has to make his own decisions. They would never have trailed me down here if I didn't want them to."

She smiled. "The captain is beyond courteous, as you can imagine. But he's still in my house. Almost all the time."

He couldn't help but laugh again.

"What?"

"Are you afraid to bring men home because of the captain?"

The pillow hit his face.

"I am not afraid."

He caught the pillow and stared at her, still smiling.

"I'm not afraid. It's…awkward. And…a good way to weed out anyone I'm less than fully interested in. It's been a long time since I've met anyone I would want to bring home to the captain."

"Great. My folks. Your captain."

She grinned at last. "And a great hotel room!" she told him. She sighed softly and lay down beside him. "Being here…it's so…so good!" she whispered.

It was. Just holding her in his arms, feeling her body curled within the curve of his.

With a sigh, he realized he had to rise.

"What is it?" she asked him.

"The captain," he said.

"He isn't here," Kody said, puzzled.

"No, I know. I want you to stay here. But I have to tell him."

She seemed surprised. "I do go out of town, or stay out with friends…"

"And I'll bet he knows when you're doing things like that," Brodie said.

The dismay on her face echoed his own as he got up, reached for his clothing, and started to dress.

She was about to do the same.

"No," he begged softly. "I walk fast. I'll be right back."

She smiled slowly and lay back down, stretched with the grace of a cat, and reached for the covers.

"I'll be right here," she promised.

Brodie hurried out.

But not so fast that he didn't make sure to lock the door behind him.

Kody couldn't believe that she'd drifted off when Brodie left. How could she sleep? He had rocked and changed her world.

He was perfect.

In his manner. In his integrity. In his belief in her.

And in the way he touched her, looked at her…

Made love.

Perhaps it had just been the impossible perfection of it all—combined with the fact that she'd barely slept since Cliff had dropped dead in front of her.

She couldn't remember feeling so alive, vital, ready to conquer the world. Sated, so happy to simply lie naked beside someone…

And yet she definitely drifted off.

When the whisper came, she thought it was part of a dream at first. Or, perhaps, Brodie had returned.

She started to smile in the dim light in the room.

"Mr. McFadden... Hey, Mr. McFadden!"

The voice wasn't coming from outside the room.

It was coming from the foot of the bed.

Kody awoke in panic, drawing the sheets to her breasts, staring down at the foot of the bed, a scream nearly tearing from her throat...

She gasped.

The ghost gasped, too—in total surprise.

"Kody?"

"Cliff?"

"Kody, what the hell?"

"Cliff Bullard, what the hell are you doing here? I've looked for you everywhere—"

"That's not the question. What the hell are you doing here? This is McFadden's room!"

"That's right."

"Oh...ohhhhhh."

"Seriously, how rude, Cliff." She wagged a finger at him, far too angry to be embarrassed that he had caught her wrapped in McFadden's sheets.

"I thought he was here alone," Cliff said. "Kody—I was murdered!"

"I know! And we're trying to do something about it. I've been trying to find you—and, you, you jerk! You've turned into a ghostly Casanova! What is the matter with you? Cliff, you were a newlywed! You're fooling around with other women!"

"No, no, I'm not... I'm just... I'm making them feel pretty. Hey, Kody, this ghost thing isn't easy. I could barely touch anyone and Rosy...my poor Rosy. She stood in the house and behaved as if wet, cold stuff was on her when I was around. She said that she was scared, so scared, of ghosts. So...well, I'm not going to haunt someone I terrify, Kody. And the others...they just needed to hear that they were pretty, that they had a life… Kody, people need to be appreciated. And that's how…that's how I got the strength to be here…to show myself… Kody, I knew. I—knew that you would sense me…see me. But I knew that about McFadden. There was something about him."

"You met him for all of two minutes."

"Right. And I knew. So I came here. For help. I surely didn't expect to find you."

"Oh, Cliff, please, I'm an adult."

"Well and good, but you're like my daughter."

"Thank you—but I'm a grown-up daughter. Cliff, come on, please!"

"Kody?" she heard her name called. Brodie had returned. He must have heard their voices. And he was worried.

"Brodie, I'm okay!" she called.

The door opened and Brodie stepped in. Tall, dark—impossible to be hers, if only for these moments, days…whatever it might be.

Concern made his ruggedly sculpted face extremely taut.

"Oh, dear," Cliff murmured.

And then Brodie saw him. Took in that Kody was fine, seated against the bedpost, sheet to her chest.

"Ghost or not, how rude!" Brodie said softly.

"I'm sorry… I didn't know, I didn't think— Hey, cut me some slack. I'm just not that good at this ghost thing yet," Cliff said indignantly.

Brodie folded his arms over his chest. "All right. This once."

"I came to you for help, young man. I don't care what they say, and I don't give a damn what they think. I was murdered. Murdered!" Cliff said.

"We know," Brodie told him.

"You know?"

"Hell, yes. And we need to know who killed you."

Cliff looked at him a long moment in surprise. Then he sank

his ghostly form down to sit at the foot of the bed. He looked at Brodie and shook his head slowly.

"Damned if I know!"

CHAPTER EIGHT

"Here's the thing," Brodie told Cliff sternly. "The way you… left us, you had to have consumed nuts or a nut product not long before you…left us."

"Died," Cliff said sadly. "Though, if it weren't for beauty of life and my dear Rosy, I wouldn't mind this so badly. That little mouse of a girl you hired to watch over the museum—she's coming into her own—because of me! And that dear girl Adia, at such a loss with her husband gone—I made her feel happy and easy, if for just one night out of her harried life."

"Cliff," Kody said, clutching tightly to her sheets, "we need your help finding your killer."

He nodded again. "I keep thinking…replaying it. Your festival had just ended. Sunday night… Key West was winding down after the weekend bachelor parties, there was also a fishing competition, and while Sunday was far quieter than the weekend… there were so many people at the Drunken Pirate that night. Jojo was serving." He shook his head. "Rosy came in with me, we sat and chatted with Bill Worth and Emory Clayton and Sonny

Atherton for a bit before I set up. Oh, then Bev got there, and then her husband, Dan...a couple of fishing captains I know."

"Your friends don't all know that you dump your drinks?" Brodie asked him.

Cliff cast him a rueful grimace. "No. Kody knows. Oh, and Jojo knows. Maybe even Liam, because he asked me once how I was still standing. And he's pretty harsh on people driving while drunk, as he should be. I told Liam he didn't have to worry about me. One sip and drinks were discreetly gone."

"You didn't actually drink any of the drinks given to you that night?" Brodie asked.

"One nut could do it," Kody said quietly.

"I had some cream thing that was tasty—I did drink most of it," Cliff admitted.

Kody glanced over at Brodie.

"Almond milk instead of cow's milk?"

"That's what I've been thinking, but..."

"I think my viewing is going to be tonight," Cliff said. "Lots of people will come. I'm so grateful for being so..."

"Beloved," Kody said.

Cliff looked at Kody. "Well, I can find my way into your museum, Kody. I'm going to be the Wandering Minstrel Ghost! How about that? Haven't figured out how to drag a guitar around as of yet, or even strum a chord, but I tell you—I will get there!"

"Wandering Minstrel Ghost?" Kody said. "Cliff Bullard, you're going to go down as the Promiscuous Ghost!"

"Kind of like that, too," Cliff said.

"Will Rosy like it?"

Cliff winced. "I just make young women with no confidence feel better. Hey, if I was being...more intimate, wouldn't be so bad—I mean, in the logical sense. No chance of a ghostly pregnancy, and certainly, no STDs."

"Cliff!" Kody said. Then she sighed. "Okay, you definitely made a change in Colleen—she does seem to be moving on."

"Aha!" Cliff said.

"Aha, and all right," Brodie said. "It's late. Cliff—"

"I'm going, I'm going. Maybe I'll hit a few bars."

"And learn how to knock in the future," Brodie told him.

"Hey, I came to find you. I didn't know Kody would be here. I shouldn't be surprised. I mean, she's a beautiful person and a beautiful soul. And you're not bad, Mr. McFadden. You seem to have some integrity and determination. If Kody is going to be with someone... She is young. I've been telling her that she needed to have some kind of life—she was turning into a spinster."

"Cliff, I'm not even sure that's a word that's still used," Kody said.

"I'll get out of your hair," Cliff said. He headed over to the door as if he would open it. He looked at it and shrugged. "That's right—I just go through those things now. Anyway..." He paused and turned back to Kody. "I love you, girl," he said softly.

"You, too, Cliff. I'm glad you've stuck around," she replied.

"We'll solve this," Brodie told him. "But we will need your help."

"Oh, I'll help you!" Cliff said. "Any way that I can!"

Then he was gone. For a moment, Brodie and Kody were silent. Brodie turned to Kody. "Well, we found Cliff."

"And he knows nothing," Kody said.

"But he will. He knows something. We're just going to have to figure out how to help him remember just what happened, exactly when and where," Brodie said.

He walked back toward the bed. Kody looked up at him; she was hugging her pillow. Her hair somehow seemed to be both wild and elegant—her look was one of being a little bit shell-shocked.

"Cliff thought he'd find you," she said.

"Well, I saw the captain. I'm glad he likes me. He seemed to approve—he was all right with you staying with me. He said you needed to spend more time with the living."

"Great, the ghosts approve," Kody said.

"Hey, my parents would love you. Nice to have the blessing of the dead?" he asked, half smiling.

"My mom is still alive. Oh, my God—" Kody said. "I have to call her. I'm a terrible daughter. I promised to call her...and I even said that Cliff could go in my dad's family's vault!"

"Call her."

"But I'm here. Naked. In a stranger's bed."

"I'm a stranger—now?" he asked.

"I mean to my mom!"

"Kody, she can't see through the phone."

Kody nodded.

"Could you pass me my little handbag?"

He handed her the bag and she dug out her phone, glancing his way with a nervous smile. He thought that if they'd been together longer—had more than a few conversations and one night—and he actually knew her mother and she had known him, he might have crawled in and teased Kody as she tried to make her call, planting intimate kisses on her bare flesh.

But he didn't touch her; he walked over to the desk and opened the computer again, determined to get some information off to Angela.

He couldn't hear what her mom was saying, but through Kody's words, he knew that someone else had already told her that the wake would be tomorrow night. And he knew that she kept assuring Kody that it was all right. And that Cliff Bullard was welcome to rest in her father's family's vault.

He thought that he was going to like Kody's mother when he met her.

Finally, the conversation ended.

He had managed to get a few things done while listening, as well. Information sent to Angela. Through his brothers, he knew just how good she was at digging up leads.

He looked at Kody.

"Really, as a daughter, I fail."

"You don't. You've been busy, concerned as a friend."

"He was my mom's friend, too. Closer even, really. Cliff kept her sane when my dad died."

"Kody, it's all right. You can't take the weight of the world, you know."

She smiled at him. "You didn't really know Cliff. And you didn't know Arnold Ferrer at all—and still, you're involved completely."

He shrugged. "It's what I do, for one. A vocation, I guess, more than anything. And this strange thing we have with the dead…somehow, it makes it all the more important. Anyway, we have help now. Real help. From the Krewe of Hunters."

"Krewe of Hunters," she repeated. "So… I guess tomorrow, you meet the one living parent we have between us. Well, wow, that was presumptive. No, I mean, you'd probably meet her anyway. I didn't mean that you had to meet her."

He stood up, walking over to her. "I will be honored to meet her," he assured her.

"They're driving back first thing in the morning. She remarried not long ago. He's fantastic—a truly wonderful man. Frank—Frank Frampton. You'll meet him tomorrow, too."

"I will be pleased to meet him," Brodie promised. He leaned toward her. "You will still stay with me?" he asked her.

She smiled. "Of course. I'm not really ready to face the captain yet."

He stripped and joined her again. He took her tenderly in his arms. "Kody, I will find the truth. I promise."

They fell asleep entwined.

"I have the documents that Arnold Ferrer meant to give to Kody," Liam told Brodie. "They're at the station. You're welcome to come and study them."

"Terrific, I'll be there soon," Brodie told him. He glanced over at Kody. She was dressed—and ready to head back to her house to shower and change.

"Anything new on Cliff Bullard?" he asked Liam.

"I think you know that he was released to the funeral home. And we've gotten the credit card receipts from the bar. I've spoken to the manager who swears that Cliff wasn't even inside where they have the salad bar. And he swears, as well, that there is never anything that even resembles nuts in the fish tacos." He was quiet a minute. "Brodie, I know that Kody isn't accepting this well. It may be that he did just get a hold of the wrong thing somehow."

"Don't you think it's strange?"

"Damned strange. But... I don't know. We've questioned everyone several times. And you can't pinpoint anyone—the credit card receipts aren't helping a whole lot. They're giving us a lot of what we already knew—half the place bought Cliff a drink that night. And, as we all know, Cliff probably dumped them."

"All he'd need was a sip of the wrong drink."

Brodie thought back to the night when he'd so briefly met the man while he'd still been alive. He'd had a drink at the table.

What had it been and who had bought it for him? Had he actually taken a sip from it? Or had he brought it back to his spot on the little dais and dumped it into the surrounding foliage, as he had been known to do?

Kody was watching him.

"I'll be there shortly."

When he hung up, Kody raised her eyebrows at him in question.

"I'm going to the station."

"I heard."

"I'll drop you off. I'm going to bring the car."

"I'm just about four blocks from here."

"Right. So I can drop you off."

"If you insist," she said, exasperated, but smiling. "Honestly, it's no problem to walk."

"I'll just take you."

They went down around the corner to the hotel's lot. He opened the passenger's side for her, and she smiled as she stepped in.

"Hey, it's just the thing to do," he said.

"And thank you," she said.

She turned to him when he got in. "And at the station?" she asked.

"Ferrer's documents are there—they searched the room, naturally, when they discovered his identity, and they have the documents he wanted to bring to Sea Life."

"Ah. So whoever killed him wasn't after the documents. Or at least they didn't get them."

"And what are you going to do?" he asked her.

"Shower, change, stop by the museum—and then I'll go to the funeral parlor and just check on everything, and from there, make a call and speak with the management at the cemetery regarding the interment. I'm sure everything will be all set. There is going to be a service at the church, and then a few words at the cemetery."

"What time is the wake?"

"Viewing hours are six to nine," Kody told him.

"I'll find you there," he told her.

When they reached Kody's house, she jumped out. "And now

to face the captain," she said. She grinned at him through the car window. "I'm a grown woman and I'm a little bit afraid of this ghost. Sad, huh?"

"No," he told her. "Not sad at all. Kind of nice."

She turned and headed up to the house; he waited until she was inside.

The captain wasn't in the hallway, but as Kody entered, he appeared, looking around the doorway from the parlor.

The television was on. He was watching a show about politics. He loved to stay in the current "know."

"Kody, you're home."

"Just to shower and change," she said. "I want to stop by the museum—and I need to get to the funeral home."

"I think I'll be there tonight, too," he said. He studied her for a moment. "Thank you," he said.

"For?"

"For sending Mr. McFadden. That way, I didn't worry about you."

She smiled, leaning against the door frame. "He's very courteous. He reminds me a lot of you."

"Oh?" Captain Hunter raised his eyebrows.

"Simple decency—integrity. And almost as dashing."

"Quite decent, I do say. Do you think he'll stay?"

"Here...in the Keys?"

"Where else?"

"I doubt it. He has a life elsewhere." She didn't want to keep going down that route. "I'm going to run up and change."

Zilla came and rubbed against her leg, meowing loudly.

"I'm going to feed the cat, and *then* run upstairs and change," she said, correcting herself. Godzilla always had a bowl of dry food, but each morning he also received a bit of vet-approved canned food. He was evidently not pleased that he had not gotten it thus far.

She went to the kitchen and took a can from the cupboard. When she had dished the food into Zilla's bowl, she looked up to see that the captain had followed her.

"I went out myself last night. Trolled the streets. The city is comparatively quiet right now. Some people were talking about the murdered man, warning each other to be careful. None of them seemed overly concerned—the general notion seems to be that Mr. Ferrer was killed because of something he knew about the *Victoria Elizabeth*."

"I wish we knew."

"Yes," the captain said. "I've been watching the news about the ship," he said. He shook his head. "The cruelty of that time, so many men and women, chained…left with no thought to their very basic and personal needs…"

"I know. If I hadn't read my history, you would have told me," Kody said, trying to be patient.

But she knew that this reminder of his past flaws had upset him—and the fact that it had upset him was a homage to his personality.

"'The only thing necessary for the triumph of evil is for good men to do nothing,'" the captain quoted. "That was said by the great Irish statesman Edmund Burke—well before even my time. But his words have run true through the centuries. We were fighting for states' rights, but in the South, slavery was a way of life. A wrong way of life—how can this be so clear to me now?"

"Because we all learn with time, Captain," Kody said.

"I will help all that I can—in all things," he assured her.

"I know that you will," she said, stroking her cat.

Godzilla purred with pleasure.

She stood and looked at the captain. "I know that you will!"

she repeated, and striding past him, she left the kitchen and walked down the hallway to the stairs and hurried up them.

In her room, she paused, and she didn't know why.

She looked around. Nothing was different, nothing was missing.

Maybe she was different herself. Maybe…

She still couldn't believe that she had all but jumped Brodie. Then again, she was still incredibly sad—she had truly loved Cliff. And she was seriously disturbed by the events that had occurred during the week. She'd needed some comfort.

But…she was a changed woman now.

And she'd had the audacity to think that Colleen was the one who needed to perk up and have faith in herself and head out and have a life.

She'd had a sort of life. She'd been incredibly busy with the museum and the festival.

She refused to think into the future; there was far too much to get through now.

She hurried into the shower. Even there, she thought about Brodie. It had just clicked. Being with him. She'd found him attractive; she had even felt drawn to him. But she hadn't admitted, even to herself, just how attracted she had been until she had basically jumped the man.

She pushed away thoughts of the night before—certain that such a night would come again—and rushed to dress.

It was only when she had donned an appropriate deep blue skirt-suit that she realized what was actually different.

Her laptop had moved.

She wasn't exactly compulsive or obsessive, but she kept the little desk in her room in a very certain order. The computer always sat squarely in the center.

It was at an angle.

She stared at it a long moment, ready to call the captain and find out if he'd been in her room.

He was never in her room.

Nor had he been there the night before—he had gone out. And he had no reason to move her laptop around.

Had someone been in her house?

It was just her computer. Maybe she hadn't noticed the way that she'd left it. And maybe she was just ridiculously paranoid all the way around.

She righted the computer, studying it.

There was nothing to see—it was just her computer. There was nothing stuck to it, no smudges or marks…nothing.

She turned and sped down the stairs. The captain was watching the news again.

The current story was about the fact that divers were working down deep, exploring and studying the *Victoria Elizabeth.*

"Bye, Captain," she said.

He turned and waved to her gravely. "I'll join you at the wake," he reminded her.

"See you there."

She managed to leave her house and head for the museum.

Arnold Ferrer's documents were incredibly well preserved.

Brodie didn't know anything about caring for historical documents—he was all for it, he'd just never owned any.

The officer who led him to Liam's office explained that they had been preserved in a very special kind of protection, not covered with glass, but rather a layer of sheeting that shielded them from mold and any other harm that might come to them.

Brodie nodded his interest—except that he was far more concerned with what was in the documents—anything that might have brought about Ferrer's murder.

"Take a look," Liam told him, rising from behind his desk as Brodie was shown in. "So far, all I've been able to fathom was

that the man was a jerk. They're all right there. Knock yourself out."

The documents were spread out across the desktop. One was
a financial sheet, Ferrer's investment in the ship itself and in the
ship's cargo.

Human life had been—compared to the man's investment in
the ship—quite cheap.

The first correspondence was to the man's wife. Brodie looked
at the documents and then glanced up at Liam.

The pages were in Portuguese.

"The translations are next to them. I asked Officer Michel
Gomez—who is Brazilian—to confirm if the translations were
good. He said they were," Liam told him.

"Okay, thanks."

He picked up the new, typewritten translation of the first
letter and read.

Dearest Isabella,
The Victoria Elizabeth *might have been built in the shipyards at*
Liverpool, but she has been outfitted quite gloriously for the cargo
we've intended. We can carry hundreds of the healthy men and
women, purchased from the tribe who enslaved them at a song. We
were informed that only the finest workers were taken for this ven-
ture; no elderly will be part of the cargo. The sick have been weeded
out. I am anxious to see their value once we reach the islands and
the colonies. I believe it will exceed our wildest speculations. We
can fit so many! Just the men and women and their chains.
With all love, your husband, Mauricio

He looked at Liam again.

"Doesn't seem human, does it? First, in Africa—one tribe
makes slaves of another. And then they are sold to the Europeans, who transport them with less care than they might horses!"

"The law forbidding the importation of slaves to the American Colonies was enacted in 1808," Brodie said. "How was the *Victoria Elizabeth* allowed to sail here?"

"That's very specific knowledge you have."

"I grew up in Virginia with a passionate teacher. There's not much about the Civil War I don't know."

"I thought maybe Kody had been bending your ear."

"I was a good student. I imagine Kody was, too."

"Better than me, I bet. But Florida didn't become a territory until 1822. The ship sailed before that, and, possibly, she really wanted to reach Cuba or one of the other islands. Though I haven't found information as to that being the case," Liam said. "Go ahead and read. I'm still going through credit card receipts and food and drink orders."

"At the Drunken Parrot?"

Liam nodded. "It was a busy night."

He turned to his work. Brodie found the second letter.

It appeared to be a potential buyer.

Senhor Gonzales,
I am delighted to assure you that all my expectations have been fulfilled; the cargo of men—between the years of sixteen and forty—is exceptional. All extremely healthy, and promising hours of work in the hottest sun. The women we have taken are all of childbearing age, and will do nicely as house slaves, or in the field. It will be extremely exciting to see them in your hands, if you so wish. On the auction block, the bidding would be fierce.

Brodie felt sickened by the words; it was difficult to imagine that people had ever felt this way. That any man could think so little of human lives.

There was an answer. It was from Mr. Gonzales.

My dear Senhor Ferrer,

*I look forward to our transactions; I will arrange purchase in a man-
ner of good faith. I will accept the healthiest men and women, to
the number of fifty. I will expect nothing less than what you have
promised for the price agreed. I trust that you have spoken in honesty; the sun here is brutal and they will be expected to work from
dawn to dusk, without falter. Their native land, you say, bears
that same humid heat; that will stand them well, as a dead slave is
a worthless slave, as I am sure that you are aware. I will expect a
guarantee for a nominal lifetime—a minimum of a decade's work.*

And then what? It didn't matter if they dropped in the fields?
In the next letter, however, it seemed that Ferrer became
something that resembled human.

Dearest Isabella,

*I began this adventure with such excitement and belief. I am sorry
to say that, while it continues, I am disheartened. At first, it
seemed fine that so many could be transported; now, I hear their
cries, and their lamentations. They are left in their own feces and
urine; I argued with the captain and he said they might be washed
down upon reaching shore. I spoke of the moaning, and the sickness aboard; he told me that there is an acceptable loss.*

I saw their faces.

*They are men and women; they are human. They hurt, they
cry, they love, as we do. They are sunk in misery. May God forgive me.*

Your loving husband, Mauricio

Brodie sat back. He felt as if he'd been punched in the gut.
Little seemed as horrible as reading Ferrer's letters—even
when Ferrer himself became sickened by what he was doing.
But the Ferrer descendant was turning these letters over to

Sea Life—he wanted them exposed. He had wanted people to know about the misery and suffering, so that history could be remembered, and never repeated. People needed to see the ugly parts of the past.

"What do you think?" Liam asked him.

Brodie shook his head. "Horrible."

"To the best of our knowledge, a few of the crew survived, but the 'cargo' died in the hold—chained together. At least, that's what Ewan believes. I spoke with him this morning. They've been exploring again."

Brodie nodded again, staring at the rest of the documents. They had to do with descriptions of the men and women—with their assets as far as work was concerned. Height, weight, age.

Maria, fine appearance, excellent for a house slave, 20.
Jose, strong, 17...field hand.
Gianna, fine teeth, wide hips, may produce excellent offspring, 15.

Brodie set the document down.

They had all perished. It was rather amazing that the island wasn't running rampant with ghosts. Then again, the Spanish moniker for Key West had been Bone Island; the bleached-out bones of a slaughtered indigenous tribe had been found on the beaches.

Natives had murdered natives.

African tribes had conquered, massacred, enslaved and sold other African tribes.

The world did not seem a very nice place when looked at through this lens.

"Anything?" Liam asked him.

Brodie shook his head. "Those who were so cruelly treated by his ancestor didn't kill Arnold Ferrer—they are long, long dead. And he was the one bringing the documents to be seen by the world. If they had belonged to someone other than the direct descendant, I could see there being some motive... Putting a man down in the wreck of a slave ship is hardly a random act of violence."

"Hardly," Liam agreed. "Any inkling, any sign—any anything—on how these two deaths could possibly be related? That is...if Cliff was murdered."

"Come on—he didn't just grab a handful of nuts."

"We'll have the chemical analysis soon enough—when we get the results on the stomach contents. Anyway, there are more documents—some relating to the ship, and the ship's captain, Angelo Montblanc, and more. Those are translation copies for you, if you want to take them."

Brodie didn't even want to pick up the papers; he'd had his fill of the horrors of the past. But he'd read them. They could lead the way to the truth. How, as yet, he didn't know.

But there were answers somewhere.

And he'd see to it that Angela got everything that he had by the end of the day.

Rising, he thanked Liam.

"Thank *you*," Liam said, a half grin on his lips. "Hey, you found the body. I guess I'm kind of counting on you to find the killer."

CHAPTER NINE

"Yes, there is a ghost at the Red Rooster Inn," Colleen said to a teenager standing in front of the ticket/reception desk. "Poor man, just home relaxing. He was slain by his wife...so unsuspecting. Just sitting there smoking his cigar. And, if you see him, he'll just look at you and smile, and slowly fade away, but as he does so, you may smell the lingering odor of his cigar."

"See, Mom! There are ghosts all over Key West. Are all the rooms haunted?"

Kody had just walked in. The young teen was with his parents, a sunburned pair, smiling at his enthusiasm.

"There's a lot of history in the museum. You can see Key West from the time we first began to keep records," Kody said. "That's where we get our guests—all the strange, eerie, violent, and maybe just sad things that have happened through history."

"And there were bones all over the island of Key West, right?" the teen asked.

Kody didn't think that the teen was particularly ghoulish—most of their guests his age tended to focus on what they saw as "creepy."

"There were bones all over the island," she agreed. "We have
what we call pre-Columbian history here in the States, which,
obviously refers to the time before Columbus sailed the ocean
blue, and we became the 'new' world. They believe that indigenous tribes such as the Tequesta held sway down here, but
that the Calusa were really dominant. And then, there were also
peoples known as the Caribes and the Matecumbes. At any rate,
there was some kind of massive battle on the island, and the
dead were left on the sands. The first Spanish explorers found
them and called the key 'Bone Island.' Some say those natives
still haunt the island, as well. Many believe that the survivors
managed to get in their boats and head south, perhaps to Cuba,
perhaps to other islands," Kody said, smiling. "There's one room
dedicated to our popular or 'known' ghosts, but in every room,
you'll get a listing of what happened in the history of the era—
and just what ghosts might remain from that time."

"Oh, cool," the teen said.

"I hope you enjoy it."

She gained a friend. The young teen and his parents were
happily starting off through Haunts and History.

"You're so good with people," Colleen told her.

"Me? You were doing a great job when I came in."

"I do love this place so much. And we're getting more and
more people every day," Colleen said. "It's barely open, and we
have twenty-three people in here!"

"And you're doing all right?"

Colleen nodded and whispered suddenly, even though they
were the only ones in the reception area.

"We need to get those cameras connected."

So far, Kody hadn't been able to afford a good alarm system.
They had rigged cameras in every room to make people think
that there was surveillance.

"We do. You're worried?"

"Sometimes, when I'm alone, I wonder if people know that we can't see what they're doing—and that they might walk out with something. We've had good people so far—we have to hope that we continue to get good people."

"We'll scrimp on something else," Kody told her. "I'll see about getting an alarm system up. I'm sure that we can get started by Monday. And, if we can keep up, I can hire us both an assistant."

"An assistant for the assistant. I like it," Colleen said. "I'm really not complaining. I just worry about the things you accumulated—bought, received as donations, inherited—being stolen. You have some remarkable pieces. Still, I think that the things you have would not be enough, if it weren't for all of your plaques with information on them. Told well—and not boringly."

"Well, thank you."

She turned to the door as it opened. A young woman of about thirty-five had come in.

"Hello, welcome," Kody said.

"So what is this place? Haunts and History?" the lady said.

"Well, we're a museum," Kody told her. "We're heavy on the history—with 'haunting' stories about it, and of course, we have one room dedicated to Robert the Doll, Elena de Hoyos and some of the other famous 'haunts.' History for those who don't believe in ghosts, and the island stories and legends for those who do," Kody told her.

"Oh, sounds great. I've read up. You have great ratings on the travel sites!" the girl said.

"Wonderful," Kody told her.

"As for me… I know the island is haunted!" she said happily. "I met a ghost last night!"

"You did?" Colleen asked her.

She nodded gravely. "I'm staying at one of the historic B and

Bs—the Sea Horse," she said happily. "And there's definitely a ghost there. A very nice one, so…sweet." She frowned suddenly and gasped. "I'd forgotten. A man staying there was murdered recently. Oh, but this was a slightly older ghost. Anyway… I've never seen one before. Oh, maybe I didn't actually see him, but I rather felt him. I dreamed him. But…you must believe in ghosts, right?"

"I believe," Colleen said.

"I don't discount any possibilities in life—or death," Kody murmured.

Cliff! Now he was haunting this girl—and at the Sea Horse! Bev and Dan probably already felt badly enough that Arnold Ferrer had been killed there.

Now all they needed were rumors about a flirty ghost.

"I always thought I'd be terrified of a ghost if it came near me, but this thing about being asleep and then feeling as if someone was with you, just making you feel…"

"Pretty," Colleen said softly.

"I— Yes, I guess, exactly." She hesitated, looking from Colleen to Kody. "I'm so sorry—way too much information from someone you've just met. And I'm usually…"

"Shy," Colleen offered.

"Yes," the woman said. "I'm Nan Merano, by the way. From Ohio. I'm a teacher. Grade school. And I never do anything exciting, but I wound up with a trip down here and I took it and… and… I'm oversharing again!"

"We're glad you're here," Kody said. "And it's a pleasure to meet you. I'm Kody, and this is Colleen. I promise you, we're a very friendly—if sometimes a bit wild—city, and I truly hope that you have a wonderful time and are happy for your adventure."

"I can give you a bit of a tour of some nice nightspots, later,"

Colleen said. Then she added quickly, "After nine. I have... I have to attend an...event tonight."

"Really? That would be wonderful!" Nan said. She held her brochure and said, "I guess I'll get started." She went in.

Colleen looked at Kody, beaming. "There are ghosts for real. He was in my dreams—and hers. And now I have a friend who wants to go out, someone I can show around the island. After the wake. It is today, right?" Colleen asked. She flushed slightly. "I do intend to come. He was such a kind man." She hesitated and grinned. "You know, it's odd. My dream guy reminds me a bit of Cliff. Maybe it's the music angle. Cliff was—like my dream guy—good to everyone."

"Yes, Cliff was good to everyone."

After he'd burst in on her and Brodie, he must have gone on to haunt Nan.

What was so bad about it?

He seemed to be making young women very happy. Feeling pretty, and appreciated.

"Go be with Rosy whenever you need to go," Colleen said. "I think you believe by now that I can honestly handle everything here. I know all the stories, and while I'll never be as good as you, I'm getting better about telling them."

"You're excellent—maybe way better than me," Kody assured her. "Okay, I'll take a run through, and then head on out over to see how Rosy is doing."

She walked down the hallway, looking to the right and to the left, observing all of her rooms.

People were reading; children were playing.

The museum was doing very well.

She went all the way to the back; everything seemed fine in the storage and staging room. She started back and then, curious, she paused to check the restrooms.

And in the one, the window was open.

She stared at it, curious, annoyed—and a little bit uneasy.

She slid the pane shut and locked the window.

On her way out she paused to speak with Colleen again. "Hey, do me a favor, will you?"

"Of course."

"When you leave, make sure both bathroom windows are locked."

"They were open?"

"Twice now."

Colleen looked at her gravely and whispered. "Guests with smelly business. I leave the air freshener in there, but…"

"Right. Smelly guests," Kody said. "Anyway, please just make sure that they're locked."

"Absolutely," Colleen promised solemnly. Then she added, "I'll see you at the wake."

Brodie stared at the wall.

He'd gone out and bought himself a corkboard, and he'd been busy pinning up what he knew about each of the murdered men.

Arnold Ferrer, a man determined to get a story out to the public. He'd been appalled by his ancestor's actions—even though it seemed his ancestor had learned a brutal lesson regarding the truth of humanity. *All men are created equal.*

He was a gay man, but he hadn't always accepted his sexual orientation. He had a girlfriend who cared about him still, and a five-year-old daughter. He'd been staying at the Sea Horse, and Bev and Dan—friends known well to Kody and other locals—had gotten to speak with him, and had really liked him. He'd been due to come into the Sea Life offices and speak with Ewan Keegan. He'd also been due to come in and meet with Kody McCoy.

Instead, he'd been killed. Struck from behind, and then murdered with something like an electrical cord. He'd fought his attacker.

He had to have seen his attacker.

Brodie had felt him...felt something! Though he wasn't appearing in the spectral flesh, something of him had remained, guiding Brodie to his body, and to the only clue they had.

The little piece of gold chain he had discovered on his second dive down to the *Victoria Elizabeth.*

Documents. Documents that included letters Mauricio Ferrer had sent to his wife—and documents regarding the cargo and the ship's crew.

He went on to the second half of his display.

Cliff Bullard. Guitar player, minstrel, songwriter—a married man, almost a newlywed, very much so in love with his wife. Good friend to Kody and others. Killed by allergic reaction. How and when would he have gotten the nuts? He knew about his allergy.

Brodie scribbled a note and added it to the board.

Last cup he drank out of disappeared.

Picked up in all the activity going on—or searched out and disposed of purposely by someone who had watched enough cop shows to know it was important evidence?

Cliff's ghost was active. He didn't know who had killed him.

Most people considered the death to be accidental.

Brodie just didn't believe it.

What in God's name could possibly connect the two men?

Arnold Ferrer had loved to play the guitar. He'd been good, according to what Liam had learned.

Someone jealous over a guitar? That didn't seem likely. Cliff and Arnold had never met.

Or had they?

He picked up his phone and put a call through to Angela.

"Hey, listen, I know you have cases, and I hate to bug you," Brodie began.

"It's what we do, and we are still hoping that you'll make the McFadden brothers a trio in the Krewe," Angela said. "Anyway, so far, I've been working your victims. Cliff Bullard, open book of a life. He's been a musician. He did work with Michael McCoy a few times—apparently, Michael was the kind of man who always tried to give old friends what help he could. But Cliff always did all right. He's got some albums—CDs and all—out there. He's always made a decent wage at doing what he loves, and once he got to Key West, he loved Key West. He married Rose Martin last year. She was born in the Tampa area and worked as a nurse's aide for years. She met Cliff on a vacation, they got married, and she became a full-time artist. Oh, she'd sold work before, she just wasn't making a living. Cliff made a decent living, and that gave Rosy a chance to pursue her love of painting."

"Anything evil in anyone's background that you can find?"

"I'm following music careers right now. Oh, and I'm looking into the names of the crew working with Sea Life. Your friend Ewan had an extraordinary military career—going above and beyond many times."

"Yes, I know."

"I figured."

"I've got parking tickets on every member of that dive crew. But that's about all."

"Hey, can you do some historical research for me, too? The captain on the ship was a man named Angelo Montblanc. I don't have a nationality on him. Though, with that surname, I'm imagining French. I suppose when it came to cargo to the New World, a ship might be from anywhere with a crew from many nations."

"Look at cruise ships today. Sure, anyone could have been from anywhere. I'll see what I can find."

He started to hang up, but then he said, "Angela?"

"Yes?"

"This might all be crazy, but the victims were both musicians, played guitar…maybe they are connected that way, somehow."

"Sure thing. I'm on all of it."

When he hung up, he looked at the time. It was getting close to six.

He needed to dress for the wake, and head for the funeral parlor.

It might be very interesting. He wondered if there were others who might realize that Cliff wasn't just there in body—but in spirit, as well.

Kody had gone straight to Rosy's from the museum, worried, and not wanting Rosy to have to go to the funeral parlor alone.

Rosy had company.

When Kody arrived, Rosy just shouted that she should come in.

Bill Worth was already there, sitting with Rosy at her dining room table—and holding her hand. Rosy had a glass of wine in front of her.

Bill was sipping a soda.

Rosy looked at Kody with a bit of guilt in her eyes.

"I needed this," she said, indicating the wine. "It was one thing when it was just us…us, his friends. But tonight… Oh, Kody, there will be so many people."

"People who loved him," Bill assured her.

"And people who just know that he's an island icon," Rosy said.

"We'll do our best to…maneuver people," Kody said.

Tears sprang into Rosy's eyes. "Tonight… Kody, will you

speak? I just won't be able to. And, tomorrow, at the church…
you'll do the eulogy for me?"

"Bill is the writer," Kody said. "He might be the better
choice…"

"But Cliff felt like he was…well, not your dad, he loved your
dad too much. But like your uncle or something. Please."

"Of course," Kody said. She glanced at her watch and then
at Bill.

He shrugged and mouthed, "I've been trying to get her to go."

"Rosy, we need to get going. They will open the doors to
the public at six—that's what's in the paper and what anyone
calling will be told. And usually…well, you might want a minute with him alone."

She nodded. "This is expected, of course. Much more hu-
mane for those remaining when…when you never see them
dead. When you get to remember them alive. I mean, I have a
picture of him strumming his guitar…and some pictures of our
honeymoon. The funeral home people had a billboard. People
will see that… I just… I mean, for me. I don't believe in open
coffins—remember that."

"Rosy, don't even think that way," Kody told her. "You have
years and years to go. And you'll get by, bit by bit, every day."

"Yes," Rosy said. "Yes, I will."

She stood, resolved. Then she picked up the glass of wine and
swallowed its contents quickly.

"I'm ready," she said. She glanced up at the clock on her
kitchen wall. "The car should be here."

"From the funeral home. It's a matter of blocks, but…" Bill
Worth shrugged. "It's part of the service. So, we'll go in the car."

"Whatever works for Rosy."

Rosy laughed softly. "We picked a cheap coffin. Still, the cost
of losing someone is absolutely outrageous!"

When they were in the car, Rosy looked at Kody and frowned. "Your mom was so close to Cliff. Is she coming?"

"Yes, she and Frank should be home by now. Frank took a last interview at 9:00 a.m. They were ready to hop in the car and head back then."

"Good," Rosy said softly. "I know he thought the world of her. Cliff, I mean. I heard that she saved your dad."

"I hear the same," Kody said softly.

The drive was short—ridiculously short. But the black sedan let them out at the entrance.

When they arrived, Emory Clayton was waiting for them. He gave Bill and Kody a rueful grimace; they had all been thinking along the same line.

They hadn't wanted Rosy to be alone.

Mr. Conway Finch—aka Shorty—was waiting for them at the door. He took Rosy's hand and nodded solemnly and told her that Cliff would be their only viewing that night; they had known just what a full house they would have for him.

"Naturally, we have the room ready for you, and your husband... Do you wish to be alone with him?" Shorty asked.

"No," Rosy whispered. She clutched Kody's hand. "And boys..." Bill and Clayton were both far from being boys, but they knew right away that she meant the two of them. "Please... don't let me be alone. I dreamed... I begged him not to haunt me. But...it's the life we'll never have now, I guess, I just... Please. Be with me."

"Of course, Rosy," Clayton said. "Whatever you need."

And so the three of them walked in together, Rosy clutching Kody's hand, Bill and Emory flanking the two of them.

As they neared the coffin, Rosy began to sag.

Bill Worth caught her.

"I can't," she whispered. "I can't see him in death."

Bill looked at Kody, just a little desperate.

"It's all right, Rosy," she said. "It's all right. This is… Some people need to see the person to say goodbye. If you don't want to…"

"I can't," Rosy whispered.

"Then that's fine. Here, just sit here, in the front, to the side."

"Tomorrow…at the church. I will give him into God's hands, and say goodbye," Rosy said. "I just… I want my memories to be of the living man, laughing, smiling, holding me."

"Of course, Rosy, that's fine," Kody said.

Bill and Emory took their cue from Kody. "It's okay."

"I'm going to tell Shorty that it's all right to open the doors now, to—" She hesitated. She didn't want to say "public." That might upset Rosy more. "To his other friends," she finished.

"Wait," Bill said. "Please."

He walked up to the coffin and knelt down. He bowed his head. When he was done, Emory walked to the coffin and did the same.

Kody wasn't sure why she didn't feel like paying her respects in this way—maybe because she'd seen Cliff in his spectral form, and she wasn't sure if she was angry with him, or if what he was doing was really…nice.

Rosy was afraid of his ghost. He probably wanted just to assure her. And he was aimlessly wandering around trying to figure out how and why he was murdered…

So why not let shy women get to feel good about themselves, gain some confidence?

When Emory rose, however, he looked at Kody expectantly. And she knew, of course, that it would appear strange if she didn't go to the coffin.

And so she walked to the front and knelt.

It was always so strange when people said that a corpse looked "good." She hadn't ever really seen anybody look "good" when they were dead—in the real form of the flesh. At best, Cliff looked as if he was at peace.

She supposed that was good.

She was startled when she heard the voice of the dead man speaking—Cliff was standing just slightly behind her to the right, in his ghostly form.

"I do look okay...leave it to Rosy. Perfect suit," he said. "Ah, Kody, thank you for helping my poor girl now. I tried to hold her, tried to hug her, but she shivered and...well, she needs you all now."

Kody inclined her head, crossed herself and stood. As she walked back to Rosy, the doors swung open and Brodie entered.

He headed first to the widow. "I am so sorry, Mrs. Bullard. I had barely met your husband. He seemed to be such a fine man."

Rosy looked at him, wiped her face and smiled curiously.

"My name is Brodie McFadden. I'm friends with Ewan and Liam and a number of your friends. We met briefly at lunch the other day."

She smoothed her hair back, managing a smiled for him. "Thank you, young man."

He nodded and walked to the coffin. Kody could see that Cliff stood by him, too, gazing over his own body. She had no idea what Cliff was saying, but Brodie, his head lowered, had a bit of a smile on his face.

Was Cliff being a funny wiseass? At his own wake?

Sonny Atherton came next, and then Bev and Dan. Then Liam arrived with Kelsey, and after that, people seemed to come in throngs.

Kody tried to remain by Rosy's side, ready to fend off anyone who made her nervous.

But then she saw her parents.

"I've got this," Emory Clayton said.

"And I'm here, too," Bill assured her.

She moved forward to greet her mother and Frank.

Her stepfather was, in her mind, remarkably like her dad in appearance—except that he wore his graying hair much shorter than her father had kept his. Michael McCoy had always looked the part of a rock musician, from the '80s up until the time he had died.

Her father had been tall, six-something. Frank was tall, too. He even had a similar build.

Sally was a beautiful woman. Kody, of course, was prejudiced, but at fifty, Sally was slim and athletic with light hair cut to frame a very nicely shaped face. Her eyes were blue; Kody knew that she had gotten her own peculiar shade of amber from her father.

"Baby," Sally said softly.

For a long moment, her mother hugged her. Kody remembered just how dear Cliff had been to her mom.

"Kody," Frank said, giving her a hug next. He was always gentle and giving. Always careful of her feelings. He had once told her that he hoped very much that she would like him; he knew he was taking her dad's place at her mother's side. Since it had taken her mom some time to date again—much less remarry—she was certainly all right with it. She wanted her mother to be happy.

And Frank was an incredibly decent man.

"We'll just see Cliff, okay?" Sally asked her.

"Of course, Mom."

But Sally still paused, looking at her.

"You're really all right?"

"I'm fine. Trying to look after Rosy," Kody said.

She watched as her mom and Frank went to stand in line—there were now a number of mourners waiting to pay respects to Cliff Bullard's earthly remains.

She saw that Brodie was off a bit with Liam. They were an interesting duo.

They were both standing with their arms crossed over their chests.

Watching.

People came, close friends, work associates—including Jojo, the bartender from the Drunken Pirate, and a number of the waitstaff and others. Colleen arrived; Kody gave her an encouraging smile.

Ewan Keegan came along with divers and staff from Sea Life.

Everyone she knew seemed to be in the room.

Anyone who was local and really friends with Cliff had come out—and maybe even some wandering tourists had made it to Cliff's viewing.

Shorty approached. "Mrs. Bullard has said that you're going to do the speaking," he said. "Cliff's priest is going to do a prayer—his actual service will be tomorrow. After he speaks, we'll be ready for you. This seems to be very hard on Mrs. Bullard. We're going to try to make sure that we usher people out by nine."

"Of course," Kody murmured.

Father Rodriguez went to stand at the front of the room. With a quick clearing of his throat, he had everyone's respectful attention. He gave a short introduction, mentioning Cliff's love of the church, and then asked them all to join in a prayer.

Kody bowed her head.

A thought was plaguing her.

Was Cliff's killer in the room?

Cliff's ghostly self was then standing just in the front, to the side. He had his head bowed in prayer.

As the prayer neared an end and there was a moment of silence, Cliff walked over to Kody.

"Make it good, kid," he said.

She didn't let herself look at him. Father Rodriguez ended his prayer and brought her up.

"Cliff was, beyond a doubt, a one-of-a-kind man," Kody began.

"A wonderful man!" Cliff's ghost said. "An extraordinary man—best ever."

Kody didn't give him a glance. She couldn't.

"A charming man, as well. A bit of a flirt, in the best way, as his wife, whom he loved beyond all measure, can tell you."

"All right, all right, so maybe not a wonderful man," Cliff's ghost said.

"A very good man, kind to all," Kody said. She talked a minute more, mentioning his ability with songs and guitar, his contribution to the local music scene, and then said, "We thank you all so very much for paying homage to Cliff tonight. We will miss him. Many will miss him as a friend. Rosy will miss him as the love of her life. All of us will miss him as a very special part of Key West."

"Why don't you ask which one of the bastards murdered me?" Cliff suggested.

"Truly loved by all," Kody said. She looked around the room. All eyes were on her.

She actually felt tempted to repeat Cliff's question herself. But then, she couldn't do that to Rosy.

"He will be missed more than words can say," she added. "And, of course, we'll always be looking for those who knew him, always seeking to exchange stories and...always..." she finished softly, because she could not help herself "...always seeking to find the truth. Thank you."

She walked away from the coffin.

CHAPTER TEN

"I always wonder what a wake just might tell us," Liam said quietly. He and Kelsey had found Brodie down near the sidewalk outside the funeral home, watching as others left.

"I wish it had told us something," Kelsey said softly. "It broke my heart to see Cliff. He loved Rosy so much."

"She seems to be having a bad time," Liam said. "Anything?" he asked Brodie.

"Not tonight. We were all watching. People seldom go to a wake and suddenly scream out a confession anyway," Brodie said.

"No, I guess not," Kelsey agreed.

"We're heading home," Liam said.

"Heading home. It's late," Kelsey said. "And, of course, we'll both stay up for hours, poring over everything we know about Cliff and Arnold Ferrer and the ship."

Brodie smiled. Kelsey was the perfect fit for Liam. She was a "seer" as well, of course—that was something that made life easier from the get-go. She wasn't just support for her husband; she was a true sounding board.

"I think we'll all do the same."

"And it works," Kelsey whispered. "I couldn't get near Kody—if you see her, give her my love. And tell her that we'll all be there tomorrow."

"Will do," Brodie promised.

He watched them walk down the path to Liam's car. And he waited.

Then he saw a group from Sea Life coming out. Ewan headed over to talk to Brodie.

"Anything else on Mr. Ferrer?" he asked.

"Liam and his team are working hard. We're getting more and more bits of information daily," Brodie told him.

"Well, you really crashed back into working—for a guy on vacation," Ewan said.

"I know you, Ewan. If you were me, you wouldn't be able to let it go," Brodie told him.

"No, no, I wouldn't. But I've got my work back down on the ship." He hesitated. "We found chains. And some human remains. Bones…bone fragment, really. After being in the service so many years, I didn't think that too much would get to me. I've gotten to see a lot of man's inhumanity to man time and time again. But when I get down there sometimes, I can't help but wonder—how could one human being do such things to other human beings?"

Ewan was clearly disturbed by the discovery and what he was seeing. Being in the actual environment was different from hearing about it. He was doing his job; doing what needed to be done. But not without empathy.

Most of the time, Brodie's sense about people was right on. Maybe that came hand in hand with seeing the dead; he wasn't sure.

"Hey, no one has cured the world of cruelty yet, and it's unlikely it will happen anytime soon," Brodie told him. "The best we can do is make and enact laws—and ignore those who run around feeling superior." He looked back toward the funeral parlor. Kody was still standing next to Rosy, holding her around the shoulders as Rosy thanked people for coming.

"It was nice that your whole crew came out, Ewan," Brodie said.

"We hadn't been working that long, but heading out to see Cliff Bullard play was something we'd all gotten into doing. It was nice at the Drunken Pirate—Cliff was funny. He was a good showman. And he strummed a good tune. But it wasn't so loud that we couldn't hear ourselves, talk over what we were doing... Anyway, we've called a moratorium on our work tomorrow, too. The parent company has sent down a few men to watch over the *Memory* and the dive site out of respect—we will all be attending the funeral."

"That's a nice gesture."

"That's respect," Ewan said. "Good night, Brodie." He started to walk away, but then turned back. "You know, you're welcome back at the dive site any time. And Sea Life wouldn't let me say that to many people."

"I'm honored," Brodie told him. "Thank you."

He walked back toward the entry to the funeral parlor.

The crowd had winnowed out.

He'd been watching the ghost of Cliff Bullard all night; he'd seen Cliff tease Kody, and he'd also seen something of the sadness and emotion in his voice when he'd suggested that she should ask which of the bastards had killed him.

He walked over to the group; he saw that Kody's mother was looking at him curiously as he approached.

Rosy stopped sniffling for a minute to stare at him, too.

"You've all met Brodie McFadden, except for my mom and Frank," Kody said. "Brodie, my mom, Sally, and her husband, Frank Frampton."

Frank immediately extended a hand. Brodie took it firmly. "Glad to meet you, sir."

"Pleasure, young man," Frank said.

"Likewise," Kody's mother said. She stepped forward, and to his surprise, gave him a kiss on the cheek. "Sorry, we're a very kissy-huggy family. We actually heard about you, Mr. McFadden," Sally said.

Everyone looked at her.

"Seriously?" she asked, a half smile on her face. Sally glanced at Rosy with sympathetic eyes. "We have been in touch with Liam and Kelsey the whole time. Our first thought had been to come straight home, but then…well, Cliff was very supportive of Frank's work, so we came this morning. We didn't want to bother you with phone calls."

Rosy smiled. "Kody has been a dream helper in so many ways!" Rosy gave a deep sigh. "I guess I need to head home. Tomorrow…"

"We'll get you home," Kody told her.

"The car is taking me home. Sonny is coming with me. She's staying at my place," Rosy assured her. "You…well, your mom and Frank just got back. Don't worry about me, Kody. I'm in good hands."

Sonny looked at Kelsey and smiled. "I'm on duty," she promised.

"And I'll head over for a few minutes, too," Bill said. "Until you've had a chance to wind down."

"It's a big car," Emory said.

"So, should we get some coffee or something?" Frank asked Kody. "Mr. McFadden, you'll join us?"

"Sure. Thank you," Brodie said.

They bid Rosy good-night, Kody giving her a warm hug, Sally doing the same. Brodie suggested the little restaurant where he and Kody had eaten the night before—they served food until midnight—not that there weren't other places, but it was a full menu, and, as far as he knew, none of them had eaten.

They ordered soon after sitting down; Brodie knew that he was being studied. He didn't mind. Frank talked about his work—the company he was with was a nonprofit, like Sea Life. "Tomorrow, I'll be back on the road, staying up in Marathon."

"I'd be going with him," Sally said. "Except..."

"Mom," Kody said, "you're still going with Frank. You don't need to stay because of me."

"We'll see," Sally said.

"We won't see—I'm fine. We have wonderful friends here. Liam is here—and Brodie is going to be here."

Had Kody told them that something was going on between them?

Frank wasn't going to get into it. "Anyway, we're going to film a documentary on all the good that is done by many of our aquariums and marine facilities. What many animal activists don't realize is how many creatures would die if they weren't cared for by such facilities."

"Tommy—he's a sea turtle," Sally said. "Poor thing was so entangled in fishing wire...he couldn't make it on his own. And Augustine the dolphin—rescued off the North Florida coast, so mangled by a boat propeller it's amazing that he has survived at all. He's very happy—loves his vet and his trainer, and when they go near his section of the water, he squeals and rushes to see him. Augustine loves people!"

"So, we've learned a little bit about you, Mr. McFadden," Frank said.

Kody rolled her eyes. Brodie smiled. "I am a PI. I'm from Virginia, but love visiting Key West. I was working with Ewan Keegan, of Sea Life. I was the one who found Mr. Ferrer's body. I've actually met Liam before and we worked together. Sad case—a boat crashed off of Stock Island and a man was killed—his body was entangled by an anchor chain that had been discarded." He hesitated. It was going to sound like all he did was find dead men in the water. "I was one of the divers who finally found him."

"Oh," Kody's mother said, glancing at Kody.

Kody laughed suddenly. "Mom, Liam is a cop. A detective. He's always involved with crime. You don't have a problem with that."

"One of the best cops on the island," Frank said. "One of the best cops we've ever had."

Brodie lowered his head, trying not to smile. Liam was Kody's friend—he hadn't asked, but he was pretty sure the two had never been romantically involved. There was a difference, maybe, in Sally's eyes, between a friend who was a cop and a man who might be more than a friend winding up in the midst of danger all the time.

"What do you think about all this?" Frank asked Brodie seriously. "Horrible—that a man was murdered, trying to do the right thing."

"Well, he's still doing the right thing," Brodie said. "The ME will be releasing Arnold Ferrer's body tomorrow, so a former partner of his is coming down. She's going to take him home to be buried. And she's going to sign over the papers that were so important to him to Sea Life and then to Kody, for the museum."

"That's wonderful of her," Sally said.

"Excellent," Frank said. "When Kody started working on the museum, I was afraid that it might be…" He hesitated, looking at Kody.

"He was afraid I was going to create the museum as something that catered to the sensationalism of some of our ghost stories," Kody said, grinning.

Frank flushed. "Well, Kody hasn't managed it that way at all. It's one of the best museums on the island, even if I am prejudiced."

"Thank you, Frank."

"And there's a beautiful memorial to your father, too," Frank said. "And, of course, other artists, actors, writers and musicians."

"Can't have Key West without music," Kody said. She smiled sadly. "I do remember when Dad and Cliff would play."

"Your father loved to play with his friends—let them be seen and heard. I think he was always surprised that he managed to gain the popularity that he did. I don't think he always thought that he was worthy of the accolades he received," Sally said. She reached across the table and squeezed her daughter's hand. "You're going to add Cliff in to the musicians of the past section, right?"

"Absolutely. I already have a great picture of him with Dad up on the wall. Of course, I have lots of pictures of the people he played with through the years"

Dinner came and went; they all lingered over coffee.

"Who is doing the eulogy?" Sally asked, after Frank and Brodie had politely argued over the bill. Frank won; Brodie didn't want to offend him.

"I'm doing the eulogy," Kody told her.

"Hmm," Sally said.

"Mom, I can do a eulogy."

"I'm sure you'll do it beautifully," Sally said. "It's just that Rosy and Bill Worth are so close, and Bill writes for a living."

"Rosy asked me. What could I say? In fact, I need to get something down on paper now."

"And we really need to get to sleep. The service at the church is at ten, right?" Frank asked.

"Ten o'clock," Kody said.

"Sweetheart, do you want to come home with us? Are you all right?"

"I'm fine," Kody said. "I just need to go mull my words. Brodie will help."

"Okay. Oh!" Sally said, as if just realizing Kody's relationship with Brodie might go deeper than she had thought.

"Sally, let's go. Let her get her eulogy written. I know it's going to be very important to her."

"All right, all right...um. Hmm. Brodie, very nice to meet you," Sally said, and she started to leave with Frank. But then she paused. "You're not from here. Are you going to stay until the murder from the ship is solved? That might take... Well, there are murders that go completely unsolved, so... You live in Virginia."

Frank gave Brodie and Kody a grimace over Sally's shoulder. "Good night, you two. We'll see you at the church."

"Good night, and a true pleasure," Brodie said.

"Of course," Sally murmured. "But—"

"We're going Sally," Frank said. "We'll see them in the morning."

They finally left, and Brodie took his seat again, smiling as he met Kody's eyes.

"She is my mom," Kody said.

"She's lovely."

"She really is. And Frank... I'll always miss my father. I know that he had very bad days when he was younger. He might not have made it. My mother was his lifeline, and he truly adored her. But I'm honestly happy for her now. Frank is a good man."

"He seems exceptional," Brodie agreed. He leaned across the table. "We are done, right?"

"I should go home, write the eulogy. Be where I can actually shower and dress in the morning."

"If that's what you want."

She smiled. "I said that I *should*. I didn't say that I *would*."

"I've got a compromise. I'll get my things. We'll stay at your place."

"I like it. Oh! But the captain."

"Kody, we just had dinner with your mom—I think you can manage the captain."

She smiled.

They left the restaurant. "I didn't see the captain at the wake," Kody said thoughtfully as they headed to his room.

"I'm sure he was there."

"Cliff was there."

"I saw. And I heard," Brodie told her.

"Do you think that's why... I always wondered why some people stay—and some go. I mean, it makes sense that you'd stay if...if there was trauma. If you were murdered, or if you died violently. If you had a reason, but...we've had a number of ghosts on this island who didn't leave the world violently. And I always wondered why..."

"Why you can never see your father?" Brodie asked.

She nodded. "You're lucky. In a way, you have both your parents."

"We are lucky," he said. "And luckiest, I guess, because they're together now as they were in life. They were lucky. Not everyone gets that kind of...not just love, but commitment."

"I really would love to meet them," Kody said. "But not tonight!"

He smiled at that. "There's no need to fear that. They're in Virginia, happily checking in on my brothers."

They'd reached his room. Brodie quickly gathered what he thought he would need for the night.

Kody hovered by the doorway, as if afraid that if she went in, they wouldn't leave.

The walk to her house didn't take long. When she opened the door, Brodie thought that she was a bit nervous.

When they went in, the captain didn't seem to be there.

The cat found them immediately, rubbing up against Kody's ankles and meowing loudly.

"Yes, you need some attention and some treats," Kody said. "But… Brodie, I don't think that Captain Hunter is here."

"He's out wandering. He said that he'd do his best to listen, to see what he could hear."

"I guess, but…"

"Kody, you can't worry about—a ghost. He's fine."

Kody agreed. Then, she suddenly seemed a little awkward. "I… Do you want anything?"

He smiled. "Just you," he told her.

They were the right words. She slid into his arms, and her lips met his.

They kissed, long, deep, hot, wet, breathless. Then she drew away. "You should go put your stuff upstairs. Stairs are to the right in the hall…there are actually four bedrooms, but one is an office, another a storage room…one guest room, and one is mine… First at the top of the stairs."

He pulled away. "I'll get set up. You go write what you want to say," he reminded her softly.

She took a step away from him. "Yes…so important. I have to make it right for Cliff…even if he can be a ghostly jerk."

Brodie turned her about and prodded her toward the hallway. She hurried ahead of him.

He went up the stairs, admiring the architecture of the old house as he did so. In the bedroom, he set down his bag and hung up the lightweight suit he'd wear the next day.

He walked down the hall to the office; Kody was busy, concentrating as she wrote.

Back in the bedroom, he set his gun and small holster he wore when working on the side table, and lay down, staring at the ceiling.

He thought about the wake, all the people on the island who had come out to pay Cliff their respects.

Even the crew from Sea Life.

Cliff had never been out on the *Memory*. He'd never worked with the Sea Life crew. He had no affiliation with the ship.

One man strangled. One man dead of a severe allergy he knew well.

As did those who knew him well.

Arnold Ferrer had loved his guitar.

Were they related through the ship somehow—or through music?

Kody entered the room. "Done," she whispered, and she closed the door and turned off the lights.

He could hear her shedding her clothing in the darkness.

She came to the bed and crawled over him. He tasted her naked flesh, his kisses soft caresses against the silken feel of her.

She moved in his arms.

And he forgot the rest of the world.

Once again, it seemed that half the island had turned out to honor Cliff.

Including Cliff himself. Kody, standing by the front pew, acknowledged his presence with a warning stare. He smiled and shrugged.

He waited as Rosy entered the church, Bill Worth and Emory Clayton escorting her, each man holding one of her arms.

They led Rosy to the front pew, where she sat down, unknowingly right next to Cliff. Both men nodded at Kody. They were leaving Rosy in her care then, heading to the front to welcome other guests as they arrived for the service.

Cliff set an arm around Rosy.

Rosy shivered.

She looked up at Kody. "This is real," she whispered. "This is…this is…real."

Kody could think of nothing to say. Cliff was watching her, heartsick.

"Tell her how much I loved her, Kody," he pleaded.

"Rosy, he loved you so much," Kody said.

Rosy nodded. "I'm cold," she said. "Why is it so cold in here?"

Cliff lowered his head, anguished. "She can't see me, Kody. She can't feel my love. I just make her frightened and cold."

Kody couldn't speak to him. He stood and moved away, just watching Rosy, so Kody took the seat next to her, putting an arm around her.

As the church began to fill, she looked around for Brodie. She saw him at the back, deep in conversation with Liam.

People began to sit, and soon, the church was full.

The priest welcomed them, and proceeded with the service.

It came time for Kody to read her eulogy. She found that she barely referred to her notes. She was able to speak from the heart. Once again, she talked about Cliff's laughing, his joking, his teasing, and his flirting—and his incredible ability to make all those around him feel good. He had the knack for saying the right thing—because he did care. He loved humanity in general; he gave his all to his friends, his beloved Rosy, and the beauty of his soul came through in his music.

Since she knew Cliff really was listening, she told him some things she wished she'd been able to tell him while he was alive. How much she loved him and was grateful for his presence in her life.

When she was done, she was happy; she thought that she had epitomized the best of the man; he didn't move mountains, he just gave the best of himself, true caring, true generosity, and thoughtfulness for others before himself.

At the end of her speech, she made eye contact with Brodie, and he gave her a look that told her she had spoken beautifully.

Then it was time to leave the church.

She discovered that Brodie—along with Liam, Emory, Bill, Frank and Sonny—had been asked to be a pallbearer and "carry" the coffin from the church to the waiting hearse. The coffin was actually on rollers; it was fine for Sonny to be along with the stronger, larger company.

Michael McCoy's ancestors had built the beautiful vault in the cemetery just years after the cemetery had opened. It was beautiful and large, with handsome Victorian lines and angels above the iron gates.

The priest said prayers again as Cliff was interred next to Kody's father.

Kody stood there and wondered if—when, perhaps, Cliff went on, or even the captain, someday—they could tell her father just how much she had loved him.

As she stood there, and Cliff's earthly remains were set into the vault, Cliff came to stand by Kody.

"I'm so sorry. It must hurt you to be here."

"It's all right," she murmured aloud.

Bill Worth, standing nearby, turned to look at her. "You okay, Kody?"

"Yes."

"You should sing for him, sing the song he loved so much," Emory said.

She shook her head. A few of Cliff's musician friends had come; they were playing "Amazing Grace."

Kody stood very still, the ghost by her side.

Why can I see so many, and not my dad?

She felt movement around her—from the living. Her mother was by her then, placing an arm over her shoulders.

The distracting note of a cell phone was almost covered by the music.

Liam's phone; frowning, he moved away to answer it.

He motioned to Brodie.

The priest invited the attendees to the Drunken Pirate for a celebration in honor of Cliff's life.

Kody turned and hugged her mom. "You okay?" she whispered.

Sally hugged her. "They're together. I like to think that there's a lovely jam session going on somewhere."

Cliff heard her. "Cool, yes…one day. A lovely jam session."

"Are you going with Rosy in the car to the Drunken Pirate?" Sally asked.

"I…"

Kody hesitated. She could see that Brodie was still talking to Liam. And she knew, even before she walked over to talk to him, that something else had happened.

"What is it?" she asked, walking up between the two men.

Brodie looked at her. "Another body," he said.

Her heart seemed to skip a beat.

"Where? How?"

"It just washed up on the beach, near Ft. Zachary Taylor," Liam said.

"Who?" Kody whispered.

"We don't know yet. I just got the call. A tourist saw some seaweed or a dead sea creature was in the waves and started pulling the seaweed…and then called 911," Liam explained. "I have to go. Kelsey will see you at the Drunken Pirate, and I'll be there as soon as I can…"

"Was it a man…a woman…young, old?" Kody asked.

"This time, it's a woman. Fifties, so my officer believes," Liam said.

"You're going with him?" Kody asked Brodie. "You must go with him."

"Kody, it looks like a drowning," Liam told her. "As sad as is any loss, we do lose people to the ocean, and every year, we have accidents on US 1, and there's no reason to believe that this death is associated in any way with Arnold—or Cliff."

She looked at Brodie sternly. "Go with him," she said softly.

"I'll be at the reception, whenever you two finish. Go, please—and find out what the hell is happening down here."

Brodie nodded.

She turned and left them, walking over to where Cliff was standing, a distance off, watching as his friends left the cemetery to head to the reception. Some had their heads bowed.

There were more than a few tears being shed.

"Cliff…" she said sympathetically.

"Someone else dead, huh?"

"An accident, they believe. A drowning."

"Right." He turned to her. "You know, people party down here. There are accidents on the road. Bizarre things do happen. But now this? Three deaths in a row? Like hell. Kody, something wrong sure in tarnation is going on down here. And, so help me, I will haunt the hell out of this island until we find out what."

CHAPTER ELEVEN

It was a perfectly beautiful day, sun shining, gentle waves washing over the sand. The tide had brought great piles of seaweed to rest on the beach. And crime scene tape cordoned off a border that kept onlookers from the body that had also been brought ashore.

As Brodie followed Liam past the small crowd and over to the body, he saw that officers guarded the yellow-tape barrier, and one watched over the body.

"Another day in paradise, huh?" Liam murmured. He shook his head. "Trust me—we're a party town. We have crime. But this..."

Brodie was surprised that Liam was suspicious—not even having seen the victim yet.

"Liam, it could be anything. Someone from a refugee boat, someone just out and partying hard—someone who just went overboard."

"Right."

They reached the body. Brodie nodded an acknowledgment to the officer standing by; if he wondered why Liam was allowing him on the site, he gave no sign. Brodie figured that being with the sheriff gave him all access.

The medical examiner down from Marathon that day was Dr. Sheila Green. She was hunkered down, but looked up when Liam walked up and introduced Brodie. Dr. Green was an African American woman of about forty, almost bone thin and currently grim. "So sad. I'd say at the moment, it's a drowning. She's in a one piece as you can see—but she's been in overnight. Probably washed up late last night, and drowned shortly before. And exact time is going to be hard to pin—since she's been in the sea."

Liam and Brodie both squatted down by her. The ME had moved the hair from the victim's face. She had been a small woman, about five-foot-two, Brodie estimated. Not heavy, but rounded. Her skin already showed signs of crab or fish nibbles. Liam shooed one away as it emerged from the seaweed that still surrounded her; the body hadn't been moved since she had been discovered.

Brodie noticed something.

"Her fingers," he pointed out.

"Her fingers?" The ME took a gloved hand and gently raised one of the dead woman's hands.

"Callused...there," Brodie said. "She was a guitar player."

"Possibly," the ME agreed. "There are other ways to callus your fingers, but...yes, possibly."

"How long since she was discovered now?"

"About an hour and a half. I happened to be down here—that's how I took the call," Dr. Green said.

The officer, patiently standing by, broke his silence. "Our first call was exactly one hour and twenty-one minutes ago," he told Liam. "The woman who discovered her is still right back there in the patrol car."

"All right, thank you. Can you get her up—any possibility of an autopsy today?"

"I'll do my best," Dr. Green said.

Liam rose and Brodie did likewise. He'd studied the body the best he could, as it lay. No visible scars—and no blood anywhere on the body. Her heart had stopped beating long before she'd washed up on the sand. She'd had a round, heart-shaped face, and generous lips. The slight wrinkling around them suggested that she'd smiled a lot.

"Sorry to say, but I think we're going to discover that she was out on some kind of a party boat," Dr. Green said, rising as well. "Most of our problems down here have to do with alcohol or partying that got out of control."

"Officer Whitney," Liam said. "Have we had any reports of a missing person off a party boat—or any missing reports, period, overnight or recently?"

"No, sir."

"Maybe they haven't discovered her gone yet," Dr. Green suggested.

"A party boat—that doesn't count heads?" Liam said.

"A private party?" Brodie put in.

"She might even have been out alone," Dr. Green said.

"Any empty boats out there?" Liam asked.

"No, sir, no reports from our people or the Coast Guard," the officer said.

"Someone has to be missing her," Liam muttered. "All right, thank you, Dr. Green. I know your office can be busy, but..."

"I'll do everything I can," Dr. Green promised.

The patrol car was parked farther up the beach, and a woman was seated in the back, the door open, her bare legs extended.

She was young, barely into her twenties, Brodie thought. A caftan covered her two-piece bathing suit; her feet were adorned with beaded flip-flops. She was sipping coffee, and looked up eagerly as they approached.

"Oh, my God, you're the detective I need to speak with, right?" she asked, rising from the car as they approached. "Detectives… Oh, my God, this is so horrible. I never imagined. I'm here with a bachelorette party… I just came out to the beach to walk along the shore…it's so beautiful. And then I saw a clump of seaweed and I looked down and there was a body in it. I dropped my phone—there was sand all over it!—but then I dialed 911. And I told the man she was dead, and he asked if I was sure, and I said yes, and he said that I should try artificial respiration and I said no, can't you understand? Dead, dead, dead!" She extended a hand suddenly. "I'm Helen. Helen Harte."

"Helen, I'm Detective Beckett. This is Brodie McFadden, a consultant," Liam told her.

"Hello. I've been here…waiting."

"Thank you. I'm sure this must have been a terrible shock for you," Liam said. "And I'm so sorry you had to go through this. Did you see anything or anyone near her? Were you by the body until police arrived?"

"I wasn't by it," she said. "Oh, my God, no! I didn't stay by the body! But… I could see it. I could see it. A couple were going to walk by with their children, and I stopped them, of course! I mean, a little kid, seeing something like that…"

"Did you look at her face?" Brodie asked.

She shook her head vigorously. "No! There was seaweed… Oh, I swear, I knew she was dead. I mean, I'm not trained, but I would have helped her if there had been any way. I knew she was dead. She was dead…right?" she asked in sudden panic.

"She was dead," Brodie assured her quietly.

"You didn't recognize her?" Liam asked.

"No, no… I told you, I'm not from here. Is anybody really

from here?" She didn't want an answer; to her, Key West was where people came to party. It was a tourist destination.

"A few," Liam said dryly.

"Miss, she was definitely dead, and it was good of you to keep the children away," Brodie said.

"Thank you, Detective," she said.

"I'm not a detective. I'm a private investigator," Brodie corrected her.

"Consulting," Liam murmured. "All right. Was there anyone nearby when you saw her? Boats out on the water."

"There were people out on the water, yes…a group on those Sea-Doo things or whatever they are. None of them seemed to see her, or know about her, or have the least interest in the shore."

"You're sure she was no one you knew, anyone with you?" Brodie asked.

She flushed. "We were up very late last night. I'm here with seven other girls. The rest of my crew is still sleeping. I—I take medication, so I don't drink. But the rest of those guys…trust me. The woman is not…was not…with me. I just came out for a walk on the beach, and there she was."

"Okay, thank you, the officer will see you back to your room," Liam said. "We have all your information, just in case…"

"In case of what?" she asked, alarm leaping into her eyes.

"Just in case there's something else we haven't thought of," Brodie said. "Please, don't worry. You couldn't have saved her. You did the right thing—especially keeping the kids away."

"Yes, thank you," Liam said. He stepped back and indicated that she was free to sit back in the car and leave the scene.

"I'm right across the street," she told them, a little baffled.

"The officer will get you right to the door," Liam said. "You're distracted…we don't want any accidents."

"Right! Right! Leave it to me—I'd find a body and then walk

into a car and become nothing more than one myself! Thank you, thank you. I'm so sorry. Anyway... I'm going to have one hell of a vacation story!"

The car door closed. The officer in the front leaned his head down and nodded to Liam.

Then the car whisked on to the road.

"No ID on her again—and she was definitely a guitar player," Brodie noted.

"Everyone in the Keys is a guitar player," Liam said. "I sure hope to hell some sick bastard isn't out for every guitar player on the island—the place will become a pile of corpses."

Brodie shook his head. "I don't think that whoever is doing this is after just any guitar players."

"Cliff's death might still have been some kind of a bizarre accident—one that no one is obviously going to want to admit," Liam said. "And this woman... We all know people die on the road, thinking that they're not drunk and they have to get back home. We all know boaters die in South Florida. And we all know that people can party too hardy."

"Yes, I understand completely," Brodie said. "But..."

"But what?"

"Usually, when someone is gone through the night, there's at least someone they were with who notices that they're gone."

The reception was going perfectly.

Colleen had posted a sign on the door, explaining that the bar would be closed for the day due to a death in the family.

Cliff had been family.

Kody had found a table for her mom and stepdad, Colleen, Kelsey Beckett and herself. There was room for Liam and Brodie if they should make it before the event ended. The Drunken Pirate was paying for the reception, though Kody knew many people had offered to help. Cliff had done all right during his life—he hadn't been rich. No one wanted the hardship to fall on Rosy.

She knew that, around the room, the conversation was about Cliff—as it should have been. And then, of course, people would talk about the weather, and the water, and what was happening in their own lives. It was a way of accepting that a loved one or a friend was gone; it was the living going on after death.

And Kody did talk about Cliff; like others, she would remember stories that involved him, and in remembering, she would smile. As she circulated around the bar, she noted that Bev and Dan Atkins were there. Ewan Keegan and the crew from Sea Life had come out—all ten of them, spread over two tables. She spoke to them all briefly, and talked with Ewan about the find and how they would make sure that everything was properly handled between maritime law, the company and her museum. They were a polite group, all of them extending sympathy and praising Cliff.

Of course, she couldn't help but wonder about Cliff's own words the other night: *Which of you bastards killed me?*

"We're working again, you know, Kody," Ewan told her. "I have pictures I'll be emailing to you. We're in a quandary now about the remains we have found. Just bones, really. No complete skeletons, but… I don't know. Maybe we'll have a service at sea, and see that the bones remain where they were found. To me, that seems proper. The sea is a grave for so many."

"I'll be part of whatever you plan," Kody told him.

She gave them all a little wave and moved on. She greeted any familiar faces; but even while listening to their stories, she was plagued with wondering about the body that Liam and Brodie were investigating right at that moment.

She went to check on the widow.

Rosy didn't need anything; there were a lot of people looking after her. She whispered to Kody that she was maintaining, but that she was more of a private person, and really wanted it all to be over.

"Cliff was a man of the people. I don't have his charm or easy ways," Rosy told her.

"You leave whenever you feel you need to."

"I need to be here until the end. For Cliff."

"I'm sure he'd be very proud of you."

Rosy smiled. She picked at the spread of food set before her. Every once in a rare while, she sipped at her glass of wine. She thanked everyone who came by.

She shivered. "It's so cold today," Rosy said softly.

What she didn't know was that Cliff was standing near her, in his ghostly form.

Kelsey Beckett caught Kody's eye and nodded, aware of Cliff as well, but they would be careful not to speak.

Kelsey had been gone from the island for a long time after her mother had died, but she and Kody had been friends before she'd left—and it had been quick to restore that friendship. Kelsey was well aware that the dead could come back in a form that only a few people were privileged or cursed to see. She also knew that Kody's mom had none of the sense—and would seriously worry about Kody if she knew that her daughter was "seeing spirits again."

Young children often had imaginary friends. It was only something to worry about when they thought it was their deceased grandparents or other known friends who had departed their earthly coils.

As Kody came back to her friends' table, Colleen suddenly said, "I feel him. I feel him—as if he were here!"

"Cliff? Well, of course you feel him, dear. He'll always be with us, in the heart, of course," Sally said. "Especially here—at the Drunken Pirate."

"Oh, yes, in the heart," Kody murmured. She excused herself; Bill Worth had brought her a glass of wine, but she didn't feel like drinking it. She wanted some water or tea.

And she wanted to be away from anyone "feeling" Cliff.

Walking over to the bar, she told Jojo, "You should have had this time off."

He shook his head. "This was what I could do. I'm working for free. It's my way of honoring a great guy. What can I get you?"

"Water."

"Wild woman."

"Yep. Can't help myself," she said, grimacing.

As he brought her a large plastic cup filled with water and ice, she asked, "Jojo—how the hell do you think Cliff's drink got contaminated? You worked with him all the time. You know how careful he was. When we went out, he always asked to make sure that his food wasn't being cooked anywhere that was used for cooking with nuts. He really was so savvy about it."

Jojo paused, shaking his head. "Kody, I wish I could remember the night better. He came in—ordered his food and started setting up. His plate went down there—right where it always goes. So many people bought him drinks—it was the end of your festival and everyone was in a great mood. I just can't see it. I don't get it. The way he died…it was almost as if he swallowed a damned handful of peanuts."

"Which he definitely didn't do. We would have seen that."

"I guess," Jojo said, "though…maybe not. I always saw to it that Cliff got his drinks—and usually watered down whatever it was, which could be anything. He knew he wasn't really going to drink it, so he'd just say, 'Surprise me!' But I can't say that I watched him."

"Do you remember what Cliff's last drink was? Or who bought it for him?"

"I wish I did. I've talked to the cops and to that PI, McFadden. I don't remember. Everyone here bought him something, seemed like. I know that he was walking around with something that looked like a White Russian, but for some reason, it seemed that everyone was ordering drinks like that the night Cliff died. White Russians, Kahlua and cream, Baileys and cream..." He paused for a minute. "Maybe Cliff picked up the wrong drink... except that I don't even keep almond milk or anything like that back here. I just don't know, Kody. I wish that I did."

"Thanks, Jojo," she said. "Hey."

"Yep?"

"Did you pick up a cup out of the foliage by the stage by any chance?"

"I don't think so. But all of us are always picking up any trash. I even throw away cups from other places all the time. Most islanders are good—but hey. People sometimes forget that they left trash around the tiki bar."

She smiled and started back to the table. Rosy was speaking softly with Bill Worth.

He was so attentive. He was great.

Great...

Was he being more than attentive?

The idea was ridiculous. They'd all been friends. And now...

"He's too close. That rascal, Bill."

Kody almost dropped her glass. She didn't know how Cliff's ghost managed to get her by surprise, but she had started.

He was watching the table, too.

"Hell, I'm barely cold, and that bastard is flirting with Rosy."

"Cliff, Bill and Emory have been trying to help her through this whole thing," she said. "And you—you've been flirting with every girl on the island."

"No, I've been like a counselor—a therapist," he argued.

"Bill is a good guy," Kody reminded him. "One of the best."

"Yeah, yeah...and old Emory is there, too. I guess I should

just be grateful, right? Nice of the Drunken Pirate to do this, yeah? And our boy Jojo, doing it all for free."

"You will always be loved," she told him.

And then she realized, of course, that people were looking at her.

It appeared that she was having a conversation with herself. And she didn't even drink. She had a glass of water.

Maybe people already considered her a little weird.

She just smiled and headed toward the table. She could see the way that Kelsey was looking at her.

Have to be careful, that look warned.

Kody kept her smile glued in place and rejoined her table.

"So, really, what do you know about this Brodie McFadden?" Sally asked her. "I mean, Liam does seem to like him. And he's very courteous. And..."

"And?" Kody asked.

"Your mother thinks he's very good-looking," Frank told her. "She doesn't want you falling for a man for his looks."

"He is really...um, tall, dark and rugged. I think you're right, Mom. He is good-looking."

"Oh, both of you!" Sally protested. "No, I mean, I even know who he is. I know about him. His parents were Maeve and Hamish McFadden, very well known in my generation. And you have to be careful..."

"Mom, my dad was Michael McCoy. That hasn't tainted me in any way—that I know of, anyway!" Kody said.

"Yes, but..."

"Sally," Frank warned.

"No, no, he seems great. Wonderful. Perfect."

"Liam says that he is all those things," Kelsey put in. "And Liam does know people."

"But what future is there in...in him?" Sally asked.

"I don't know what the future is with anyone," Kody said.

"And please, please, please—don't go asking him what his intentions are, or anything like that."

"Well, of course not," Sally said, but she looked sheepish.

Kody glanced at Frank and grinned. "What were you doing, Mom, fooling around with a rocker like my dad?"

"Oh, Kody!"

Frank laughed. "Hey! Let's call a truce here. We're not going to ask about his intentions!" He was silent for a minute and then added softly, "You know, though, it's the kind of thing Cliff might have done."

Kelsey smiled. "I'm sure, in his spiritual way, he's looking at us all—and certainly at Brodie McFadden."

Kody narrowed her eyes at Kelsey.

Kelsey grimaced.

Cliff's ghost was now with them again, leaning against Kelsey's chair.

"I know his immediate intentions!" he said. "They were crystal clear. He'd just better remain…well, a gentleman!"

Kody smiled at Kelsey. "Right, because if we'd seen Cliff flirting around, we'd be certain to ask his intentions!"

"Ah, Cliff! He was a flirt—a sweetheart of a flirt," Kody's mom said.

"But," Frank added, "he loved his Rosy!"

"And, oh, indeed he did," Cliff's ghost said sadly. He stepped back, his expression changing.

One of the entertainers for the evening—a young guitarist Kody didn't know—approached the table.

"Miss McCoy?"

"Yes?"

"These guys were all hoping you'd do something with us."

"Oh, no, no. My dad—"

"Was the singer, but you did sing with Cliff."

"Yes, I was singing with him when he dropped dead," Kody said flatly.

"Yeah, we know. One of your dad's tunes. But we were hoping you'd do that one Cliff was so well known for doing. 'Love in the Sun.'"

"Oh, um, no…it's…"

"Oh, Kody," Cliff's ghost said softly. "Please!"

She let out a long sigh and nodded. She walked with the guitarist to the dais where she had been so recently—with Cliff.

But Cliff was still there…

And he wanted this.

The guitarist announced that she was going to do "Love in the Sun." It was a beautiful song, a ballad. About the days of youth and love and believing in living forever…and then how love could live on forever, even when someone was gone.

Kody gave it her all. When she finished, the room was silent; then there was wild applause.

But then, she glanced at Rosy, and she was looking at her so strangely. Tears fell from her eyes.

Kody hurried over to her table. "Oh, Rosy, I'm so sorry. I shouldn't have—"

"No, dear! You should have. That was beautiful," Rosy said.

She stood and hugged Kody.

Long minutes passed before Kody could return to her own table.

A sketch artist was going to be called in, but it turned out not to be necessary.

When the body reached the morgue—which happened while Liam was still deep in paperwork and Brodie was reading documents—she was identified by one of the medical assistants, and the identification was accepted as correct.

Her name had been Mathilda Sumner. She lived in Marathon. By day, she worked in the local grocery.

Two nights a week, she played at Tortoise Cove, a little sea shanty bar on Grassy Key. She had been born in Miami and moved down to the Keys just about ten years earlier.

Liam listened to the call from the station and then repeated what he had learned to Brodie. "She was single—no family left, not that anyone knew about. She was well liked—loved where she worked, both in the grocery store and when she played."

"Was she down here with friends? Why wouldn't they have reported her missing?" Brodie asked.

"Well, so far, we have nothing on that. She was just recognized by one of the morgue staff as soon as she came in. She was very upset—she didn't know her that well, but said she always had a smile for everyone, and just really loved living in Marathon. This had to have been some kind of an accident."

"Yeah, maybe," Brodie said. "She was out with friends, and she fell overboard—and no one wants to report it because they're afraid that they might be accused of manslaughter or worse?"

"That is possible."

"Someone had to know that she was going out—that she was doing something."

"I'll probably have to take a trip back up to Marathon to find out," Liam said. "We'll put out an appeal to the public."

Liam parked in the public lot near the hotel and the Drunken Pirate. "I'm guessing the reception will be winding down soon," Liam said. "It was good of the owners and management to plan this in memory of Cliff. But I don't suppose they can let it go on forever."

They were walking in when Brodie's phone rang. He noted that the call was coming from Krewe headquarters, and he answered it quickly.

"Angela?"

"It's me."

"Please, say you have something."

"I went through the names you gave me. Then I started cross-referencing with the names you had given me that had to do with the sinking of the *Victoria Elizabeth*. It wasn't easy," Angela said. "Very confusing following the lineage."

"But?"

"One of the names on the list of locals connected to Cliff Bullard has a relationship to the ship."

"Who? How?"

"Gonzales," Angela said.

For a moment, Brodie's mind was blank. Then he remembered. Of course, Mauricio Ferrer had addressed one of his letters to a *Senhor Gonzales*. Gonzales had answered; he had been interested in buying the slaves who had perished on the doomed ship.

"You found a real connection?" he asked, very impressed. He hadn't even given Angela a first name; he hadn't had one to give her.

"Yes, I researched rich men living in the south during the months before the ship went down. Hector Gonzales had a spread of land in southern Georgia. He already owned a hundred plus slaves and hundreds of acres. He grew cotton. I was able to find a few pieces on him. He was hated—even by his neighbors. One of them sent a complaint to a local politician. He was appalled by the man's treatment of his slaves, which, of course, Gonzales considered to be his property—his to use as he would. Anyway, the neighbor, one Samuel Martin, stated in very eloquent language that no man should treat a mule so cruelly. Now, Samuel Martin was a slave owner himself. But it seems, according to records, he must have, at the least, been a kind man. His plantation—burned to the ground in the Civil War, during Sherman's 'March to the Sea'—was just as massive, but his records showed that he actually allowed his people to work only so many hours and that he never allowed families to be split up. I believe for his time, he was trying very hard to be a moral man."

"He was, in his way, but…what about Gonzales?"

"Hector Gonzales married a young woman named Massie Belaire. They had one daughter."

"Back in the early 1800s," Brodie said.

"Yes. They were too old to fight, really, but both Gonzales and Martin created companies and fought in the Civil War. They were both killed in the fighting. Gonzales's wife and daughter were his heirs, but…by 1865, they were heirs to nothing. Anyway, Gonzales's daughter moved out to California. She married a man named Tillerson. She also had one daughter."

"Angela…"

"I'm getting to it. Gonzales's granddaughter married a man named Worth."

"Worth?" Brodie repeated. Worth.

As in Bill Worth?

"It's a common enough name," Brodie said.

"Yes, it is," Angela said. "And God knows, this could just be happenstance. The man may not know anything about all this. Gonzales's great-grandson is a William Worth. He moved to Seattle. The family was in that area from that time on. We're talking about something that occurred almost two-hundred years ago. Generation after generation."

"That's what I mean. Angela—"

"You asked me. I researched. Like I said, nearly two centuries have passed since the sinking of that ship. We usually know something about our parents and even our great-grandparents. Gonzales was Portuguese, but over two hundred years in America, any family winds up mixed to the gills. Brodie, I followed a paper trail. Okay, a paper trail now a digital trail, but the documents are listed at various churches and in county registers. I was careful. Your William Worth is a descendant of the *Senhor Gonzales* who was interested in buying the *Victoria Elizabeth's* wretched human cargo."

"Maybe Ferrer wanted the truth out—but Worth didn't," Brodie said.

"Possibly," Angela said.

"But even so…decades and generations have passed. A man living and working down here wouldn't have any reason to kill over that—even if someone found out. I mean, you had to dig and dig to find that fragment of history, right?"

"I did. It was tricky. I'm good at what I do. Naw, really, not to totally leave all realms of humility, I'm very good. Someone else, of course, could have come upon the information, but it wouldn't have been easy."

"Still, it's a motive," Brodie said.

"Like I said, family trees are like spiderwebs. Especially in America—that's one of our greatest strengths—everybody may be just about everything by the time three or four generations have come and gone. Mr. Worth may not even know that he has any affiliation with the ship."

"He may not, but it's definitely worth looking at," Brodie said.

"There's something else," Angela said. "And," she told him, hesitating slightly, "you may not like this piece of information."

"Whatever it is, shoot."

"I culled information of the ten men on the Sea Life crew. I looked up anything that resembled a boat owned by any of them. Only two men in the group actually reside in Key West."

"Right," Brodie said evenly. "Ewan Keegan, and Josh Gable."

"Yes. None of the other men live in the Keys. Both Ewan and Josh keep boats. And both of them have GPS systems—a great safety measure. Anyway, on the night when Arnold Ferrer's body was taken down into the hold of the wreck, Ewan Keegan's boat was out on the water. That doesn't even mean that Ewan was aboard—but his boat was out near the dive site. I can send you the information I was able to pull up. I'll get it all into your email."

"Thank you," Brodie told her.

"I'm sorry."

"He may not be guilty of anything—except for omission. But then again, it's possible to see omission as a lie," Brodie said.

He hung up; Liam was watching him.

Brodie sighed inwardly and shared the information he'd been given.

"Time to check into both men more closely," Liam said. "But we can't stay here long. Arnold Ferrer's ex-girlfriend, Adelaide Firestone, has arrived—she called the station. I told my officers to let her know that we'll come to her. I take it you want to meet her." He paused. "We—as in the police—were going to put her up at one of the big chain hotels on the south side of the island—but she received a better offer."

"A better offer?"

"She's going to stay at Bev and Dan's bed-and-breakfast—the Sea Horse. Apparently, Bev was taken with Arnold, and she and Dan want to do anything they can to help us. They thought that offering his ex-girlfriend a place to stay that was comfortable, in Old Town, and near Arnold's last place, would be the right thing to do."

"I believe Bev and Dan are at the funeral reception," Brodie said.

Liam nodded. "They might still be here. They have a live-in manager who handles things when they're out."

"Let's pay our respects—and then go meet Miss Firestone."

CHAPTER TWELVE

"They're here," Cliff's ghost whispered to Kody.

She looked up, finding the way she felt a little alarming—so incredibly glad that a man had arrived. But then, nothing to do with Brodie had been anything that might be considered "usual" for her. She was still amazed that she had all but attacked him. But there was something between them.

He walked in with Liam. There was something about both of them, really. They never entered a room without being noticed. She'd known and loved Liam all her life—he was close to being the big brother she'd never had. They'd even squabbled upon occasion—though he had been older, more mature—in his mind, at least.

With Brodie…

Was it special just because he also saw the dead?

No. She'd been attracted to him before she'd even known.

They stopped by to see Rosy, as had everyone, offering her their sympathy again. Watching Brodie, she frowned. He seemed to be looking at those around Rosy's table intently.

Focusing on Bill.

But he didn't seem to be engaging in a heavy conversation with him.

Kelsey got up to greet her husband as Liam and Brodie came to the table. Frank quickly rose to greet the newcomers and Kody stood as well—suddenly a bit awkward, not knowing if she should be quite so obvious. But they bustled about, drawing in chairs.

Cliff Bullard, who had anxiously joined the group, asked, "What's happened? What's going on?"

Neither Brodie nor Liam gave him notice, but in his way, Liam answered him. "A woman from Marathon was found on the beach. A drowning. We're investigating, of course. She wasn't reported missing and we don't know exactly when she washed up on the beach—or where she'd been before she washed up on the beach."

"Do you know her name?" Kody asked anxiously.

"Mathilda Sumner," he said, and Kody knew that he was hoping that the dead woman hadn't been a friend of hers.

"I recognize the name… I think I've seen ads around," Kody told him. "She was a performer somewhere?"

"She was a grocery store clerk who worked a few nights a week playing guitar and singing," Brodie told her.

"Like Cliff," Colleen said. "That's frightening. That's…well, tragic."

"How very, very odd," Sally said.

She realized that everyone at the table was looking at her. "Well, three strange deaths in one week." She shook her head and looked at Liam sadly. "You couldn't even make it through the day when you had to say goodbye to a dear friend."

"It is strange, for our island," Colleen said. "But…sad, mainly. We are surrounded by water. I guess… I guess people drown."

"You can't be careless around the ocean," Sally said.

Liam looked at Kelsey. "We came by to see Rosy and pay

our last official respects," Liam said. "And to let you know what happened."

"Of course," Kelsey said. She smiled at her husband. "I'll hang with these guys…for a while, and then, if you're looking for me, I'll probably head home."

"You can hang with me as long as you like," Kody said.

"See, there you go. I'll be with Kody."

No one said anything, and Kody realized that it was already assumed that Brodie—although he had no real authority at all—would be going with Liam.

She looked at Brodie.

"We're headed to see Adelaide Firestone," he said.

"Who?" Sally asked.

"The mother of Arnold Ferrer's child, and his very good friend," Liam told her. He pushed his chair back. Brodie did the same.

"We'll be in touch," Liam said.

And then they were gone.

So now, Kody thought, they knew. A woman had drowned; her body had washed up on the beach. She hadn't been from Key West, but from Marathon—a whole fifty or so miles north. She couldn't have washed all the way from Marathon down to Key West, could she? Kody really had no idea. But it was more likely that she had come down, or that she had been on a boat just off of Key West, or…

"Well, I think it's time," Frank said, looking at Sally. Kody realized that many people had already left.

Sally turned to Kody. "Sweetheart, I can stay. I mean, we aren't leaving until tomorrow morning, but we need to pack. And I really don't have to go—"

"Mom. Yes, you do."

"Kody and I will stay," Kelsey said.

"And… I'm here," Colleen told them.

"Yes, of course," Sally said. She seemed so concerned when she looked at Kody. Kody rose and went to her mother, hugging her where she sat.

"I love you so much. But I'm okay—I swear to you, I'm okay. And, hey… I have friends all around."

"And Mr. McFadden," Sally said.

"And Brodie, yes. Mom, he's a good guy."

"I believe that. And I'm glad that he's with you. It was just so…sudden."

"When something is right, it's just right," Kelsey said.

"And really, Kody has done nothing but work on that museum for the longest time," Colleen said. "She accuses *me* of not getting out!"

"Trying to find a murderer is not my idea of getting out," Sally said. She looked up at Kody. "You are worried about what happened to Cliff, aren't you? I know you. You're worried that…"

"Mom!"

Her mother lowered her voice. "Dakota McCoy, you be careful. Stay with that new man of yours…please!"

"What a blessing," Cliff piped up. "A blessing—from your own mom. Okay, I like the guy, too. And he will find out who gave me the damned nuts."

"Mother, you're not heading out to Alaska. You're going to be an hour away, still in the lower Keys. I can reach you in no time, and you can reach me. All is well."

"Not really," Cliff said. "I am dead. And someone made me this way."

Kody ignored him. Kelsey looked as if she'd kick him—if she could.

Kody hugged Sally fiercely. She drew back and looked at Frank.

"Take care of *her* for me, please?"

"That I will do," Frank vowed, setting his hands on his wife's shoulders.

"It's just that…" Sally paused, glancing back at Frank apologetically. "Cliff and your dad, they were such good friends. I know that Cliff meant so much to you back when we lost Michael. Kody, I'm just worried about…"

"Please, Mom, go pack. Go. You can't help Cliff or me by staring at me, okay?"

"Okay, one last hug!"

Sally hugged her tightly again. Then she turned with a little sob and started out, Frank casting Kody a quick smile and then hurrying after her. They paused to say goodbye to Rosy. The women were emotional.

Cliff watched them. "Such magnificent women in my life," he said. He sank his ghostly body into the chair Sally had just vacated. "In my life," he repeated. He looked from Kelsey to Kody. "I have to know the truth."

CHAPTER THIRTEEN

At the Sea Horse, the manager greeted Liam and Brodie. Bev and Dan were out; they were at the reception for Cliff, of course. Miss Firestone was expecting them, and they were to go right to her room.

"First room on the pool level," they were told.

"Yes, thank you," Liam said. "It's the same room Mr. Ferrer had. I've been in it."

The bed-and-breakfast consisted of the main house—another of the old Victorian two-story homes on the island—and a string of rooms that were all pool-front stretching out on either side of the main house. In the fifties, apparently, a young entrepreneur had bought up the warehouse structures next to the house, ripped them down, and put in the "motel" type rooms.

"This was nice of Bev and Dan," Liam said as they headed around to the left extension. "They're usually full—before anyone else—because they have great free parking just on the other side of the rooms. They held the room. We never even collected Ferrer's things—after our crime scene people went through it—

because we reached Adelaide before we did so. They were kind
to keep the room for her—with all of his belongings."

"Bev did seem to like him very much," Brodie agreed. "And
sometimes, people are just nice."

"They can be," Liam agreed. "Too bad some are also murdering assholes."

"Well, now, there's a piece of truth," Brodie agreed.

A woman opened the door to the room before they could
knock. She was a slim brunette with warm brown eyes and
freckles, wearing cutoff shorts and a T-shirt.

"Detective Beckett?" she asked.

"I am," Liam said, and he introduced Brodie.

She shook their hands. "I'm Adelaide. And I..."

Brodie was nearest, and so he wound up holding her for the
spasm of tears that came until she gained control again.

"Sorry! I'm so sorry."

"Please, don't be. You loved him."

She nodded. "I did. He was such a good man, and such an
amazing father. That's been the hardest, making Haley realize
that her daddy can't come and play with her anymore. She's just
five. And Arnie didn't have any relatives...no one. The good
thing is that she does love the man I'm dating now— Arnie even
introduced us, do you believe that?"

"Is your daughter with you?" Liam asked her.

She shook her head. "No, no. I was waiting for my mother to
come and watch her...that's what took me so long to get here.
Please, come on in."

The room was a good size, offering a king bed in the middle,
and a mini kitchen off a small hallway to the bath. There was
also a sofa bed by the window, and a desk with a chair.

"Sit, please," Adelaide offered, indicating the sofa. She perched
at the foot of the bed. "I don't know how I can help you, but I
will do anything that I can."

"Mr. Ferrer talked to you before coming down here, right?" Liam asked her.

"Of course! We had the best shared parenting you can imagine. Go figure, right? I have the nicest guy who trips over himself to accommodate me while still being an active parent and… this. This happens. I have friends who have had wretched divorces, and their exes are alive and kicking and mean. I guess that's life. And death."

She kept trying not to cry. A closet door was open; Brodie could see that a man's clothing was still hanging there. She hadn't begun to pack up yet.

"Did he talk to you about what he was doing?" Brodie asked.

She nodded. "He planned on seeing a Mr. Keegan, head diver and in charge of the expedition for the *Victoria Elizabeth*. And he'd corresponded with Miss McCoy, who was going to do an exhibit on the exploration, the discovery—and the history of the ship. He thought his documents were really the most important for her. She would be displaying them. But then again, he didn't know if anything he had would be useful to the Sea Life crew. He had plans of the ship, building designs—and the proposed 'storage' of the 'cargo.' It really bothered him; he was such a humanitarian. He fought for human rights. And it was so important to him that people see what was done."

"Yes, we do know that," Liam said softly. "Did you talk to him once he got here?"

"Of course—we talked to each other any time we were traveling. When he left on a trip, he let me know when he was on a plane—and when he landed. I did the same for him. It's nice, knowing that someone cares that you get somewhere safely." She swallowed. "He came in at night and called me because he just loved this place—said he loved the couple who run the place, Bev and Dan. I think they own it. He had never stayed anywhere like this before, where it was like visiting family, where everyone was really nice, where they talked to you…"

"Bev was very quickly fond of Arnold Ferrer," Brodie acknowledged.

She nodded. "That's it—to know him was to love him. This makes no sense to me. No sense whatsoever. I mean…it couldn't have been random violence, right? You don't kill a man and stuff him down into a ship in a hundred feet of water, right, just randomly?"

"No, we certainly don't believe that it was any kind of a random act," Liam said. "As far as you know, was Arnold talking to anyone else?"

"I've gone over this in my head a million times," Adelaide said. "He called when he landed, and he called the next morning, telling me how great the B and B was—which I understand. It was so sweet of them to just keep this room until I could get here. When I walked in, though, it took a minute. It was almost as if Arnie would appear…but…"

"Adelaide," Brodie prodded, "did he talk to you about anyone else?"

"That night," she whispered. "He was here the one night, woke up and called. And then, later in the day, he called again. He was so happy! He said that he was hurrying out—he had a meeting. He was very excited. He said that people wanted to be helpful—in fact, he said that 'people were coming out of the woodwork' to be helpful."

"What people?" Liam asked.

She shook head sadly. "I don't know… But I had a feeling that the meeting had just popped up—he wasn't seeing Ewan until the next day, and then he wasn't going see Miss McCoy until the day after. If only he'd spoken to me more plainly…if only I had been more curious."

"Do you think that he had an early meeting with someone he was planning to see?" Liam asked.

"Or someone new? Someone who 'came out of the wood-work'?" Brodie asked.

She shook her head miserably. "I have no idea. Haley was running around when I was talking to him, and I went to see what she was up to in the kitchen. I just said great—have a wonderful time and tell me about it all later!"

"Don't feel bad, please," Liam told her.

"Even if he'd given you a name, it most probably would have been something made up," Brodie told her.

As he spoke, he noticed a guitar against the wall near the closet; it was halfway covered with a jacket.

"He brought his guitar," he murmured.

Adelaide's eyes widened. "Oh, yes. He loved playing—and he was very good. I'd always promised him that he could take Haley to lessons when she was a bit older. Now I'll be the one doing it. But she will play, and if she plays like he does..."

Brodie got up and wandered over to the guitar.

Since Ferrer's death, another musician had drowned. He hadn't seen bruises on her body—as if she'd been held down. But then, maybe the bruises would appear by the time of the autopsy.

And again, maybe she hadn't been forced into the water—maybe she'd been pushed in. And at such a distance from the shore that she wouldn't have had a prayer of making it in, unless she was an incredible swimmer.

"Please, you can pick it up—the police finished with this room. They have all of Arnie's documents at the station and they've looked through everything else."

Brodie lifted the guitar. He played a little. He'd never be considered much of a musician, but he did love the instrument.

"A Fender," he said.

"He traveled with that guitar—yes, his Fender. He had others, one that had belonged to a famous guitar player, and I can't remember which. He took very good care of his instruments."

Brodie hit a few chords. It was perfectly in tune. Even the man's travel guitar was a good guitar.

He set it down and turned back to Adelaide and Liam. "Do you have pictures of your little girl? And of Arnie?"

"Oh, of course! In this digital age?" Adelaide asked.

He smiled. "Of course."

She pulled out her cell phone—a nice big one—and touched the screen to bring up her gallery of pictures. Liam and Brodie came to stand by her. "There's Arnie, holding Haley at a toddler's gym, and there he is with her at the fair... Oh, and there he's playing with friends at his service club. And here...well, that was the two of us about seven years ago..."

It was a nice picture. They'd taken a "photo op" at Walt Disney World. A castle rose high behind them, along with shooting fireworks. They were arm in arm, Adelaide looked lovely in a cool white halter dress, and Arnie handsome in Mickey Mouse T-shirt and black jeans.

"Mind if I keep going?" Brodie asked her.

"Not at all!"

One picture had Arnie in front of a giant stage.

"Where was this?" Brodie asked.

"Oh, the arena. One of his favorite old '80s bands was playing and he knew one guy in the group and—it was amazing—they let him come up and play," Adelaide said.

"You don't know what group?" Liam asked her.

She shook her head. "It was right before we met, actually. I saw the pic on one of his social media pages and just loved it. I downloaded it to my own page, and I keep it... I keep it in with these. Oh, I'm not trying to come off as if I weren't traumatized when I realized I was in love with a man who did love me—but had no interest in me sexually. I had to wrestle with my own demons, but his were so much worse. It was good then that he didn't have any family left—he said that his father was one of the homophobic men who would have rather seen him... dead than gay," she added in a whisper. Then she grew angry. "What a foolish man! I wonder how much of his son's real love he lost before he died."

"Well, hopefully, we've reached an age where we're learning not to be so foolish," Liam said. He sat across from her again. "Miss Firestone—"

"Adelaide."

"Adelaide, please. I need you to keep thinking. I know that you've been thinking of little else since you received word about Arnold, but... You've already given us so much today. No matter how small you think it is, we need to know."

"Definitely. I'll be here a few days. I've spoken to the medical examiner—he said he can release Arnie to the funeral home as soon as I've made arrangements. I'm going to have him embalmed down here, and then take him home. I'm putting him with my family—we go back forever in Georgia, and we're just out of the city of Atlanta and have a beautiful and peaceful graveyard... Anyway, I'll be here another few days. In fact, I'll check with you before I leave. Calling well before the plane."

"Thank you," Liam told her.

They both headed to the door of her room.

"Hey. Can you tell me some things to do on the island? I should have gotten a book. I just—wasn't thinking."

"Of course," Liam said. "The little aquarium, the Conch Tour train. The Mel Fisher Museum, a walking tour, Ripley's."

"And we have a friend who owns a museum. It was just opened," Brodie said.

"Haunts and History," she said. "That's where Arnie was going to donate his documents."

"Right," Liam said.

"Thank you for reminding me. I wouldn't want to leave without going there—without seeing her, meeting her."

She studied Brodie for a long minute. "You're not a detective," she said. "But you were introduced to me by Detective Beckett as a private eye. Who are you working for?"

Brodie took a deep breath. "I found Arnold Ferrer, Adelaide. I'm working for him," he said softly.

She smiled. Tears sprang into her eyes again. "Thank you."

It was a strange day, indeed. A funeral, a dead woman, and Cliff…incredibly capable of appearing to others, but only managing to give a shivery chill to the woman he loved.

They were almost down to the last of the mourners at the reception.

"Colleen," Kody said, "you're more than welcome to come to my house for a while, too. Kelsey and I will just be…there."

"I'd love to come to your place for a bit," Colleen said. "You don't need to go with Rosy, or do you? I think more than one or two people will be too much for her after today, but you may be the one person she wants."

"I'll ask, but I think we're good," Kody said.

Kody walked over to check.

"Are you doing okay?" she asked Rosy.

Rosy nodded. "I'm good. Sonny is going to be staying with me."

Sonny smiled at Kody. "I don't have a house down here anyway. Actually, I never need to have a house when I'm here—I have so many good friends." She squeezed Rosy's shoulder.

"We'll see them safely tucked in," Emory said. "Bill and me, we'll walk them home."

"Good night, then," Kody said.

She started away from the table. Rosy called her back. "Kody?"

"Yes?"

"Thank you again. I mean, the McCoy tomb is really one of the finest in the cemetery. I especially love the guardian angels at the entry. But mostly, whatever the next step might be, I'm grateful that Cliff is lying next to your dad."

"My dad would like that, too, Rosy. He always loved having his real friends around."

Kelsey and Colleen had already risen as well and were waiting their turns to give Rosy their sympathy and best wishes again.

"We'll be getting all kinds of pictures up and information about Cliff," Colleen said. "He'll be in the display for famous men and women of Key West! I know that Kody will have him up, and we'll have his songs right along with Jimmy Buffett, her dad, and the rest!" She flushed suddenly. "I mean, I know Kody will, and I'll help her every step of the way."

"Thank you," Rosy said. She glanced at Kody, maybe a little amused. Colleen had been coming into her own; the last time Rosy had stopped by the museum, Colleen had been shy and awkward and almost afraid to speak with her.

"Oh, and I love your artwork, too!" Colleen said.

Again, Rosy thanked her.

Kelsey gave Rosy a kiss and a hug and bid the others good night. Then, the three of them left. Kody felt a little badly—maybe she should have stayed until Rosy and her crew had left, until the very end. But Rosy was in good hands.

In a way, it was a bit tricky that Colleen had chosen to come with them; alone, Kody could have said just about anything to Kelsey. She wanted to be careful around Colleen. Still, she thought it was important that Colleen knew that she wasn't alone in the world, and that she did have friends. She was glad that Colleen had been getting out. But that wasn't the same as being with steady friends who lived near her.

When they reached her place, Kody brought Kelsey and Colleen into her living room and parlor. There had been food and drinks all day, but it seemed the natural thing to offer coffee and tea.

Kody went about fixing the drinks. She had a box of shortbread and decided that she would set them out, too.

When she carried the little tray holding all out to the living room, she was surprised to see Kelsey looking a little pained—and Colleen leaning toward her as if she had just divulged a great secret.

"Um…drinks," Kody said, looking at Kelsey.

Kelsey cleared her throat. "Colleen was just telling me that she is certain that Cliff Bullard is still with us."

"Oh?" Kody said, looking at Colleen.

Colleen nodded solemnly.

"You've—seen his ghost?" she asked.

Colleen shook her head, and then frowned. "No, you remember the dream I told you about? Somehow, today, I started thinking that the man in my dream was Cliff."

"I see," Kody murmured.

"And I sense…something," Colleen said.

"Well, if he is a ghost, he's a good one," Kody said.

Colleen remained solemn.

"I think I know why he's still here," Colleen said.

"You do? And why?"

She waited to hear Colleen declare that she believed Cliff had been murdered.

"He's here because he loved his Rosy so much. And he's here…like an angel. Just to help poor girls like me, helping out."

"A flirty ghost," Kody murmured.

"Oh, no! An angel of a ghost!" Colleen said.

As she spoke, the "angel of a ghost" joined them, walking through the doorway from the hall as if he were alive and well and solid flesh.

Colleen put her hand to her heart. "He's here! I think he's here. And I will love him forever!"

"Bravo," Cliff said. He beamed at Kelsey and Kody.

Then his smile faded, his expression lost and hopeless.

"I wish… I wish that's why I was here. But… I know now. I don't know for certain. But I'm starting to think I might even know exactly who murdered me."

CHAPTER FOURTEEN

Brodie had spoken to Liam about the discoveries Angela had made.

And although Brodie was finding it impossible to imagine that Ewan Keegan could have murdered anyone in cold blood, they'd have to follow the lead and confirm his alibi, considering where the GPS placed his boat.

"Damn. She's good," Liam said. "My squad has been hoofing it around, trying to find out what boats might have been out in the area. And as for Bill... We'd never have known. I'm going to say they both need to be interviewed. Oh, yes, and then tomorrow, a trip up to Marathon for another autopsy."

"Then maybe we should stop in on one of them tonight," Brodie said.

Liam hesitated. "I have a better idea. Let's actually get something to eat."

"You want to go to that seafood restaurant Ewan said he was at the other night?"

"And then we can barhop. We can bring Bill in tomorrow.

He and Emory and Sonny seemed to be heading to Rosy's house with her."

"Sounds like a plan," Brodie agreed.

The restaurant was down on Duval, about a block south of Front Street. Liam was greeted warmly by the hostess, who obviously knew him.

"Is Lizzy working tonight?" Liam asked.

"She is." The hostess looked at Liam with worried eyes. "She spoke to an officer yesterday, I think. Nothing is wrong?"

"No, no, Lizzy is great," Liam said.

The hostess studied Brodie as well, smiled and led them to a table.

A moment after they sat, a woman came over to them. She had a broad smile, blond hair cut in a short bob, and big green eyes. "Liam, hey. And…hello. Welcome!"

"Thanks. What's good tonight, Lizzy?" Liam asked.

"The grouper special."

"I'll have it."

"I will, too," Brodie said.

"Right away. Anything to drink?" she asked.

"Iced tea?" Brodie asked.

"Sure thing."

Liam ordered the same. "Lizzy, I need to ask you some questions."

"Oh." Her smile faded. "You know, I talked to the police already, Liam."

"Yep. But I just wanted to talk to you myself."

She nodded, glancing around at her other tables. She seemed satisfied that everyone was doing well. "Okay," she said. She looked at Brodie. "Are you a new cop down here?"

"Private investigator," Brodie said.

"Oh. Oh! You're the man who found the body."

"Yes," Brodie said.

"That wasn't on the news," Liam said.

Lizzy laughed. "It was on the 'Keys' news. Someone from the ship told someone in a shop and you know how that goes!"

"Ah, yes," Liam murmured. "So, how was Ewan that night? He was here, right?"

"He was here, alone. He was... Ewan. Nice, polite, reading away the whole time he was here."

"He didn't look anxious—as if he was waiting to meet anyone or anything like that?" Brodie asked her.

"Nope. He had one of his dive magazines for company. Like I said, he was courteous, he was... Ewan. Not a big talker, but just fine. Wish all our customers were like him. Did you guys really want the grouper?" she asked them.

"Yes, we're just about starving," Brodie said.

"We forgot to eat today," Liam explained.

"Oh, yes...the funeral was today. I got to the wake last night... Cliff was such a great guy. I guess he's up in that great jam session in the sky!" she said.

She started to head into the kitchen to put in their order.

"Hey, how late was Ewan here?" Liam asked her.

"Nine? Quarter of nine—or nine-fifteen. Somewhere in there," she said. "Is that good? You want your food?"

"Yes, thanks."

"How the hell could he have been on his boat if he was here?" Brodie asked Liam quietly.

"We'll see if they remember him as well at the Irish bar," Liam said. "We know from Adelaide that Ferrer was excited, that he was going to go out and meet someone. Whoever he met must have lured him out somehow—and then killed him."

"Or, whoever was going to meet him was overheard—and Arnold Ferrer went with this person, headed back to the bed-and-breakfast, and was ambushed by someone else."

Liam glared at him. "That isn't helping."

Plates of fresh grouper excellently prepared arrived; they ate, barely speaking. And when they were done, they thanked Lizzy for her help, and headed out, walking down the street to the Irish bar.

Music was playing loudly. Most of the crowd within was young, mostly tourists.

"It's not that locals don't like this place—they do. They just usually come out when it's a little quieter," Liam shouted to Brodie.

"I imagine," Brodie said.

They made their way to the bar, an oblong in the middle of the restaurant. There was a bandstand where the group was playing—old '80s hits, so it seemed—and tables all about. Immediately around the bar, though, there were no tables. It was the dance area.

Making their way through was interesting.

Lots of bopping, bumping and very happy slightly inebriated girls made a maze of their path. They smiled as they cut through; Brodie very politely extricated himself when one very happy young lady slipped her arms around his neck, determined that he would dance with her.

"Hey!" Liam called to the bartender.

"Hey!" the bartender called back. Brodie thought he might as well be Ireland himself; he had fire-red hair, freckles and hazel eyes. He was finishing up with his mixology—very impressive as he tossed shakers into the air and caught them with the skill of a juggler—but headed over to Liam right after he'd passed over the drinks.

"Liam, how you doing? This has to be a professional call, I'm thinkin'."

The man's speech was a lilting brogue; his smile was genuine and seemed to emphasize his red hair and sparking eyes.

"Sorry, Sean, it is," Liam said. "This is my friend, Brodie McFadden."

"McFadden, pleasure," the bartender said.

They shook hands.

"We're here about Ewan Keegan," Brodie said.

"Oh, aye, yes. Some of your coppers already asked me about him, Liam," Sean said gravely.

"Bartender!" someone called.

"A minute." Sean excused himself.

He was back quickly, having only had to hand over a few bottled beers. He studied Brodie. "You're the chap found the body, eh?"

Brodie nodded. "Everyone knows," he said dryly.

"Well, now, there's not that many six-foot-plus men with dark hair and brick shoulders walking around with Liam, eh? Aye, of course, the word is out. A murder, you know? A man found dead on a slave ship. Aye, everyone would be talking about it."

"You talked to officers about Ewan. I know you told them that he was here the night before we found the body."

Sean nodded. "Oh, indeed. I served him myself."

"Do you know how long he was here?" Liam asked.

"Oh, he was here a bit—standing right over there, watching the band. We had a group in from Dublin. Ewan was loving them."

"How late was he here?" Brodie asked. "Did you see him with anyone else?"

Sean laughed. "Did I see him with anyone else? You know that group you passed through to reach me? The place was even crazier that night. He talked to lots of people. He was dancing—I happened to notice him because of where he was standing."

"Any idea of what time he left?"

"I'm thinkin' it was midnight."

"Hey, Irish!" someone called.

Sean winced. "Okay?"

"Yes, yes, go to work. And thank you," Liam said.

Brodie nodded a thanks, as well. They left the bar, and headed out.

"So, Ewan's boat's GPS puts him near the *Victoria Elizabeth* the night that Arnold Ferrer was murdered and taken down to the ship. But witnesses have him in the restaurant and bar."

"I'm going to have to get back to Angela. The question is going to be precisely when," Brodie said. He paused, looking at Liam. "You know, though, there's one thing I know about Ewan Keegan that might…might wind up clearing him as much as his alibi corroborations."

"What's that?"

"The man can't play a guitar to save his life."

It was impossible to out and out ask Cliff what he was talking about. Colleen was there—going through a bit of a mystical thing, trying to convince them that she could "feel" Cliff.

Neither Kody nor Kelsey agreed with her—or disagreed.

Kody managed to glare at Cliff's ghost, indicating that he was to follow her into the kitchen.

The captain was there; Kody didn't know where he'd been, but he had returned from wherever, and he nodded to Cliff.

"Sir, you're doing quite amazing with your appearance and your abilities," the captain said, addressing Cliff. "It took me… well, months, at least, to materialize and, through the years, find those who knew I was there."

"I think I'm so angry—and, quite naturally, disturbed," Cliff said. "Guess that makes me motivated. And I guess, too, I always had a feeling about Kody. Her mom told me once that she'd seen her grandmother. Poor Sally had been worried as hell."

"Well, whatever the cause, you're doing remarkably well," the captain said.

"Thank you," Cliff told him.

"He thinks he knows who murdered him," Kody explained, talking softly. She hadn't closed the kitchen door entirely.

"Oh?" the captain asked.

"Bill Worth," Cliff said.

Kody was stunned. She couldn't help but remember the strange way Brodie had behaved when he and Liam had stopped by Rosy's table.

"Bill?" she said.

"He was too close to Rosy," Cliff said.

"You're kidding me, right?" Kody asked. "Cliff, all of us have been doing what we can—for her!"

"He was too close," Cliff said.

"It's not right at all, and the man has quite a point. Not right that a friend should be close to a dead man's wife, that man barely cold," the captain said.

"But that's all that you're basing it on?" Kody asked.

"That's not enough?" Cliff asked.

"His head was close to hers because they were talking," Kody told him. "Cliff, you can't…you can't pin a murder on a man for that. Did you follow them tonight? I'll bet you did. I'll bet you went to your house—and watched."

Cliff was silent for a minute.

"You did!" Kody accused.

"All right, all right, I did!" Cliff said.

"And, sir, what happened?" the captain asked.

"Nothing," Cliff admitted. "Emory and Bill saw that Rosy made it safely home with Sonny. Then the two of them left together."

"So, you're just angry because Bill had his head close to Rosy's as they were talking?"

"He still might be trying to make a move," Cliff said.

"And you have a young woman out there fascinated and half-

way in love with you—because you come to her at night!"
Kody said.

"Really? Sir, a gentleman does not go into a lady's room un-
announced," the captain said.

"I *tried* to see Rosy. She freaks out!" Cliff protested.

"Sir, still…"

"I made her happy," Cliff said softly.

"Yes, and next week, she's going to be buying a crystal ball
and become a medium," Kody said.

Cliff sighed. He shook his head and turned around and walked
out.

"I'll follow him," the captain offered.

They were barely gone when the half-closed kitchen door
opened and Colleen came in.

"Are you all right?" Colleen asked her anxiously. "I heard
you talking to yourself."

"No, I was just…singing," Kody said.

"Oh. One of your dad's songs?"

"No, actually, one of Cliff's songs," Kody said, smiling, thinking quickly. "'Love in the Sun.' Well, I guess he and my dad
wrote it together, but I think it's really Cliff's song."

"Oh, that's the one you did today, at the funeral reception,"
Colleen said. "That was beautiful. You made Rosy cry—I think
you made everyone cry."

"Great," Kody murmured.

Kelsey popped around the corner of the kitchen door. "The
guys are back."

"Oh, excellent," Kody said. "Come on, let's see…how they're
doing."

In the hallway, Liam slipped an arm around Kelsey, then
looked at Kody. "I'm so sorry we had to head out like that."

"You've had a lot going on this week," Kody said.

He nodded. "See you in the morning?" he asked Brodie.

"Whenever you're ready," Brodie told him.

"Seven too early?"

"Seven is fine."

Liam turned to Colleen. "Should we get you home?"

"Yes, how nice of you."

"Colleen, you can stay longer if you wish," Kody told her.

But Colleen shook her head. "It's been a long day," she said. "And I'll be opening the museum right on time."

"I'll be there tomorrow," Kody told her.

"Great. It is a lot more fun when there are two of us," she said cheerfully. Then she added anxiously, "But if you need to be somewhere else—"

"I need to be at the museum. I have to see how I'm going to rearrange the Civil War Era room and then the Artist's Corner," Kody said. "It will be wonderful if we have a chance to work at it together."

"Right. Well, then, I can't wait to get home," Colleen said. "I mean, I'm so tired!"

Kelsey and Liam bid them good-night; Colleen did the same.

"Oh! That Cliff! I'd smack him if I could!" Kody said when the door closed on the trio.

"And why is that?"

"He came in announcing that Bill Worth was his murderer—and do you know why?"

"Why?" Brodie asked, frowning as he looked at her.

"Because his head was too close to Rosy's when they were talking," Kody told him.

There was something odd in his expression.

"What?"

"Nothing, really. Nothing yet," he added.

"That means something. Damn it, Brodie, tell me."

"Angela Hawkins was doing some research for me at Krewe headquarters..."

"I thought your brothers were in the academy—not you."

"I know a lot of them...naturally. Especially Adam Harrison and Jackson...and therefore Angela, his wife. She traced every name I could give her that had to do with the *Victoria Elizabeth*."

"Oh?"

"Bill Worth is a descendant of one of the men with whom Mauricio Ferrer was corresponding—one of the men for whom he was buying the slaves."

"And—he killed the diver *and* Cliff Bullard because of something an ancestor did?" Kody asked, incredulous.

"Kody, some people wouldn't want to be associated with something that negative from the past."

"I'm telling you—that would be ridiculous. Besides, Bill was involved in our festival. On the Saturday night when the diver was killed, Bill Worth was at our event. We did a dinner-show thing. The artists worked on our little 'sets,' the musicians played for it, the actors performed it—and Bill Worth and a few other men wrote it."

"And what time did your dinner show end?" Brodie asked her.

"I don't know—late."

"Midnight?"

She let out a breath. "A little before."

"And then..."

"People hung around, talking to one another."

"And you saw Bill all the time?"

"No, but I'm sure others did. He wouldn't have headed back to his own house until very, very late." She narrowed her eyes, looking at him. "Was that the only name that came up in Angela's research?"

He hesitated—just slightly.

"No. She did research on every man involved with Sea Life—including Ewan. And she found that Ewan's boat was out all night—out near the *Victoria Elizabeth*."

Kody threw her hands up. "There you go! Hey, I like Ewan, too. We had a great working relationship going over the discovery of the ship and how it would be displayed at the museum. But he is a phenomenal diver. He knows that ship now better than anyone else."

"He has an alibi, too."

She stared at him. "But..."

"But what?"

"Why would he have killed Cliff Bullard? They weren't that close at all."

"Mr. Ferrer was a guitarist, a musician—a good one," Brodie said.

"So it isn't likely, though, that Ewan, who doesn't play a guitar and whose life is the water, would kill Cliff. None of it makes sense. And now...we have a drowning victim. The woman on the beach they found this morning," Kody said.

She turned around and headed up the stairs.

He followed her. She was upset; she thought that he was upset.

But the minute they were in her bedroom, he pulled her into his arms.

And she folded into him willingly.

It had been the kind of day when emotions had come to a pinnacle, and somehow it made making love more important. More urgent. More necessary.

And even more passionate.

She wondered how she could live if she believed that she would never feel that touch of his kiss upon her naked flesh again...

Know the way he looked at her when he moved over her, came into her...

They didn't speak more that night—except for urgent little whispers.

And so, it wasn't until the morning—long after Kody had

rolled over to say goodbye for the day, receiving Brodie's assurance that he would keep in touch—that she rose, stretching, and noted the picture of her and her father she kept on her dresser.

It had moved.

She was certain, absolutely certain, that it had moved. For a moment, she was in a panic in her own home.

Who the hell had been in there? Was she going crazy? Had Brodie looked at it, picked it up, put it back down in not quite the right spot?

She threw open the door to her bedroom, almost ready to run out of the house, wrapped in a sheet.

"Captain!" she called.

She met him at the foot of the stairs. "Kody— Oh, dear, Kody, what's wrong?"

"The house!" she whispered. "There was someone in the house!"

"No," he told her, shaking his head. "I go through the entire house every time I return home. There's no one here."

"You're certain?"

"Absolutely certain."

She swallowed hard. "Dakota McCoy, I swear to you, on my honor. There is no one in this house."

"Oh…okay. Thank you. I'm going to take a shower. Get dressed, head to work."

He looked at her with concern. "Kody, I will not leave today. I will watch. And if anyone comes near this house, you will know immediately."

"Thank you," she told him.

She still showered and dressed faster than she had ever done in her life.

And when she left the house, she was afraid.

Even when she walked down the street, she was afraid. Very afraid that someone was watching her, haunting her…

Someone who was not dead, but who might very well have caused the death of others.

They reached the morgue very early, but the autopsy of Mathilda Sumner was well underway, Dr. Sheila Green—the ME they'd met at the beach—presiding.

They suited up; Dr. Green was already on the stomach contents.

"Welcome, Detective, Mr. McFadden," she said, nodding to them both as they came into the room. "I believe I'm glad to tell you that, while death is a tragedy in one yet to see her golden years, the cause of death was definitely drowning. I'm assuming accidental."

"Assuming?"

"I can only work with what I see. There are no bruises on her anywhere, suggesting that she might have been held down."

"No bruises, no defense wounds," Liam said.

They were both close to the corpse. Brodie, his hands gloved, said to the doctor, "May I?"

She nodded.

He lifted the victim's hands, making a pretense of looking at her hands, fingers and fingernails.

The ghost of the woman did not pop into the autopsy room.

But as he had with Arnold Ferrer, he had a feeling that Mathilda Sumner was not *completely gone*. She hadn't managed to stay with an instant talent for haunting, like Cliff. Yet he wondered if there hadn't been some type of shadow about her... something that whispered in the wind or compelled one with a flash of light, bringing them to the body.

Murdered, needing to be discovered.

"As you can see, there's no reason not to believe this was an accident."

"Except, of course, we have to find out how a woman from

Marathon managed to die on a beach down in Key West—no clothing, towel, or anything else left on the beach, no ID of any kind."

"Perhaps she fell off a friend's boat," Dr. Green said.

"Perhaps. But usually, if you fall off a friend's boat, they fish you back up—or, at least report what has happened," Brodie said quietly.

The doctor paused and looked at them. "You want me *not* to say that this was an accidental drowning?"

"Not as yet. Give us some time," Liam said.

"Okay...well, I guess I can wait. But from what I see here... no one forced her under."

"But she might have grown tired out at sea, unable to see the shore, perhaps. Once you're out there, the waves—even when they're mild—can be something to fight," Liam said.

"Even a good swimmer can drown," Brodie added.

Dr. Green paused again, staring at the two of them. "You know you're probably chasing a mystery where there is none."

"Well, let me chase it," Liam told her. "And thank you."

"You can see Misty Cahill—she should be out in reception by now. She's the one who recognized Miss Sumner when she came in."

"Thank you," Liam told her.

"Oh, and I know Dr. Bethany—who did the autopsy on your friend, Cliff Bullard—has sent you the reports on the stomach contents."

"I don't have the reports yet," Liam said.

"He just completed them after receiving the results from the lab. You can ask Misty for a printed copy."

Again, they thanked her.

And left her working over the body of Mathilda Sumner.

"Misty?" Brodie asked at the reception desk. "Brodie Mc-

Fadden, PI, and Detective Beckett. We're here about Mathilda Sumner."

The woman was young—probably right out of college. Brodie remembered that she'd been back working in a filing room when they'd been at the morgue before.

"Hello," she said, looking at them solemnly. "Are you going to find out what happened with Mathilda?"

"We're going to try," Liam said. "We won't just forget her as a sad accident," he promised.

"How well did you know her?" Brodie asked.

"Not that well—or well enough, I guess. I saw her at the grocery store. And she was so sweet. I'd hear her play at the bar sometimes. Friends came with me. We all enjoyed her. She liked to joke, her voice was kind of throaty—and she could really play the guitar."

"So, you wouldn't have any idea how she wound up dead on a beach in Key West?" Liam asked.

"Well, I'm assuming she went down there with some friends. Or…maybe she just wanted to go down to the beach."

"She didn't get there on her own. The local police found her car up here," Brodie said.

"She drove down with someone else? You might ask at the grocery store where she worked—or at the bar where she played. I liked her—very much. She was friendly, and so kind to the elderly at the store, to anyone who needed extra help in any way. She should have been a professional musician—I mean, she was the kind of good where she shouldn't have had to bag groceries to make ends meet. She could really play!"

"One more thing, Dr. Bethany just finished a report," Liam said.

"Yes," she said, looking at them.

"Could you get us a hard copy, please?" Brodie asked.

"Oh, sure!"

They waited while she printed up the report. She started to hand it to Brodie; he stepped back. Liam was still the detective down here. Liam read them first.

"Almond milk?" Brodie asked. "Easily exchanged with cream in a White Russian or other cream drink."

Liam looked up at him. "Yep. He must have taken in just enough...right at the end."

"He had that drink with him when he was at the table with us," Brodie said.

Liam nodded.

They thanked Misty and headed on out.

"Definitely a murder, I'd say. Somehow, I think death had to be the intent," Brodie said dryly.

"Okay, so...and now Mathilda Sumner. How the hell could these deaths possibly connect? Maybe they just don't."

"Guitars. Somehow, I can't help but believe, it all has to do with music."

When they reached the car, Liam checked notes on his phone and then looked up at Brodie. "We're meeting up with Detective Lacy, from the sheriff's department. He's the one who put the search out for Miss Sumner's car and did the bit of research on her. We'll meet him at the grocery." He paused a moment. "Anything?" he asked. "I mean, back in there, in the morgue, with Mathilda?"

And Brodie knew what he was talking about.

And he understood why Liam, minus his partner, had been so accepting of Brodie heading out with him as an interim co-worker.

They'd both been looking for something a bit different, touching the body of the dead woman.

"Something, but I don't know what," Brodie told him. "It was strange. My brothers and I might be late bloomers in this thing. I hadn't begun to see a ghost—until my parents died, and they came in full blown, just as dramatic in death as they'd been in life. But when I was down in that ship, there was some kind of a dark shadow in the water—it led me right to the corpse."

"Figured something like that," Liam said. "And now?"

"I just don't get the sense that she's completely gone."

"I felt that, too," Liam said. "Damn, I wish to hell someone in this group would walk around like Cliff and know exactly what the hell happened to them."

Yep, would be nice. But it seldom happened.

Actually, in Brodie's experience, it never happened. Often, but not always, the dead remained because they needed help for closure. They didn't know what had happened to them—why they had so suddenly been jerked from life.

And sometimes they stayed because their love for family or friends was so strong, they had to make sure that they were all right, that they were there to help others through trials or troubled times.

"Both she and Arnold Ferrer are…still with us, somehow, in a sense," Brodie said.

Liam nodded.

"Let's see this Detective Lacy. Someone, somewhere, knows just where and how Mathilda Sumner wound up washing up in Key West."

CHAPTER FIFTEEN

Kody's museum had been a labor of love for a long time.

She'd left the islands long enough to attend college up in Orlando, but she'd always known that she'd live back in Key West. She had received her degree in fine arts, with dual majors in history and hospitality.

That was what one needed in the Keys.

She spent several years working for various different tour groups and with local inns and bed-and-breakfast establishments; she'd helped Bev and Dan out at the Sea Horse at one time. All of it had been leading to her museum. She'd been lucky, gaining so much community support. With Colleen going through the other rooms, Kody concentrated on the Artist's Corner, a room of the museum dedicated to those who were performers or creators in the many different arts that were, in Kody's mind, the finest part of humanity. She had always particularly loved music. It would have been impossible to be her father's daughter otherwise.

There was one wall and a display case dedicated just to her father.

The wall was adorned with his album covers, concert posters and pictures of Michael McCoy with the Bone Island Boys—his two fellow bandmates in the '80s. Ben Woodrow, drummer, had died of a sudden heart attack when he'd been very young for such a death, just forty. George Fallow, bassist, had passed away soon after, complications from AIDS.

She knew far too much about her father's life. Being as successful as he'd been had become a challenge for him. There were people with the strength and will to survive the lifestyle that often came with fame and fortune, those who learned and came out of it okay. If it hadn't been for her mom, she didn't think that her father would have been one of them.

He had told her as much.

Her father had been, though, a savvy businessman. He had kept control and owned all of his music—he had created the tunes and written the lyrics himself on the numbers that had been done with the band. Kody was incredibly proud that he had been, no matter what, a humanitarian. His music often called on people to fight for justice, and, always, to be kind to one another.

He'd written more than a few love ballads, too.

She stopped in front of a large poster that featured her father's face. She'd gotten her eyes from him—a strange yellow-brown-green color that was hazel but also amber. She had his light brown hair. In this particular poster, he'd been a very handsome man.

A total heartthrob in his day, which had, of course, gotten him into a bit of trouble at times.

He stared down at her from the poster, a serious expression on his face, his beloved guitar held in his hands.

"Why?" she whispered softly. "Why? I often feel like I'm walking in Grand Central for the dead, but I don't get to see you!"

She hoped desperately that there was a heaven.

That he was there, playing away. He had, oddly enough, been a very spiritual guy, though he hadn't adhered to a particular church.

He'd gone often enough to services with Cliff—and had brought her with him. While Cliff had gone to the Catholic Church and her mother had gone to the Episcopalian, neither of them cared which she went to—or if she attended Temple with Jewish friends or any other house of worship. They believed in the basic tenets of goodness, and her father once told her, "Most religions teach us to be good people. It's only what men can do with religions that make them bad."

"Love you so much," she whispered. "Wish you were here… I think you'd love Brodie. Of course, I don't know what the future will bring."

She was still staring at the poster when Colleen found her.

"All is well. Hey, when we close, can I give you a few ideas?"

"You know I always value your opinion," Kody assured her.

She pointed to one of the display cases. "I like the way you have your dad's notes displayed. I think it's really cool to see how a major talent like your dad went about his creations. You know, we still have that box in back that you haven't gone through yet."

"I'll get to that—very soon. I think I'm going to move some of these posters…get them closer together. And then gather the pictures of my father and Cliff and let those segue into a section on Cliff. What do you think?"

"I think it's great. And we can get another of those cases you have for your dad's guitar—and put Cliff's guitar next to it."

"Well, we'll have to see. Rosy may want to keep Cliff's guitar."

"Oh, well, you're right…we'll see. I kind of ran back here— I'm going to run back to the front."

"I'll spell you in just a minute. I'm going to go through the

Civil War Era room and figure out more on the artifacts and documents from the *Victoria Elizabeth*," Kody told her.

Colleen left the room. Kody stared at the picture of her father a moment longer, and then started to turn away when another picture caught her eye.

It was one of more than a dozen that had been set in handsome five-by-seven frames and arranged in what Kody hoped were artistic rows that created the shape of a guitar on the wall.

He was with the Bone Island Boys in several; others featured various top '80s and '90s bands he'd sat in with.

Still others featured her father playing with friends, lesser known musicians, those he was trying to help along.

She peered closely at one picture.

There was her father—with a very young Arnold Ferrer.

Detective Lacy was an older man—one with twenty-seven years of experience with the Monroe County sheriff's office. He was both laid back and thorough, a man who was more interested in facts than in speculation. He'd brought them to the store where Mathilda Sumner worked.

"Mathilda's car was parked right in front of her house. She owns a little ranch place off of Mile Marker 54," he told them. "I've been in the house, but as far as I can see, nothing went on there—nothing is in disarray. There are no notes on the kitchen counter, nothing to indicate that she was going out. I've talked to her manager already, but he's promised to gather those who are closest to her so that they can speak with us now."

Liam thanked him.

"We've got to keep it together here, right?" Lacy asked. He eyed Brodie suspiciously.

"Mr. McFadden is a private investigator working with local concerns," Liam explained.

Brodie was pretty sure Lacy wasn't about to embrace him fully, but at least Lacy made no protest about his being there.

They went into the grocery store.

It was a local shop, not a big chain. There were two checkout counters. There were signs above some of the refrigerator containers. One read "Fresh dolphin—the fish, not the mammal, for all our northern guests! Caught by Jim Beacon last night!" Another advised, "Yellowtail! Off the boat of Big Pat O'Malley!"

A man approached them. He was of medium height, a bit stout, and in his mid-fifties or so.

He wore an anxious look on his bulldog face.

"Hello, I'm Syd Avila. This is my place. I'm closing the door while you're here and calling out the staff. Mathilda was one of ours," he added in a whisper.

Brodie liked the man right away; he obviously really cared. He was willing to shut down his business to help.

"Thank you," Brodie said.

"Hey, I'm going to do my grocery shopping up here from now on, even if I live in Key West," Liam told him.

Detective Lacy grunted.

A minute later, the door was locked and they were gathered in the back office and storeroom. Avila's staff consisted of two stock boys, plus Mrs. Avila, his wife, and another Mrs. Avila, his daughter-in-law.

"Thank you all," Liam said. "What I need to know is who saw Miss Sumner last. Did any of you have any idea of what she might have been doing?"

"She told me she was going to be fixing up the house," Mrs. Avila, the owner's wife, said.

"She left here right about six—we don't close until eight," Syd Avila said, "but Mathilda was here until six—she played at night sometimes, so…she'd need to be at the bar for their entertainment hours. But she wasn't due to work last night—there was a band down from Miami—probably not nearly as good as Mathilda—but the owner's son wanted to shake everything up a bit." He made a face. "We don't need that new hopped-up stuff at our tiki bars. But… Mathilda was glad of a night off. Said her place needed some freshening up."

"Mathilda was awesome," one of the stock boys offered.

"She was the best," the other agreed.

"But did anyone see or hear from her after she left the store?" Brodie asked.

The younger Mrs. Avila spoke up softly. "She drowned, right? She must have gone down to the beach and…"

"Was that her custom—to come down to Key West at night and go to the beach?" Brodie asked.

"No…no one goes to the beach at night," Syd said.

"She could swim," younger Mrs. Avila offered. She looked from Detective Lacy to Liam to Brodie. "She was a good swimmer, and a diver, but not by night. She loved the sun. She was so happy to live here, in Marathon. But she said she never wanted to dive at night—or to swim at night. You couldn't see at night."

"Was she meeting with any kind of a friend, maybe?" Liam asked hopefully.

They all stared at him blankly.

"She was going home. She was going to clean," Mrs. Avila—Syd's wife—said, shaking her head at a total loss. Tears popped into her eyes. "We will miss her so much."

"None of you knows anything else?" Liam asked. "She just left here—and told you she was heading home to clean."

They all stared at Liam. Their eyes were big and moist.

Liam thanked them all; Brodie echoed his words. Detective Lacy led the way out, saying, "Syd, you're the best. You can open back up now."

Brodie trailed on the way out. He was startled to feel a hand on his upper arm; he turned back.

The younger Mrs. Avila had followed him.

She glanced past him to make sure that Detective Lacy had gone on ahead.

"He thinks it's a simple drowning—I don't. Mathilda was such a good friend, we did nails together, movies...times out. And, like my mother-in-law said, it's true. When she left here, she said she was going home to clean."

"But?" Brodie asked softly.

"She was excited about something. She told me a great opportunity was coming up, that a friend had called her about putting together a special gig. That was a few days ago. I bugged her, but she wouldn't say more. She promised I'd be the first to know. I don't know if that means anything or not, but I wanted to tell you. Without our fine Detective Lacy thinking I'm just a hysterical woman."

"Thank you," Brodie told her. "That could mean nothing, or everything."

Detective Lacy and Liam were staring at him. He smiled and hurried on out—after discreetly handing Mrs. Avila his card.

"On to the bar?" he asked.

Lacy shrugged. "We can, but as they told you, Mathilda was off that night."

"She still might have talked to a friend there," Liam pointed out.

Lacy shrugged. "I've talked to them. The manager, the bartender, the waiters and waitresses...they all acted as if I was crazy. Said they were far too busy for chitchat or phone calls. But then again, we don't have anything at all. You are welcome to give it a go."

Tortoise Cove was just a few miles south, near the Seven Mile Bridge.

It was a small place with a large overhang, a very tiny bandstand, and, as with many such places, a bar in the middle.

An early lunch crowd was seated around the bar; two bartenders were working, and it seemed that there were three girls on the floor. A man sitting at the bar rose when the young bartender pointed out the three men coming toward the bar.

He strode over to meet them. "Detective Lacy," he said, shaking his hand, and then looking at Liam and Brodie. "I'm Harry Wallace, manager here. Mathilda worked for us here two to three nights a week, depending on what was going on. Great woman. Our locals loved her. Goes to prove, huh, no matter how good a swimmer you think you are, you can always get caught in a current."

"We're just trying to figure out who she was with—and how she wound up in Key West," Liam said. "She didn't drive down by herself. Her car was parked in front of her house."

"I talked to the detective already," Wallace said, indicating Lacy.

"We know. We'd just like to find out if she said anything to anyone else. If she mentioned going out, anyone she intended to meet."

"My staff are busy," Wallace said.

"We'll be discreet, and we'll split up," Liam said.

Brodie drew the bartender and two of the girls working the floor. The bartender stopped what he was doing when Brodie approached him; he must have known that he was coming to talk about Mathilda.

"Ah, man. It's such a bummer. She was the sweetest," he said.

"Yeah, I know—bummer," Brodie agreed. "Thing is, we're trying to find out what happened. We're hoping she said something to one of you."

"No, I didn't see her night before last. She wasn't working. We had a band in from Miami."

"I know. But I mean, at any time, in the days before, did she say anything about meeting a friend, going to the beach?"

He started to shake his head. "Oh, well, I don't know if this means anything, but…a couple of days before she…drowned, she gave me a wink when we were talking and said that she might be involved in something very special."

"And she didn't say what?"

"Something special…to Mathilda, that meant music. It might have meant that she was trying to score some great concert tickets—she loved to play, but man, she loved to watch other musicians, too. I…wish I knew more. I'd give a lot to help you."

Brodie quietly handed him a card. "If by any chance…"

"You bet, man. I'll call you right way."

His one waitress was older; she was nice, but harried, and just told him that she never really got to spend much time with Mathilda and didn't know her very well.

The second waitress, a bone-thin younger girl, was more interested in speaking with him. "Mathilda was a doll. We'd have coffee now and then. I thought she might drive up to Miami with a night off, or, come to think of it—down to Key West. But she was sad, I think—a friend of hers who played down there died. I don't think she'd still be going…but…maybe in honor."

"Cliff Bullard. Does that name mean anything to you?"

Balancing plates in her hand, she cocked her head to the side. "Cliff…yes, that might have been it. Clive or Cliff…yes, a C name, I'm certain."

"Did she tell you about doing something special?"

"Oh, yes, but that was several days ago. She told me to cross my fingers for her. But what it was, I'm so sorry… I don't know."

Brodie met up with Liam and Detective Lacy back at the front. They thanked the manager and left.

"How about the neighbors? Were they able to tell you anything?" Brodie asked Lacy.

Lacy shook his head. "Only found one of them. An old, old man living next to her. He had no idea, but told me that a bomb could go off and he wouldn't know—he's almost deaf and on medication."

"Care if we go door to door?" Liam asked him.

"Be my guest," Lacy told him. He hesitated—as if he really didn't want to say what he was about to, or maybe that he knew he was about to sound like a completely heartless dick. "Look, she drowned. No defensive wounds or marks. Maybe someone we can't even think of dropped her at the beach. But probably she just drowned."

"Were any of her belongings found on any beach here?" Brodie asked.

Lacy shrugged. "Look, we're not without our problems—and not without our homeless. She might have brought nothing but a few bucks with her and a towel. And if that was the case... Look, I'm sorry. Really sorry. She was probably a good person. But the best I can see, it was an accidental drowning and her body got caught in the currents. God knows, water does strange things. But please feel free to investigate. Even if this is Marathon, Detective Beckett, and you work down in Key West."

Brodie smiled at him. "I'm a private investigator. Reciprocal privileges," he said. "I'll be working this until we discover just what did happen."

"Knock yourself out," Lacy said. "Just don't get in my way." He turned and walked off, heading for his unmarked car.

"Well, I think you pissed him off pretty good," Liam noted. "Sorry."

"Hell, no, don't be sorry. He was pissing me off, too. Want to check with the neighbors?"

"You bet. I doubt that everyone in the neighborhood is deaf. And, anyway, what the hell is he talking about? The body showed up in your territory."

"That's right. He'd best not get in my way," Liam said softly.

Brodie hesitated, letting out a sigh.

"We have to get into her house, too, Liam. Wish to hell I'd thought of that before I pissed him off."

"We'll get the key. I'll go in. You stay in the car."

"Will do," Brodie promised.

The museum was very nicely busy.

As Kody talked to people, drew pirates with a few children and talked about the Civil War in Key West and pirates and wreckers in the islands, she struggled with the dilemma of calling Brodie now—or waiting to show him the picture when he returned.

She knew he was busy with Liam. She didn't want to interrupt him when he was questioning someone or, perhaps, even getting close to the truth.

She didn't know how long he'd be in Marathon.

Finally, he called her.

"Hey, how's it going?" she said.

"Like all such things—slowly," he said.

"Anything solid yet?"

"Not really. I'm waiting for Liam to get a key. Then, we'll see if we can find notes or anything in Mathilda Sumner's house, or…anything to suggest how she was found with just a bathing suit on. Anyway, how are you doing?"

She almost asked him if he'd picked up the picture of her and her father that was on the dresser; but in the busy museum, with people all around her, she was beginning to wonder if she wasn't being a little bit paranoid.

"Things are fine here, but… Brodie, I did find something!"

"What?"

"In the 'Artist's Corner,' I have pictures of my dad on the wall… Arnold Ferrer is in one of them! You know…maybe you don't know, but my dad was great with fellow musicians—always trying to get them out there, give them a venue for playing. I can't really tell when…maybe a little more than a decade ago… Arnold Ferrer played with my dad."

"In Key West?"

"I don't know—I don't know when the picture was taken or where. You can see it when you get back."

"Interesting. You're sure it was Arnold Ferrer?"

"His picture was in the paper and on the news—yes, I'm sure."

"All right, thanks, Kody. That does sound very interesting. When you have a chance, see if you can find anything with him and your dad and Cliff. Ask Cliff, if you see him. I'm willing to bet he might remember if he played with Ferrer. Anyway, I'll be back later. Keep in touch. Call me if anything comes up that might be something that pushes us in the right direction." He hesitated a minute. "Stay safe," he said.

"Of course," she told him, and then added, "You, too."

"Liam is back, heading to Mathilda's house. Talk to you soon."

The call ended.

"Can you help me draw a pirate?"

She looked up; a little boy was standing there, staring at her hopefully.

She realized that she'd sat down at one of the tables they'd set up for children's activities.

"Of course, I'd be happy to help you draw a pirate," she assured him.

And when she was done, she'd hurry back to the "Artist's Corner" and study every picture she had on the wall.

Mr. Eli Quill was deaf; they knocked on the door for a long time before he answered.

He was old—and a big grouch.

"Hold your horses, hold your horses!" he called out. A minute later, the door opened. His mushy beard and mustache were whiter than snow, as was the hair on his head. He walked with a cane, and he stared at them with serious annoyance.

"Hello, sir, and our pardon," Brodie said politely. "We've come to see if you know anything at all about your neighbor, Mathilda Sumner, and where she might have gone the night before last, or if, by any chance, she said anything at all to you."

"Cops already came and talked to me," he snapped. "I didn't see anything; I didn't hear anything."

"Did you know her well?" Liam asked.

"Well enough," he said gruffly, and then he shook his head, eyes lowered. "Good girl, nice girl. Woman—too old to be a girl, right? She'd come and play for me sometimes."

"That was nice."

"Darned tootin'!"

"Then...did she tell you about anything she wanted to do, anything special that was going to happen?" Brodie asked.

He shrugged, and then rubbed his beard. "She was pretty excited the last few days. Something about playing somewhere or doing something with old friends... I don't know what it was. She wasn't as happy when that friend of hers died down in Key West, but...she was still up to something."

"With who, do you know?" Brodie asked.

He shook his head, and then peered at them closely. "Why are you asking? I heard that she went swimming and drowned."

"Her body was found down in Key West. We don't know how she got there," Liam said.

"Oh, she's a cruel mistress, the sea. Water travels, you know."

"We do know, of course," Brodie said. "The way she was washed up, though...she was a good swimmer, I heard. Good swimmers don't usually go too far out. Especially at night. Especially when they don't like dark water."

"I didn't see her leave the house. I'm sorry."

They thanked him, and started knocking on other doors.

They came upon a young mother who hadn't really known Mathilda. "Two toddlers. I'm afraid I don't know anything about anyone anymore."

The next person they talked to was a construction worker, a man walking home, still in his hard hat and carrying an old lunch pail.

"Mathilda, what a shame," he said.

"Did you see her leave the other night?"

He shook his head. "No, I'm sorry. She drowned, right?"

Liam glanced at Brodie.

"She drowned. We don't know how." They would have to answer that question every time they spoke to anyone, it seemed.

Detective Lacy really had put it off as nothing more than an accident.

"Time to try Mathilda's house?" Liam suggested.

"The house," Brodie agreed.

The kitchen was spotless except for one coffee cup in her sink. Her bills were neatly kept in a stack on her counter. Her bedroom was just as tidy.

Brodie went through her closet; she had several purses and shoulder bags. As he moved them aside, he realized that one was heavier than the others.

Liam had given him gloves—they didn't know just what they were dealing with, and, if it should prove to be a crime scene, they didn't want to contaminate anything. "Not that anything happened here," Liam mused. "No defensive wounds—she didn't know she was in trouble when she went into the water."

Brodie opened the heavy bag; it must have been the one she'd been carrying last.

Her wallet was in it, with her ID. Also her car keys, along with a compact, tissues and a few guitar picks.

"Liam!"

"Yeah?" Liam had been in her den.

"She didn't bring a purse. Everything is here—license, keys, everything."

"I think we knew that, but now..."

There was a slip of paper in her purse.

There was nothing but a name written on it, and the word, "Yah!"

The name was *Michael McCoy*.

The day was winding down.

Sometimes, people came to the door late—thinking that since it was Key West, everything was open late.

A few people were still walking around in back, but Colleen wasn't allowing any new visitors in. Kody started to take a walk herself, just to count those who remained in the various rooms.

When she came back to the "Artist's Corner," she saw that a woman was standing there—much as she herself had been earlier—staring at the wall. She was a petite brunette and, when she turned, Kody saw that she had huge brown eyes and freckles, and an easy smile.

"Hello," she said, walking straight toward Kody as if she knew her. "You're Dakota McCoy, right?"

"Yes, I am. Hi, how do you do? Nice to meet you." She arched her brows, smiling—the implication, of course, being that she needed to know who she was meeting.

The young woman laughed softly. "Adelaide. Adelaide Firestone. I came down here to... I came down because of Arnie."

"Oh, Adelaide! I'm so pleased to meet you—and so very sorry! I never did get to meet Arnold. We corresponded through email. I would have met him last week..."

And she hadn't. The reason was obvious.

Adelaide nodded. "It's horrible," she whispered. "No good deed goes unpunished, right?" she asked. "I'm so glad that the police have taken this so seriously. I couldn't help but wonder at first if it was a hate crime, but I don't believe that the police think that's the case. I don't care what the motive was—this was a horrible crime. People say it all the time, but the world is really a lesser place without Arnie in it."

"I believe you, from what I know," Kody said softly. "I wish I could say something."

"I'm all right, really." She looked around the room. "Arnie and I were together for a few years. I knew that something wasn't right and that we weren't going to make it as a couple, but..."

"I know, Adelaide. I've seen that same situation with people before. I had a great friend in college, and I would always be pretending to date him when his dad visited. His dad never did accept that his only son was gay. His loss. I still hear from my friend. He's actually a police chief up in north Florida now. He tried, like your Arnie, to be what he wasn't. And he, like your Arnie, too, is one of the best human beings I know."

She was surprised when the young woman walked over and impulsively hugged her tightly. Kody responded.

"We have a daughter. Haley. I just couldn't bring her down here for this. She's turning six soon."

Adelaide pulled away, wiping her eyes. "I just wanted to come in and speak with you, meet you, and tell you that I intend to honor everything that Arnie wanted to do. And that's to tell the truth about history. I'm just afraid, sometimes, that there's someone out there who doesn't like what we're doing. Or, they're afraid of their part in it—oh, not their part, obviously, but you know what I mean—the sins of the fathers and all that."

"They'll find the truth," Kody promised her.

Adelaide smiled. "I was just looking at that picture of your dad and Arnie. It's so nice that he's part of your museum! I have another one, by the way. If you'd like it, I'd be happy to get it to you."

"I'd love to have another picture," Kody assured her. "I'm

going to be redoing the display here." She paused. "Another friend died…another musician. I'm trying to figure out exactly how best to showcase people. Of course, Arnie will have his place in the Civil War Era room, too. Along with the *Victoria Elizabeth*."

"Thank you. One day, I'm going to bring Haley here. She'll get to understand just how terrific her dad was." Adelaide looked as if she might start crying again; instead, she turned back to the wall of photos.

"These are just great! You must have pictures of your dad with just about everyone—and still, you put up lesser-known musicians."

"My dad went through a very bad period—he struggled with drug and alcohol addiction in his younger years. To me, though, the best thing about my dad was that he was always just a man who really loved his music—and he was happy to share with others."

Kody walked over to stare at the wall again. She found herself looking at one in particular, wondering why something about it drew her attention.

She had always seen it as a picture of her dad, out in front. He was in the Keys, at a tiki bar, and it had been taken maybe two or three years before his death.

Cliff was in the picture, in the background. She'd always known that.

At the bottom of the picture, though, was a hand—as if someone had been speaking emotionally and gesturing with their arms and hands—and the hand had just been caught in the image. Kody hadn't had any of the pictures retouched; they were her father in his natural element. Like Tom Petty was known to suddenly play in Gainesville coffee houses or bars, her father had often just wound up playing at places in the Keys.

Something in the shot bothered her, and she didn't know what. What was it about the hand?

Adelaide wandered over to her. "Hey, Arnie's in that one, too," she said.

"What? Where? Do you mean—that's his hand?"

"No. See, back there. Far right corner near the stage. He's holding the neck of a guitar, and he's turned away, you can only see a bit of his face. But that is Arnie."

"So, my dad, Cliff and Arnie. And…"

The hand.

That meant that Cliff had known—or at least met—Arnold. Why hadn't he said something?

"Anyway, it's an absolute pleasure to get to know you," Adelaide said. "I'm going to head back to the house. I'm going through Arnie's clothing, sorting it for Goodwill or the Salvation Army. That would make him happy."

"Thank you so much for coming to visit, Adelaide. I'm glad I got to meet you."

Adelaide smiled, and left the room. Kody turned to stare at the picture again. Then she suddenly knew who belonged to the hand.

Bill Worth. She recognized the ring that he wore on his third figure; it was a gold ring with the initials WW engraved on it, a present from his father.

She felt chilled, but then wondered just what it might mean.

She knew that her father played with other people; her father had been close friends with both Cliff and Bill. It meant nothing that the man was there, in the picture.

Surely, nothing at all.

Except that according to Special Agent Angela Hawkins, Krewe of Hunters, Bill Worth was a descendant of a man named Gonzales, a man who meant to purchase the best slaves possible, and work them until they collapsed beneath the hot Georgia sun.

And here was proof he'd been in the same room with a murdered man, the descendant of the owner of the very same slave ship.

"Ridiculous," she said aloud. She'd known Bill forever. He'd never kill—period. Much less over something that a long-gone ancestor had done.

"Kody?"

She'd been staring with such determination at the wall of pictures that she hadn't heard Colleen come into the room.

"Shall I help you now?" Colleen asked Kody. "I think I've got everyone out."

Kody smiled, hoping Colleen hadn't seen how she'd jumped.

"No, not today," Kody said. "I'm just not ready, I guess. But we will start tomorrow."

"Want to head out with me?" Colleen asked.

"No, you get home. You've gone above and beyond. Get some rest. You know what I'm going to do? Just a bit of reading. Liam sent me email translations of some of the documents that Arnold Ferrer left. I'm going to go over them."

"Okay."

"You going out on the town?"

Colleen grinned. "Maybe. For a bit. But hey, I like being home."

"Your dream ghost, right? And you think that he's Cliff," Kody murmured.

"Oh, he's so sweet. Such a gentleman."

"He was married," Kody reminded her.

"Yes, I know. He's just kind and gentle and makes me feel good. That doesn't hurt anyone at all."

"No, it doesn't," Kody agreed.

"I'll lock up. You have your keys, right?"

"I do. Good night."

Colleen left. Kody kept staring at the wall. *Three people dead. Did those deaths have anything to do with one another? The drowned* woman… *Mathilda Sumner. Did she have anything at all to do with the* Victoria Elizabeth?

Only one slim factor joined them all together.

They had been musicians who played guitar.

She moved closer to the wall, searching the images. There were several women in the different pictures. Differing ages, differing years. She hadn't known Mathilda Sumner, and she didn't know what she'd looked like. Thus far, her image hadn't been on the news or in the papers—not that Kody had seen.

She walked to the front, sliding back behind the little counter. She chose not to use the work computer, and drew out the laptop she kept beneath the desk. She pulled it out and keyed in Mathilda Sumner's name.

All kinds of information on her popped up; Kody went to the musician's website and looked under "Photos."

And right there, the very first of the photos, was a duplicate of one picture that Kody had on her wall.

Mathilda Sumner, her eyes expressing awe as she stared up at the man who had an arm around her, grinning at the camera—Michael McCoy.

"I probably met her myself," Kody muttered. She even recognized the venue in this one—it had been a time when Michael had been playing at Mallory Square. Kody had been about fourteen. It had been billed as "Michael McCoy and Friends." He had Cliff up that day, and all kinds of performers. She remembered the day because her dad and Cliff had insisted that she showcase Cliff's song—"Love in the Sun." It was one of the first times she'd sung in front of such a large crowd.

"So," she said aloud softly again, "every one of you had a connection to my father. You knew him, played with him. But my dad has been dead for a decade!"

There was no answer, though.

As she scrolled through the rest of Mathilda's pictures, she heard a noise from the back. She frowned. Colleen had said that the museum was cleared out.

She walked to the hallway. "Anyone there?"

No answer.

She went room by room; no one seemed to be there.

She was uneasy; nervous, even. She tried to tell herself that she was being jumpy—too much had happened too quickly.

She ran her check again.

Finally, she went back to the front, trying to find some kind of logic in what had happened.

She now needed to do what she had told Colleen they would do; read everything she could about the *Victoria Elizabeth*.

Ewan Keegan wasn't home; Brodie figured that he might be out on the *Memory*, since the Sea Life crew was exploring the wreck again.

They wanted to know what his boat had been doing out on the water the night Ferrer had been killed—and find out if he'd give them his permission to search his boat.

Ewan might also be at the Sea Life offices, and so, while the hour was growing late, they decided to try there.

"There should have been something more," Brodie murmured, as they walked down the street heading for the Sea Life offices.

Someone, somewhere was warbling out a Journey song. Karaoke, in Key West, always seemed to be a fun thing for people to do—even if they never stood up to sing anywhere else.

Ewan's sister-in-law had a karaoke place south on Duval—but it was a bit of the lower Duval party route, and O'Hara's tended to draw more of a local crowd.

"Gotta love Journey," Liam said dryly. "Actually, I do. I just wish the karaoke crowd would learn a few more numbers." He grimaced.

"There was nothing," Brodie said. "Nothing but that bit of chain. And I couldn't find anyone who even knew anyone who had broken a necklace. Of course, even if we found one of the divers had lost one…there's no guarantee that it arrived right along with the body of Arnold Ferrer."

"You're sure Ewan didn't break such a chain? He's the only one who regularly wears one while diving. Sorry to suggest it, I like the man myself."

Brodie shook his head. "Ewan has always worn one chain. Just one. It's still around his neck."

"If he took his boat out, it had to have been late—really late."

They reached the offices of Sea Life, and Ewan was there.

"Hey," he said at first, opening the door for them. Then he groaned. "Okay, what did I do now? I know that I must be a 'person of interest.' That's been established. But I told you where I was and when. I know that people can vouch for me."

"People did vouch for you," Liam said. "Until about midnight."

"And what do you think I was doing after midnight? I'm not a twentysomething party guy, and I've lived down here far too long to play a drunken tourist."

"Ewan," Brodie said, "we have reason to believe your boat was out on the water—near the *Victoria Elizabeth*."

Ewan frowned. "My boat is out there most of the time. I let the guys head over there sometimes, and I go over myself. I keep it out there on purpose."

"But you weren't on it."

"If my boat was out there… Oh, I see. You think that I killed Ferrer, and just hailed a water cab to take me and the body out there?"

"Ewan, I know this is hard, but please don't be defensive. You know as well as I do that we have to check out anything and everything and use that to *eliminate* potential suspects," Brodie said.

"Yeah, sure. Dammit, Brodie, you know I didn't do this," Ewan said.

"You're right. I don't believe you could have done this. We have to check everything."

Ewan walked around in a circle and then plopped down behind his desk. "My boat was out there. She's a thirty-five-footer with a master's cabin and a second bedroom—they'd be fore and aft. Oh, and the galley seats can stand as beds. Sometimes, when we've all been worn to hell, some of the divers have crashed there instead of going all the way back in."

"And they use dinghies from the *Memory*, right?" Liam asked.

"Right. And sure, I could have motored myself in one of the dinghies from the *Memory*, and then taken it back to my boat, the *Great Escape*."

"Conceivably, you could have," Brodie said.

Ewan didn't deny the words; he frowned more deeply.

"The guys would know if one of the dinghies was gone," he said. Brodie thought that he wasn't being defensive.

He was worried.

He shook his head. He leaned forward. "Unless you think Ferrer's murder was perpetrated by my entire crew, that would be about impossible. Unless..."

"What?"

He shook his head.

"Dammit, Ewan, what?" Brodie pressed, leaning toward him on the desk.

Ewan sighed. "You can row a bit...and then turn on a motor. But I'm telling you, everyone on my crew was fascinated with Arnold Ferrer—they couldn't wait to meet him. They didn't want him hurt in anyway—he was making our discovery all the more significant."

"Who else might know about how everyone functions on the *Memory*?" Ewan asked.

Liam answered for him. "Anyone. When the dive first started, a local journalist did a documentary report on the *Memory*, Sea Life, and even featured Ewan."

"We'd like to search your boat," Brodie said. "Without having to get a warrant. And, of course, the dinghies on the ship."

"Go for it," Ewan said. "I'll sign anything you need."

"Just need your permission," Liam said.

Ewan lifted his hands. "You've got it. And you already know all of the men… Whatever you need. Do it."

Liam and Brodie left the office.

"That was easy enough," Liam said.

"Easy—and hard. Now, we have a whole new list of possibilities."

"You still can't rule Ewan out, you know."

"I don't—not in the way I work," Brodie assured him. "But I have to say, I just don't think it's possible—and I don't even believe we're going in the right direction."

"Because…"

"Because—I think I told you—Ewan Keegan is just about tone deaf. The man is truly a horrible singer, and he loves to sing the National Anthem. He can't play an instrument."

"The music connection. It just…"

"What?"

"This can't be someone murdering guitarists. It just can't be. You do know that I don't think a single behavioral scientist— not just with the FBI, but anywhere—would believe that these murders could possibly be related, right?" Liam asked him.

Brodie nodded. "And you do know that even the very best of the best have never been able to completely solve the human mind or human nature?"

"So, three separate murders. Three separate methods of death. Two that might not have been murders at all, but rather, accidental deaths. Great. Let's get to it. Let's find Bill Worth."

★ ★ ★

Senhor Gonzales,
I am delighted to assure you that all my expectations have been ful-
filled; the cargo of men—between the years of sixteen and forty—is
exceptional. All extremely healthy, and promising hours of work
in the hottest sun…

Kody read the words and wondered how there had ever been a world in which people were so callous when it came to others.

She knew that slavery had existed throughout history. She'd attended a great lecture in college given by a visiting Moroccan professor; slavery went back to the times when the first hunter-gatherers had begun to form cities. Babylonia recorded the medical treatment of slaves, and there, too, slaves could own slaves. The first well-recorded history of the process, according to her professor, had been in Ancient Greece.

War tended to be the greatest provider of slaves throughout history.

One tribe decimating another and making slaves of the survivors.

Modern-day slavery existed. It was now referred to as "trafficking in persons," and her professor had taught them that it still happens around the world—in the free world, men and women of responsibility should watch for the signs and make sure that any suggestion of the trade be reported to the police. He taught them the signs to watch out for.

And still it was hard to imagine.

She read the reply to Senhor Ferrer.

…A dead slave is a worthless slave, as I am sure that you are
aware. I will expect a guarantee for a nominal lifetime—a mini-
mum of a decade's work.

And that had been written by a man who was supposedly one of Bill Worth's ancestors.

But then again, what had her own ancestors been doing? What had anyone's ancestors been doing, and could any man, of free mind and will, be blamed for the sins of the past?

She stared at the computer. There was more. A diagram of the ship that showed how human beings were basically stuffed in the hold—like sardines in a can.

Thump!

Kody sat straight, desperately trying to figure if she had heard the sound, if it had come from the back of the museum—or, perhaps, been caused by somebody or something falling near the museum.

It sounded as if it had come from inside.

She stood up and peeked into the hallway. There was nothing there.

"Where the hell is one of my good old ghosts when I need one, huh?" she murmured aloud.

Get out, she told herself.

Whatever was going on, it was beginning to make her think that the strange deaths and occurrences were making her paranoid. She thought people had been in her house, and now she was thinking that people were in her museum.

Get out, idiot, just get out.

But who the hell would be in the museum? Or in her house? She had *email* that contained translations of documents—she didn't have any of the artifacts, documents, letters—anything. The police had taken the information that Arnold Ferrer had been bringing. There wasn't really anything to steal.

She found herself walking down the hallway. Great—she'd turned off most of the lights earlier. The auxiliary floor lights were on, but the rooms were in shadow.

She was an idiot.

She was also angry. Was someone coming in and out her bathroom window? She could swear that she locked the damn thing every day.

She began to stride toward the back; she'd worked really hard for the museum. She'd defend it.

She was just suddenly certain that someone *had* been breaking into her house and into the museum—and no one had been hurt.

As yet.

She suddenly stopped walking. There was something ahead of her. It was like a dark mist in the air, floating.

It wasn't the captain. It wasn't Cliff.

She stood still, swallowing.

The ghosts she had known had all been good…lost. Wanting to help, or to be helped.

And this…

"Get out, get out…"

It seemed that a voice sounded, like the wind, or a wave, gruff and rusty, echoing the thoughts she'd had earlier.

She turned and fled back to the front, not at all sure if the voice had been a warning—or a threat.

She ran the length of the hallway, out into the reception area. She tried to throw the door open, but it was locked. Without missing a beat she turned and grabbed her bag from beneath the counter, opened the door, and flew out into the street.

She flew so hard that she nearly knocked down the man standing there.

Bill Worth.

CHAPTER SIXTEEN

Brodie was at the end of the block when he saw Kody fly out the door from the museum—and smack right into a man.

He hurried forward, realizing as he did that the man was Bill Worth.

He quickened his footsteps.

Bill was smiling, Kody was apologizing.

"Hey, what happened?" Brodie asked, reaching the two.

"I guess I didn't expect anyone, and I was hurrying," Kody said. "Long day… I'm so sorry, Bill."

"Not at all, Kody," Bill said. "I saw that the lights were still on in your reception area there. I thought I'd stop by and see you…see how you're doing."

"I'm—fine," Kody said.

She wasn't fine. There was something bothering her.

"I'm…just supertired," Kody said.

"Okay, kid, I won't bug you. I'll come by and see you tomorrow or the next day. I have some great pictures of Cliff—thought you might want them. I know you. I know that you're going to give him a big spot in the museum. You need some help. You know I'm your man!"

"Of course, Bill, thank you."

Bill eyed Brodie. "I guess you were coming to meet Kody."

"I was," Brodie said.

"I see," Bill murmured, and smiled. "Well, see you guys later."

He started down the street. Brodie looked at Kody. "What?" She waited, watching until Bill was far down the street.

"Someone was in the museum."

"You mean…"

"Right, sorry, lots of people come to the museum. But I closed…well, Colleen closed, and I was still in there. I was reading over the letters. On the computer. And I started hearing a noise, I went to the back… Brodie, something…someone…appeared. Like a black shadow. It—spoke. It said, 'Get out!' And I know I'm getting a little paranoid, but I don't know if it was a warning—or a threat."

"But you heard something?"

"I know. It sounds crazy."

"No," he told her firmly. "Let's go see."

He opened the door and went in, and then paused, looking back at her. She was certainly safe; there were still plenty of people on the street, walking to and from restaurants and bars.

But he wanted her with him.

"Stay behind me," he said, catching her hand.

"Oh, you bet," she promised.

They headed in, past the counter and entry, into the hallway. He was pretty damned sure that if someone had been in there, in the back, they were gone now. But he was curious. A black shape. And it spoke. Maybe the spirit of Arnold Ferrer had remained behind.

If so, he'd given Kody a warning and not a threat.

They went room by room; he turned on lights. No one was in any of the rooms. He hadn't expected that they would be.

They reached the storeroom, and he made a thorough check, going behind every box, even looking beneath the work tables.

No one.

"Brodie... I swear..."

"I'm not doubting you."

They checked the bathrooms. The windows were closed. Neither window was locked.

"Did you check these today?"

She let out a breath. "No, not today. I did yesterday. Colleen locked up, but she always forgets the bathroom windows. I should put bars on them."

"They lead to the back alley?"

She nodded. "Brodie, Bill could have been in there. He could have come out to the alley, and quickly veered around to the street."

"He could have," Brodie agreed. "And it could have been someone else, someone who headed on out to the opposite street."

"How could anyone be doing all these things? Oh, Brodie... I don't even know if anyone is doing anything. No one could be interested in what I have because I don't have anything yet! Artifacts are still with Sea Life, and I don't have any documents—the police still have them. This is insane!"

"It is insane," he agreed. "But..." He hesitated, looking at her. "Kody, I think that whatever you saw—the shape, the mist, whatever—could have been Arnold Ferrer. He doesn't seem to have the ability to show himself. But I do believe he's helping."

"So...it wasn't anything evil?"

"No."

She let out a sigh. "Let's go," she said. "Let's please go home."

"Right now."

He carefully locked the windows, then they went back through the hallway, checking each room once again, turning off lights and heading out. Kody used her keys at the front, and secured the museum.

They started walking.

"I can't believe this," she said. "I can't believe that Bill…"

"Kody, you don't know that he did anything."

"You told me about his ancestor. And I read about the man."

"It still doesn't mean he did anything."

"You're the one who brought him up as a suspect."

"His association with the ship does make him a person of interest right now, but there are others who are of interest, as well," he assured her.

"You're saying that to make me feel better."

"I'm saying that because it's true."

They reached her house. The captain didn't seem to be there. Only Godzilla came up to them as they entered, rubbing against Kody's leg.

"All right, my boy. Dinner," Kody promised.

Brodie followed her into the kitchen. She fed the cat. Then she reached up into a cabinet and pulled out a bottle of whiskey.

"Want a drink?"

"No, I'm good."

She poured herself an inch of the liquor and swallowed it down in a gulp. He walked over to her, set the glass down and took her into his arms. She seemed to melt into him, shivering.

"Let's go to bed," he suggested. "I like to think I'm a lot better than a shot of whiskey."

She pulled back and smiled at last. "I just can't feed your ego, you know. I will say that I'll bet you're incredible…and the shot of whiskey wasn't bad. Feel free to follow me."

She walked ahead of him. She was either very, very nervous,

or the one shot of whiskey had made her playful. She stripped off her shirt and let it fall to the floor.

And then, as they passed through the parlor, her bra. But before he even had a chance to follow her, she suddenly came rushing back, picking up the bra.

He collected her shirt as she reached down for it. Their eyes met, and she said, "Sorry!"

"Ah, the captain. Well, we'd best hurry up in case he returns."

"Living with a ghost isn't easy."

"Tell me about it!" he murmured.

She smiled, turned and headed out of the parlor to the hallway, and then raced up the stairs.

He followed her, working at his shirt as he did, letting it fall when he reached her room—then closing the door before going any farther. Just in case.

And grateful, of course, the captain was a gentleman of a ghost, the kind who would always knock at a closed door.

He gave no more thought to the dead; his mind was then upon the beautiful creature before him, stripped down, flushing slightly, and ready to fly into his arms again.

"I've never been like this before in my life," she whispered, just before finding his lips.

"Then I'm awfully damned glad that you're like this now," he told her. They entwined, kissed and fell on the bed. She was electric; she was always filled with such sweet passion. He had a feeling that she was telling the complete truth; she seldom gave of herself.

So when she did, it was completely.

As always, the taste of her was exquisite. Fantastically arousing. And yet, even as she shimmied her body down his, doing amazing things to him, he thought that it was more than her ability to tease, arouse and seduce. He was falling in love with her mind, cliché though that might be. He loved her view on the world, the way she talked, her ability with people...

Then, he ceased to think about such things. Because she really did have one damned natural talent. And all he could think about was his lips upon her everywhere, the caress of her tongue upon his flesh, moving into her, and moving together.

Later, she lay easily against him. She didn't speak. And he realized that she had fallen asleep, curled against him. He was exceedingly glad of just the way she lay against him, sleeping so readily...trusting him so completely.

He didn't sleep so effortlessly; tomorrow, he and Liam would search Ewan's boat, the *Great Escape,* and they'd board the *Memory* again, and search the dinghies and speak with the men.

But first, he'd find a way to have a talk with Bill Worth.

Brodie's phone rang at seven. Kody was still half asleep and luxuriating in the feel of his body, which was spooned around her own.

He moved to answer the phone.

His voice was deep and groggy. "Liam?"

He listened for a minute, and then answered.

"Sure. But I want to see Kody into work first."

He ended the call.

Kody said softly, "I don't go to work at seven," she said. "And you don't need to see me into work."

"I don't like what happened last night."

"I don't, either. But it's daytime—the streets will be filled with people, and Colleen will be working with me. Well, it's not really daytime yet, but it will be. And some people—obviously Liam—seem to think that this is daytime."

He laughed, kissing her quickly, but rising. "Trust me. It's daytime," he told her. He started to walk away. She felt a rush of something warm settle over her; she loved just watching him walk away. It certainly wasn't everything, but even from behind, he had an impressive appearance.

He came back and leaned over her.

"We have to start early—we have a lot to do."

"With Bill?"

"With Bill, for one. With Ewan's boat, with the dinghies off the *Memory*."

"You think one of the divers, or one of the techs, or… Ewan?"

"Told you—we have to explore all the possibilities."

"Okay."

"Do you want to get up and open early? No, that wouldn't work. I don't want you there alone. Come to think of it, I don't want you here alone."

"This is my home. I worked hard for it. I can't let myself become afraid of it," she said, and she wasn't sure if she was telling him—or herself.

He looked at her a moment. "I'm going to shower and dress. And then go through every room here, like we did last night. And then, when I leave, you lock the door. And you don't open it until you're ready to go straight to the museum."

"Actually, I'm going to go ahead and get up—and stop by Rosy's first. She's always up by seven—she likes to paint with the first light of day."

"All right."

Twenty minutes later, he was showered and dressed. Kody slipped into a robe and came out with him to go through her house.

He was more thorough than she would have ever imagined possible; no closet was left untouched—anything that might even fit a five-year-old was checked out.

She saw him to the door to lock it after he left. He paused. She thought that he was going to comment on the fact that they hadn't seen either of their ghosts—Cliff or the captain.

But instead he asked her softly, "What are we going to do?"

She looked at him, curious at first, and then realized what he was saying.

What *were* they going to do? He was from Virginia; she was a Conch. And this time that they were together would not be endless.

"I..."

Tell him the truth? That she'd barely been living as a full human being, and she hadn't even known it. The museum, the past, work...she'd been driven, and maybe that was not even a bad thing, because she'd been waiting...for someone just like him.

"Something," she whispered honestly. "We're going to have to do something. I mean..."

"Something," he replied. "Because I don't think I can go back."

She thought that he would kiss her goodbye; she was surprised by the emotion that seemed to be holding him away.

"Something. We'll figure it out," he said, and he turned to head down the street.

Kody locked her door and turned around. She jumped. She'd been missing her resident ghost; he was back.

He seemed very grave. "I've been watching," he said softly.

"Me?" Kody exclaimed with shock.

"Lord, no!" the captain said, horrified. "No!"

"Watching...?"

"I've been about, first, trying to see what the chatter might be around the island, and that was what I discovered, nothing but chatter. I have spent time observing Adelaide Firestone, and she seems to be nothing but a lovely young lady. I have been around your friends, Rosy, Bill and Emory...and I am worried."

Kody stared at him. "And you think that Bill is somehow involved."

"It's curious, I will say. Rosy tries to be strong. She tells Sonny that she is all right, that she is doing fine, and that she will be all right alone—she must learn to live again. Emory comes to the house, and he stays and leaves. Bill comes, and stays and leaves."

"Why does this disturb you?" Kody asked. "They're all friends. Sonny is being an especially good friend; she doesn't even live down here."

He didn't reply to that. "I went down by the water, first, by Mallory Square and the hotel, and over by the docks. I listened to the men, the way they talked about the boats out by the wreck of the slave ship. They talked about the men working for Sea Life, they wondered if there isn't something more on that ship, something that someone might be looking for. Gold? I don't imagine that such a thing could be—the time was way before my era, way before the war. There would be no reason to be smuggling anything of great value." He seemed to take a long ghostly breath. "I thought... I thought that I could help you. And what I have discovered is nothing that you don't already know. There is a connection, but what it is, I cannot figure."

"I wish I could hug you," Kody told him softly. "You're trying, and we're trying, and that's the best that anyone can do."

"You think that someone has been in this house. I've failed you. I haven't seen anyone. I don't know who could have been in here, or why."

"It's all right," Kody said softly. "I'm just going to shower. I'm going to stop by Rosy's myself, and then head into the museum."

"I will be in the parlor, watching the news. With the cat. He is a very good cat. He has come to accept me quite nicely."

She smiled and walked over, trying to hug him. She embraced nothing, and yet she was certain he felt her love.

★ ★ ★

Brodie was ready to head out with Liam to Ewan Keegan's boat, the *Great Escape*.

While he was headed out to meet Liam, his phone rang. It was Angela.

"Anything else?" he asked her anxiously.

"Nothing new on the ship, but I have looked into the woman who drowned," Angela said.

"And?"

"Well, the only connection I can find between the victims has to do with music—and Michael McCoy. Mathilda Sumner played with Michael McCoy down in Key West."

"Yeah, I figured as much. We're still following up on Ewan Keegan's boat and the Sea Life crew, as well."

"You've got some help coming," Angela said.

"Help?" he asked, curious. "You know, I'm homing in on this myself."

"It's all cool. Adam Harrison called the powers that be down there. Jackson is either on his way, or he's there already. He has some of our forensic people down from Miami. Not Krewe people," she warned, "but a great forensic team."

"Oh. I just wonder if the Key West police—"

"Detective Beckett has welcomed federal help. It's a national issue, really, because of the history of the ship."

"That's great—thanks."

"Well, your brothers—"

"Oh, Lord."

"They wanted to come down. But they're in the academy. Jackson swore that he'd handle things—and try to twist your arm. Hey, Brodie, trust me, it's good to work with others who see the dead," she said flatly.

"I know." Liam Beckett had proven to be a hell of a man, allowing him to be a temporary partner.

"Thank you," he told Angela.

"It's the way we do things," she said. She hesitated. "The Bureau lost a man down there a few years ago, and we've had agents who were involved with Key West before. And as far as the Krewe goes, well, some people think there are certain meccas for areas where spiritual activity is heavier than others, often involving crimes of the day, and Key West is one of those places. Anyway, no one will step on anyone's toes."

"I'm not worried about that. If someone has answers, I'm all for it."

"I knew you'd feel that way. So does Beckett—I imagine that was why he was willing to let you in from the get-go."

"And I found the body."

"That, too."

"Tell my big brothers…"

"Yeah?"

"Just tell them thanks."

"I think your mother was getting antsy," Angela told him. "And your father even bugged them about what was going on with you."

He groaned. Sometimes it was a tough thing to be haunted by one's dead parents.

Then again, he knew that they were incredibly lucky; Maeve and Hamish had been incredibly loving parents. Busybodies at times, but that was worth the care.

Even in death.

"Just tell them all thank you—and that we will find the truth."

She agreed.

He met up with Liam at the coffee shop just down from Kody's and told him about the call he'd just had, and that FBI agents might soon be joining them.

"Here's the thing," Liam said. "The US Marshal's Office

has just a couple of men here—the local bases for them and the FBI are up in Miami. The police department is usually clogged with lesser crimes. We all depend on each other down here, FBI, Coast Guard, you name it. So, your friend bringing down some guys to really be thorough, hell—damned good thing."

"And that leaves us free to see if we can't catch Bill Worth at home."

"My thoughts exactly, my friend."

Bill didn't open the door immediately. But they had waited long enough. They banged and rang the bell until he came to the door, answering it like a man only half awake and completely confused.

"Hey. What are you all doing here?" he asked.

"We need to talk," Brodie said.

"We need to talk? I hardly know you. Liam—"

"We need to talk," Liam said.

Bill shrugged. "Come on in. And be grateful that I have a coffeemaker that's set on automatic. I may have a cup and be able to talk." He was still standing in the doorway in briefs and a plaid terry robe. He stepped aside and let them in.

Once they were in the house, he headed to his dining room. He disappeared into the kitchen and returned with a coffeepot. "You want cream or sugar? You're cops, you're not supposed to. Oh, McFadden, wait. You're not a cop."

"Black coffee is fine," Brodie said.

"What's all this about? Why the hell are you two looking at me like that?" Bill asked them. "Good Lord, you don't think I somehow gave old Cliff nuts as a joke or something, thinking that he'd just choke up?"

"The past," Liam said.

"What about the past?" Bill demanded. "Hey, I've been clean for years. I didn't do anything to anyone else in the old days— just beat the hell out of myself."

"Gonzales," Brodie said, waiting for the man's reaction.

The name fell heavy on the air, and Brodie was certain that Bill Worth knew he was a descendant of the man.

Hell, he wrote about history, and he certainly knew how to research.

"Gonzales," Bill repeated. Then he leaned back, apparently having thought it out quickly—and determined that the truth might serve him best.

"You're talking about my wretched ancestor, right? Yeah, I do know all about him. He was a bastard. Ran a massive cotton plantation in Georgia—there are letters out there that condemn the man as one of the most vicious slave holders who ever lived. He thought human beings were expendable and easily replaced. What about him?"

"He was planning to buy slaves off the *Victoria Elizabeth*," Brodie told him.

"What?" Bill seemed honestly surprised.

"Arnold Ferrer was in possession of an exchange of letters between the two men," Liam added.

"Well. That's not entirely a shock," Bill said. "Naturally, I knew about the man. But I didn't know how he procured all his people. I only know about him because I studied my family tree and dug in and found out. Oh, by the way, I also had a relative responsible for helping to break Nazi code during World War II. That's the past for all of us—some good guys back there, and some bad guys back there."

He looked at the two of them and then groaned. "That makes me a suspect in Ferrer's murder? I don't run around being proud of the guy, but if someone asks me, I admit it. What good would it do to try to hide that past by *killing* someone in the present? That's ludicrous."

He seemed to be telling the truth.

But murderers could be damned good liars, too.

"Are you interested in Rosy Bullard?" Liam asked him flatly.

Bill frowned. "Rosy. She's a sweet and beautiful woman. Am I interested in her? Yes, she is a very good friend. And I'm interested in Sonny, and in Kody, and in all my friends. And Sally McCoy Frampton, and her new husband—they are friends. And if I'm really interested in anyone…"

He broke off.

"Go on," Brodie prodded.

"It's none of your damned business," Bill said flatly. "Hey, are you done here? Because if you're not arresting me for having an asshole for a great-great-great-whatever grandfather, I want you out of my house."

"Right," Brodie said. "But, Bill, bear in mind—you were close to Cliff Bullard. You were here when he dropped dead."

"So were you. And you, Liam."

"But we didn't buy him any drinks," Liam said.

"Get out! And what—I left the festival that Saturday night, got my dive gear, lured a guy out, killed him, made my way out to the depths where the Sea Life crew is working, dove a hundred feet with a body, and made it back for Sunday morning?"

"Something like that, yeah. That's what we're looking at," Liam said.

Bill threw his hands up. "You can ask! I was at that damned festival!"

"We know you were there," Liam said.

"We just don't know if you left."

"Get out, get the hell out!" Bill said.

They started to the door and then turned back. "You weren't in Kody's museum yesterday, by any chance."

"You saw me, McFadden. She ran out. I never got a chance to go in."

Again, the man seemed to be telling the truth. But he could just be one damned good liar.

"Thanks, Bill. We'll be in touch," Liam said.

"Yeah, well, hell, we're always in touch, huh? Happens when you live down here."

They saw themselves out.

Liam looked at Brodie, one eyebrow quirked in question.

"Hell if I know," he said.

"Ditto."

"Well, let's get on out to the *Great Escape* and the *Memory.*"

Kody felt guilty that she hadn't checked in on Rosy in a while, so she stopped by before heading to the museum. Sonny opened the door.

"Kody, girl, come on in."

"How's she doing?" Kody asked.

"Oh, she's okay. I think she's actually longing to be alone. She's in the back, with her artwork. Emory is with her," Sonny said. "I guess it is time for me to go on home."

She seemed to be hesitating.

"What?"

"Well, nothing. Nothing at all."

"What? You were thinking something."

"Just that…well, I think that…someone is a little bit in love with her. Not my place to say, anyway…and there's nothing going on that's not appropriate—I've been here. I can tell you that. I know that Rosy needs her own time, too. She's gone out walking, for coffee, down to the water…alone. Maybe we're kind of smothering her."

"Oh, I can't believe that. I'm sure that, when Rosy did want to be alone, she went out for one of her walks. Maybe that made her feel a little closer to Cliff."

"Maybe. Anyway, I've stayed while I've thought that I should. Now, it's time for me to let her live on her own."

"You know that you're always welcome at my house, if you want to be close by but feel that you're crowding Rosy now."

"Ah, sweetie, I do know that I'm always welcome, and I love you for that."

"Anytime."

"I really do need to get home. I think I'll pack up while you and Emory are talking to Rosy."

Sonny disappeared into a bedroom. Kody headed on to the back.

Emory was seated in a chair.

Rosy was sketching him.

Emory had been saying something, and Rosy was shushing him—he was messing up her work.

Kody greeted them both with kisses on the cheek—apologizing for the interruption. "I just felt that I need to get by to see you."

"You're a love," Rosy told her. "And it's fine. We'll get back to it. How are you doing, Kody? You okay?" Rosy asked anxiously.

"I'm fine. And I'm grateful you've had so much company," she said. She smiled at Emory. "Have you been taking time off work?"

"Helps to be the boss. I can push people around from afar," Emory said. "And, hey, I just manage money and people. My absence isn't going to impede the saving of a sea mammal or revolutionizing fish farming."

Kody smiled at that, mouthing that she was glad he was with Rosy.

"We've all been around as much as possible," Emory assured her.

"I know."

Rosy looked over from her stool and smiled. "Get out of here, go to work. And I'm getting Sonny out of here, too. I'm so grateful—but I'm a big girl. And I must now manage on my own."

Kody hugged her. "You're not on your own. We are all here. Anytime you need us."

"I'll go to the museum again soon. I want to see what you have on Cliff—and what I can add."

"Perfect," Kody told her.

She waved to Emory and headed to the door; Sonny met her in the hallway. "I've got some Miami friends down here, vacationing. I'm meeting them for a late lunch today. But remember, I can pop down anytime you need me."

"Thank you, Sonny. I'll keep you up-to-date with everything happening."

"And if you need help with the wall for the artists...with the Civil War Era room—I'm your man. Woman, I mean. Just call me."

"Will do, Sonny."

Kody realized, as she walked to the museum, that she was going to let Colleen manage the front entirely that day.

She thought that someone had been in her house—and someone had been in the museum.

But they hadn't been in the Artist's Corner, and they hadn't been up front—getting into her computer where the information on the *Victoria Elizabeth* could be found.

They had been in the back.

The storage room...

The place where she had papers, pictures and things that she hadn't even been able to go through yet.

Today, she was going to find just what it was that someone seemed to be looking for.

CHAPTER SEVENTEEN

Jackson Crow was one of the most interesting men Brodie had ever met. He'd been with the FBI for years, and Brodie was aware that a brutal trauma—the loss of his first wife—had sidelined him for a while. He'd been chosen by Adam Harrison to take the lead on the Krewe's first case in New Orleans.

He was tall, lean, but ruggedly built; his face was a fascinating character study. His father's Native American heritage was clearly visible in the structure of his cheekbones and his ink-dark straight hair; his eyes were a sharp blue, contrasting vividly with his coloring.

When Brodie and Liam met up with him on the *Great Escape*, Jackson had been working for hours. But then, after finding Bill and speaking with him, and finally getting out on the water, Brodie realized that it was already well past lunch time. He was glad of the help; even with Liam's fellow detectives and officers preceding them and gathering all possible suspects and speaking with them, it seemed that he and Liam couldn't get places fast enough.

They still had nothing. Nothing new at all on Mathilda Sumner. Except that she had somehow cleanly disappeared from her house, leaving behind her wallet and car and anything else that someone might bring with them to go out—even just to the beach.

They stood on the deck speaking with Jackson, bringing him up-to-date. Brodie knew Jackson and was well aware that he had kept up, through Angela, with everything going on. He was thorough; he had the resources to investigate from afar.

It was still good to rehash events with what detail they had. When they had finished the complete update, they moved on to the matter at hand.

"If anyone was dragged out here and kept on this boat, the forensic team hasn't been able to find any evidence to that effect," Jackson told Brodie and Liam.

"I don't think that this boat was used," Brodie said.

"We can't clear Ewan as yet," Liam said quietly.

"I'm not saying that. What I think is that, even if Ewan was involved—murdered Ferrer in cold blood—I don't think he'd have used his own boat. That it's here is happenstance, one way or another. Whoever it was took some kind of a small boat from the docks. One person at least had to have been a diver, and, I believe, have a deep-diving certificate—the body was below a hundred feet down. The whole operation had to have taken some time—no diver could have gone down there and just come up without having the bends. Or dying. It was planned from the get-go."

"But," Jackson suggested, "the fact that your suspects were seen until midnight doesn't mean much. The whole operation might have taken three hours, but that could have been at any hour. Say, between 1:00 a.m. and 6:00 or 7:00 a.m."

"True, and there's a dilemma," Liam noted.

"We're going to move our operation over to the *Memory*,"

Jackson told him. "With your blessing, of course, Detective Beckett."

"Help me solve this—and I'll bless you from here to eternity," Liam told him.

Jackson nodded.

"I'm going to take a look below myself," Brodie said.

"What are you looking for?" Jackson asked.

"I have no idea. The kind of thing I'll know when I see."

He headed belowdecks. The boat was a really nice one. Ewan had spent his life loving the water, so it was only natural.

He introduced himself to the four FBI forensic techs, and promised them he would stay out of their way. He wasn't even sure what they were looking for, but he went into the master's cabin—which they had already gone over—and found nothing suspicious. He headed to the guest cabin at the aft.

By then, the techs had gone topside. Brodie stood in the combo galley/living area/dining room and wondered just what the hell he thought he was going to find himself.

He went to the trash; the forensics team had taken any contents.

He shook his head, and then opened the cabinets.

That's when he saw what he hadn't known he was looking for.

It was a cup. A plastic cup that advertised the Drunken Pirate tiki bar.

His heart seemed to miss a beat. Of course, Ewan had been to the bar dozens of times. It might be natural that he had a cup from the tiki hut.

But Brodie took a paper towel and reached up behind the other cups and glasses and slipped his hand around the cup.

Something of a milky color was still stuck to the rim.

Something like a cream drink might well have been in the cup—and stuck if it was poorly or hastily washed.

Something like a cream drink—tainted with almond milk.

★ ★ ★

Guitarists.

Brodie seemed to think that it all had something to do with guitars.

But she knew for a fact that her father, Cliff and Arnold Ferrer had each had their own beloved guitars. She knew, through her dad, that each man loved something different about a guitar— she couldn't believe that anyone was killing anyone over a guitar.

Maybe guitars were worth more than she thought?

She had a box of her father's belongings that she really wanted to go through. She had everything he'd left. Since her father had been so famous, she'd been careful from the beginning to display what she thought was most relevant.

There was one box that contained all manner of his papers. Some of them receipts, some of them thank-you letters from people he had worked with. Some of them were just notes. When Michael McCoy had written songs, they often came to him at odd times. He'd write music or lyrics on whatever was handy—cocktail napkins, the backs of envelopes—whatever was near him.

She remembered when her dad had died, her mom had tried hard to keep what was important, and clean out what wasn't. She'd been going to dispose of a number of the crumpled napkins and other brief notes. Kody, devastated, had quietly picked them all up.

She hadn't been able to let go of anything.

She began to dig through the napkins, lost in thought. She found his initial lyrics for a Bone Island Boys hit titled "War and Peace." It was a ballad that might have pertained to any war; it was about Johnny coming home from battle, wanting to kiss his wife's lips—but having no arms to hold her. Wanting to walk by her side, but having no legs with which to stride.

It was a beautiful song—and incredibly sad. The lyrics began with his love for her, and then, bit by bit, the listener learned his condition.

She set the handwritten words down. She would never let go of that crumpled piece of cocktail napkin.

"Hey, Kody!"

She looked up. Colleen asked her, "Do you know how late it is?"

"Ah, closing?"

"Want to come out with me?"

"Um, no. I'm going to stay a bit. Will you do me a big favor, though? Make sure that the place is all locked up."

"Sure thing. Oh, Bill Worth came by. I told him that you were busy."

"Good. Thank you. I am busy. Just lock up for me, please?"

"Sure thing."

Colleen left her alone.

She looked back at the box she was searching.

She picked up the next scrap of paper.

It was one of their best rock songs—not her favorite lyrics, but the song remained a hit. The music her dad had written was just the kind that made people move, want to dance—out on the floor, or just in their chairs.

She smoothed out paper after paper, and then paused, reading one she knew exceptionally well.

"Love in the Sun."

It was Cliff's song, she had always thought. But here it was, in her father's handwriting.

It was sand and sun, til she walked in,
The moment I saw her, I came undone.
I saw it anew, all the sand, all the sun,
Paradise gained, my heart on the run.
The world became my love in the sun,

For paradise comes when love walks in,
And God knows, there is nothing like
My love in the sun.

There were more verses, and she knew them all by heart—
she sang the song often enough. She knew that her father had
been involved in the creation of the song, but she'd never realized that he had set down the first lyrics.

In a fury, she suddenly dumped the box. And as she quickly
shuffled and inspected paper after paper, she found another napkin.

The second verse.

In her father's handwriting.

"Kody. I didn't cheat your dad out of anything."

She nearly jumped sky-high; she had thought she was alone
in the back.

Cliff's ghost was looking at her, appearing extremely worried.

"This is his handwriting—I know it."

"Kody, I swear, please. Don't look like that. I would never
hurt you! I would die before I'd hurt you."

She realized that she had been afraid of him when she'd first
seen him there. Cliff. She'd been afraid of a ghost—Cliff's ghost.

"Kody, so help me God, I… I would never hurt you. And
I…that song…"

She realized that he was in turmoil. And that it was true he
never would hurt her.

"My dad worked it with you, right?"

Cliff's ghost came closer and sank down into the chair by the
desk, looking down at her where she sat on the floor—in her
pile of cocktail napkins.

"Your father was truly a good man—an exceptionally good
man. He wanted all of his friends—his musician friends—to
make a living at their passion."

"I know that."

"He did do most of the work on 'Love in the Sun.' It should have been his song."

"He wanted you to have it," she said softly.

"Yes, he did. That song is what's kept me floating all these years. It's the one thing I've done that has continually made me an income. Well, that did make me an income. It's—it's all I really had to leave Rosy."

"That's okay, Cliff."

"Kody, if you or your mom had ever wanted to…well, you could have taken me to court."

"Why would we ever do that?"

He smiled. "You wouldn't. I know that you wouldn't."

He looked at her with such affection and love that she smiled. "My dad's legacy left my mom and me just fine. She keeps the trust fund and gives every year to his charities, just the way that he would have done. Cliff, my dad loved you."

"I know." He was silent for a minute. "I wonder if I'll get to see him soon. You know, Kody, I loved my church. And in my church, we have always believed…well, I do believe there is a heaven. I'm not ready for it yet, apparently, but…"

"Cliff," she asked, puzzled, "were you aware that you had played with my father and Arnold Ferrer?"

"Ferrer?" he asked

"There's a picture on the wall—you, my dad and Arnold Ferrer are in it."

He shrugged. "Your dad always had us playing with someone. I don't particularly remember everyone. He was…hell, he just loved to drag anyone in on a set."

"I wish you remembered," she told him.

"I'm sorry, Kody. There were so many people—so many years."

She nodded. She looked back at the napkin in her hands.

"I'd have been nothing without him," Cliff said. "People didn't know me or care about me until your dad helped me up, gave me that song."

"Cliff, you were a wonderful entertainer. Everybody gets a start somewhere. I'm glad that my dad gave you a boost. I loved you both, you know."

He nodded, and then rose, frowning.

"What?" Kody asked.

"I thought I heard something."

Kody froze. "What?"

"Oh, I don't know. Maybe you have one of our Key West roosters running around in here," he said lightly.

But he was concerned.

Then, they heard a knocking.

Cliff headed out to the hallway. Kody followed him on tiptoe.

Colleen had done a good job of locking up—the lights were out just about everywhere. Only the auxiliary lights were on in the rooms.

She made it to the end of the hallway.

Bill Worth was at the front, banging on the door, calling her name.

She remembered the captain's words that morning, that he'd seen nothing really wrong, but that it seemed that Rosy's male friends were maybe being a little too attentive.

She remembered Cliff at the reception following his funeral, watching Bill, saying that he was too close to Rosy.

Bill had been there when Cliff had died.

Oh, God, no. Had he *killed Cliff to be with Rosy*?

She held still, not going anywhere near the door. He would go away. Even as she stood there, watching him, she was in turmoil.

It was hard to believe, but surely, many murders had been committed in the name of love. If Bill had been secretly worshipping Rosy from afar, he might have gone over the brink.

But that made no sense, not if they were right that the murders committed had all been associated. But maybe they weren't associated, maybe they were looking for different killers, and maybe…

She turned around and whispered to Cliff.

"I'm going to go out the back."

He nodded. She started down the hallway, but paused. There was a strange lump on the floor in the Artist's Corner.

"Cliff," she whispered.

She couldn't help herself. She walked into the room, dreading every step.

And then she knew why; the lump on the floor was Colleen Bellamy.

"Colleen!"

She didn't whisper; she cried out the name. She gathered the girl carefully in her arms, digging in her jeans pocket for her cell phone. But it wasn't there—she'd left it on the table back in the storage room.

She couldn't tell if Colleen was dead or alive at first. Then, she thought she felt a faint pulse. She had to leave Colleen and get to the landline on the ticket counter.

As she stood, though, she saw the shadow again, the black mist-like shadow.

"Cliff…" she said.

"It's Ferrer, has to be," Cliff whispered. "Arnold Ferrer."

Then she heard the man's raspy words again. "*Get out, get out, get out.*"

"I have to help Colleen," she said.

And then, someone walked through the mist, oblivious to it. Someone smiling, and wielding a knife.

"Kody. Dakota McCoy. The amazing Miss Dakota McCoy. You never could just let things be, could you? Oh, Kody, perfect Kody, voice like a lark, energy, kindness, smiles… God, how I hate you!"

★ ★ ★

Brodie had turned the cup over to Crow's FBI forensic team. They were starting on the dinghies.

Ewan Keegan had been down with his divers. Brodie was waiting for him when he came up.

Ewan looked at him as if he were a protective pit bull—who just got kicked by his master.

Brodie waited until Ewan had unstrapped himself from his tank and set it down.

"What? What the hell?" Ewan demanded, standing on the deck, dripping.

"There was a cup in your cabinet, Ewan. It's from the Drunken Pirate."

Ewan shook his head. "I don't keep those plastic cups, Brodie. But if you're looking for one, you'll find it in the bags of half the tourists down here."

"This one is encrusted with something creamy. Cliff Bullard was killed with almond milk."

"Cliff Bullard, what the hell? I thought I was being accused of killing Arnold Ferrer!"

"How did that cup get in your cupboard?"

"I—I don't know! I told you, I don't keep cups like that."

"But it's your cupboard."

Ewan stared at him, shaking his head. "Brodie, you know that I let these guys use the place. Hell, almost everyone on the island knows that the boat is here. It's been here since just about the time we started. Anyone could have put it there."

"Someone washed it out—poorly—and put it on a shelf," Brodie said.

He walked closer to Ewan, not wanting to be heard by anyone else. "I don't think you put it there. But I don't know who did. They are going to check it for fingerprints, everything else."

He hesitated. "I'm going to have you go with Jackson. If one of these guys is guilty, he'll be glad and give himself away, maybe."

"You want me to go with the FBI guy—as if I'm under arrest."

"We'll be polite about it, but… Ewan, help us here. I believe in you."

Ewan shook his head. "Brodie, you know me, dammit. I'm not a killer. And neither are these guys… We're careful when we hire people."

"Help me out."

Ewan stared at him another moment.

Jackson walked over to him. "Mr. Keegan, are you ready?"

Another crewmate, the local guy Josh Gable, had come up after him. "Toss me a shirt?" Ewan asked, stripping off his half suit. In his swim trunks, he accepted the shirt and slid it over his head. "Yeah. Let me get my shoes."

Those onboard watched as Jackson Crow led Ewan to the starboard side of the ship where a Coast Guard cutter was waiting to bring them back to shore.

"That's bullshit!" Josh Gable exclaimed.

"He's just being questioned," Liam told him.

Gable looked at Brodie and then at Liam. "Bullshit!" he repeated.

Others just stared. Then, man by man, they left the deck.

Brodie looked at Liam. "I know he was framed."

"Then we need to prove who did do it."

Brodie nodded.

Four of the dinghies were up on their hoists.

Two were in the water.

"Guess I'll start that way—the one the crew isn't in," he said.

Liam nodded. "I'll see that we get the others down."

Brodie went to the aft and the dive platform. One of the dinghies was tied to the staff on the port side.

He hopped over, feeling irritated—and weary. He couldn't believe it. Couldn't believe that Ewan—who had spent so much of his life defending mankind—could have become a murderer.

He jumped down into the dinghy. It was empty except for one broken flipper.

He moved the flipper.

And then, to his amazement, he saw something else. Small, fragile, glittering gold.

He picked it up; it was another piece of the chain. Except that it was more than a chain.

It was a gold charm the shape of Key West. It had the words "Conch Republic" written on it.

And a name.

Suddenly, the pieces fell together for him.

He leaped out of the dinghy, shouting for Liam, digging out his phone.

He dialed Kody's number.

It rang and rang.

And rang.

Kody stared at Rosy Bullard, emotions running through her like electric bolts.

"You've got to be kidding me," she said.

"Precious Kody, no, I'm not kidding. I'm so sorry. No, I'm not. You've always had everything. Born to a rich and famous father…and just so damned sweet and good and everybody loves you. Well, that's a nice life—when you just fall into it."

"You married Cliff for his money? But…you? You did all this? Or…or you just killed Cliff?"

Cliff was standing near Kody.

"Rosy killed me?" he said, his voice incredulous, broken.

He had really loved his Rosy.

"I don't have to explain anything to you. You're going to get me the song."

"The song?"

"The damned song, Kody. Cliff told me that your father had a copy in his own handwriting. All right, the plan hasn't been to kill you, Kody. Even if you are a royal thorn in my ass. I want the original copy of the song. I looked in your house—I've searched here, I've gone over this wall… Where's the damned song, Kody? Your ever-so-sickeningly sweet mother told me that you could never let anything go, that you kept everything—even when she would have thrown the stupid napkins and whatever else shit out! So, you have it. And you know you have it."

"She killed me!" Cliff repeated, tears in his voice.

The knife Rosy was wielding was a big one. A Bowie knife. Very sharp.

Kody was younger and probably stronger, but could she get a big knife away from Rosy?

"I want the song, Kody."

"So, you're going to kill me, but you want me to give you the song first. Rosy, what a fool you are. I would never have gone after the rights to that song. And what a seriously soul-sucking bitch! He loved you—really loved you."

"He was an investment," Rosy said simply. "And then someone else came along and…and it was time the investment paid off."

"Oh, my God!" Cliff exclaimed, walking over to Rosy. He tried to hit her. Rosy saw nothing at all—but she did shiver.

"Damn it, you people freeze these places to death," Rosy said. She took a step toward Kody. "I'm actually really good with this. I can carve up your pretty, pretty face until you're ready to scream."

"And maybe I can get the knife from you. And if I'm dead, I promise you—Liam and Brodie will catch you and you might well be executed in the State of Florida for the premeditated killing of so many people."

"He will not catch me. Right now, he thinks that his friend Ewan is guilty of the other murders, and he's going to think that the sweet little Adelaide girl killed you. I've set that up, too. They'll never prove that Mathilda was murdered. She was, of course, but they'll never prove it."

"Why the hell did you kill them? How did you kill them?"

"Want to know the truth? It was unbelievably easy. All I had to do was tell the idiots that we were meeting about a show, about getting together for a tribute to the great Michael McCoy. They came running. Oh, we weren't good at it with Arnie—we were sloppy. But you see, Ewan let anybody on that boat—people came and went all the time. I figured if I put Arnie down below in the ship, everyone would think that it was a social issue—that someone was disgusted with what he did. Or someone was trying to hide something. And they did. Anyway…"

"Why?" Kodie demanded.

"You foolish girl. *They* all knew that your father had really written that song."

She couldn't help but remember the way Rosy had appeared to be in tears when Kody had sung the song.

Tears!

She had been edgy, of course.

But laughing.

"They all played together one day, and they all knew what Michael was writing. I need the song, Kody. I'm starting my new life now, a real life."

"You killed people—*over a song?*"

"Not the song—the money! Do you know what it brings in each year? As Cliff's widow, it comes to me now. I need that song, and that money, Kody. Now!"

"Come get me," Kody said.

"Watch out!" Cliff warned.

There was someone coming behind Kody. Someone else in the museum.

Colleen had never had a chance to lock up. They had ambushed her, and now...

Strong arms suddenly gripped her even as she tried to turn.

"I've found it," a male voice exclaimed. "We don't need to do any cutting. We just need to get them out of here!"

"I want to cut her!" Rosy said.

"Dammit, no. Do you want to get away with this, or not? Oh, screw this!"

Something slammed down on her head. Kody didn't even have time to think that she might really die.

Everything went black in an instant.

"Her name is right on the damned thing," Brodie told Liam. "*Rosy.* Cliff must have bought this for her- -he was so in love with her. Thing is, she couldn't have acted alone. She isn't that strong -or, she may be strong, but she didn't maneuver the physical part of this by herself. Rosy isn't a diver."

"Bill?" Liam asked.

They were heading back to shore as fast as they could go.

Brodie had already called Jackson; Liam had called it in to dispatch.

Brodie's heart was beating in a deadly race.

She hadn't answered her phone. She hadn't answered her phone...

"So Rosy and her lover killed her husband—but why Ferrer, and why Mathilda?"

Brodie shook his head. "I'm not sure, but...it goes back to Michael McCoy. His music, something. I don't know. That's been the link all the way through this."

His and Liam's phones rang at the same time.

He answered. Jackson.

"There's no one here at the museum except for her assistant—the girl is in bad shape, EMTs are already here. But Kody is gone. I'd say she might have just left, except...the back room is trashed. Boxes dumped everywhere. We're heading out—cops heading out in every direction."

"We're on the way," Brodie said.

Kody heard water...water, splashing against the hull.

She hurt.

Her head was killing her. Her body...

She opened her eyes just a slit. She had been dumped at the aft of a small motorboat in a curled up and knotted position.

That's why she hurt so badly.

But what was the plan? Throw her out in the water—as they had done with Mathilda Sumner? No, they had been subtler with Mathilda. They must have lured her out, then pushed her.

Maybe Rosy had done it herself one of the times when she'd slipped away from Sonny.

They had killed together, and they had killed alone.

At the moment, it didn't matter. Because they were going to kill her, too.

With her head pounding, she cracked her eyes. She saw Rosy, alone at the helm.

But she hadn't been alone. Where was...

She knew that Rosy still had her knife, and now, she wondered what shape she was in for a knife fight. And then she saw it—shoved against the starboard side of the little motorboat was a spear gun. If she was going to use it, she was going to have to be fast.

If it had been left loaded.

She waited, trying to make sure that her head was steady, that she could manage to twist and turn and...

The purr of the motor began to wane.

They were coming out to a point where Rosy was probably going to act...

Kody used all of her strength to unwind, come to her knees, and grab the spear gun.

Rosy heard her. She let out a scream of anger, looking like some kind of ancient evil witch.

She leaped up, her knife high.

No time! Kody maneuvered the spear gun with little precision. But the projectile flew out. It hit Rosy—in the arm. The wrong arm. While she screamed in pain, she still gripped the knife.

Kody threw herself into the water.

She dove deep, swimming hard into the water, darkening now, as the spectacular Key West sunset began to turn to blackness.

They were still on their way in to shore when Brodie's phone rang again.

"You've found Kody?"

"No, no. But we did find Bill Worth."

"And? Where is she? Demand that he tell you where they took her."

She couldn't be dead, dear God, she couldn't be dead!

"Brodie, Bill never saw her. He says that he tried to visit her today, that he wanted to talk to her about his ancestor. Tell her that he knew—but that he was sorry as hell, he really didn't have anything on the man, and it wasn't something he bragged about. Brodie, he also told me something else."

"What's that?"

"He believes that Rosy...that Rosy was falling for another man. It just wasn't him."

"And something else. I went to her house. There's a ghost there named—"

"I know about Captain Hunter. What did he say?"

"He knows who the man is—he saw him with Rosy. Nothing overt, but he knew."

"Emory Clayton," Brodie said dully.

"Yes. We have APBs out on both of them. But the captain thinks that they have some connections at one of the marinas, and little motorboats bought under assumed names. Oh, and get this—they make sure, unless it's the dead of night, that they're seen, and seen apart. They've used Ewan's name with dockmasters when they have to."

Where the hell was Kody?

He watched a motorboat, making its way through the waves. And another, following...

"I think we have something," Jackson said.

"If not, we'll keep going."

Boats, two of them, moving over the water, lights low in the falling dusk, as if they didn't want to be seen.

Brodie swore out loud, dropping his phone.

They had her. He knew where they had her.

But he had to be careful.

Because, it they were accosted, they would still kill her. Just out of spite.

"Liam, this is what we have to do!" he exclaimed.

Kody swam hard, but she was afraid she was losing consciousness. Her head throbbed. She was all right, she was all right...

She wasn't all right. Everything hurt. And Rosy could maneuver her boat, get to her before Kody could swim far enough. No matter how many times Kody managed to go under, holding her breath and feeling as if she would black out again, Rosy could find her.

There was another boat nearby.

She swam to it. Swam hard. She clutched the hull. She tried to hike herself up.

"There you are!"

She looked up. Emory Clayton was reaching down for her, a grim expression on his face.

"Oh, Kody, I don't hate you the way Rosy does. And, I am sorry. This is no fun for me, I can assure you," he said.

He'd pulled her up.

"Sorry?" she spat out. "Is murder usually fun?"

Why the hell hadn't he just left her in the water?

Hadn't they intended to drown her?

He threw her down and she collapsed onto the bottom of the boat. She was at just about the end of her reserves.

There were other vessels out on the water. It was Key West. She could see party boats and night-dive boats, and...

"Emory, you're in love with Rosy, Rosy is in love with you. Great. Why didn't she just get a divorce?"

"The money, Kody. I'm about to lose my job. They're bringing in another scientist to manage the place. And Rosy...she was always broke, always working...don't you understand? It's our time, it's finally our time."

She looked past him. There was something dark on the water. Like a shadow.

The ghost of Arnold Ferrer? The man who had tried to warn her...twice.

No, it was something—solid.

And she realized that, impossibly, Brodie was there. In the water, coming up as quietly as possible, getting his hold on the boat.

She could hear Rosy's boat swinging around.

"Kill her! Do it! Smash the hell out of her— *Now!*" she called over the sound of her engine.

Emory Clayton raised his arms over his head. He was wielding his boat's anchor.

Brodie leaped onto the boat. He slammed into Emory with a physical force that sent the man pitching into the water, screaming.

Suddenly there were lights on the water, where there had been none.

And Liam was on a bullhorn, shouting out, "Rosy Bullard, Emory Clayton, you're under arrest for the murders of Arnold Ferrer, Cliff Bullard, Mathilda Sumner and the attempted murder of Dakota McCoy."

Kody smiled. Brodie reached for her.

And she came up, unaware of any pain as he folded her into his arms.

"They thought it out—from the time they heard that Arnold Ferrer was involved with the *Victoria Elizabeth* and coming down to Key West. His goodness did him in," Jackson said.

They were gathered around the bar at the Drunken Pirate: Sonny, Bill Worth, Kelsey and Liam—and Jackson, Kody and Brodie.

It was the following night. Colleen was still in the hospital. They thought they had left her dead, but luckily they had not.

They had set everything up. When Rosy had come through the bathroom window one night, she'd found a few little things that had belonged to Colleen—a brush, a compact and a notepad.

Emory—visiting a hapless Bev at the Sea Horse—had managed to plant the things in Adelaide's room, and they'd taken hair from Adelaide's brush to leave on Colleen.

They had thought themselves incredibly clever.

"Thing is, they were getting away with what they were doing," Brodie said.

"My dad would be heartbroken that his music caused such pain," Kody said.

"Your dad's music didn't cause any of this—greed caused it," Jackson said firmly.

"Rosy said that marrying Cliff was an investment—she only intended to be with him so long. But…my God, did she marry him, intending to kill him?" she asked.

"We'll see what the prosecutors tell us on that," Liam said. "Their fate is in the hands of the law now. But this is a death penalty state. They may well plead out to multiple life terms. Rosy wanted a new life—she's going to get one."

"The thing is, they were holding a reign of terror—and it's over," Brodie said firmly.

"I'm almost surprised they didn't try to pin things on me," Sonny said.

"Maybe they were smart enough on that front—if they tried, we'd have disproved them too quickly," Liam said.

"In light of all this…" She looked across the table at Bill.

Bill cleared his throat. "We never got to tell anyone. But… Sonny and I are a couple. We were actually going to say something right after the festival, but then Cliff…"

"It didn't seem right," Sonny said.

"But it does now. We're going to get married," Bill said.

Congratulations went around. And then they were silent.

"Thing is, it is over," Brodie said. He looked over at Kody. "And just beginning."

"What are we going to do?" she asked.

Jackson cleared his throat. "I have a plan—if you're interested."

"Shoot," Brodie told him, smiling.

"Brodie goes into the academy when it starts up again. Until then, he's a consultant. It will take some time, so he can stay down here and help you get the museum up and running as it should be. Then, of course, Kody keeps her museum. But Colleen...she also loves the museum. She almost gave her life for it. And, from what I understand, she was very shy. Now, she's coming out of her shell. She would be a wonderful manager for the place. Of course, you two can spend your time going between places so that Kody doesn't lose what she worked so hard to obtain."

There was an awkward silence at the table.

Then Brodie shrugged, smiled and looked at Kody.

"I like it," he said.

"I like it, too."

"Yay!" Sonny said.

Jojo walked over.

"Hey, the band is asking if you'll do one of Cliff's or your dad's songs," he said.

She hesitated. She wasn't sure she ever wanted to do a song again.

And then she did.

Jackson was right. Music hadn't caused the horror—it had been greed.

So she got up on stage and sang "Love in the Sun," attributing it to Cliff Bullard and Michael McCoy.

They talked awhile longer. And then, Sonny and Bill headed off, hand in hand.

And when they were gone, the others were quickly joined by the captain and Cliff Bullard.

"I'll still watch over the house," the captain said.

"And, I believe I'll stay awhile myself. And I'm going to be a very promiscuous ghost—improving the lives of young women any time I can!"

They all laughed at that.

Cliff thanked Kody for the accolades.

"I love you. Like I loved my dad," she told him.

"And when I do go, I will tell him that—and tell him what a spectacular young woman he raised, and just how beautiful you are."

Soon, the living finished their food and drink.

Cliff was taking the captain for a stroll. He might just make a good promiscuous ghost, too.

And the others split.

Brodie and Kody returned to her house, walking through the streets of the city she loved so much.

At her house, Brodie suddenly swept her up into his arms.

"You know that I'm going to marry you," he said. "This may be a bit premature, but I'm going to carry you over the threshold. And up the stairs. Maybe not the stairs—they're old and narrow. I might hurt you. Or me! But...time and place...tomorrow, next year...you choose. But I am going to marry you."

He looked at her, waiting for an answer.

She smiled. "Okay." And then she laughed softly. "My mother will be relieved, of course. And you will have to let the captain know your intentions soon."

"And you're going to get to meet my diva mom and my ever-patient dad," he told her.

"I am so glad they're still in your life!"

He carried her into the house, but not up the stairs. He caught her hand and they ran up together, and they made love, and it was the sweetest thing in the world.

Love in the sun...

Or wherever.

It was more intense, more passionate than ever before.

Because now they knew it would be forever.

The next day, they visited the cemetery together. Kody set up flowers for her father—and for Cliff.

The reality of death was especially hard for him, knowing the way his life had ended.

"Looks nice," Brodie told her softly.

She nodded as they walked away.

She looked back. One of Key West's famous sunsets was streaking the sky, casting light and shadows down on the beautiful old McCoy tomb.

And for a moment, just a moment, Kody thought that she saw her father.

Lit up in a second of Key West mauve and golden light.

He smiled at her, drew his fingers to his lips, and sent her a kiss.

It couldn't be…

But maybe it was.

She blew a kiss back, and then took Brodie's hand.

Michael McCoy had given her so much. He'd taught her so much.

And, she knew, he would be happy.

He would have liked Brodie very much. If only he'd seen him, met him.

And she wondered if, maybe, in a way, he had.

★ ★ ★ ★ ★

Keep reading for an exclusive preview of
Undercover Connection
A thrilling new romantic suspense from
New York Times *bestselling author*
Heather Graham

An undercover cop and a deep-cover FBI agent
have to team up to take down an organized crime ring on the sultry
Miami Beach strip…

Available November 20, 2018,
only from Harlequin Intrigue

Chapter One

The woman on the runway was truly one of the most stunning creatures Jacob Wolff had ever seen. Her skin was pure bronze, as sleek and as dazzling as the deepest sunray. When she turned, he could see—even from his distance at the club's bar—that her eyes were light. Green, he thought, and a sharp contrast to her skin. She had amazing hair, long and so shimmering that it was as close to pure black as it was possible to be; so dark it almost had a gleam of violet. She was long-legged, lean, and yet exquisitely shaped, and amazing as she moved in the creation she modeled—a pastel mix of colors which was perfect and enhanced by her skin coloring, bare at the shoulder and throat, with a plunging neckline—and back—and then sweeping to the floor.

She moved like a woman accustomed to such a haughty strut, proud, confident, arrogant and perhaps even amused by the awe of the onlookers.

"That one—she will rule the place one day."

Jacob turned.

Ivan Petrov leaned on one elbow across the bar from Jacob. Ivan bartended and—so Jacob believed thus far—ran all things that had to do with the on-the-ground-management of the

Gold Sun Club, the burning hot new establishment having its grand opening tonight.

"I'd imagine," Jacob said. He leaned closer on the bar and smiled. "And I imagine that she might perhaps be…available?"

Ivan smiled, clearly glad that Jacob had asked him; Ivan was a proud man, appreciative that Jacob had noted his position of power within the club.

"Not…immediately," Ivan said. "She is fairly new. But…all things come in good time, my friend, eh? Now you—" he said, pouring a shot of vodka into a glass for Jacob. "You are fairly new, too. New to Miami Beach—new to our ways. We have our…social…rules, you know."

Jacob knew all too well.

And he knew what happened to those who didn't follow the rules—or, who dared to make their own. He'd been south of I-75 that morning, off part of the highway still known as Alligator Alley, and for good reason. He'd been deep in the Everglades where a Seminole ranger had recently discovered a bizarre cache of oil drums, inside of which had been a cache of bodies in various stages of decomposition.

"I have my reputation," Jacob said softly.

Ivan caught Jacob's meaning. Yes, Jacob would follow the rules. But he was his own man—very much a *made* man from the underbelly of New York City. Now, he'd bought a gallery on South Beach; but he'd been doing his other business for years.

That was the information that had been fed to what had become known as the *Deco Gang*—because of the beautifully preserved architecture on South Beach.

Jacob was, for all intents and purposes, a new major player in the area. And it was important, of course, that he appear to be a team player—but a very powerful team player who respected another man's turf while also keeping a strict hold on his own.

"A man's reputation must be upheld," Ivan said, nodding approvingly.

"And, of course, give heed to all that belongs to another man, as well," Jacob assured him.

A loud clash of drums drew Jacob's attention for a moment. The Dissidents were playing that night; they were supposedly one of the hottest up-and-coming bands not just in the state, but worldwide.

The grand opening to the Gold Sun Club had been invitation only; tomorrow night, others would flow in, awed by the publicity generated by this celebrity-studded evening. The rich and the beautiful—and the not-so-rich but very beautiful—were all on the ground floor, listening to the popular new band and watching the fashion show. Jacob took in the place as a whole, noting an upstairs balcony level that ran the perimeter, with a bar at the back above the stage. That bar was closed; the guests that night were all downstairs, and Ivan Petrov was manning the main bar himself.

The elegant model on the runway swirled with perfect timing, walking toward the crowd again, pausing to seductively steal a ripe and delicious-looking apple from the hands of a pretty boy—a young male model, dressed as Adonis—standing like a statue at the bottom of the steps to the runway.

"I believe," Jacob told Ivan, turning to look at him gravely again, "that my business will be an asset to your business, and that we will work in perfect harmony together."

"Yes," Ivan said. "Mr. Smirnoff invited you, right?"

Jacob nodded. "Josef brought me in."

Ivan said, "He is an important man."

"Yes, I know," Jacob assured him.

If Ivan only knew how.

JASMINE ADAIR—Jasmine Alamein, as far as this group was concerned—was glad that she had managed to learn the art of walk-

ing in ridiculous heels without tripping—and observing at the
same time. It wasn't as if she'd had training or gone to cotillion—did they still have cotillion classes?—but she'd been graced
with the most wonderful parents in the world.

Her mother had been with the Peace Corps—which had
maybe been a natural course for her, having somewhat global
roots. Her mom's *parents* had come from Jordan and Kenya,
met and married in Morocco, and moved to the United States.
There, Jasmine's mom, Liliana, had been born and grown up in
Miami, but had travelled the world to help people before she'd
finally settled down. Liliana had been a great mom, always all
about kindness to others, and passionate that everyone must be
careful with others—words could make or break a person's day,
and truly *seeing* people was one of the most important talents
anyone could have in life.

Declan Adair, Jasmine's dad, was a mostly-Irish-American
mutt—her father's own words. He'd been a cop, and had taught
Jasmine what that meant to him: serving his community.

They had both taught her about absolute equality, color, race,
creed, sex, and sexual orientation, and they had both taught
her that good people were good people and, in all, most of the
people in the world were good, longing for the same things, especially in America—life, liberty, and the pursuit of happiness.

They sounded like a sweet pair of hippies; they had been anything but. Her father had also taught her that those who appeared
to be the nicest people in the world often were not—and that
lip service didn't mean a hell of a lot and could hide an ocean
of lies and misdeeds.

"Judging people—hardest call you'll ever make," he'd told
her once. "Especially when you have to do so quickly."

He'd shaken his head in disgust over the result of a trial often
enough, and her mother had always reminded him, "There are

things that just aren't allowed before a jury, Declan. Things that the jury just doesn't see, and doesn't know."

"Not to worry, we'll get them next time," he assured her.

Jasmine scanned the crowd. Members of this group, the so-called Deco Gang, hadn't been gotten yet. And they needed to be—no one really knew the full extent of their crimes because they were good. Damned good at knowing how to game the justice system.

Fanatics came in all kinds—and fanatics were dangerous. Just as criminals came in all kinds—and they ruined the lives of those who wanted to live in peace, raising their children, working—enjoying their liberty and pursuing their happiness.

That's why cops were so important—something of course, she had learned when sometimes, her dad, the detective, hadn't made it to a birthday party.

Because of him, she'd always wanted to be a cop.

And she was a damned good one, if she did say so herself.

At the moment, it was her mother's training that was paying off. Because, as a child, she'd accompanied her mom to all kinds of fund-raisers——and once she was a teenager, she'd started modeling at fashion shows in order to attract large donations for her mom's various charities. She had worked with a few top designers who were equally passionate about feeding children or raising awareness when natural disasters devastated various regions in the States and around the world.

So as Jasmine strutted and played it up for the audience, she also watched.

The event had attracted a who's who of the city. She could see two television stars who were acting in current hit series. A renowned Italian artist was there, along with the Chinese businessman who had just built two of the largest hotels in the world, one in Dubai, and one on Miami Beach. A matriarch of old, old Miami society and money had made it, along with a famed English film director.

And amid the gathering of the rich and famous, the club's grand opening was also a meeting of the Deco Gang.

The Miami Dade police had labeled the loosely organized group of South Beach criminals the Deco Gang. They had gathered together beneath the control of a Russian-born kingpin, Josef Smirnoff, and they were an equal-opportunity group of very dangerous criminals. They weren't connected to the Italian Mafia or Cosa Nostra, and they weren't the Asian mob, or a cartel from any South American or island country. And they were hard to pin down, using legitimate business for money laundering and for their forays into drug smuggling and dealing and prostitution. Crimes had been committed; the bodies of victims had been found, but for the most part, those who got in the way of the gang were eliminated and, because of their connections with one another, alibis were abundant, evidence disappeared, and pinning anything on any one individual had been elusive for the police.

Jasmine had used every favor she had saved up to get assigned to the case. It helped that her looks gave her a good cover and way in.

Her captain, Mac Lorenzo, probably suspected that she had motives. But he didn't ask, and she didn't tell. She hadn't let Lorenzo know that her personal determination to bring down the notorious Deco Gang—long suspected of murder, extortion, and many an offense—had begun when Mary Ahearn had disappeared. Her old friend vanished without a trace or clue after working with the nightclub that was most probably a front for a very high-scale prostitution ring.

She could see Josef Smirnoff in the front of the crowd; he was smiling and looking right at her. He seemed to like what he saw. Good. He was the man in charge—and she needed access to him. She needed to be able to count out his body guards and his henchmen and get close to him.

She wasn't working alone; Jasmine was blessed with an incredible partner, Jorge Fuentes.

Along with being a dedicated cop, Jorge was also extremely good-looking, and thanks to that, that he'd been given leeway when he'd shown up, supposedly looking for work. He'd managed to hire on just for the day; Jasmine had told Natasha Volkov—manager of the models who worked these events or sat about various places looking pretty—that she'd worked with Jorge before, and that he was wonderfully easygoing. Turned out the show was short a man; Jorge had been hired on easily. They'd cast him as Adonis and given him a very small costume to wear.

She was afraid of the fate of the man he was replacing.

He'd been trying to get a moment alone with her as preparations for the fashion show had gone on. Jasmine had been undercover for the better part of a month in the lead-up to the show and party, and briefings had been few and far between. The opportunity hadn't arisen as yet, but they'd be able to connect as soon as the runway show part of the opening was over. She was curious what updates he had, but they were both savvy enough to bide their time. Neither of them dared to blow their covers with this group—such a mistake could result in an instant death, with neither of them even aware or able to help the other in any way.

She'd started working a few weeks back; her cover story was complete. She had a rented room on Miami Beach which she took for several days before answering the ad for models—one that would be going through various police sources on the streets. She'd been given an effective fake résumé—one that showed she'd worked, but never been on the top. And might well be hungry to get there.

After a lightning-quick change of outfit backstage, she made another sweep on the runway. She noted the celebrities in attendance. South Beach clubs were like rolls of toilet paper—people used them up and discarded them without a thought. What was popular today might be deserted within a month.

But she didn't think that this enterprise would care—the showy opening was just another front for the illegal activities that kept them going.

She noted the men and women surrounding Josef Smirnoff. He was about six feet tall, big and solidly muscled. His head was immaculately bald, which made his sharp jaw even more prominent, and his dark eyes stood out.

At his side, on his arm, was an up-and-coming young starlet. She was in from California, a lovely young blue-eyed blonde, hoping that Smirnoff's connections here would allow her to rub elbows with the right people.

Jasmine hoped that worked out for her—and that she didn't become involved with the wrong people.

Natasha was with him, as well. She had modeled in her own youth, in Europe. About five-eleven and in her mid-fifties, Natasha had come up through the ranks. One of the girls had whispered to her that Natasha had always been smart—she had managed to sleep her way up with the right people. She was an attractive woman, keeping her shoulder-length hair a silvery white color that enhanced her slim features. She kept tight control of the fashion show and other events, and sharp eyes on everyone and everything.

Rumor had it she was sleeping with Josef. It wasn't something she proclaimed or denied. But there were signs. Jasmine wondered if she cared for Josef—or if it was a power play.

Jasmine had to wonder how Natasha felt about the beautiful women who were always around. But she understood, for Natasha, life hadn't been easy.

Power probably overrode emotion.

The men by Smirnoff were his immediate body guards. Jasmine thought of them as Curly, Moe and Larry. In truth, they were Alejandro Suarez, Antonio Garibaldi and Sasha Antonovich. All three were big men, broad-shouldered, and spent their off hours in the gym. One of the three was always with Smirnoff. On a day like today, they were all close to him.

Victor Kozak was there, as well. Victor was apparently the rising heir to receive control of the action. He was taller and slimmer than Josef, and he had bright blue eyes and perfectly clipped, salt-and-pepper facial hair. He was extremely pleasant to Jasmine—so pleasant that it made her feel uneasy.

She knew about them all somewhat because she had talked to Mary about what she was doing. She had warned Mary that there was suspicion about the group on South Beach that ran so many of the events that called for runway models or beautiful people just to be in a crowd. Beautiful people who, it was rumored, you could engage to spend time with privately. Mary had described so many of these players before Jasmine had met them.

Before she had disappeared.

The club manager was behind the bar; he didn't often work that kind of labor himself. He usually oversaw what was going on there. He was like the bodyguards—solid, watching, earning his way up the ranks.

Still watching, Jasmine made another of her teasing plays with Jorge—pointing out the next model who was coming down the runway. Kari Anderson was walking along in a black caftan that accented the fairness of her skin and the platinum shimmer of her hair. Jorge stood perfectly still; only his eyes moved, drawing laughter from the crowd.

As Jasmine did her turn around, she noted a man at the bar. She did not know him, or about him. He was a newcomer, Kari had told her. A big man in New York City. He was taller and leaner than any of the other men, and yet Jasmine had the feeling that he was steel-muscled beneath the designer suit he was wearing. He hadn't close-cropped his hair, either; it was long, shaggy around his ears, a soft brown.

He was definitely the best-looking of the bunch; his face was crafted with sharp, clean contours, high, defined cheekbones, nicely squared chin, and wideset, light eyes. He could have been up on the runway, playing "pretty boy" with Jorge.

But of course, newcomer that he might be, he'd be one of "them." He'd recently come to South Beach, pretending to be some kind of an artist and owning and operating a gallery.

The hair. Maybe he believed that would disguise him as an artist—rather than a murdering criminal!

When she had made another turn, after pausing to do a synchronized turn with Kari, she saw that the new guy had left the bar area, along with the bartender. They were near Josef Smirnoff now, as well.

Allowed into the inner circle.

Just as she noticed them, a loud crack rang out. The sound was almost masked by the music.

People didn't react.

Instinct and experience told Jasmine that it was indeed a gunshot; she instantly grabbed hold of Kari and dragged her down to the platform, all but lying over her. Another shot sounded; a light exploded in a hail of sparks—just as the *rat-tat-tat* of bullets exploded throughout the room.

The crowd began to scream and move.

There was nothing orderly about what happened—people panicked. It was hard not to blame them. It was a fearsome world they lived in.

"Stay down!" Jasmine told Kari, rising carefully.

Jorge was already on the floor, trying to help up a woman who had fallen, in danger of being trampled.

Bodyguards and police hired for the night were trying to bring order. Jasmine jumped into the crowd, trying to fathom where the shots had been fired. It was a light at the end of the runway that had exploded; where the other shot had come from was hard to discern.

The band had panicked, as well.

A guitar crashed down on the floor.

Josef Smirnoff was on the ground, too. His bodyguards were near, trying to hold off the people who were set to run over him.

An absolute melee had begun.

Jasmine helped up a white-faced young man, a rising star in a new television series. He tried to thank her.

"Get out, go—walk quickly," she said.

There were no more shots. But would they begin again?

She made her way to Smirnoff, ducking beneath the distracted bodyguards. She knelt by him as people raced around her.

"Josef?" she said, reaching for his shoulder, turning him over.

Blood covered his chest. Covered him. There was no hope for the man; he was already dead, his eyes open in shock. There was blood on her now, blood on the designer gown she'd been wearing, everywhere.

She looked up; Jorge had to be somewhere nearby.

That's when she knew she was about to be attacked herself.

There was a man coming after her, reaching for her.

She rolled quickly, avoiding him once. But as she prepared to fight back, she felt as if she had been taken down by a linebacker. She stared up into the eyes of the long-haired newcomer. Bright blue eyes, startling against his face and dark hair. She felt his hands on her, felt the strength in his hold.

No. She was going to take him down.

She jackknifed her body, letting him use his own weight against himself, causing him to crash into the floor.

He was obviously surprised; it took him a second—but only a

second—to spin himself. He was back on his feet in a hunched position, ready to spring at her.

Where the hell was Jorge?

She feinted, as if she would dive down to the left, dove to the right instead, and caught the man with a hard chop to the abdomen that should have stolen his breath.

He didn't give; she was suddenly tackled again, down on the ground, feeling the full power of the man's strength atop her. She stared up into his eyes, blue eyes, glistening ice at the moment.

She realized the crowd was gone; she could hear the bustle at the doorway, hear the police as they poured in at the entrance.

But right there, at that moment, Josef Smirnoff lay dead in an ungodly pool of blood—blood she wore—just feet away.

And there was this man.

And herself.

"Hey!" Thank God, Jorge had found her.

He dived down beside them, as if joining the fight.

But he didn't help Jasmine; he made no move against the man. He lay by Jasmine, as if just floored himself.

"Stop! FBI, meet MDPD. Jasmine, he's undercover. Jacob… Jasmine is a cop. My partner," he whispered urgently.

The man couldn't have looked more surprised. Then, he made a play of socking Jorge, and Jorge lay still.

He stood and dragged Jasmine to her feet. For a long moment he looked into her eyes, and then he wrenched her elbow behind her back.

"Play it out," he said, "nothing else to do."

"Sure," Jasmine told him.

And as he led her out—toward Victor Kozak, who now stood in the front, ready to take charge, Jasmine managed to twist and deliver a hard right to his jaw.

He swirled her around again, staring at her, and rubbing his jaw with his free hand.

"Play it out," she said softly.

The Feds always thought they knew more than the locals, whether they were team people or not. He'd probably be furious. He'd want to call the shots.

But at least his presence meant that the Feds had been aware of this place, they had listened to the police, and they had sent someone in.

It was probably what Jorge had been trying to tell her.

Jacob was still staring at her. Well, she did have a damned good right hook.

To her surprise, he almost smiled.

"Play it out," he said softly. And to her surprise, he added, "You are one hell of a player!"